ASH & BRAMBLE

ASH & BRAMBLE

SARAH PRINEAS

HARPER TEEN

An Imprint of HarperCollinsPublishers

HarperTeen is an imprint of HarperCollins Publishers.

Ash & Bramble
Copyright © 2015 by Sarah Prineas
All rights reserved. Printed in the United States of America.
No part of this book may be used or reproduced in any manner whatsoever
without written permission except in the case of brief quotations embodied
in critical articles and reviews. For information address HarperCollins
Children's Books, a division of HarperCollins Publishers,
195 Broadway, New York, NY 10007.
www.epicreads.com

Library of Congress Cataloging-in-Publication Data
Prineas, Sarah.
 Ash & Bramble / Sarah Prineas. — First edition.
  pages cm
 Summary: After Pin and Shoe escape from servitude in the Godmother's
fortress, they learn that she has taken control of Story, which can warp
the world around it, forcing people into its shape, and they decide to try
to break out and create their own destinies in this tale that features many
familiar characters.
 ISBN 978-0-06-233794-8 (hardcover)
 [1. Fairy tales. 2. Fairy godmothers—Fiction. 3. Characters in literature—
Fiction. 4. Storytelling—Fiction. 5. Memory—Fiction.] I. Title. II. Title:
Ash and Bramble.
PZ8.P94Ash 2015   2014041198
[Fic]—dc23   CIP
                                                                            AC

Typography by Carla Weise
15 16 17 18 19   PC/RRDH   10 9 8 7 6 5 4 3 2 1

First Edition

To my dear, genius editor, Toni Markiet

ASH
&
BRAMBLE

YOUR WORLD IS DARK.

You fear the dark. You fear pain and sickness and loss and sorrow; you fear that your life is meaningless. You fear death, that most terrible of endings.

You huddle around the brightly burning fire in the hearth, and you tell stories. Your stories are about good people finding happiness, about bad people getting what they deserve, and most of all, you tell about true love. Your stories make the fire burn brighter; your stories push back the darkness.

I am the Godmother. I know your greatest fears; I know your deepest desires. I have taken your stories and added magic and wonder and, oh, perhaps a dancing slipper made of glass. A poisoned apple. A sharpened spindle. A glittering ball gown.

An ever after.

I give them all to you. Tell them around your meager fires. Tell them again, for they are light in the darkness. Tell and retell them, for they have power.

Live them, and their power grows.

I am the Godmother. I give you Story.

PART
ONE

CHAPTER 1

I KNOW THIS PART OF MY STORY, THE BEGINNING, MAYBE.

I am Nothing.

All is darkness and pain, radiating from an icy touch in the middle of my forehead, the frozen, dazzling ache of it flashing through me.

When I open my eyes, I look through tears at strands of dark hair looped around my bare feet. My own hair, I realize slowly, dimly, as if I am waking after a long sleep. It has been cut off. I am naked, shivering. A furred hand grips my arm, keeping me on my feet.

Then a bucket of ice-cold water comes down over my head, and I gasp. Somebody behind me gives a harsh bark of laughter, and a bundle of cloth is shoved into my arms. I have something in my hand, a little metal knob about the size of an acorn. It has warmed to my touch, and I somehow know they must not find it. Whoever *they* are.

Keeping the metal acorn clenched in my fist, I put on the shift they've given me and pull the shapeless dress over my head, followed by the apron, which I tie at my waist. My movements are stiff, jerky, as if my body isn't really mine. The shift scratches against my skin—it is made of undyed wool. My neck feels cold and defenseless. The stone floor is icy under my bare feet. My hand finds the pocket of my apron and hides the metal acorn away. And then the paw grips my arm, and I am dragged, blinking, dazed, down a long passageway and into a dank, dim room.

As I stand there, I hear voices, but I can make no sense of the words. My feet go numb and I can't feel the floor beneath me. The walls recede. Darkness gathers around me. I am Nothing, and the horror of it makes my skin shrink with cold, makes shadows echo through my head. Trembling, I close my eyes, and to keep myself from flying off into the Nothing I wrap my arms around myself. It is some comfort, but not enough.

Rough hands grasp my arms and shove me onto a bench.

"You are Seamstress," a sharp voice says. "Undersssstand? Seamstress."

The room returns, and the feel of the floor against the soles of my feet, the coarse shift on the skin of my body, the smell of tallow candles. I cling to the words. Seamstress. I am Seamstress.

Cloth is put into my hands, and a threaded needle.

"Stitch," the voice orders.

I am Seamstress. I must stitch.

The cloth is light and fine, the purest virgin white. A hem has been started along one edge. With trembling fingers, I add a stitch. Then another.

"The stitchesss," the voice adds, "must be no bigger than a grain of sand."

Squinting at the delicate white cloth, the thread as fine as spider silk, I take another stitch. My fingers do not know this work; my stitch is awkward, uneven.

"Sahhhh," hisses the voice.

I look up, and see a woman dressed in a simple gown like mine. She wears a cap that covers a perfectly bald skull. She has no eyebrows; her eyelids are lashless; her pupils are slitted. With a forked tongue she licks her lips. "I am the Overseer," she says. "You are Seamstress. Stitch."

For a long time I work. My stitches march on, inevitable, a straggling, wandering line of foot soldiers, with here and there a casualty where I accidentally prick my finger on the needle and the tiny bead of blood is blotted by the cloth. My fingertips ache; my hands grow stiff. My bottom is sore from sitting for so long on this hard bench. A spool of spider-silk thread appears at my elbow when I need it. A tallow candle burns lower, gutters, and is replaced. Slowly, so slowly, pushed back by my attention to my work, the Nothing recedes, the room becomes real around me, and I become real in the room.

I am Seamstress, and I am not alone as I labor. Next to me on the bench is another Seamstress, one who bends her head to her work and does not glance aside. The room is long and low-ceilinged, with cracked plaster walls. A table runs the length of the room; a row of Seamstresses sits along each side. Using silken thread and silver needles, the Seamstresses sew seed pearls onto damask that glows like sapphires in the golden candlelight. They stitch cobwebs of lace onto petticoats. They sew stays of whalebone into wasp-waisted ball gowns.

The Overseer slithers up behind me. "Eyes on your work, Seamstresss," she hisses. There's a rustle and a swish, and a burning line of pain slashes across the back of my neck. A quick glance over my shoulder, and I see the Overseer blink her slitted eyes and fold her arms. She holds a long switch, which twitches as if she's eager to hit me again.

I bow my head and try to make my stitches tinier, neater, more like grains of sand than disobedient soldiers. My neck burns, a line of fire left by her switch.

Oceans of silk and satin ebb and flow from one end of the table to the other, washing up here for an embroidery at the hem, there for a fall of ruffles, and back to the Seamstress next to me for another spangling of seed pearls. Our own dresses are made of gray wool with a plain white apron over the top. Most of the other Seamstresses are old women, bent, gray, their eyesight failing in the dim light. I am the newest, and the youngest, and I am still slim and straight, but soon

I will grow, like the others, humpbacked from bending over my work and crook-fingered from gripping the needle.

We stitch. I find myself drifting with the tidal flow of flounces and furbelows. The Overseer's breath is cold on my neck; her forked tongue flickers at my ear. *Swifter! Smaller stitches! Straighter seams!*

I sew. My stitches are not smaller; my seams are not straighter.

Thwack comes the burn of the switch on the back of my neck.

A CLOCK STRIKES, a hollow, echoing boom that makes the walls of the sewing room shake.

"Up," the Overseer orders. "Exercise."

With weary sighs, the Seamstresses around me set down their work. Following their lead, I do the same, rubbing fingers that feel stiffly clenched like claws. Slowly we get to our feet, stretching our backs, blinking tired eyes. Without speaking, we shuffle from the sewing room down a long hallway, and out to a walled courtyard.

As we stumble into the gray light, I pull the knobby acorn-thing from my apron pocket to see what it is. A thimble. It warms at my touch. Silver, dimpled, as a thimble should be, with tiny roses amid brambles engraved along the base. A thimble would be useful, but somehow I know that I must keep it hidden, so I quickly tuck it back into my pocket.

Under the eyes of the Overseer and a few guards, we

Seamstresses are ordered to stand and bend and stretch. As I move, reaching high toward the gray sky and then twisting at the waist, I feel my sluggish blood begin to pulse in my hands and feet. I blink away the dim monotony of the sewing room and notice my surroundings.

Looming over us is a fortress dark as a storm cloud; a clock set in its tallest square tower watches grimly over all. Around the courtyard is a high, bramble-covered wall. In the middle is a wooden post with chains and manacles hanging from it. A place of punishment.

I glance down the row of Seamstresses. They all have an inward look. They stare blankly ahead as they stretch. We are a line of gray-faced, gray-dressed, bony clockwork females. It's as if the individual part of each of the others has been stripped out, leaving behind only their skills. I was Nothing, and then I was Seamstress, like them, but . . . I have a secret, a silver thimble hidden in my apron pocket.

I reach for the sky again, feeling the ache of the work leach from my bones. My thimble came from somewhere. I take a deep breath of cold air scented faintly with pine. My thimble came from somewhere outside this place, and so did I. There was something before this. Just as I know I must hide the thimble, I know instinctively that I must keep this knowledge hidden as well.

Perhaps the other Seamstresses have hidden themselves away, too. Maybe it is safer in this gray fortress to hide your essential self deep within, where no one else can see it.

I wonder if I can tell one Seamstress from another. Glancing down the bending, twisting line, I see beside me the oldest and frailest of the Seamstresses, the one who was sitting next to me in our room. She had to bring her sewing right up to her watery blue eyes in order to see her own stitches. Next to her is a Seamstress who has age spots covering her gnarled hands. Then comes one who hunches under the burden of her humped back.

I wonder if inside their minds where they keep their own thoughts hidden, they wonder why they are here. Or perhaps they just do their work. I have to wonder, because my straggling stitchwork makes me guess that I am something else and not a true Seamstress, as they are.

The clock strikes the half hour. Beside me, the Oldest gasps for breath as we finish our exercises, and Spots, beside her, holds her side as if she's got a stitch.

A stitch. I smile at my little joke. The Overseer, catching my eye, frowns, and I make my face blank again.

In silence we leave the courtyard, still in a neatly hemmed line, and file into another room. A kind of dining hall with a low ceiling and long wooden tables. Like the other Seamstresses, I take a spoon and a dented tin bowl from a stack on the table by the door. We hold the bowls in front of us. The guards and the Overseer are always watching. The Seamstress with the hump is sneaky—she's cut into line behind me, and when one of the guards looks away, she reaches out and rakes a cruel fingernail down the welts on the back of my neck.

I gasp and take a quick glance over my shoulder. Maybe she can tell that I am not like the others. Her face goes blank except for a hint of satisfaction around her mouth. I wouldn't mind if she hid her essential self a bit more deeply inside.

The Seamstress ahead of me, Oldest, takes an unsteady step toward the food hatch and holds out her bowl. A ladle half filled with lentils and oats emerges from the hatch; Oldest catches her dinner in her bowl and wavers as if she's about to stumble.

As I reach out to steady her, Hump takes the opportunity to knock the empty bowl out of my hands; it tumbles to the stone floor, landing with a harsh clatter. I glance over my shoulder, but Hump is staring straight ahead.

Of *course* the guards didn't see her. Gritting my teeth, I retrieve my bowl. As Oldest hobbles away from the food hatch I step forward.

Before I can get my dinner, the Overseer slithers up. "This Seamstress has none," she hisses, laying her switch across my bowl. "Seek to mend yourself," she tells me.

For the merest half second I think about protesting, but I can see that the Overseer is waiting for it, hoping for it, perhaps. I must keep myself hidden, so I bow my head meekly. My stomach gives a hollow, hopeless grumble, and with my empty bowl I follow the other Seamstresses to the long table, where we sit. The room is silent except for the scrape of spoons scouring every drop of dinner from the tin bowls. Next to me sits a Seamstress with saggy skin, as if she'd once been plump; she edges her bowl closer to mine. A silent invitation to share. Then Hump sits across from us, banging down her bowl. She glares at Once-Plump, who edges her bowl back in front of herself and starts spooning up lentils. Hump kicks me hard under the table. I glare at her, but I don't kick back.

FROM THE EATING room we go to a laundry. We are made to strip naked, leaving our shifts, dresses, and aprons in a pile. I keep my silver thimble hidden in my hand. Shivering under the eyes of the guards, we go down the hallway to a cleaning room, where we are doused with icy water. The soap they make us use has some sort of fleabane in it; it scours the skin, leaving us scraped raw and red. Then we are doused again. Still dripping and naked, we are inspected, rough hands checking our shorn heads for lice. After that we file into a room for sleeping. We each take a rough woolen blanket from a pile by the door and go to one of the cots.

As one of the Seamstresses passes me, she pauses, and I brace myself in case she enjoys petty cruelty as much as Hump does. After a quick glance to check for the Overseer, she slips something cold and wet into my hand—a strip of ragged cloth.

"For your neck," the Seamstress breathes, looking straight ahead.

I don't dare thank her, for the Overseer is gliding toward me.

Under her slit-eyed gaze, I lie stiffly down on a cot. One by one, the lights in the sleep room are put out, until just one lantern remains lit by the door, where a guard with furred ears stands at attention. In the near-darkness, I carefully unfold the cloth and lay it against the welts on my neck, and it isn't really soothing, as chilled as I am, but the unexpected kindness of it warms me.

We are supposed to sleep, but I steal a little time for myself. I put the silver thimble onto my finger. It glows warm; with it I trace my bones—ribs, collarbone, a jutting hip. I reach up to rub my short hair, then run the thimbled finger-tip over my eyebrow. I don't know what I look like. Just like the others, I suppose, only younger.

If I could, I would savor this time alone with my thoughts, but the weight of the work presses down on me. Warmed by the touch of the thimble, I fall asleep.

It is still dark when we are wakened by the tolling of the fortress clock and a guard's barked orders.

Wearily I pull myself from the narrow cot, joining the other Seamstresses as we file out, leaving the blankets in a pile by the door so they can be laundered for the next shift of sleepers.

Again we go to the cleaning room for the cold shower and caustic soap.

Whoever runs this place has a horror of dirt and bugs, I imagine, as the icy water pours over my head.

In our line, we are given clothes, and after we have put

them on we shuffle silently down the passageways to the sewing room, where we go immediately to work.

The muslin night-dresses that I have been hemming need to be redone. The Overseer gives me another stinging welt on my neck and orders me to unpick all of my stitches. "The Godmother sees," she hisses. "Straighter thisss time."

The Godmother.

Words rattle around in my head like pebbles in a cup. I open my mouth and speak for the first time. "The Godmother?" I whisper.

The Overseer's slitted eyes narrow. "Seamstress serves her."

"This is her fortress?" I dare.

"Sahhh," the Overseer hisses. "Silence. Stitch."

Swallowing the rest of my questions, I bend to my work. So passes a day, and another day, and then more days. We clockwork Seamstresses are wound up, and our gears engage, and we work until we wind down into our narrow beds. It's all carefully calculated, I realize. Not quite enough food, not nearly enough sleep, a little exercise, and punishments now and then to keep us from getting too dull.

More time passes. A question here, a sharp ear there, and I learn more about the Godmother. She takes ragged, smudged girls—girls like me?—and turns them into beautiful princesses. Why, I don't know. An obsession? A calling? A passion for neatly tied-off threads?

As I sew my awkward seams, I tell myself a story. It goes

like this: the Godmother in all her glory glides into the sewing room and surveys us, one slender finger on her perfect lips, and she chooses the one who is different, special—me, of course. She plucks me out of the row of humpbacked, squinting Seamstresses and makes me, too, a beautiful princess. With a gown sewn by . . . well, by the poor wenches too old or ugly to catch the Godmother's eye.

But that story is not meant to be. Here I sit. Have sat. Will sit. Time passes; we stitch.

THE BOOMING OF the fortress clock tells me that it's two in the afternoon when the door to our room opens and a guard comes in. A gruff whisper to the Overseer, and we are ordered to put down our work and stand. Like the others, I obediently get to my feet. The guard leads us to the cobblestone courtyard where we do our exercises. The fortress looms at our backs, gray and impenetrable, the clock like a blank face in its tallest tower; the bramble-covered wall surrounds it. The sky overhead is cloudy. Flecks of ice fall from the clouds and prick at us like needles.

In the middle of the courtyard is the stout wooden post, but this time someone is chained to it. A young man, a boy really, about the same age that I seem to be, with sandy hair. I can't see any more of him because he has his forehead pressed against the post and his eyes closed. He is shirtless and shivering in the icy wind.

We Seamstresses are lined up to watch, joined by other

workers, all dressed in gray. The Overseer stands beside me; a row of guards in light-blue, lace-trimmed uniforms faces us.

"What is happening?" I dare to whisper to the Overseer.

Her slitted eyes gaze straight ahead, at the boy chained to the post. "A chastisement is necessitated."

A punishment, she means. "Who is he?" I ask.

"Shoemaker," she answers.

"What did he do?"

"Asked too many quessstions," the Overseer hisses, with a meaningful glare at me. "Stay silent, Seamstress."

We wait. My bare feet are frozen and I am shaking with a combination of cold and fright. I open my mouth to ask another question.

"Hush," the Overseer breathes, and strangely, she sounds frightened, too. "She comes."

A subtle change washes over the courtyard. The guards straighten, the air grows more chill. At the post, I see the Shoemaker stiffen; his manacled hands clench into fists.

The Godmother enters. I know at once that it is her; she is exactly as I imagined. She wears a swansdown cape and muff, white as snow. She glides past the other workers, then past us, the Seamstresses. As she passes, to keep from trembling, I grip the thimble in my apron pocket; as always, the silver warms under my fingers. At the same moment that I peek up at her, the Godmother glances aside at me, hesitating ever so slightly. Her eyes are silver-blue and as beautiful and cold as ice. Her glance hits me like a wash of freezing water, and for a moment I am Nothing, not even a Seamstress, and I look quickly down again. I am lost, adrift, and then the thimble in my hand flares with heat. I cling to it and the Nothing recedes.

When I look up again, the Godmother has seated herself in a carved chair on a dais raised above the cold cobblestones. She makes no speech; she simply waves a languid hand, and a pig-snouted guard steps forward, takes one or two practice swings, and proceeds to whip the Shoemaker bloody. The courtyard echoes with the sound of braided leather meeting flesh. I can't help but keep count. Ten lashes is enough. At twenty I am sure the guard will stop. At twenty-five I find myself flinching with every blow. At last, at thirty, the guard stops. All is silent. On the dais, the Godmother gets to her feet, smooths her gown, and steps onto the cobblestones.

My face feels stiff as I watch her leave. A group of workers follows.

"Hatters," says the Overseer, unexpectedly. She points out the other workers as they depart. Lacemakers, Bakers of gingerbread, Candlemakers, Glovers, Spinsters of gold into straw, and the Jacks of all trades, who can make anything, she says, from a sharpened spindle to a glass coffin.

"Why are we here?" I ask desperately. "What are we for?"

The Overseer blinks, a slow flick of a lid sideways across her slitted eye. "We serve her. That is all."

That is all. And now I know that drawing the Godmother's attention is the last thing I'd ever want to do.

FOR ANOTHER LONG stretch of time I sew. My stitch-soldiers line up at ragged attention and then wander off on missions of their own instead of marching in perfectly straight hemlines. At the striking of the fortress clock, I go with the other Seamstresses to the courtyard for exercise; I eat unsalted lentils and oats twice a day; I sleep on a cot under a scratchy woolen blanket.

And I stitch.

Then one afternoon, the door at one end of the sewing room flies open and someone bursts inside. The candle flames waver in the wind of his arrival. The Shoemaker from the courtyard.

I sit up and take notice. He has clean features, and I can't quite see what color his eyes are. He carries himself stiffly, his shoulders slightly hunched, and he is thin—too thin, as we all are.

"A glass slipper?" the Shoemaker protests, holding up a scrap of light-blue paper. "A shoe made of *glass*? I'm a Shoemaker, not a Glassblower!"

At the Shoemaker's unexpected fierceness, a few heads bob up, surfacing from the placid stitch-stitch-stitch for a moment, bleary eyes taking in the scene, hearts beating with the pitter-patter of curiosity and fear. Then the heads jerk down again.

The Overseer glides up to him. The shoes he makes must be matched to the dresses we stitch, so she's not surprised to see him. "Certainly some mistake," she hisses. "Show me the requisition." She peers at the blue square of paper. "Sahhhh. A simple misspelling. The slippers are supposed to be fur. Fur slippers."

The Shoemaker frowns and runs a hand through his ragged hair. "I don't know. It says *verre*, that's glass."

"Yesss, but it's supposed to be fur. *Vaire*. See?" The Overseer taps the requisition form with her switch.

"I don't think so." The Shoemaker shakes his head, decisive. "No. Last time I tried doing it my way I was sorry after."

He's talking about the thirty lashes at the post. Through careful questioning, I'd found out his crime. He'd made *dogskin* slippers instead of the *doeskin* ones that had been ordered. The Overseer told me he claimed he'd misread the requisition, but I have my doubts about that. The Shoemaker is like me, someone who asks questions when he shouldn't. I wouldn't put it past him to design subtle mockery into a pair of slippers, even though he must have known how dangerous even such a small rebellion would be. But lashes with a whip are far worse than welts from a switch, and apparently he's learned his lesson.

"Could you do it with a pattern?" the Overseer asks. "Using mirrors, perhapsss?"

The Shoemaker gives a stiff shrug, suddenly resigned. The blue requisition form flutters to the floor. "I'll work something out." As he turns to leave, he catches me looking at him. I slide my hand into my pocket and grip the silver thimble. It gives me strength. I don't dare offer up a smile, but he must understand the suggestion in my eyes, for he frowns and then gives the slightest nod in return.

Green. His eyes are green. How could I have failed to notice it before? His eyes promise that there really is something outside the grim gray of the Godmother's fortress. The green of a forest. Escape.

I feel a strange, faint flame kindle in my heart.

After the Shoemaker goes, the Seamstresses are unsettled. Whispers are heard; the Overseer's watchful gaze darts here, there, trying to catch us out.

The Seamstress next to me, the one who gave me the cloth for my welts, leans over and speaks without taking her eyes from her work. "Do you think the Shoemaker is good-looking?"

I sit up straighter. Sneaking a quick sideways glance, I realize that she is not much older than I am. Her short hair is chestnut brown and her fading blue eyes might once have been merry.

At the far end of the room, the Overseer's head comes up, alert, her mouth open to sense the air. I bend over my work. Without looking at my neighbor, I breathe, "Do you?"

Her only reply is a faint snort. A short time later she whispers, "We had much better-looking young men in our village. I had one myself."

The Overseer's head swivels toward the sound. The switch twitches.

We sew furiously at our seams until her slit-eyed gaze slides away.

I sneak another glance at the Seamstress beside me. She bites off a thread and casts me a wink.

"Do you remember your village?" I whisper.

She gives an almost-imperceptible nod. "Some things. I remember my name, too. It's Marya."

I think about that for a while. None of us is supposed to remember anything. How could she sit here stitching her life away if she had any memories of a Before? I decide that she's lying.

"Well, do you think he's handsome?" Marya whispers, when the Overseer is busy inspecting another Seamstress's work.

She's back to the Shoemaker again. She must not remember the time when he was flogged for the dogskin slippers.

I will never forget it. He was hanging in his chains by the time the whipping was over, but he never cried out.

Yes, he is very good-looking.

But *handsome* is not the word I would use to describe the Shoemaker.

What would I call him? Resilient, maybe? Or stubborn? Or perhaps stupid, to take the risks that he has. Yet the little candle flame of hope that burns in me leans toward him, as if it senses that he bears the same flame within himself.

Marya makes her impatience for an answer known in the abrupt way she ties and bites off a thread.

Finally, I shrug.

"My young man was a farmer's son," Marya whispers, "and I was the best seamstress in the village, well known for my fine needlework. We were to be married, and I was sewing my wedding gown. I chose the softest pink wool, and embroidered the sweetest roses around the collar, and sewed tiny mother-of-pearl buttons up the back."

This is too real a memory she's describing—she can't be lying. She really is from outside, and she was torn away from that life because of her skills, I guess, brought here to labor for the Godmother.

Unlike Marya, I do not sew well. Why, then, was I brought here? Did the Godmother make a mistake? What am I? What life did I have before this?

My Before is a blank emptiness. For just a moment the Nothing looms like a darkness at the edge of my vision. I take a shaking breath and push it back. I stare down at the white cloth in my hands. It is smooth under my fingers. The needle is a sliver of silver. The flame burns warm in my heart. I take another, steadier breath. The Nothing recedes.

Marya gives me a nudge and a sly wink. "I couldn't wait until my wedding night." She opens her mouth to whisper something else. But in her enthusiasm she's lost vigilance.

"Sssso, something to say?" The Overseer peers over Marya's shoulder, her tongue flicking eagerly in and out of her mouth. A scaly hand raises the switch and *thwack*, a red welt slashes across the back of Marya's neck. Then another and another.

Marya cringes under the blows. "N-no, Overseer," she whimpers, all trace of daring gone.

The Overseer draws back her head and narrows her eyes. "Sahhh. Possibly a chastisement is necessitated. Yes?" It is the post in the courtyard she means, and the whip.

Marya bites her lip; her hands are trembling and her face has gone petticoat-white.

"A Seamstress's purpose is to stitch," the Overseer says, pushing her face up to Marya's. "Stitch and stitch. Not to gosssssip, not to speculate. Stitch."

Marya sits frozen.

"Seamstress has nothing Before," the Overseer continues. "Nothing to come. Understand?"

Tears drop from Marya's eyes, watering the silk that has gusted onto her lap. She nods and takes a trembling stitch.

The Overseer opens her mouth to continue her harangue.

I poke my needle into a pincushion and turn to face the Overseer. "I asked if she can see well enough." My voice seems to echo in the silent room. No one has ever dared to speak up before. The rows of Seamstresses pause for a moment in their work, then commence stitching again. But ears are pricked.

The Overseer jerks around to face me. "Sahhh?"

"I said that we haven't enough light to sew by." I point to the guttering tallow candle at my elbow. "We could do finer work if we had better light."

The Overseer blinks. She closes her mouth and straightens, gazing at me as if hypnotized. The switch twitches.

I hold my breath.

"So," she says at last. "I see."

To my relief, she lowers the switch and glides away to resume her watchful duties.

I stitch, and I think about the Shoemaker. That single brief glance that we shared—in this place where hardly anyone dares to speak, a glance like that is like an entire conversation. It asks, *how long have you been here?* and *do you wonder?* and *what if . . . ?* I think about the smell of pine that wafts over the courtyard wall. About my thimble. About my certainty that there was something before the Nothing, before the Seamstress.

And if there was something before, there must be something after, for stitched seams have beginnings, and they have tied-off ends, too.

After a time, two horned, goat-footed guards bring in boxes of fresh waxen candles, which are lit and placed at our elbows. The other Seamstresses cast me wondering glances. Marya sits like a stone beside me, and stitches.

"Are you all right?" I whisper.

She stares at her work and does not answer.

For a time I sew my straggling stitches, which aren't anything like grains of sand, and think. My history is a blank. Marya remembers a village, a handsome boy, her name. I don't know what I would do if I had all that in my Before and nothing ahead.

The candles burn down and are replaced with new ones. A silver needle breaks and I reach for another, threading it with white silk to match the nightgown I am hemming.

An odd stillness interrupts my thoughts. Marya has stopped working. She sits beside me on the bench staring at her unmoving hands. The Overseer's back is turned, but when she looks around she will see.

"Are you all right?" I ask again.

Marya does not answer. Slowly she sets down her needle and pushes a pile of scarlet velvet off her lap. Her movements fluid with remembered grace, she gets to her feet.

The Overseer, distracted by another's stitches, does not see.

Marya turns and walks to the sewing-room door.

Don't! I want to scream. *Stop!* I grope for the thimble in my pocket.

The Seamstresses pause in their work, following her with their squinting eyes. This cessation of motion the Overseer notices. She snaps around.

At the same moment, Marya throws open the door and flings herself into the passageway. A spate of activity follows: the shouting of guards, a scuffle, the sound of blows, Marya's high-pitched screams. Followed by stillness and silence.

We Seamstresses are on our feet, our faces to the door,

our eyes straining to see. The Overseer re-enters, smoothing her dress; there is no sound but the susurration of her footsteps. She looks up, sees us staring.

"Sssssew."

We bow our heads, resume our seats, and sew. We are all wondering what will become of Marya. Most of us imagine the flogging post. Some of us might even look forward to witnessing such a punishment, as it breaks up the monotony of our work.

We stitch. A day passes.

Late in the afternoon the guards come again. Between them walks Marya, her eyes blank, moving awkwardly, like a collection of sticks pulled by strings. The guards push her onto her seat beside me on the bench; the Overseer places a threaded needle into her hand and sets her to hemming an apron.

The guards depart. Marya stitches. I watch her out of the corners of my eyes. Her stitches, I notice, are wide and sloppy, far worse than mine. A thread of drool escapes from her mouth and stains the cloth, but she sews on, unnoticing.

I have thought of doing what Marya has done, but no one has ever tried to escape the fortress. I can see why the Godmother has sent Marya back again, even though she has been made useless. Just like the Shoemaker, I suppose, she has learned her lesson, and now she serves as a lesson for the rest of us.

I wonder what I will learn from it.

We stitch on. My fingers cramp around the needle. The Overseer gives me a few more *thwacks* with her switch. My shoulders hunch, and I stretch to get the ache out of my back, rub my burning eyes, and then stitch some more.

I am unpicking yet another crooked seam when the door opens. Three guards bustle in and whisper to the Overseer. We Seamstresses are made to stand in rows before our table, heads bowed, hands folded neatly before us. The thimble burns in my apron pocket. Just an inspection, the Overseer says, as if trying to reassure us.

For a moment there is silence. Then the Godmother enters. I don't dare look at her, but her presence is obvious in the way the room feels suddenly smaller and colder, and taut with held breaths.

The Godmother stands in the doorway, surveying us.

"Good girls," she says, even though some of the so-called girls are old enough to be grandmothers. The Godmother sweeps into the room, trailed by the Overseer and the nervous guards. She pauses to inspect a bit of Hump's fine embroidery, then proceeds down the row. She passes Marya without even a glance, and comes to me.

I keep my gaze on the stone floor. The welts that stripe the back of my neck burn.

"Show me your hands," the Godmother says.

The sound of her voice makes me jerk in surprise; my body tingles as if I've been dropped into an icy river. For a second I grip the thimble. Then I let it go and pull my shaking hands out of my apron pockets, holding them palms up for inspection.

The Godmother takes one of my hands in hers. It is like being touched by a marble statue; her skin is that cold and smooth, white veined with palest blue. Her fingers stroke the callus on my thumb.

"The Overseer says you speak for the others, Seamstress," the Godmother says, still holding my hand.

I suppose she's right. I do speak for the others. Even though admitting it is dangerous, I nod.

"Well then," the Godmother says. She turns my hand, inspecting each finger. Her delicate nose wrinkles slightly, as if she smells something she doesn't like. "Is there anything you want? Or need?"

Ah. They don't want us thinking about escape, as Marya did. They want us to be happy, or at least compliant. Good little workers.

But I will not ask the Godmother for anything. What could she give us that she hasn't already taken away?

I can sense the other Seamstresses' anticipation, their unspoken requests. "Nothing," I say, and risk an upward glance.

The Godmother regards me with her silver-blue eyes. Her expression says that she is wondering if my refusal to ask her for anything is a veiled rebellion. Her dress is the same frozen color as her eyes; I remember Marya sewing the tiny crystals onto the overskirt. She leans closer.

I hold myself still.

Her breath is cold against my cheek. "I wonder about you, my dear," she whispers into my ear. "What you remember. And what you forget."

"I forget everything," I breathe. "I remember nothing."

She straightens and drops my hand. Her eyes narrow as she inspects me closely. Too closely.

I bow my head. My flame fades to the faintest ember, hiding. I make myself the very image of a good and obedient Seamstress.

Her attention fixes on my bare feet. "Your feet are sufficiently small," she says. "The Overseer reports that the Shoemaker has requested a model for his latest task. You are excused from your duties until he has finished with you."

The Godmother stares at me, waiting. I bob a quick curtsy, and she glides regally from the room. The walls step back and take a deep breath after she's gone.

The other Seamstresses cast me jealous looks as they resume their seats.

Marya stays on her feet, staring blankly at the wall across from her, until I take her arm and pull her to the bench.

"Here," I whisper, and put a threaded needle in her hand. Her fingers stay loose until I fold them around the needle. Then I pick up the apron she's been stitching and put it back into her lap. I let my touch linger against her hand for a moment, a bit of warmth for her, and for me. "I'll be back soon," I say.

"Sahhh," the Overseer interrupts, and I straighten. She ushers me to the door and tells me how to reach the Shoe-maker's workshop. I go out the sewing-room door, down the passageway, and out to the courtyard. As always, the sky is gray, and the air is swirling with tiny snowflakes. Shivering, I cross the courtyard without looking at the post or the bramble-covered wall beyond it, and re-enter the fortress. I follow the Overseer's directions, making a left turn here, following that empty corridor to its end, climbing this narrow staircase, until I come to the Shoemaker's door. As instructed, I knock and enter.

CHAPTER

2

SHOE LOOKS UP FROM THE WORKBENCH WHERE HE'S BEEN
sketching out some plans for the blasted glass slipper ordered
by the Godmother.

The stick of charcoal drops from his fingers.

The new girl, the one from the room of the Seamstresses,
stands in the doorway. She'd caught his eye before, and her
gaze had been piercingly, speakingly direct. And now she is
here. She has a hand in the pocket of her apron as if she is
holding something but keeping it hidden.

He gets to his feet, wiping smudged fingers on his trousers. He nods a greeting.

"Hello," she says. Her voice is slightly rough—because she
doesn't use it often, he knows. She is tall—his own height—
with pale skin and hacked-short hair as dark and shiny as shoe

leather, and red welts across the back of her neck. Her features are strong, not pretty, he thinks, but sharply distinctive. She looks around the room with assessing gray eyes. "You're all alone here?"

He nods, still trying to find his voice. There had been another Shoemaker once, a young man, but a long time ago he'd gotten a requisition for twelve sets of dancing slippers, and then twelve more, and then more and more without end, and was beaten by their Overseer when he couldn't keep up. In the end all he could do was rock back and forth on his bench, muttering to himself while stabbing an awl through a mangled piece of shoe leather over and over again. Guards had taken him away, and he'd never come back.

Yes, he is alone.

"No Overseer?" she asks.

He clears his throat. "Sometimes. They trust me to get on with it."

"You must have been here for a long time, then," she observes. "What's your name?"

He shakes his head. "Call me Shoe. We don't have much time, so you'd better sit down." He points to the three-legged stool beside his bench.

She stays on her feet. "Aren't you going to ask my name?"

"You don't have a name," he says roughly.

"Still," she says, and cocks her head as if waiting.

He sighs. "What should I call you?"

She gives a one-shouldered shrug. "I don't know. Stitch?"

No, she is too sharp for a name like that. "You're more of a Needle," he mutters. "Or a Pin."

Without warning she smiles, not a cool, sharp smile, but a wicked grin that makes him step back and catch his breath.

"Pin will do very well," she says.

He notices, then, that her way of talking is sharp, too. Like cut glass, he would say. He is the Shoemaker, and in the Before he must have been an apprentice to a shoemaker, because even though he remembers nothing from then, his hands know what they are doing when it comes to making shoes. But her—in the Before, she wasn't a seamstress. She's too keen; she burns too brightly. In the Before, she'd been something else.

Pin steps closer, and he smells her: clean, caustic soap and something of the wind and snow in the courtyard. She reaches out and takes his hand in hers.

He feels her touch as a shock, the warmth of her fingers scorchingly hot against the skin of his own cold hand. He grits his teeth as she holds his hand in both of hers and turns it over, inspecting it. With slender fingers, she traces lines of fire along the tendons on the back of his hand, then strokes coals against the calluses on his thumb. She has calluses too, on the tips of her fingers.

He pulls his hand away. This is dangerous. *She* is dangerous. If this kind of thing goes any further, he'll end up under the whip again, or she will, and he can't face either one of those things. "You'd better sit down," he repeats, and points at the stool.

With a shrug she sits, first sweeping her skirt aside, an almost regal movement, as if she is used to wearing a fuller, richer dress with layers of petticoats. Maybe in the Before she did, and her body remembers it. Now she wears an apron over a loose woolen dress that comes down to her ankles.

He sits, and she pulls her skirt up to her knees and plops one of her bare feet onto the low workbench. "Well, Shoe," she says. "I suppose you'd better get on with it."

The glass slipper—or fur one, he hasn't gotten that cleared up yet—has to fit perfectly. He will measure each of Pin's feet and then carve a model of them, and then build the shoes. A girl can dance all night long in a shoe he's made and never feel footsore; her toes will never be pinched; she will never feel the slightest blemish of a blister on her heel.

He'll know about it if they do, the mysterious girls who wear the shoes he makes. He'll be punished for any mistakes, and know better next time. He gets out the calipers and measuring tape and a fresh piece of paper and his charcoal pencil and starts making notes.

CHAPTER

3

I LIKE THE NAME HE'S GIVEN ME. *PIN*. I LIKE HIS NAME, *Shoe*. From the way he moves, and the depth of his concentration, I can see that he's very skilled at his craft, just as the Seamstresses are. That makes sense; the Godmother would take only the best. Except for me. It makes me wonder even more why I'm here when I'm of no use to her.

I like the way Shoe's room smells of cured leather and tallow candle, and I like the way his tools are carefully put away on a rack on the wall. His workbench is neat, with everything to hand. Clearly he takes pride in his work, which strikes me as being odd, somehow. Something about him makes me feel wide awake and alive, not at all the gray, exhausted, dull Seamstress.

He bends over my foot, taking a precise measurement

with some metal device, inspecting it, then making notes on a piece of paper.

"Why are shoemakers called cobblers?" I ask, for something to fill the silence.

He glances up, wary. His green eyes are a strange flash of forest in this dim gray room inside a gray stone fortress within a foggy gray world. "We're not," he says. "Cobblers fix shoes, they don't make new ones. They're not supposed to use a whole piece of leather, they only repair shoes by cobbling together odds and ends. It's—" He opens his mouth as if he'd like to say more, but then shakes his head and closes it again. Shoe is a talker, I realize; he's just out of practice.

"That must be from the Before," I note. The Godmother does not deal in scraps and rags. For the Seamstresses it is only the richest fabrics and finest of threads. I can see, stacked on a table in the corner of the room, that Shoe has rolls of the best materials to work with, mottled leather from some reptile, a snake perhaps, shiny black leather, creamy white doeskin, and sables and rabbit fur and thick felt.

He blinks and bends his head to the measurements again. His voice has been rough, but his hands are gentle as he cradles my foot, turning it this way and that.

"Shoe, do you remember anything from the Before?" I ask softly.

"No." He pauses to write something down on the paper. "Just the Now. I forget everything before this moment."

I can understand this. His recent past includes the post,

after all. Time is tricky here, but it can't have been too long since then. The lashes on his back must be barely healed. "And will you forget this moment when it has passed?" I ask.

He shakes his head. "I don't know. Maybe."

"What about this, Shoe," I ask. "Do you know why we're making these dresses, and the shoes, and the rest of it? They're not all for the Godmother, are they?"

He gives me a frowning glance. "You ask a lot of questions."

"Ones that you won't answer," I say.

"I don't know the answers, Pin," he says wearily, and suddenly I notice that his face is too pale, too thin, and his green eyes are shadowed with exhaustion. I wonder if I look the same, stretched to skin-over-bones by too much work and too little food. I examine my own hand. It *is* too thin, too pale. We cannot live long, I think, in service to the Godmother.

I put my too-thin hand into my apron pocket. The thimble slips onto my finger, and it warms my hand. My hope flares; a knot of determination forms in my chest. "Shoe, something is out there, beyond the walls around this fortress. I think we should try to get to it."

He drops the metal measuring device—it clatters against the stone floor—and jerks to his feet, eyes wide. Staring at me, he backs away until he is pressed against the cold stone wall of his room. "No," he says, and I can see that he's shaking. "If she caught us, she'd kill us. Or worse. Curse it, Pin, she'd kill us if she knew we were even talking about it." He glances around as if expecting a listening ear to spring out of the stone walls of his room, or an accusing finger to appear and point him out as a rebel.

"You know it exists, don't you?" I challenge. "We had to come from somewhere, didn't we?"

He shakes his head. "No. I'd better get started on the slipper pattern before it's too late."

"All right," I say. But it is already too late. For I am more than a Seamstress, and I have decided what I am going to do.

Shoe finishes his measurements, his movements jerky, his shoulders stiff. Then he stands and pulls on a shapeless coat made of the same gray wool as my dress. "I'll walk you to the sewing room," he says.

Oh, so gallant. Or maybe he wants to be sure I won't get into trouble on the way back. I give him a pert curtsy that makes him frown, and then follow him from the room and down the narrow stairs. At the bottom we're supposed to go right, toward the courtyard; I go left.

I hear quick footsteps, and he catches up to me. "What are you doing?" he whispers.

"Just curious," I answer. Curiosity is a new feeling, and I want to indulge it. I want to see what sorts of rags and scraps I might find lying around the Godmother's fortress so I can stitch together a plan. The hallway we're in is wide, lined with closed doors, lit by smoky lanterns, paved with smooth stone that is cold under my bare feet. I pause and try turning a doorknob. It's locked.

"We shouldn't be here," he breathes.

"You don't have to come with me," I reply. I try another door. Also locked.

I know nothing about the Before. I don't know my name or where I came from, but I do know that I am a person who asks questions and risks pushing against the boundaries of obedience. Shoe could leave me now; if he is smart, that's what he'll do. My plan will unravel, likely enough, and I'll end up at the post. But he's stubborn—I know that much about him, even not really knowing him at all—and he stays with me, a grim shadow at my back.

I reach another door, and this time I pull the thimble from my apron pocket.

"What is that?" Shoe asks at my shoulder.

With anyone else, I would hide it, but for him I open my hand; the thimble gleams silver on my palm.

"It's from the Before," I whisper.

His eyes widen as he stares down at it; then he looks soberly at me, and I feel as if I could fall into his green eyes, into the promise of the forest outside. My knees wobble and I clench my hand around the thimble. He takes my arms, steadying me, and for just a moment my faint flame kindles to his; between us, the thimble burns with a sudden flash of light that leaks from between my fingers. Suddenly I can feel how strange the thimble is—its power, its potential.

He closes his hand over mine. "Keep it hidden," he says, his voice ragged.

I nod, knowing he means the thimble *and* the flame.

"What can it do?" he whispers.

"Let's find out," I answer, and slip the thimble onto my finger. Turning from him, I try the doorknob again. It turns. I glance at the thimble and it flashes a gleam at me, as sly and secret as a wink. "Thank you very much," I tell it. Opening the door, I poke my head inside. The big, high-ceilinged room is busy, smelling of sawdust and burned feathers and linseed oil. It is the workroom of the Jacks of all trades. The air is noisy with the sound of hammering and the whoosh and rush of a bellows. I step inside and look around. In the center of the room, four Jacks are using a rope and pulleys strung from a hook in the ceiling to maneuver a feather mattress onto the top of a teetering stack of mattresses piled on a sturdy bed frame. They don't notice me and Shoe standing just inside the doorway.

But another Jack does, and scurries over to us, his face lined and pinched. "We're busy," he snaps. "And our Overseer is due to check on us in less than an hour. Do you have a requisition?" On a nearby table, I notice blue requisition slips impaled on a metal spike.

"That depends," I say. "Could you make me a metal hook about this big?" I hold out my hands to show him.

The Jack stares. "A *hook*? You want to know if we can make you a *hook*?" He barks out a scornful laugh. "Missy, we could make you a spinning wheel to spin thread as fine and strong as a cobweb. We could make you wings that will fly you to the moon to get cream for your tea. We could make a music box out of pure gold that can sing like a nightingale. A hook! Hmph."

At the center of the room, one of the Jacks reaches the top of the bed piled with mattresses. "Have you got the pea?" he shouts down to the other Jacks. One of them scurries off, presumably to fetch a pea, though what that has to do with such a strange and impractical bed, I have no idea. I ask the Jack. "Why a pea?"

He blinks and glances over at the mattress-stacked bed. "Godmother's orders, of course," he says.

I seize at once on his words. "But why? What does she want it for?"

The Jack looks blank. "The Godmother's orders. That's all I know, missy."

"And you don't know why?" I say to our Jack.

He shrugs. "Not my job to know."

Of course it's not. I go back to the reason I came in here. "I need you to make me a hook, Jack. One with an eye at the end to put a rope through, and prongs that will hold tight to the top of a wall that someone might want to climb."

From half a step behind me, I hear Shoe take a breath, as if he's about to say something.

"A grappling hook, you mean." The Jack rubs his nose. "You got a requisition?"

"No," I answer.

"Then we can't make you any hook."

"Pin," Shoe says in a low voice, a warning.

"It's all right," I say to him. Then to the Jack, "I thought you could make anything."

"We *can* make anything," the Jack protests. "But you've got to have a requisition!"

In the center of the room, one of the Jacks wails; another one comes climbing down from the tall bed. One of the mattresses has sprung a leak; feathers swirl around them.

"Oh, curse it," our Jack mutters. "Just a moment." He scurries away to confer with the other Jacks.

"I'll be right back," I say to Shoe, and I join the Jacks. A mattress at about head-height in the pile on the bed has split at its seam, which is still unraveling, and feathers are spilling out of it—bursting out—and floating down to the floor like snow. As I reach them, a seam on another mattress splits, and then another. The Jacks are frantically trying to stuff the feathers back into the mattresses, holding the unraveling seams together with their hands, wailing, arguing, blaming one another for the mistake.

"Come on, lads," our Jack orders. "The requisition says this must be ready tonight."

"It'll never be ready in time, Jack," one of the other Jacks says, and sneezes as a bit of fluff goes up his nose. The tall stack of mattresses wavers as if it's about to topple over.

"Oh, we're in for it," our Jack moans. "Our Overseer will be here soon. It'll be the post for all of us."

The other Jacks moan, and a few of the younger ones

start to cry. Bits of feathers and fluff stick to their damp faces.

"Have you got a needle and plenty of stout thread?" I interrupt.

Our Jack glances aside at me and makes a shooing motion with his hands. "Go away," he says. "You can't help."

"Seamstress," I tell him.

He blinks. "Jack," he orders, with a snap of his fingers. "Needle. Stout thread."

The fluff-covered Jack brings them, and a ladder. As I thread the needle, I push the other Jacks out of the way and climb the ladder. Here it doesn't matter if my stitches are tiny and straight, and quick as a flash I stitch up the seams of the leaking mattresses. Then I run the thimble along each seam. I don't know what its powers are, but perhaps this will help. "They'll hold," I say, hopping to the floor.

Our Jack looks up at the teetering stack of mattresses. Then he gives me a brisk nod. "That was well done." He lowers his voice. "You want that hook, do you?"

"Yes, I do," I say. I can see it; the Jack has the same rebellious flame in his heart that I do. Just a spark, but it's there. I give him a quick grin.

He gulps. "When she catches you, don't tell her it was us you got it from. Right?"

"She's not going to catch me," I say.

"Well then," the Jack says slowly. "We'll make your grappler, right enough."

"Thank you." On my finger, the thimble gives a warning

throb, and I know it's telling me that it's time to go. "I'll come fetch it soon," I say, and I lead Shoe out into the hallway. This time I turn right, toward the sewing room, and Shoe falls into step beside me.

He is furious. I can see it in the set of his shoulders, in the line of his jaw.

"I have to try," I explain. Hook or no hook, I am going to try. I stop and face him. "I have to escape from here."

"Where?" he asks roughly. "Even if you could get away, there's nowhere to go."

"Yes there is," I assure him. "There's the Before."

"No." He shoves his fists into his coat pockets and frowns at me. "There's no Before. It's gone."

"An After, then," I tell him, and point down the hall to where a door leads to the courtyard, past the post, over the wall, and beyond. "To whatever's out there."

"There's nothing out there for you," he says bleakly, and shakes his head. "It's too much of a risk."

"Staying here is the biggest risk you could ever take," I tell him.

"I can't—" he starts, then breaks off and closes his eyes. "There's worse things than the post, Pin."

"Shoe," I say. "We get barely enough to eat and hardly any sleep, we're not permitted to speak, we're frightened all the time, and we will work here until the day we die." Now I step closer to him. We are much the same height, and as I lean in to whisper into his ear, my cheek brushes against his, and he flinches. I put my hand on his shoulder to steady him. "We don't touch," I breathe. "We don't kiss. We don't love. How could anything be worse than that?"

He closes his eyes. Then he bends his head, leaning against me, taking comfort. I can feel the tension in his body, the weight of his hand on my arm. I lean into him, giving him warmth for warmth. "Come with me," I whisper.

"Pin . . ." After a long moment, he takes a shuddering breath, as if he's going to say something else. But he doesn't. He opens his eyes, steps away, and I see that his pale face has turned even paler. "Don't do it. She'll find out. She'll catch you. You'll end up . . ." His voice breaks, and he shakes his head.

He really has learned his lesson. "You don't have to come, Shoe," I say, trying to keep my voice light even though I'm far more disappointed than I thought I'd be.

And I leave him there and go back to the sewing room, where I will stitch and stitch and plan my escape, and Marya's, into the Before, or perhaps the After, that waits for me beyond the Godmother's fortress walls.

CHAPTER

4

SHOE TRUDGES UP THE STAIRS TO HIS WORKROOM. HE takes off his coat and hangs it on its hook, gives the door a savage kick to close it, and sits down at his bench. The measurements of Pin's feet are marked neatly on the piece of paper he's left there.

Pin. She is braver than he is, with her plan to escape. She has no way of knowing what is outside, beyond the walls of the fortress. Even if she manages to get over the wall, the Godmother will track her, and catch her. Then it will be Pin chained to the post, feeling the icy wind on her bare skin, and the deep bite and burn as the whip slashes into her back.

On the day he was flogged, the guards left him chained to the post until the sky turned black with night. He'd gotten so cold that the blood from the lashes he'd been given had frozen on his back. The cold hadn't been enough to numb the pain, though. He hunches his shoulders and presses the heels of his hands over his eyes, trying to put that memory back into the past, where it belongs.

Taking a shaky breath and opening his eyes, he stares down at Pin's measurements. A very neat foot, she has, and cold, he imagines, on the stone floors of the fortress.

Outside, winter is coming.

He has glass slippers to make for the Godmother—and fur ones, just in case. He picks up his tools and gets to work.

SOMETHING PERHAPS ONLY a Seamstress—even a poor one like me—would know is that even though silk is light and lovely and flows as smooth as moonbeams over the skin, it is a very strong material. It is good for making ball gowns, and it is good for making ropes.

In the sewing room, I keep my head down and stitch. I have filched every scrap of silk cloth and silk thread that I can, and when the Overseer is busy with the other Seamstresses I work it. My rope is narrow and braided and well stitched, and with every hour that passes, it gets longer, but it is not yet long enough. When the Overseer slithers closer to see what I am up to, I hide my silk rope workings under my apron, and she blinks her slitted eyes and flicks her forked tongue and goes away again. The other Seamstresses cast me sidelong looks, and some of them pass me scraps of silk under the table, but they say nothing. Even Hump stays silent, though perhaps she is waiting until later so my crime will be all the greater when I am caught.

Except that I don't plan on getting caught.

I lean closer to Marya to whisper. "I'll take you with me when I go."

Marya doesn't answer. She stares down at the apron she is stitching, her face blank. With a chill, I realize that she is not really Marya anymore, just Seamstress.

"You can go back to your village and marry your handsome boy," I whisper when the Overseer's back is turned. "You will be happy again, after that."

Marya's faded blue eyes blink. But she doesn't speak.

To my surprise, on one afternoon when a damp chill is lurking in the corners and my fingers are stiff with overwork, Shoe comes into the sewing room. His glance at me is swift, just a flash of green, but it is enough to set my heart pounding.

I keep my head carefully lowered, but my skin prickles with awareness of him. The set of his shoulders. His frown as he discusses a requisition with the Overseer in a low voice. Like picking at a loose thread, I have been thinking of him since we parted ways. I imagine him up there in his little room, his fair head bent over his work, his hands quick and competent. I'm curious about him. What does he think about? Does he ever imagine the world outside the fortress walls?

We don't kiss, I told him before. I wonder what it would feel like to kiss him.

But I stay rooted to my seat with my head lowered over my work. Before he goes, I steal one quick glance at him. The skin over his high cheekbones is flushed, and I know that he is as aware of me—of my every move and breath—as I am of him.

And then he goes.

I barely know Shoe, really. Yet I don't want to leave here without him.

I KEEP MY ears pricked, and when the Overseer is busy, I scoot forward to sit on the edge of the bench so my skirts come down to the floor. I play out my thin, silken rope to see how long it is, hiding its coils under my skirt as I measure it. How many arm's lengths will I need? More than this, I think. Carefully I reel in the rope again, coiling it on my lap, under my apron. It makes a heavy heap no bigger than a curled, sleeping cat. It is not enough, but it is almost enough.

It will hold Shoe's weight, I think. If he will come with me.

A sudden movement jolts me out of my calculating. Marya lurches from the bench. Her eyes are wide and staring; her mouth is a determined line. The apron she's been hemming falls to the floor.

Across the room, the Overseer's back is still turned.

Marya stands, swaying.

"Wait," I whisper.

With a trembling hand, Marya presses my shoulder,

keeping me in my seat. She does not speak. Then she stumbles to the door, opens it, and slips out. For a moment I stare after her—it's too soon—I'm not ready—does she *want* to end up at the post?—and then I jerk my eyes back to my work so I can pretend I didn't see her go. But my every muscle, every nerve, is clenched with dread. My ears strain to hear a sound from outside the sewing room, the sound of Marya's screams as she is captured again.

But there is nothing. Only silence.

Candles flicker. The other Seamstresses keep their heads lowered as they work, but I can feel their tension as they wait. The Overseer is busy with a mistake made by the Seamstress with the gnarled, age-spotted hands; she hisses as the trembling old woman unpicks a seam under her slit-eyed gaze.

At last, the Overseer straightens. She turns and surveys the room. And she sees that Marya's place is empty.

"Ssssahhhh," the Overseer breathes, and I see a flicker of something—is it fear?—in her eyes. In a flash she is at the door, flinging it open and calling for the guards, and then from outside there is shouting, and the rush of feet and paws in the passageway, and then . . .

Silence.

For a long time, nothing happens.

Marya's seat remains empty. I hide my rope beneath a pile of scraps under my bench. We are taken out for our stretches, our meager meal, our sleep; we come back and stitch. The old Seamstresses make more mistakes. Their hands shake and their eyes run with tears, and the Overseer hisses at them with increasing urgency. The tension in the air gets thicker and darker. They pass me more scraps of silk, more than I can use. I keep my head down and wonder what happened to Marya. She has been gone for a long time. She must have gotten away. My rope, finished, is coiled on my lap.

THE SOUND OF footsteps and curt orders is heard outside. The door flies open and several guards rush in, their naked tails waving behind them. The Overseer slithers up, hissing her displeasure. A lesson, she is told.

The Overseer wrings her scaly hands. "Stand silently," she orders.

We Seamstresses set down our work and get to our feet. I hide my rope on my bench under the dress that I am hemming. A knot of tension tightens in my chest. Where are they taking us? The Seamstress beside me, Oldest, puts her gnarled hands on the table to push herself up, and I steady her with a hand on her arm. She leans against me as we are ushered out the door.

Two pig-snouted guards are waiting in the passageway. Four more guards with twitching furry ears join us as we come out into the courtyard, blinking at the light. The sky overhead is gray—is it always gray? I wonder—and I shiver as I walk beside the shuffling old Seamstresses. The guards lead us across the courtyard—past the post, its chains and manacles clanking against the wood—to the high wall that surrounds the fortress and the courtyard.

The wall is what they have brought us to see.

It is the height of two tall men, I would guess, and covered with gray brambles about the thickness of my arm. The brambles are studded with thorns as long and sharp as daggers.

Halfway up the wall, impaled on thorns that are crusted with dried blood, is Marya's body. It looks like a giant rag doll. Its back is to us; its head lolls to the side; its arms and legs are splayed and pierced by the bloody thorns. Marya was stabbed by the thorns as she climbed the wall. And she was left there to die.

The guards say nothing. The Overseer stands with her mouth slightly open, and I see her forked tongue testing the air, as if she can taste the smell of blood. The other Seamstresses glance quickly at Marya's body and then stare down at the cobblestones.

I can't pull my eyes away. My arms and legs feel cold as lead. My heart trembles in my chest.

The arm of the body twitches. I blink and hold my breath. The air is still and heavy, and then I hear, faintly, a moan. A bead of blood—fresh blood—trickles down Marya's impaled foot, gathers at her toe, and then drops, splattering on the cobblestones.

I turn to the Overseer. "She's still alive," I gasp.

The Overseer's slitted eyes glance aside at me, but she does not speak.

I dare to reach out and touch the Overseer's sleeve. "We

must get her down from there," I say, more loudly.

"It's a lesson," the Overseer says. "She stays."

"No," I say wildly, and make a move toward the wall, but the Overseer grips my arm and snakes her other arm around my waist, holding me beside her.

"Stop," she hisses, and I feel her forked tongue flicker against my ear. "Stop. Or you will be punished." She nods at the wall, and I see what she means—if I protest I will be impaled on the thorns beside Marya.

Trembling, I stand beside the Overseer. My ears strain, listening for another moan, but I hear nothing. I want to help Marya, to climb the brambles and ease her from the thorns and wrap her in a blanket so she'll at least be warm as she dies. I want to whisper that her handsome young man is waiting for her. But it is too late for that.

This lesson, I feel suddenly and coldly sure, is meant for me. A wave of prickling dread washes over my skin. Shoe said that the Godmother would know I was planning to escape, and she does—she *must*. Even now, her guards are discovering the hidden rope; they are questioning the Jack about the grappling hook. They must know about Shoe, too. I've dragged him into more trouble and he can't bear any more—I know it—and he'll be broken, the way Marya was broken. Shoe was right. I feel hot and cold at once, and shivery with terror. When we go back to the sewing room, they will be waiting for me.

My heart is pounding, and my knees are shaking. The

healing welts on the back of my neck burn. But all I can do is stand silently with the other Seamstresses. I put my hand into my pocket, seeking strength from my thimble, but for the first time, it stays cold.

Drops of blood from Marya's bone-white foot fall onto the cobblestones. One drop, two drops, a third, and fourth.

After a long time, the drops stop falling. Quietly, softly, what was Marya has gone, and she is just a body now, hanging limply from the thorns.

The Overseer hisses, and the guards lead us back across the cobblestones to the sewing room. I hold my breath, waiting for the accusing finger, for the guards and the screaming, but all is quiet. We settle at the long table. With trembling fingers, we take up our needles, our thread, our damask and velvet.

My silken rope, undiscovered, is a weight on my lap, under my apron. Now that I have seen the wall, I am sure that my rope is long enough.

Maybe the Godmother knows.

It doesn't matter if she does.

They will not take Marya's body down. It will hang there, this lesson.

But here is the irony: the lesson I am learning is not at all what they intend. Their lesson has made me even more determined to escape.

THE WAX CANDLE at my elbow gutters; it's burned down to a stub. Until this moment, I am not sure how to continue planning my escape, but as my candle flickers out, I hide the rope under the bench and get to my feet. The Overseer sees and glides over to me.

"We need more candles," I explain, bowing my head with false meekness. "I will fetch them, if you like."

The Overseer fixes me with a long stare. "Sssahhh," she breathes. Then she writes out a blue requisition form and leads me to the door, where she tells me how to find the Candlemakers.

I go straight to the workrooms of the Candlemakers. In exchange for the requisition, they give me a box full of the best wax candles, and, when I ask, a few extra. I start to carry the box back to the sewing room, but on the way I make a few stops, have a few words with the Spinsters of straw into gold, and with the Bakers, and do a little sniffing around. More rags and patches for my plan.

It's getting late and I should stay away, but I can't. If I'm going to escape from here, I at least need to see Shoe again before I go. So I climb the stairs to his workroom and, setting the box of candles on the floor, tap on his door.

No answer.

Quietly I open the door. The room is not large, just his shelves of supplies and racks of tools, a work bench, and a table and chair. Shoe is at the table with his head down, resting on one arm. I ease inside the room and close the door behind me, and come around the table to see him better.

He's fallen asleep while working. One relaxed hand is

holding a charcoal pencil; on a piece of paper he's been noting numbers, shoe measurements, I assume. His handwriting is neat, and he's made a sketch of a shoe. *Blue-green satin*, it says. *Match to tea dress. Low heel.*

I study his face. A lock of shaggy hair has fallen over one eye, and my fingers itch to brush it aside so I can see him better. I lean closer.

Marya was right, I realize, and my stomach gives a little flip. He is very good-looking. I still wouldn't call him handsome, exactly, because *handsome* is really just a bland regularity of features. But even in sleep, there is something about Shoe's face that draws my eye. Maybe it's the clean line of his jaw, or the set of his mouth, so grim and almost stern when he is awake, but softer now, or the way his stubbornness is belied by the surprising length of his eyelashes.

The pencil falls from his hand, rattling against the tabletop. His eyes blink open, and he stares at me, barely awake, as if he can't quite believe that I'm here.

"Hello," I whisper, my voice shaking.

He straightens, rubbing his forehead, making his hair stick up. "Hello," he says blearily. He shakes his head and his eyes focus. "Pin," he says more sharply, pushing himself to his feet. "What are you doing here?"

I steady myself, leaning my hip against the table. "I had to ask again. I want you to come with me." Carefully I reach out and rest my hand against his chest. Under my fingers I can feel the rough weave of his shirt and then the warmth of his skin, and the accelerating beat of his heart.

His hand reaches up to cover mine. Then he shakes his head, as if he can't speak.

"What do *you* think is out there?" I ask. I step closer and turn my hand in his so we are palm to palm. Our fingers interlace.

"I don't know," he says. "Wolves on the hunt. Fog and nothingness."

"You're afraid," I say starkly.

"Of course I am." He pulls his hand away from mine. "There's no Before for the likes of us, Pin, and no After, either."

He truly believes that his entire world is bounded by the bramble-covered wall that surrounds the fortress. "So you really won't come?" I ask.

He looks down at the floor and shakes his head.

Tears prickle at the corner of my eyes. I blink them away. "Can you just do me one favor?"

He gives me a wary nod.

I lift my bare foot and waggle it at him. "In a few days, call for a model again. That'll give me an excuse to leave the sewing room so I can get out of the fortress. Will you do it?"

"Yes," he says, his voice rough.

The tears threaten again, and I turn away because I don't want him to see me crying, I want him to think that I am strong. He doesn't speak as I move to the door, turn the knob, and go out into the hallway, where I bend to pick up the box of candles.

Then the sound of a quick step and as I stand I feel his warmth at my shoulder. "Pin," he whispers. "Come and say good-bye before you go."

I nod and hurry away.

THE OVERSEER IS nervous; the guards come in and out of the sewing room, extra vigilant. Marya's attempted escape is being whispered about throughout the Godmother's fortress, even though we are warned that to be caught mentioning it is a crime that will be punished by fifty lashes at the post. There will be inspections, we are told, and extra vigilance, and punishments.

I have been ready and waiting for a long time—or what seems like a long time in this place where time passes so slowly—before Shoe calls again for his model. The thin silken rope that I made is coiled around my waist under my loose woolen dress and shift. My silver thimble is clenched in my hand, and it burns like a hot coal. I carefully get to my feet, bow my head when the Overseer hisses her orders, and slide out of the room.

Outside, the sky is dark gray and snakes of freezing fog slither across the courtyard. On the way to Shoe's room, I stop at an out-of-the-way closet I found when fetching the candles, and collect my other supplies, carrying them in my apron.

It is time.

CHAPTER

5

Shoe is just finishing one of the fur slippers when Pin knocks on the door and slips into his workroom.

She is different now; he can see it at once. Before she was sharp and a little teasing; now she looks sharp and determined.

"You were right, by the way," Pin says. She dumps a pile of things out of her apron. A wax candle rolls across the floor and bumps against his foot. Then, to his alarm, she bends over and, pulling her skirt up to her knees, reaches under her dress. He relaxes a little when he sees that she is unwinding a thin rope from around her waist; it falls in a heap at her bare feet. "There. I think it's long enough." She crouches and starts coiling the rope.

He sets an awl on his workbench and clears his throat. "I was right about what?"

She glances up at him. A lock of her short, dark hair falls over her eyes, and she brushes it impatiently away. "That there are worse things than the post," she says shortly.

He nods. After Pin's visit, a Jack had come with a requisition for some leather, and whispered to him that a Seamstress had dared the wall. For a moment he'd felt a stab to the heart; he'd been sure it was Pin.

"No, not her," the Jack had said. "Not that girl you were with. A different one. Our Overseer took us Jacks to see her, stuck on the wall. She's meant to be a lesson."

His own Overseer, an over-busy, rat-tailed man, hadn't bothered taking Shoe to the wall. Shoe had already learned his lesson at the post.

The Jack had glanced furtively around. "Tell her, your girl. Tell her the hook is ready."

Pin has finished coiling the rope, and stands. "I came to say good-bye," she says.

He bends and picks up the candle, holding it out to her. When their hands meet, he feels the searing heat of her lingering touch. She gives him a long look, and he knows she is asking again. *I can't*, he wants to say, but the words stay caught in his throat. She nods and adds the candle to her pile of things. Feeling as creaky as an old man—he's been hunched over his workbench for too long—he pushes himself to his feet and goes to the darkest corner of his workroom. From under his bench he pulls the boots he cobbled together when he should have been making glass slippers. "Here," he says, and thrusts them awkwardly at her. "They're for you."

Pin's eyes widen. "Oh." Abruptly, she sits on the floor and pulls a boot onto her left foot. "It fits perfectly."

"Of course it's perfect." He's used her foot for a model, after all. He's lined the boots with sable, for warmth, and he's made them sturdy, too, not dainty or fragile like the dancing slippers he has to make for the Godmother. They are boots for walking long distances, boots for running while pursued by trackers.

With quick fingers she is slipping the other boot onto her right foot and tying the laces. "Won't you get into trouble?" she asks.

"No," he answers. "They're cobbled. I only used leftover scraps." In truth, if she gets away clean, he'll be fine. If she is caught, though, as she is sure to be, with his boots on her feet, he will be in trouble—they all will. But he knows that even if the Godmother herself questions Pin, she won't tell that he made the boots especially for her escape. He might get another trip to the post for it, and that will be bad enough, but there are worse things.

She stands and stamps each foot to test the fit. "Well, they're wonderful. Thank you." She bends and puts the coil of rope over her arm and gathers her things into her apron. The candle escapes again and rolls away. As she stands, a square, paper-wrapped package that smells like gingerbread drops to the floor. "Oops," she says.

He bends to pick them up. "I'll carry them for you," he

offers, because he can't bear to say good-bye to her quite yet. "Just to the Jacks' workroom. They said to tell you that your grappling hook is ready. They'll have a sack you can use, too."

She gives him the wicked grin she gave him once before and hands him a small velvet bag that makes a metal clinking sound when he takes it.

"This, too. It's gold from the Spinsters," she tells him. "I'll need money when I get to the Before."

She really believes she is going to get out.

He knows she won't. But he puts on his coat and stows the bag of money in his pocket, and, carrying the packet of gingerbread and a few candles, follows her out of his workroom.

NOW THAT THE moment has come, my candle flame of hope has flared into a bonfire. Marya had nothing, she'd been broken, and she'd made a desperate dash for the wall. But I have a plan; I have supplies. I am going to make it, and then I will come back for Shoe and rescue him and all the other slaves from this place.

I lead Shoe through the dim hallways of the fortress and down the stairs, where I turn left toward the Jacks' workroom.

From behind us comes a rush of footsteps. Before I can turn to see what's going on, Shoe has grabbed me and dragged me into another, darker hallway. I start to protest, and his hand comes over my mouth. I can feel the calluses on his palm and fingers, rough against my face. "Shhh," he breathes into my ear. The footsteps clatter past the end of the hallway. Releasing me, he edges to the corner and peers around. Then he leans his shoulder against the wall. "Something's happening."

"I have to go on," I say, gripping the corners of my apron.

He gives me a grim nod, and after peeking around again, pulls me out of the dark corridor. Silently, keeping our ears pricked, we ghost through the hallways to the workroom of the Jacks of all trades.

Holding the corners of my overloaded apron with one hand, I slip the thimble on my finger and try the knob.

"Quietly," Shoe whispers.

I nod and open the door the merest crack.

The room inside is chaos. The sound of the Jacks' wailing leaks out the door; I catch a glimpse of sawdust and feathers swirling through the air. One of the Jacks spies me at the door and hurries over. It is our Jack, from before.

"*Shhh, shhh,*" he whispers, glancing over his shoulder. "You shouldn't have come here."

"I need the grappling hook," I whisper through the crack in the door. "And a knapsack, if you've got one to spare. What's going on in there?"

"Surprise inspection," the Jack replies in a shaking voice. "Wait here." The door eases closed.

I lean against the wall beside Shoe. He's wound tightly, his head cocked as he listens to sounds coming from elsewhere in the fortress.

"If you squeeze that candle any harder," I whisper, "it's going to melt into a puddle of wax."

He gives me a dark look and hands me the candle.

The door opens, and the Jack quickly passes me a knapsack, which I give to Shoe, and then something heavy wrapped in rags. "That's your hook," he whispers. "Hurry. They know. They are searching for you."

My heart quivers in my chest like a hunted rabbit. Beside me, Shoe has gone as white as chalk.

From the workroom behind the Jack comes the sound of a guard shouting.

"Curse it," mutters the Jack. "We're headed for the post, all of us." He glances over his shoulder. "They are coming," he whispers urgently. "*Run!*" He reaches through and shoves me away from the door and slams it closed.

I stumble into Shoe, lose hold of a corner of my apron, and all my supplies tumble to the floor.

"Oh, curse it, Pin," Shoe says in a strangled whisper. He's already on his knees gathering the things, stuffing them into the knapsack. I keep hold of the grappling hook, and I have the rope over my shoulder. He snatches up a candle and shoves it into the bag.

"Shoe, leave it," I say. "You have to get back to your workroom." I reach out to take the knapsack from him, but he jerks it away and, wincing, slings it onto his back.

"No," he says. In the dim light, his eyes are intensely green. "I'm coming with you." He grabs my hand and pulls me down the hallway, toward the courtyard. Behind us, I hear pounding at the workshop door. The Jack must have blocked it somehow; the guards are trying to get through, to come after us.

"Come on," Shoe says.

We race around a corner. From behind, I hear the workshop door burst open, and the pounding of feet.

Panting, I follow Shoe. He rounds a corner. I grab his arm. "No, this way," I gasp, and he whirls and follows me down another corridor to another, smaller door, one that I scouted when I was sent out for candles. He flings the door open and pulls me through, and we set off across the courtyard. Halfway, I pull Shoe to a stop.

Wild-eyed, he pauses. "Pin, they're coming!"

"Just a moment," I say, and I set down the rag-wrapped hook. I can hear shouts and crashes coming from the fortress. "Shoe, face in the direction of the wall," I order. "Know exactly where it is so we don't lose it." Without arguing, he does it.

I grope in my apron pocket for the thimble. As I slip it onto my finger it flares with heat.

Crouching, I tap my thimbled finger against the slick courtyard cobblestones. "I need more than heat," I whisper. "Give me smoke." For just a moment I close my eyes; if this doesn't work, we won't even make it as far as the wall. "Thick smoke to hide us." Quickly I stow the thimble in my pocket, pick up the hook, and take Shoe's hand. "Don't let go," I tell him.

As we start toward the wall on the other side of the court-yard, a heavy smoke seeps from the cobblestones. With every step it grows thicker. I glance behind us, and see the fortress as if through a foggy curtain; when I look again it is gone, and we are surrounded by a hot, billowing cloud. I pull closer to Shoe. "Do you have the wall?" I whisper. My eyes water in the thick air.

He coughs, then nods, and we go on.

The smoke swirls around us. From the direction of the fortress I hear guards calling to one another; their voices sound very far away. My stout boots are sure on the cobbles, and Shoe guides us steadily onward. The air grows quieter; even our footsteps are muffled. Suddenly a tall, thin shape looms at our left. The post, with its chains hanging down. I check to be sure Shoe is all right, but he grips my hand and keeps his face set resolutely forward, and he leads us on.

At last we reach the wall. Shoe releases my hand. The smoke is another wall behind us; above us the sky lowers, dark gray and threatening. Thick gray brambles snake across the wall, naked but for a few grayish leaves. I can't see any thorns; I can't see Marya's body, either. Quickly I drop the grappling hook onto the cobbles and unwrap it from the rags. It is matte black metal and has four sharp prongs for cling-ing to the top of the wall. Once it's anchored, we'll be able to climb up, and over. Uncoiling my silken rope, I tie an end through the eye at the bottom of the hook. Then I stand and face the wall. It is very high.

"I'll do it," Shoe says. I trade him the knapsack for the rope and hook. He steps back, settling the rope so it will fly free, taking the measure of the wall, and whirls the hook, faster and faster, and then releases it. The hook, trailing the rope, flies in a perfect arc, up and up, and lodges at the very top of the wall.

My hope flares again. Escape is possible. We're going to do it.

Shoe cocks his head, listening. "Pin, they're coming. Hurry."

I can hear it, too: barked orders and the sound of running footsteps on cobblestones. The smoke behind us swirls, thins. Shoe tries to take the knapsack, but I saw how he winced when he put it on before, so I shrug away from him and grip my lumpy silken rope, step onto a loop of bramble, and pull myself up. The knapsack heavy on my shoulders, I climb higher, and then feel Shoe's weight on the rope below me. I glance down and narrow my eyes. "You're not looking up my dress, are you, Shoe?" I say.

"Shhh," he says, and to my surprise, he flushes.

I hoist myself higher, holding tightly to the rope, my feet braced against the thick brambles. And higher still. Fog swirls above my head, obscuring the top of the wall. It can't be too much farther. My hands cramp as they grip the rope; the muscles in my arms ache. The knapsack feels like it's full of rocks. I pull myself higher. Tilting my head back, I peer up through the fog. Surely I should have reached the top by now.

I glance over my shoulder. Shoe is right below me. Beneath him, I can't see the ground, only fog. A chill, damp tendril brushes the back of my neck, and I shiver. "Onward," I tell myself, and pull myself higher. The muscles in my arms and shoulders are burning now. "Just a little farther."

From below, I hear a gasp. The rope jerks. I lose my footing and, clinging desperately to the rope, I slam against the wall. "Pin," Shoe whispers urgently. "Be careful. Thorns."

As he speaks, a thorn as long as my hand and as sharp as a dagger bursts from the bramble vine, stabbing past my face. I jerk away, and my hands slip on the rope. As I sway toward the wall again, another thorn slashes at my arm; the cloth of my dress rips, and a line of fire burns across my wrist, leaving a bleeding gash behind it. I pull away. A thorn jabs at my foot, and my sturdy boot deflects it. All around me, knifelike thorns erupt from the brambles, seeking my blood.

This is how Marya's escape ended.

But mine will not. Ignoring the pain in my wrist and gripping the rope, I look over my shoulder to be sure Shoe is all right, but the fog has crept between us. "Keep going," I say, hoping he can hear me. I pull myself higher and higher, my muscles burning, flinching when a thorn stabs at me. As the thorns fail, the brambles start to writhe under my feet; thick tendrils reach for me, and I duck under them, and climb on.

I pause, panting, and look up. The fog swirls aside. The wall stretches above me, endless, gray, and crawling with thorny, tangled brambles.

The Godmother's magic.

As I realize this, the clouds overhead blacken, and a few drops of icy rain fall. Thunder grumbles, the clouds lower, and rain pounds down, trying to wash us from the wall. In a moment I am drenched, my dress a heavy, wet weight on my arms and legs. Cold radiates from the wall, and the rainwater freezes, coating every surface with a thin, slippery layer of ice. My hands go numb. Blood drips from my throbbing wrist, rivulets of pink washing away with the rain.

I close my eyes for a moment, a hairbreadth from despair. The Godmother won't let us escape. We'll be another lesson for the workers in her fortress. After this, nobody will ever try to get away again.

A hand closes around my ankle. I look down and see Shoe's determined, rain-wet face, looking up. His coat is torn in two places from the thorns, but I don't see any blood. "Keep going," he gasps.

I take a deep breath. In my hands, the rope is solid, taut, created with scraps of silken ball gowns, and it is stitched with thread as strong as spider silk. My will is even stronger. Clinging to the rope with one hand, keeping my feet braced, I reach my other hand into my pocket and slip the thimble onto my finger. "Enough of this," I whisper, and, flinching as a wickedly sharp thorn slashes at me, I reach out and touch the wall. The wall shudders; the brambles writhe, the thimble burns. The silver turns molten red, and then flares into a fiery white.

In answer, a bolt of lightning rips across the sky; thunder crashes; and I look up, blinking the rain out of my eyes, to see the Jacks' grappling hook just over my head. With Shoe pushing my boots from below, I haul myself up the last few feet, and over the grasping brambles that are slippery and crackling with ice. I crouch on the top of the wide wall, gasping for breath. A moment later, Shoe joins me, and we cling to each other, panting, as the icy rain slams down around us.

CHAPTER

6

THE GUARDS ARE STILL COMING. SHOE TEARS HIMSELF
away from Pin's burning warmth, and with shaking hands he
pulls up the rope and jerks the hook out of the fortress side
of the wall. Then he turns and jams it onto the outside of the
wall, low enough so that it won't be seen from the courtyard.
The rain has turned to ice. He is soaked to the skin and numb
with cold.

"C-c-c-" he stutters, his lips too cold to form the words.
Come on, Pin. We're not safe yet. He points at the rope hanging down, and Pin swipes the rat tails of wet hair out of her
eyes, grips the rope with bloodstained hands, and swings
herself over the edge of the wall. The thorns got her, he realizes with a prickle of worry. Hand over hand, bracing her
feet against the wall, she climbs down the rope, fast, and

he follows. There are no brambles on this side of the wall, just ice-slick stones. Shards of ice flake from the rope as it stretches under his weight. He gets halfway down and checks over his shoulder to see Pin waiting on the ground, her face a pale oval in the darkness. Then his foot slips on a patch of icy wall, and his numb hands stop gripping, and he slithers down the rest of the rope, landing in a heap at her feet.

She crouches beside him, her gray eyes wide and shadowed. "Are you all right?" she asks.

The ground, saturated with rain, is soft. He'll have a bruise or two, but nothing broken. Nodding, he climbs to his feet, flexing his frozen fingers to drive out the cold. "Th-thorns?" he manages to get out, and takes Pin's hands in his. A nasty gash crosses the inside of her wrist, dark red against bone-white skin; it drips blood.

"It's all right," she says, and closes her other hand over the wound to stop the bleeding.

Shoe turns to see what kind of land lies outside the God-mother's fortress. The wall, gray stone with darker patches of ice and water, stands at their back. Before them is a dense forest of pine trees, dark and menacing under the swollen black clouds, crowded with ferns drooping under a crust of ice. The damp, pine-needle-covered forest floor is studded here and there with mossy rocks.

Holding her wrist, Pin is looking up the wall. Her short hair is plastered to her head from the rain. Her lips are blue with cold. "It's a sh-shame to leave the rope and the hook," she says, shivering. "I wonder if my thimble could bring it down."

Shoe finds his voice, speaking through chattering teeth. "Leave it, Pin. We don't have time. They'll be coming."

"There's no gate in the wall," Pin answers, "so they can't come after us unless they come over, and that'll take them a while to work out." She gives her sudden wicked grin. "That's irony for you."

"What's i-irony?" Shoe asks. He shivers convulsively and wraps his arms around his chest.

"It's when something is supposed to work a certain way, but it turns out just the opposite," Pin explains. "The wall is meant to keep us in, but now it's keeping the Godmother inside instead."

"If the Godmother wants a gate," Shoe says darkly, "there will be a g-gate. That's reality for you."

"I suppose you're right." Pin faces the forest. "Let's go."

MY SODDEN DRESS hangs heavily on me, and the knapsack feels heavier with every step. Drops of blood leak from the throbbing gash on my wrist. I feel frozen through. We're out of the fortress, but we're not yet free of it. Still, hope burns through me, for I have the thimble, and I know that I'm only just beginning to discover the extent of its power. I push through knee-high, ice-encrusted ferns and into the pine forest. Almost at once the wall disappears behind us. The trees' trunks are wet, and the pine-needle-covered ground is damp, but the branches grow so thickly that they protect us from the worst of the rain. It is gloomy here, but not frightening. The forest feels wild, unmanageable, like something outside of the Godmother's control.

I lead Shoe onward, winding between the tree trunks, ducking low branches. We walk for a long time, leaving the fortress behind. The forest seems to gather us in and lead us on as the pine trees are joined by slender trees with white-barked trunks slashed with black, and golden leaves that shiver in the chilly wind. The land grows steeper, and we meet a tumbling stream and follow it up a hill. My feet are dry in my perfect boots, and the walking warms me; the thimble in my pocket warms me too. My wound is still oozing blood, but I feel as if I can keep going forever.

Shoe, evidently, does not feel the same pull toward whatever lies beyond the forest. I can hear him behind me, stumbling and muttering to himself. I stop, and he runs into me, and we both stagger a few steps. I turn and put my hands on his shoulders to steady him.

"Only if the thorns . . . ," he says, his voice ragged. "And— and you think the Before is there, Pin, but it's not, or it's not what you think it is, anyway, and—"

He's not making any sense. I lay my chilled fingers on his lips and he stops talking. He stares at me with shadowed eyes, with drops of rain beading his eyelashes, and I can see that he's too tired and too cold. I want to wrap my arms around him and share with him the warmth from my thimble. And,

I have to admit, I want to feel his arms come around me, too; I want to feel his lips warm against mine. It's something I've never felt before, and I'm curious. "Just a little farther," I promise.

He jerks out a nod, and I lead him on beside the rushing stream, looking for a place to rest. The icy rain has stopped, and night is gathering under the eaves of the trees. The moss-covered tree trunks are shadows in the darkness. We stumble on. Now and then I pause to dig under a particularly thick clump of ferns or fallen branches, pulling out moss that has stayed dry, or a bundle of twigs, carrying it all in my apron. Shoe keeps his hand on my shoulder, stopping when I stop, trudging on when I continue.

At last, looming out of the darkness, blocking our path, is the huge trunk of a pine tree that has fallen in a storm. I follow it to its end. In falling, its wide roots have pulled up with them a canopy of moss and dirt that form a low, snug hollow edged by snaky roots hanging down. "In here," I say to Shoe, and push him ahead of me into the dark cave.

He collapses with his back against the rooty, dirty wall, and puts his head down on his knees, shivering uncontrollably. Unslinging the knapsack, which is dark with rain, I crawl into the cave after him, dumping my load of dry moss and wood in a heap by Shoe's feet. I pull the knapsack in after me. Crouching, my head brushes the rooty ceiling; the opening is a low arch that shows only gathering night. The air in our cave is heavy and damp. I sweep the lumpy ground with my hand until I've made a flat place by the low opening and, working mostly by touch in the darkening cave, I make a pile of the moss and bark and the smaller twigs. With chilled, dirty fingers, I reach into my apron pocket and pull out the thimble.

"If ever you've helped me," I whisper to it, "help me now." I hold the thimble to the tinder. "Burn," I tell it.

For a moment, the cave stays dark. Then a faint spark falls from the thimble into the dry moss. The tiny feathers of moss glow orange and curl, and a wisp of smoke drifts up. Quickly I add a few peels of bark to the moss, and the coals lick up into flames, and then I add sticks, and in a moment a warm fire is burning merrily.

"Thank you," I whisper to the thimble. In the flickering light, I take a moment to inspect it. Reflected in its smooth, silver base is my face, tiny, wreathed by etched brambles. "You came from somewhere," I murmur. "And I'm going to find out where."

Opening the knapsack, I find that even though it's wet on the outside, the things within are dry. Clever Jacks—it's waterproof. First I pull out a candle and light it at the fire, and stick it in the dirt by Shoe's foot. Now for my wrist. The skin is purple around the gash, which is about as long as my pinkie finger. As I squint at it, another drop of blood oozes from it and falls to the dirt. My apron is filthy, covered with dirt and flakes of moss and bark, but it's the best I've got. I tear a strip from the bottom of it and use it to bind up the wound. There, all right and tight. Then I start pulling things out of the knapsack to see what we've got: the bag of money, which is no use to us at the moment, a few more candles, a paper-wrapped package of gingerbread, and a row of pins stuck in paper that I stole from the sewing room. That should be everything, but the knapsack isn't empty. I pull out a rough woolen blanket and two packets that smell like food of some kind and a stoppered bottle of water.

The Jack. He must have had the bag already packed when we came for the hook. I know how much the Jacks fear the post: I hope our Jack hasn't gotten a flogging for what he's done. I close my eyes and clench my fists. "If I make it out," I whisper, a promise to the Jack far away, who might already be dead, "I'll figure out a way to come back for you." And for the other Jacks and the Seamstresses who passed me scraps of silk under the table, the Spinsters who snuck me a bag of gold coins, and the Candlemakers who spared a few extra candles. All of them. It's a big promise, and one I probably can't keep, but I am the first to escape, and so I must try. Shoe will help me, I know.

After feeding the fire another knot of wood, I take my treasures and settle next to Shoe. He has his eyes closed; he is still shuddering with cold.

"Here," I say, and carefully ease the sodden coat from his shoulders, replacing it with the Jack's woolen blanket. I spread his coat next to the fire to dry and join him under the blanket. The fire blazes away. The pine wood is full of sap, and it pops and hisses; sparks leap up, and the comforting smell of woodsmoke fills the cave, but most of the smoke is pulled out of the opening. Every now and then Shoe gives a convulsive shiver as if he's throwing off the last of the cold. Then, finally, he is still.

I watch the flames, safe in our cocoon of warmth and light.

"I know it's wretched," I say to him, "and that I shouldn't have dragged you into this. But I don't wish you back at the fortress."

"No," he agrees, "I don't wish either of us there," and I see that his eyes are open now, reflecting the warmth of the fire. He shifts, and his arm comes around me. I lean into him.

My stomach rumbles. Back at the fortress, the God-mother's workers are eating tasteless lentils. It's the only food I can remember.

"Here," Shoe says. He takes the warmth of his arm away and opens the packet of gingerbread. He breaks off a piece, catching every precious crumb in his hand, and holds it to my lips.

The ginger-spice smell fills my nose, and my mouth starts to water. I take a bite. Its sweetness is so overwhelming, it's almost painful. It fills me with another kind of warmth as I chew and swallow.

More, my stomach demands.

Shoe is eating the crumbs off his hand and gazing at me with an almost-smiling look in his forest-green eyes. Even though he is exhausted and dirt-smudged, with twigs snarled in his ragged hair, looking at him feels to me like a bite of gingerbread—sweet, and a little painful. Because I've never seen Shoe smile. His face is beautiful to me, but it is too pale, too bleak. A smile will be my new goal, I decide, even if an actual smile from him might be more sweetness than I can bear.

My stomach gives a loud growl. "It wants more," I say.

"Try giving it a bit of this." Shoe hands me a piece of cheese that he's taken from one of the Jack's packages.

I close my eyes as I savor it, then eat the cracker Shoe gives me, and drink some water, and then I'm full and warm and leaning into Shoe as he settles against the cave wall again.

"All right?" he mumbles. I can hear the exhaustion in his voice.

"Mmm. You?" Suddenly the escape and the thorns and icy rain and long walk through the forest catch up to me, and I feel the heavy weight of sleep pressing down on my body. My eyes fall shut.

I feel the vibrations in Shoe's chest as he answers, talking more than he has before, as if being outside the Godmother's fortress has finally made him feel more like himself—but my ears can't sort out what he is saying.

I resist the pull of sleep for a moment, afraid of the darkness that is a little like the Nothing. Then its peace and warmth surround me, and with a sigh I let it pull me down into its soft and velvety depths.

SHOE WAKES UP with the solid wall of their tree-cave at his back, curled around Pin, who is sound asleep. The coals of their fire smolder. For a moment he watches the last tendrils of smoke drift up, and he feels safe and warm. It is as if they are two rabbits in a snug burrow. The opening of their cave is a low arch in the darkness framing a forest that glows emerald green and gold.

He pushes up onto his elbow and looks down at Pin. She looks different in sleep. Sweet, somehow. When awake she is so sharp, her gray eyes keen under her level brows, her mouth ready to quirk into a teasing smile. Truth to tell, she *has* dragged him into this, and they aren't clear yet, but he is glad to be filthy and afraid and still aching with weariness—and warm next to her in their tree-cave. Better here with her than making endless pairs of shoes in the Godmother's fortress.

He frowns. She has her hand curled under her chin, and he can see the dark stain of blood soaking the bandage she's wrapped around her wrist. Surely it should have stopped bleeding by now. He'll have to talk to her about it when she wakes up.

Quietly, trying not to disturb her, he eases out from under the woolen blanket and tucks it around her, rummages in the knapsack, then crawls out the opening of their cave.

The sun is just coming up; the sky overhead, what he can see of it between the tall pine trees, is the pale blue of early morning. The air is cool and smells richly of dirt and green growing things. The rising sun shines through the trees, sending shafts of golden light to pierce the shadows. He sees moss-covered tree stumps, and pine branches dripping with another kind of moss, and green billows of ferns, and, among the pines, trees with yellowing leaves as big as his hand. The forest feels welcoming, a place where they will be safe.

After the gray stones and cloudy skies of the Godmother's fortress, it is too much all at once, and he closes his eyes as he creaks to his feet, then looks again. Off to his right, he hears the rustling of a stream. Leaving Pin to sleep, he finds the stream and follows it, climbing over moss-covered rocks, winding between pine trees as big around as he is tall, until the stream widens into a pond fed by a waterfall that tumbles from a notch in a high gray cliff. For a moment Shoe stands mesmerized by the falling water.

Then his stomach growls. "Oh, sure," he tells it. "Give you a bit of gingerbread and some half-moldy cheese for dinner, and you just want to eat again in the morning."

A kingfisher darts past, a brilliant flash of blue. Where there are fish hunters, he reasons, there must be fish, and where there are fish, is breakfast. He finds a big rock that juts into the pond, and there he unravels a thread from the bottom of his ragged shirt and ties it to one of the pins he found in the knapsack. He bends the pin and sticks on a crumb of cheese, then settles himself in a sunny spot and drops the baited hook into the water. The lightest spray from the waterfall wafts over him as the breeze shifts.

He doesn't remember fishing from the Before, but when

the bait is taken, his body knows exactly what to do, jerking the flashing, silver fish from the water, holding it behind the gills while he takes out the hook, then stunning it against the rock. He baits the hook again and catches another fish. He and Pin will have a feast for breakfast.

As he makes his way downstream, he comes to a sun-warmed clearing not far from their tree-cave. To his alarm, he sees Pin's gray woolen dress spread on a rock to dry. And her apron, which is dripping wet from a washing. Pin's clothes, but no Pin.

She is right, he realizes. In the Godmother's fortress they'd only had the monotony of work; they never talked, never touched, never felt anything but fear. Now he feels something else, a longing for Pin that sweeps over him, leaving him feeling a little breathless.

After peeking into the cave, he goes to the stream. There he finds Pin, wearing only her shift, lying on a flat, moss-covered rock, eyes closed, basking in the sun. She's washed her short hair, and it is curling as it dries. He creeps closer, wanting suddenly to kiss her, to feel her skin under his hands. It is a strange, unremembered feeling, but his body knows what to do with it.

As his shadow falls across her, she opens her eyes. "You could use a wash too, Shoe," she says, smiling. The sun reflecting off the water is dazzling, and she shades her eyes with her hand.

He is about to smile and answer, when he freezes. The

fizzing excitement of seeing her suddenly drains away. She has rebandaged her wrist with a clean strip torn from the bottom of her shift.

The bandage is already stained with blood.

One thing he's learned from his time at the post is how long a wound like that should bleed. Setting down the fish, he goes to his knees on the rock beside her. She sits up, still smiling. He takes her hand, turns it over, inspects her wrist.

"It's still bleeding," he says.

She glances down at it, then back at him. "It's all right."

"No, it isn't all right. Does it hurt?"

"No," she answers, and tugs her hand out of his. "It just drips."

"It drips," he repeats. With a stab of terror, he realizes what that means. As he speaks, his lips feel stiff. "It left a trail."

Her gray eyes widen. "The thorns."

He nods, knowing what she means. The thorns are the Godmother's. They were meant to slash, to make a wound that will not heal, so that if anyone ever managed to get over the wall, they would be easy to track.

Pin has gone pale. She climbs quickly to her feet. "We have to go farther into the forest," she says. "She won't be able to find us. Don't worry, Shoe. We'll be safe." She hops from the rock to the shore, hurrying away to the clearing.

Shoe follows, the fish forgotten. There is no help for them in the forest, he feels certain.

But the Godmother is coming, and they have nowhere else to go.

MY DRESS IS still clammy as I wrestle it on over my wet shift. As I pull on my boots and tie the laces, my hands shake.

The Godmother has guards in her fortress. Some of the guards have scaly skin, like the Overseer, and some have pig snouts, and some have naked rat tails that wave behind them as they walk. Still others have the keen noses of dogs and lean bodies made for running. Trackers.

I stand and jerk my apron around my waist, fumbling with the ties. They *will* be coming, of that I am certain. So much for my promise to get everyone out of the Godmother's fortress. I may be going back there myself, sooner than I would like, as a prisoner.

Shoe comes from the cave with the knapsack slung on his back. He carries himself a bit stiffly, so I know those wounds aren't fully healed either, but there is no time to argue about who should carry the pack. Without speaking, he hands me a bit of cheese and cracker, and I eat them as we hurry away, deeper into the forest.

We hike all that day, uphill and down, along a narrow valley cut by a rushing, icy-cold stream, then up another steep hillside that gives us a view, as we top it, of gray, snowcapped mountains in the distance.

We hear nothing of pursuit. During a brief rest, I try sealing the wound on my wrist with the thimble, but it continues to bleed. We press on, stopping only to fill the water bottle and to eat more gingerbread, which tastes to me now like ashes.

"Maybe we've gotten away," I say as we pause, panting, at the top of a hill. Ahead of us, a path overshadowed by trees leads toward the distant mountains; behind us, the path has disappeared, swallowed up by the forest. "I think the forest is helping us escape," I realize.

Shoe glances back, but he doesn't say anything.

As the sun slopes toward setting and Shoe and I are both stumbling with weariness, we hear, in the distance, the baying of hounds.

We exchange a glance, but we don't speak. We both know what it is that hunts us, and we know that they are close. He holds out his hand and I take it for a moment, and then we go on as fast as we can manage.

With the sunset comes the cold. Our clothes are still damp. "My feet are warm, at least," I tell Shoe, but it doesn't make him smile.

No, of course it doesn't. He's felt the Godmother's punishments before. I haven't, but I know that if she catches us, our punishment for escaping her fortress—her prison—will not be as simple or as easy as death.

We press on. Night falls, and we feel our way through the trees. First I lead, with Shoe's hand on my shoulder, and then he leads, guiding me over rocks and stumps. In the middle of the night a full moon rises. A hunter's moon.

As we cross a clearing, Shoe stops me and pulls up the sleeve of my dress. The moon stands directly overhead. In its light the bandage looks black with blood. He frowns, then bends down and rips another strip from my apron—which is growing short—and wraps it around my wrist.

"I think—" I start to say.

"No, Pin," he interrupts. He knows what I am going to suggest, that he should go on while I lead the trackers away.

"Shoe, there's only one way this can end," I tell him, and hold up my wrist as a reminder.

"No," he says stubbornly, and I know there's no changing his mind.

He comes closer, opening his arms, and I step into his embrace. I put my face against his, feeling on my cheek the light stubble along the line of his jaw, leaning into his neck to breath him in. He smells of woodsmoke from our fire, and sweat, and of the caustic soap used to launder our clothes back in the fortress, and over it his own clean smell. This is what I wanted. I wish it could last, and last, until it became our After.

But there's going to be no After for us.

"I'm afraid," I whisper, hating to admit it.

"So am I," he whispers back. "But we'll face it together."

Blinking back sudden tears, I nod. He tightens his arms around me. I feel his strength and determination, and in return I give him my warmth.

Then, holding hands, we stumble on through the night.

DAWN STAINS THE sky red. The wound on my wrist drips a steady trickle of blood. The howl of the trackers draws ever nearer.

My head is spinning; maybe I've bled too much, or maybe it's exhaustion.

Beside me, Shoe bends over, hands on his knees, catching his breath. His head jerks up as a hunting howl echoes through the pines. "We could find a stream, maybe," he pants.

"To throw off the scent. Yes, that might work." I look wildly around, trying to get my bearings. Black spots waver before my eyes.

"This way," Shoe says, and he takes my hand.

We stumble-run down the side of a steep hill, dodging trees, until we reach the bottom of a valley where a stream runs swift and clear. As I plunge into it after Shoe, the cold water sloshes over my perfect boots. We splash upstream, hoping the water will wash away the smell of blood. My wrist throbs with every stumbling step. I hear Shoe's ragged breaths as he pulls me steadily on.

As we climb higher, the stream flows faster, tugging at the bottom of my dress. The frigid water has turned the color of milk; my feet are blocks of ice. The stones lose their blankets of moss and grow sharper. The pines on the stream bank thin, and I look up to see, ahead of Shoe, that the stream slices through a narrow ravine bare of trees. We're leaving the protection of the forest. The stream is leading us higher and higher to a looming mountain, its broad peak capped with snow, its sides gray with ash—an old volcano. We struggle higher, and the ravine turns sharply and doubles back on itself. It feels as if the water is rushing past us and we are climbing in place.

We come around another bend and I see, just ahead, that the stream leaps toward us over a ledge, a waterfall just taller than I am. Shoe stops, staring at it, his breath coming in desperate gasps. I push blindly past him, stepping knee-deep into an eddy, and scrabble at the rocks. I hear Shoe shout something, but I find a ledge for my feet and start climbing up the waterfall. Icy water sprays over my head.

Then his hands are on my shoulders, and he jerks me from the stream, dragging me dripping and shivering out of the water until we are standing on ash-covered ground, surrounded by gray rocks, the gray flanks of the mountain looming at our backs.

I will go up the bank then, I think. We must hurry.

"Pin," Shoe says urgently, and I realize that he's been repeating my name. With his hands he frames my face, and he feels so steady, so true that I close my eyes and lean into him.

I feel his breath on my cheek. "They're coming, Pin," he says into my ear.

Blinking the black spots from my vision, I look back, but the stream disappears around a bend in the steep ravine.

A howl echoes from just around the corner. I grope for the thimble in my pocket, clench it in my fist. It can't help us now, but it warms my hand.

And then I am clinging to him, and he to me. "Pin," he breathes, and our lips meet and linger, and like wildfire through dry grass our kiss sweeps through me until I am nothing but flame, and it is not just a kiss, but a promise.

I lean into him, and, without him seeing, I slip the thimble into his coat pocket. Another kind of promise.

A chorus of howls echoes. They will be here in a moment.

"Listen," I start.

"No, I already told you," Shoe says fiercely. He brushes shaking fingers over my lips, as if to silence me. "I'm staying with you."

"You are *not*." I grip the front of his coat; blood from my wrist stains the cloth. "Shoe, she will break you."

"I don't care," Shoe says. His mouth is a straight, uncompromising line.

Suddenly I feel a flare of fury. I push Shoe, and he stumbles back, slipping on the ash, falling to his knees. "You have a chance to get away, you stubborn idiot!" I shout, and point upstream. "Go, curse you!"

He glares back at me, scrambles to his feet. "Not without you, Pin."

I hold up my hand. The bandage on my wrist is soaked with blood; drops spatter on the ashy ground. "Shoe," I say. "If you care about me at all, you won't follow me." Then I turn my back on him and start downstream. I don't look over my shoulder to see if he's gone. My booted feet are sure on the ashy bank of the stream. I tumble downhill, picking up speed, and I still don't look back.

Ahead, the stream bends sharply around a fall of rocks.

A tracker appears. He is naked, gray-skinned, man-shaped, with lean flanks, running on all fours. His dog-snouted face snuffles along the ash-covered bank of the stream.

I stumble to a stop.

Hearing me, the tracker freezes. He sniffs the air. He sees me.

At the same moment, four more trackers appear from around the bend. With them is the Godmother, mounted sidesaddle on a tall, white horse. At her back are three grizzled Huntsmen dressed in leather, riding sturdy horses. One of the Huntsmen pulls an arrow from a quiver, nocks it, and holds his bow ready. At a curt word from the Godmother, all five trackers hurtle toward me. In a moment I am surrounded. The trackers' bodies are smudged with ash; their backs are ridged with bleeding whip marks; their tongues loll from their panting mouths. They smell rankly of sweat and of fear.

One of the trackers sniffs past me, as if he's following another scent—Shoe's.

I fling my arms open, and my blood spatters in a wide arc. Then I wipe my wrist down the front of what's left of my apron, leaving a smear of blood. When I edge sideways, away from the stream, away from Shoe's trail, all the trackers follow, watching keenly, their noses a-twitch.

"That's right, you dogs," I whisper. "It's me you want, not Shoe." Who, at this very moment, had better be hurrying upstream as fast as his feet can take him.

Darkness edges my vision. I stay on my feet, swaying. The Godmother guides her horse around a rock, then jerks it to a halt. The horse snorts, breathing heavily, and hangs its head.

The trackers are snuffling at my skirt. One of them nuzzles at my boot. "Stop that, you," I tell him. The dog-man glances up at me, gives a low whine, then puts his nose to the ground again.

The Godmother studies me from atop her horse. She is holding the reins in one gloved hand. Her riding dress is made of ice-blue velvet with fur at the collar and cuffs, all of it beautifully stitched, of course, though its hem is mud-stained and ragged. "Where is your friend, the Shoemaker?" she asks. Her voice is rough. The skin of her face is finely wrinkled, and her silver-blue eyes are smudged with the shadows of lost sleep.

Though I know I look far worse, exhausted and filthy as I am, stained with blood, wearing a tattered, wet dress, I feel a flash of triumph, knowing that her hunt for us has not been easy. "Who?" I ask.

The Godmother huffs an impatient sigh and climbs stiffly down from her horse. After brushing at a stain on her skirt, she wades through the trackers, kicking at one of them when he snuffles too close to her foot. The dog-man yelps and cringes away.

She is taller than I am. Graceful and beautiful. Dazzling, like a cruel, cold sun across a field of snow. She looks me up and down, then gives an annoyed sniff. Abruptly she turns away, gesturing to her Huntsmen. They nudge their horses, coming closer. One of them, I notice, has a whip jammed into his belt.

"You." She points at one of the others, a burly man with dark brown skin, an enormous mustache, and an ax strapped to his saddle. "Take two of the dogs and go after the boy. Bring him to me alive."

"Yes, Mistress," the Huntsman says, bowing from the back of his horse. "Jip, Jes," he calls two of the dog-men. "Get on with you." He kicks his horse and it trots upstream, trailed by two of the weary trackers.

I follow them with my eyes. I hope Shoe is running. I hope he can stay ahead of them.

The Godmother starts taking off an ice-blue leather glove, one dainty finger at a time. "He will be caught, you know, and then he'll have to be punished. I don't suppose he'll be of any use to me after that."

I am too tired, now, to be frightened of her. "You won't catch him," I say.

"Don't be silly," she says. "Of course I will, even if the forest interferes." And she shrugs as if she's already bored with the conversation. Her eyes narrow, and she studies me.

"What did you think you were doing?"

"Escaping," I admit. "Finding out where I came from."

She looks faintly amused. "Those things are lost to you."

"No," I say, shaking my head, refusing to believe her.

"So certain," she chides. "I do wonder what prompted you to think that you were anything but a Seamstress." Behind her, the two Huntsmen watch from horseback. The three remaining trackers have flopped to the ground, where they lie still, panting. "You must have something," the Godmother says softly, leaning closer. "Some magical thing that helped you escape my fortress. Am I correct?"

The thimble. I swallow down a gasp. The thimble that is in the pocket of Shoe's coat. "I have nothing," I say truthfully.

"Mm. At any rate, here we are," the Godmother says. She holds the empty glove in her other palm, and flexes her bare hand.

No, it's not bare, I realize. On the tip of her finger she is wearing a silver thimble.

A *thimble*.

She steps closer, and taps the thimble against her front teeth, as if thinking. "Given who you are, I should have known I'd have more difficulty controlling you. I suppose I thought you were too young to resist. I shall simply have to be more careful this time. We'll start again from Nothing."

Nothing. What I fear most. "No," I say, and my voice shivers, betraying me. I stare up into her silver-blue eyes. "I'll remember." I will remember who I am. I will remember Shoe.

"No, you won't," the Godmother says calmly.

Raising her hand, she brushes aside a lock of my hair. Her touch is almost gentle, but I can feel the cold radiating from her marble-white fingers. My heart is pounding so hard it is shaking my body. "Don't be so afraid." The Godmother rests her thimble against my forehead. "I am only giving you what every girl wants." The chill of the thimble's touch spreads into me. "And then you will cause me no more trouble."

Suddenly I know with a horrified certainty that Shoe was right. There are worse things than the post. Worse things than being stabbed to death by thorns. I try to jerk away, but it is too late. Cold radiates from the touch of the Godmother's thimble. Darkness swirls around me. *Shoe*, I think, as I fall.

And then I am Nothing.

PART
TWO

CHAPTER

7

I WAKE UP IN THE CINDERS.

It is the sound of a distant clock that wakes me, striking the hour. Morning.

I am curled on my side, practically in the hearth itself. One hand, flung out, rests against the cold grate; a bandage enwraps my wrist.

There is the clank and rattle of a coal scuttle being set down. "Lady Penelope," a housemaid says, shaking my shoulder.

I blink. "What?" I croak.

"Lady Penelope, wake up." The housemaid, dressed in a dark-blue uniform with a starched white apron over it, crouches on the carpet next to me. She shakes my shoulder again. "The clock has struck the hour. You can't be here now."

Creaking in every joint, I sit up and put my hand to my head, which aches like fury. Blinking, I take in the room. The walls are covered from floor to ceiling with bookshelves; the room is filled with an overstuffed, doily-covered velvet sofa, spindly tables holding vases billowing with dried flowers, and a desk of polished mahogany. A book lies beside me on the hearth. Oh. The library. The memory of it comes back to me. I must have fallen asleep while reading again.

"It's just gone eight, my lady, which means breakfast, and if you're late again your stepmother will be angry," the maid says. With her hands, she brushes ineffectually at my dress.

I look down at myself. I'm wearing a black silk dress, black lace at the cuffs and collar, with three petticoats under it and black button-up shoes that pinch my toes. All of it slightly shabby and covered with a thin, gray layer of ash.

A flurry at the door, and a big woman bustles into the room. My stepmother, I realize after a blank moment. She has a broad, red face made pale with powder, and a wealth of chestnut hair shot with gray, covered by a lace cap. She is the kind of woman people call *handsome*. She wears a fashionable blue-and-white striped silk morning dress with three flounces at the hem, a narrow waist achievable only through ruthless corseting, and a wide hoop skirt that sways as she sails across the carpet toward me. "Oh, Penelope," she says, her voice shrill with exasperation. "I might have known you'd be in here." She makes shooing motions at the maid. "Go on, girl; you heard the clock strike. Go on with your duties."

The maid heaves up the coal scuttle and hurries out. My stepmother stares down at me. "Get up at once," she orders.

Picking up the book I used as a pillow, I climb to my feet. I feel strangely weary down to my bones, and ravagingly hungry. Did I remember to eat dinner last night? "Have I been ill?" I ask. I feel as if I've been asleep for a long time, like an enchanted princess in a bramble-wrapped tower.

"No, you have not, you silly girl." My stepmother huffs out a sigh of vexation. "Oh, for pity's sake, look at you."

Adrift, I stare blankly back at her.

"Come here," Stepmama says, and when I move too slowly, she reaches out and grabs my arm and drags me to the desk. After rummaging in a drawer, Stepmama pulls out a hand mirror and holds it up. "Just look at yourself."

Squinting, I peer at my reflection in the mirror. A stranger looks back at me. Her face is too thin. Her chin-length dark hair is tangled. Her gray eyes are shadowed. I turn my head, and so does the girl in the mirror. It is me. Maybe I *have* been ill; I certainly look it.

"Do you see? Wretched. Smudged with cinders. Up all night reading, I expect." Stepmama turns toward the door, a ship under full sail coming about. "You are a very foolish girl. So much like your father."

I catch my breath as unexpected sorrow sweeps through me, a stabbing realization that I've lost something precious and I'll never find it again. Find *him* again. It must be . . . is it . . . grief for my father?

"Come along to breakfast, Penelope," my stepmother orders. "Hurry now; the clock has already struck eight. And then you must go up to your room and change." She sweeps out of the library.

I close my eyes for a moment. Taking a deep breath, I try to remember my father's face, but I can't. The sadness is there, though, aching and deep and surprisingly immediate.

"Come to breakfast *now*," Stepmama shrills from the hallway.

I clench my teeth and will myself not to cry. I am alone, and no amount of grieving is going to change that. I straighten my spine and head for the library door.

The fashion is for blue, and so stepping into the breakfast room is like being closed into a blue box. The ceiling and walls are painted the color of robins' eggs; the carpet is sky blue and matches the velvet curtains at the tall windows. Even the pictures on the walls feature blue scenes—seascapes and sweeping skies and landscapes brimming with bluebells. I blink. This room is like the library—like everything here. Only half familiar, as if it's been described to me, but I've never actually seen it for myself. It makes me feel shaky, as if the floor isn't quite solid under my feet.

My stepsisters—also oddly sharp around the edges, as if I'm seeing them for the first time too—are already at the table. They are both excruciatingly elegant and polite, and somehow I know that even though they never show it, they despise me.

That's all right. Apparently I don't like them very much either.

The sisters are dressed in blue—of course—chestnut-haired Precious in royal-blue silk with an embroidered slate-colored overskirt, blonde Dulcet in a woolen riding dress in palest cerulean to match her eyes. Though they are both naturally slender, they are corseted within an inch of their lives.

Precious butters a morsel of toast. "Good morning, sister," she says, and takes a dainty bite. "You're covered in cinders."

Dulcet holds an eggshell-thin teacup to her lips. "She looks a bit watery, too, don't you think, Precious?"

Precious raises a perfect eyebrow. "I believe she does, Dulcie."

Stepmama has taken toast at the sideboard and seated herself at the table, where she rings the silver bell at her place. "More tea," she tells the maid who appears. Then she turns her gimlet gaze onto me. "Really, Penelope. It's been almost a year. You don't see me weeping into my teacup, do you? Six months is the allotted time for mourning. It is time to stop all this silly crying."

I grit my teeth. I am *not* actually crying. Instead of pointing this out, I give my stepmama and stepsisters a stiff smile and go to the sideboard, where the food is laid out in chafing dishes warmed by paraffin candles. The smell of breakfast wafts from them, and suddenly, despite everything, I am still ravenous—as if I haven't eaten for days—and I fill my plate with eggs and grilled mushrooms and five pieces of crisp bacon, adding two pieces of toast. I am barely seated when I begin eating. "Pass the jam, would you, Dulcie?" I ask through a mouthful of toast.

My stepsister raises an eyebrow and passes a jar with an ornate label on it.

Raspberry. "Ta," I say, and add a spoonful of jam to my next bite of toast. Mm, and the bacon is delightfully crisp.

At the head of the table, my stepmama stares. "Penelope, you're eating like a dock worker. It's hardly attractive."

Thanks to the food, I am feeling more like myself. "I have absolutely no interest in being attractive," I say, and pour out a cup of tea.

"Yes you do," Stepmama insists. "You're seventeen years old, and that means old enough to marry. You need to be thinking about attracting a husband, and believe you me, *no* man wants to see his wife eating like a pig at the trough when he comes down to the breakfast table."

I take a gulp of tea and ignore my stepmother, who gives an exasperated sigh. "Hopeless!" she says.

"Mama is right," Dulcet says primly, forking up a tiny bite of egg, inspecting it, and then setting it down.

"She also needs to put off her mourning clothes," Precious adds.

"Oh yes, very much so," Stepmama agrees. "Penelope, we were all dreadfully sorry when our dear duke died, but you look like—"

"Like a crow with shabby feathers," Precious finishes for her.

"Yes, exactly so," Stepmama says. "Well put, my dear. And so, Penelope, after breakfast you will find that all of your mourning clothes have been taken from your room and put properly away in the attic."

I freeze, and the bite of bacon and egg I am about to eat suddenly doesn't smell quite so delicious. The grief and loss that I feel are too immediate; I'm not ready to put off my mourning clothes.

"She's getting watery again," Dulcet notes.

I am *not* going to cry. "You had no right to do that," I protest.

Stepmama places a hand on her wide bosom. "I have every right!" Her voice grows shriller. "This is my house, after all, and you are living in it on my sufferance!" She goes on, listing the ways in which I am an ungrateful, unnatural child, so difficult compared to her own daughters, such an expense, a burden, a trial, and so on.

I close my ears and grimly eat more toast.

It isn't actually Stepmama's house. It is mine, or it should be, except that I am only seventeen and my father died unexpectedly and without leaving a will, and Stepmama is very rich—and so my place in the world is a little uncertain, except that I am Lady Penelope because I am the daughter of a duke.

It must be one of the reasons my stepsisters hate me. They

have more money than they know what to do with, and I have no money at all, but they're not Lady Precious and Lady Dulcet; they're just ordinary Misses.

"It's settled then," Stepmama says with a self-satisfied nod.

I look up, my toast forgotten. What is settled?

"I shall write to Lady Faye at once," Stepmama goes on. She sees my blank look. "About setting you up with a husband, of course," she adds.

"The last thing I want is a husband," I say. And I don't need this Lady Faye friend of my stepmother's telling me I need one, either.

"Don't be silly," Stepmama corrects. "Every girl wants a husband. Just leave it to me, and to Lady Faye. She is an expert matchmaker. We'll have you out of this house and settled with a fine man in a trice."

"I'm perfectly settled as I am," I say. I don't feel too much alarm. Stepmama can't actually *force* me to marry somebody I don't want to.

"Oh!" Stepmama makes shooing motions with her hands. "You're impossibly contradictory. Leave the table at once, Penelope. Go to your room until you can behave properly."

I get up and, snatching two muffins from a plate on the sideboard, leave my stepmama and stepsisters to tell one another all about what a horrible girl I am.

In my room, the maid is standing before the wardrobe folding a pair of black stockings and setting them in a trunk. After a blank moment her name slots into place: Anna. I shake my head. My memory is behaving so strangely; it's like a worn cloth, full of holes and unraveling threads. Seeing me, Anna bobs a curtsy. "I'm sorry, Lady Penelope, indeed I am, for I knew you wouldn't like it none, but your stepmother ordered it, and—"

"It's all right," I say, and Anna heaves a sigh of relief and keeps packing.

I lean against the wall and nibble at a muffin and feel twitchy, as if there's something else I'm supposed to be doing, but I can't remember what it is. It's like an itch in the middle of your back, that feeling. An itch you can't scratch.

My room is large and full of light, but shabby, too. Even though he was a duke, my father didn't have much money, but when he married wealthy Stepmama I refused to let her redecorate my room—I don't like blue—though she offered more than once to pay for it. I still don't regret saying no, because Stepmama would only add it to her list of the many things that her ungrateful stepdaughter owes her.

A bed takes up some of the space, with a chipped wardrobe beside it and, under the window, a small writing desk covered with books and papers and a pot of ink. I must be a scholar, though I don't recognize the handwriting on the pages. Opening the top drawer of the desk, I find an embroidery hoop and an impossible knot of silk threads. Only one edge of the cloth is filled with an awkward jumble of stitches. I have calluses on each of my fingertips, but clearly I am no seamstress. I wonder how I got them.

I try to think back to what happened yesterday. A kind of blank nothingness waits for me there, and I flinch from it. For a moment I feel as if I am falling. A sudden pain lances into my forehead, and I lean against my bedroom wall and close my eyes. The wall is solid behind me. With my fingers I can feel the nubbled silk of my dress. My too-small shoes pinch my toes. An ordinary day, I tell myself. Yesterday was ordinary. I don't need to think about it.

At a scraping sound, I open my eyes. The maid Anna is dragging the packed trunk out of the room.

I take a deep, steadying breath. "Anna."

She straightens. "Yes, Lady Penelope?"

"Do you remember my father?" I ask. "The duke?"

She frowns, and for a moment she looks flustered. "I—" Then she looks primly down. "I remember just what I ought to," she says, her voice wooden.

A strange answer.

"Will that be all?" she asks.

"Yes," I say, and I can't help adding a sharp retort. "If you're done taking all my dresses away, that is."

With a flush, she bobs a hasty curtsy and leaves the room.

Sighing, I rub my forehead. The ache lingers, as if someone is pushing against it with freezing-cold fingers. I catch sight of the ash-smudged bandage on my wrist. I don't remember hurting myself. I turn my hand over and unwrap the bandage. It reveals a mostly healed gash on the inside of my wrist. It doesn't hurt, so I find an old stocking in my wardrobe and wrap it up again. As I try to remember how I got the gash, my head aches even more. I know what will comfort me, and I reach into the pocket of my dress for my thimble.

But the pocket is empty. Frowning, I check my other pocket, and then the purse in the wardrobe where I keep a few coins. The thimble isn't there, either. I know it isn't in my desk with the disastrous jumble of embroidery, but I check it just in case.

I couldn't have lost it, could I?

Now I really am getting watery. The thimble is real, solid—I know it. It's the only thing that I am really certain of. Everything else is slipping away from me. I can't remember anything about my father, not even what he looked like, and the only thing I remember about my mother is that the thimble was a special present from her. It is silver, engraved along the bottom with the roses among thorns that are the symbol of my mother's family, and it has been passed down, mother to daughter, for many generations. Just having it in my pocket gives me strength. And now to lose it!

If I can find the thimble, I will have something to hold on to. Something that will make this strange place feel solid and real to me; something that will make me feel real to myself.

The thimble is surely somewhere in the house. It *must* be. Where else could it be?

CHAPTER

8

His lips are still burning from their kiss, and yet Shoe is furiously angry with Pin.

"You have a chance to get away, you stubborn idiot," she shouts, and points up the stream toward the mountain. "Go, curse you!"

Glaring at her, he scrambles to his feet. *She* is the one being the stubborn, stupid idiot. Neither one of them is going to escape—hasn't she realized that yet?—and they might as well be together when it comes. "Not without you, Pin."

She holds up her hand. The bandage on her wrist is soaked with blood; drops spatter on the ground and are absorbed by the ash. Her face is thin and determined, and seeing it, maybe for the last time, makes Shoe's heart, which he'd thought was a frozen, shriveled thing about the size of a burned crust, pound in his chest. "Shoe," she says. "If you care about me at all, you won't follow me." Then she turns her back and heads down the ash-covered stream bank.

Shoe stares after her. *If you care about me at all* . . .

His legs quiver with weariness, and the rest of him is shivering because he knows what the Godmother will do to them—she will break them to her will, each of them in different, slow, special ways, and she'll take pleasure in doing it, too.

Pin starts to run, leaping over rocks, stepping lightly over the ash, and she's running right into the arms of capture. Her boots, Shoe notices, are making her steps surer than they would be without them. There might be irony in that. Pin would know if there was or not.

She disappears from view, and the shock of it is enough to get him moving, scrambling like a scared rabbit up the bank past the waterfall, then around another bend, his feet leaving easy-to-follow prints in the ash. *Pin*, he thinks with every step, but he can't help but fear for his own skin, too.

The backpack is heavy, and it rubs against his old friends, the still-healing welts from his time at the post, but that just reminds him to go faster. As he told Pin, there's worse things than the post. When he sees a sort of notch in the side of the ravine, he runs for it, knowing that the Godmother will follow his trail easily, but knowing, too, that to stay in the ravine is an even surer way to be captured. He climbs the slope, ash as fine and soft as sable sliding down around him and filling his boots, until he makes it to the notch that takes him up and out of the ravine, scrambling along a rocky shoulder of the mountain. What he really needs is to get down into the trees again; out here he's too exposed.

The first jolt of energy has worn off, and he can feel how tired his body is; it's a candle burned almost down to the socket, a flickering flame about to go out. The backpack weighs more with every step. The ash-covered slopes have turned to wiry brown grass, and below him he can see the tree line, which is dark and welcoming, as if he'll be safe there, which he knows he won't.

Carrying the backpack is stupid. He pauses and slips it off, dumping it behind a rock, but taking out the cheese and gingerbread first, just in case he lives long enough to want to eat again. The relief from the pain of carrying it takes him the rest of the way down the slope to the edge of the forest, but then the weariness catches up to him again. About to plunge into the trees, he pauses to catch his breath and looks back over his shoulder.

A jolt of fright flashes through him. A man on a big brown horse is at the top of the spur of the mountain where Shoe left the backpack. Two creatures that look something like dogs and something like men crouch at the horse's knees; they have their heads to the ground as if they're sniffing. As Shoe stares at them, the man sweeps a look over the tree line; his gaze stops, fastens on Shoe. Slowly, deliberately, he nudges the horse into a walk, and they start down the slope.

The Godmother's Huntsman and two trackers.

Shoe stumbles into the forest and jerks himself into a run. The Huntsman has his trail. "I'm not getting out of this, am I?" he mutters to himself. But he isn't going to hand himself over to them, either.

The trees are spaced widely here, this high up the flank of the mountain, so he has room to run, ferns brushing his knees, slipping and sliding now and then down a steeper, pine-needle-covered slope, always finding a path, as if the forest is clearing a way for him. Clouds have moved in to cover the sun; it must be after midday, he guesses. The Huntsman can't be very far behind. His stomach growls, and he puts his hand into his coat pocket to find the packet of cheese. Something else is in there; he pulls it out.

Staggering to a stop, he stares down at Pin's thimble. She must have slipped it into his pocket. Why? It's magic— he's figured that much out at least, he's not completely an idiot—and maybe Pin thought it would help him. "That was stupid," he mutters. Because the thimble would have helped her more.

The Huntsman and his trackers are coming, he reminds himself. Taking a quick bite of cheese and then wrapping it back up again, Shoe stumbles on, holding Pin's thimble tightly in his fist.

The sky overhead has turned darker gray, the sun going down behind the clouds. Shadows gather among the trees. Shoe's run isn't a run anymore, it's just a dull shuffle, his muscles one big weary ache. Now and then he trips over a gnarled root and has to find the will to pick himself off the ground so he can shuffle on. In his fist, the thimble feels warm, and it seems to pull in one direction. Maybe Pin created some kind of magic with the thimble so it will lead him to safety.

He hears the *shuff-shuff* of hooves on soft ground. He's got his head down, watching for tree roots to trip over. At the corner of his vision, he sees the Huntsman pull even with him, the horse at a plodding walk. The horse's head is hanging, Shoe notices, as if it's just as exhausted as he is. The trackers that hover at the horse's heels are tired too, their tongues lolling.

Clutching the thimble, Shoe stumbles on. He's good and caught, he realizes through the haze of weariness, but he's too tired to be afraid. The twilight advances. He bumps into a tree, then stops, staring at it for a moment.

Tree.

Tree?

What to do with a tree? Oh. Yes. Go around it. Slowly he shuffles around the tree and keeps going. Another root trips him and he goes down hard, but keeps his hold on the thimble, then slowly peels himself off the soft, welcoming ground.

He hears the Huntsman beside him, the snorts of his tired horse, the creaking of his saddle, the occasional low whine from one of the trackers.

"Aren't you—" Shoe starts, and stops, alarmed at how

rough and weary his voice sounds. He catches his breath. "Aren't you going to capture me?" he asks the Huntsman.

The man clears his throat. "Aye, we're getting to it," he answers, his voice deep and gravelly.

Oh. Shoe trudges on. His feet aren't sore, he realizes. Well, of course. He's wearing boots he made himself.

"Just waiting for you to run yourself out," the Huntsman adds.

"This isn't exactly running," Shoe mutters.

To his surprise, he hears a huff of a laugh. "No, that it's not," the Huntsman says. "Not to worry, lad. It won't be long now."

"It'll be longer than you think," Shoe whispers, not sure if the Huntsman hears him. His shuffle is a walk, now, and he has to think about every step. Pick up his extremely well-shod foot. Drag it forward, set it down again. Lean forward—but not too far. He's hunched over like an old man. Pretty soon he'll be crawling.

But Pin is right. He is stubborn; he'll crawl if he has to.

After a long time, it comes to that. He stumbles again, and falls, and this time he can't make his legs work. Try as he might, they won't let him stand. Crawling, he goes on. The pine needles are prickly against the palm of his hand and the fist that is clutching Pin's thimble. There is just darkness, the ache in his muscles, the dragging weights of sleep and hunger, and the pull from the thimble. If he can keep going until morning, he promises himself, something will happen.

"Had enough yet?" the Huntsman asks, just a deep voice in the darkness.

No. He can't muster up enough strength to say the word out loud.

He crawls on through the night. Until he finds himself with his face pressed against the rough bark of a pine tree and can't figure out what he's supposed to be doing.

One of the trackers whines, a pitiful sound.

"Shhh," the Huntsman tells it. "We're almost done." His voice is closer; he's not on the horse anymore, but has been walking patiently alongside Shoe, waiting for him to stop.

No. Not stopping. Slowly, his arms and legs dragging, Shoe shifts away from the tree. As he crawls past it, his shoulder bumps the trunk and he goes down, face-first in the pine needles.

This time, he can't get up. The candle flame flickers out; he's used up. A heavy weight of despair presses down on him. The Huntsman will take him to the Godmother now, and he, and probably Pin, too, will be turned into lessons for the rest of the slaves at the fortress. *See?* the Jacks and the Seamstresses and the new Shoemaker will be told, as the guards point to his body and Pin's hanging from thorns on the wall. *This is what happens to those who try to escape.* It'll hurt a lot, Shoe thinks fuzzily, but then it'll be over.

As if he's a long way from his body, he feels, distantly, the Huntsman's big hands on his shoulders, turning him onto his still-healing back, and even the pain of that isn't enough to return him to himself. From far away he hears the whining of the trackers and the Huntsman's deep voice calming them. Then sleep comes like a black bag over his head, and he's out.

SHOE WAKES UP in the morning wrapped in a blanket with his own backpack for a pillow. He's curled on his side next to a crackling fire. The air smells of pine smoke and browning sausages. An early dawn light filters through the tree branches.

He's still got the thimble clenched in his fist.

As he lifts his arm to look at it, his whole body is seized with a muscle cramp; he grits his teeth until it passes.

"Awake, are you?" asks a deep voice.

The Huntsman. The weight of despair crashes back into Shoe. Suffering, death, the whole lot of it. That's what today has in store for him. Slowly, so as not to trigger the cramps again, he opens his hand to examine the thimble. It gleams silver against his dirty palm. At its base are etched brambles—thorny vines like the ones that covered the wall around the Godmother's fortress. Amid the brambles, though, are dainty roses. Pin's thimble. It reminds him of her—prickly, with occasional glimpses of sweetness. In his mind he can see her face so clearly, her dark hair tangled, her gray eyes weary, but still sharp. When he'd first seen her, he'd thought she wasn't pretty—and no, she's not. *Pretty* is too small and light a word for what she is. Missing her is an ache in his chest. He turns the thimble, letting the light burnish its dimpled surface, then puts it into his coat pocket. His eyes drop closed. He's been captured, just as she has. The one consolation is that it means he'll see her again before they die.

"Sausages?" the Huntsman asks.

He cracks his eyes open again.

"Expect you need a bit of help there," the Huntsman says from the other side of the fire. He gets up from the log he's been sitting on and comes around the fire. He's a big man, and he looms; Shoe tries to scramble away, and his muscles cramp again.

"Now then, now then," the Huntsman says in a soothing voice, and with strange gentleness helps Shoe sit up, leaning him against a tree, then tucking the blanket around his shoulders. He turns to the fire, and turns back with a steaming mug of something that smells like coffee. "Start with this," he says, helping Shoe close his hand around the tin cup.

The cup is hot under Shoe's fingers. For a moment, all he can do is sit and hold it; then he manages to lift the cup to his mouth and take a sip. The coffee burns a warm and bitter path to his stomach, which responds by demanding something to eat.

Shoe eyes the Huntsman warily. He has an enormous, drooping mustache, brown skin, and a shiny, bald head. He is busy at the fire; he skewers a fat sausage with a fork and holds it out to Shoe. "Careful, there. It's hot."

For a moment Shoe hesitates; then, slowly, he reaches out and takes it. He doesn't remember having sausage before, so it's the best one he's ever eaten, and he savors every scrap of it, trying to ignore the two drooling trackers that are keenly watching him eat it. The Huntsman's big brown horse is tethered to a low branch, he notices, and there's an open saddlebag on the ground near the fire, and another bedroll.

"I'm your prisoner, aren't I?" Shoe asks through a bite of sausage.

"So it would seem," the Huntsman answers.

Finishing the sausage, Shoe wipes a bit of grease from his chin with the corner of the blanket. "Why didn't you stop me walking last night?" he asks, and takes a sip of coffee.

"Well now, that's the strange thing, isn't it?" the Huntsman says. He is busy dabbing a thick, greenish salve on the trackers' backs where they've been whipped. "You're leading us straight as arrow-shot to where we're supposed to be going."

The words are like a blow. All that struggle to get away, and he was going *toward* his own suffering and death? "Oh, that's definitely irony," he mutters, his voice shaking. "Trying to escape the fortress by running directly toward the fortress."

"The Godmother's fortress, you mean?" the Huntsman asks, setting aside his pot of salve. At Shoe's nod, he goes on. "No, you're not going there. You're heading for the city, and that's where I'm ordered to bring you."

Shoe stares. "The city?" he repeats, as if saying the word again will make his brain understand it.

"Aye." The Huntsman sets a large tin bowl filled with porridge on the ground. "The Godmother's city." The two trackers, both moving stiffly, come to the bowl and, dipping their heads, begin to lap up the porridge. "She's got plans for you there, most likely."

"I expect she does," Shoe says morosely.

The Huntsman fries two more sausages and adds them to the trackers' bowl; they look up, their dog faces grinning, and then plunge their muzzles back into their breakfast. "They'd wag if they could," the Huntsman says with a sad sigh. "But she didn't give 'em tails."

Feeling better now that he's got breakfast and coffee in him, Shoe studies the thimble again. He's seen it do magic, when Pin lit the fire in the cave, and when she made the smoke arise from the cobblestones outside the Godmother's fortress. He frowns. It's Pin's thimble. "It's leading me to Pin," he whispers, feeling stupid for not realizing it before.

If the thimble is leading him to Pin, the same place the Huntsman's been ordered to take him, then the Godmother must have plans for both of them in this city, whatever it is.

Shoe realizes that his hands are shaking. He clenches his fist around the thimble.

The Huntsman is sitting on his log, drinking coffee from a tin cup. "Afraid, are you?"

Of course he's afraid, but he's not going to admit it to his captor. Shoe shrugs. He doesn't want to think about what's going to happen to him. His story is going to be very short, and it will have an ugly ending.

"Hmm." The Huntsman maneuvers the cup under his

drooping mustache and takes a sip of coffee. "What if you could do something else. Like, say, join up with other people who've escaped?"

Shoe looks up. "You know people like that?"

"I may," the Huntsman answers. "They might be hiding away in a place where the Godmother can't find them. You interested?"

Before he can stop himself, Shoe nods.

"I can take you to them," the Huntsman offers. "We've got a place in the forest."

Shoe's noticed how the Huntsman has switched from the vague *maybe I might know some people* to the more certain *we've got a place.*

He frowns. The Huntsman is the Godmother's man, isn't he? His offer of escape is much more likely to be a trap. But . . . he seems kind. Gentle, even. And he'd put the salve on the trackers' backs, where they'd been whipped.

Maybe the Huntsman is a rebel, and he's offering a way out. In Shoe's fist, the silver thimble warms. He can feel it pulling him toward Pin. Toward his own death. The thought of that makes him tremble down to his bones.

This fear isn't doing him any good. In the fortress he was afraid all the time, especially after the post. He'd kept his head down and worked hard, and he hadn't done anything to change the horror of it all until Pin had come and led him out.

He can't be afraid anymore. He takes a deep breath to

steady himself, to face what he's got to do. Stiffly he sheds the blanket and, leaning against the tree, levers himself to his feet. "No," he tells the Huntsman. "I need to go on."

The Huntsman shakes his head. "She'll kill you."

"Pin is there," Shoe says stubbornly. "The girl who was captured by the Godmother. I can't get out unless she does, too."

"Your Pen—" the Huntsman starts.

"Pin," Shoe corrects.

"Right-o." The Huntsman nods. "This girl of yours. Pin. It's clear enough that she's been chosen for a special fate." He gives a grim shake of his head.

"It's bad, this special fate?" Shoe asks.

"The worst," the Huntsman says.

"Then we'll have to hurry." Shoe grips the thimble, feeling its pull. "Do you think we can get there today?"

"Maybe, if the forest wills it." With a huff, the Huntsman gets to his feet. "Well, come on, Jip, Jes," he says to the two trackers. "Our desperate criminal here is bent on meeting his doom before dinnertime."

While the Huntsman packs up his bags and saddles his horse, Shoe shoulders the knapsack and sets off. He can only hobble through the trees at first, with his muscles so stiff and sore, so it isn't long before the Huntsman catches him.

"Off to find your Pen," he comments, after riding in silence for a while.

"Pin," Shoe corrects again. "Yes. I, um . . ." It feels strange to be saying it out loud. "I think I might love her."

"Ah." After a silence full of cogitation, the Huntsman adds, "You're not a Prince in Disguise, are you?"

"Nothing like that," Shoe says.

"Didn't think so." He gives Shoe a pitying look. "Here, I'll carry this for you." He reaches down from the saddle and takes the pack from Shoe's shoulder. "Listen, lad, you don't want to go to the city. Come with me. The forest will protect us."

"I can't," Shoe says, and, free of the weight of the pack, shifts from a walk to a slow shuffle.

The Huntsman nods sadly. "All right, then. I see how it is. I'll get you secretly into the city. The wheels'll be turning, though, so you won't have much time to find your girl."

Pin, Shoe thinks as he trudges along, knows who she is. Somewhere inside her head, she's got her self—her own self—hidden away, a girl who sweeps her skirts aside when she sits, a girl with a proud tilt to her chin, a girl who laughs at irony even when she's dirty and bloodstained and exhausted after running through the forest for a day and a night. Shoe hasn't any idea who he is, except that he's a shoemaker, not a secret prince. He could be somebody's son, or brother, though he doesn't know about lover, because if that were the case he's sure he would've been better at kissing Pin.

He'd give anything, he thinks, to be able to kiss her again.

CHAPTER

9

I SEARCH THE ENTIRE HOUSE FOR MY THIMBLE. I START IN the library, where I spent all night in the cinders—thinking maybe it fell out of my pocket while I was sleeping—but the hearth is cleanly swept. Then the blue breakfast room, drawing rooms, dining rooms, a vast ballroom, all of it only half familiar, as if I've been told about this huge mansion of a house but never actually walked the hallways or peered into any of the rooms. It's a strange, disconnected feeling—that itch, again, that tells me I'm supposed to be somewhere else.

Having explored the entire upper house, I head down a set of narrow stairs to the servants' areas—the kitchens and wine cellars and storage rooms—where the servants exchange sidelong glances as I ask the maid Anna if she found my thimble. She says no, and I go back upstairs. The music room was empty when I searched before, but as I step softly past the door, I hear a faint note played on a piano. A moment later, the note is echoed by a voice. Catching a tune, the voice soars into a ripple of notes, a quick breath, and then a leaping, joyful song full of trills and high notes.

Quietly, I turn the knob and ease the door open. Through the crack in the door I see my stepsister Dulcet, her back to me, standing by the piano singing. Her voice is so rich it fills the entire room like golden sunshine and spills out into the hallway. What would it be like, I wonder, to open my mouth and have such glorious music come out? Somehow I am sure that my own singing voice is more like frogs croaking.

Dulcet is my stepsister, and we seem to be settled into certain roles—her proudly disdainful, me the cinder-smudged annoying one who is disdained—but what do I really know about her? She, and her sister and my stepmother, too, are like the house—only half familiar to me. It's as if I know perfectly well what a stepsister is, but I don't know Dulcet at all.

The floor under my feet squeaks and the music stops. Dulcet holds herself absolutely still; slowly she turns toward the door. Seeing that it's me, she lets out the faintest relieved breath, and then she is her usual carefully controlled self.

"That was beautiful," I tell her. "I didn't know you could sing."

Dulcet takes a breath. "Oh, that," she says, with a false-careless wave of her hand. "I hardly call that singing."

"It was glorious," I say. "You should sing so others can hear you."

Dulcet's face turns cold. "In public, you mean?" Her every move elegant, she closes the lid of the piano and crosses the room toward me. "Certainly not. A lady never performs in public. It would not be attractive or at all appropriate. It's a terrible suggestion." She brushes past me, takes two steps down the hallway, and then pauses. Without turning to face me she adds, "You don't need to mention this to my mother, Pen."

"I won't," I promise, and I mean it. It's Dulcet's secret, and now it's mine, too.

My thimble search ends in a picture gallery on the third floor of the house, which is a far grander mansion than I realized. The gallery is a long hallway with floor-to-ceiling windows on one wall, windows that look out over a parklike square edged by other grand houses. On the other wall is a row of oil paintings, each one as tall as I am, almost life-size portraits of people who, I guess, are ancestors who once lived in this house. Most of them I don't recognize, stiffly posed women in old-fashioned dresses, solemn-faced children, bearded patriarchs.

Then I come to the end of the gallery. One last painting is leaning against the wall, as if placed there as an after-thought. In the picture, a woman is standing in the midst of what looks like an untamed forest that is a riot of fir trees and ferns, vines and moss. She looks directly at me. Her dark hair is braided and pinned into a severe style. Her face is not softly pretty, but sharp-featured and lined with care, though I can see a wicked smile lurking at the corner of her mouth. She has blue eyes set under dark brows, and the wildness of the forest is reflected in them, almost hidden, but still there. A coil of brambles and roses twines around her feet and up the sides of the picture, almost like a frame. Her hand rests on the skirt of her simple dress, and on one finger she is wearing a silver thimble.

The thimble.

My thimble.

This must be my mother.

I step closer to see. The setting sun comes in through the gallery windows, shining over my shoulder and illuminating the thimble, which is painted in exquisite detail. Silver, dimpled, thorny brambles and roses, just as I remember it.

And I *do* remember it. I can almost feel the weight of the thimble in my hand, heavier and more solid than it should be, really, as if it carries with it portents and power. Absent, it is more real to me than anything in this house. I could never have lost it. *Never.*

I examine the rest of the painting from top to bottom, but I cannot find any more clues. Except that my mother and her wild forest seem strange and out of place here in this grand house.

From outside, in the city, comes the sound of an enormous clock striking the hour. The muffled booms make the air tremble; dust motes rise up and swirl around, glinting gold in the light.

Somehow I'm sure that my mother, watching with that knowing smile, could answer all of my questions. "I expect you know where I lost my thimble," I mutter. She smiles on. "Stop looking at me like that," I tell her.

A bustle and thump from the end of the gallery interrupts me. A tall footman dressed in dark-blue livery hurries toward me. "Lady Penelope," he gasps.

"Yes?" I say, and raise my eyebrows.

The footman pauses, looks from me to the painting and back again with his mouth open, then catches his breath. "Lady Penelope," he repeats. "Your stepmother wants you in the blue drawing room right away. She's right tetchy, m'lady, that you weren't in your room when she wanted you."

"All right," I say. I'm not going to hurry for Stepmama, so I turn and take one last look at my mother's picture before following the footman along the gallery and down the stairs to the blue drawing room.

As I enter the room, my stepmother turns from the mantel, her face flushed and peevish. "Penelope, where *have* you been?" she chides.

"Looking for something," I say absently. Sitting in a brocade chair next to the hearth is a woman who, I guess, is Stepmama's friend.

Lady Faye gives me a careful, assessing look, from the tips of my scuffed shoes to my tousled hair.

I study her just as carefully. Stepmama is all bluster and impatience. Somehow I am sure that Lady Faye is something else altogether. She is wearing an ice-blue velvet morning dress that is shaped perfectly to her form; priceless lace as fine as cobwebs edges the low-cut bodice and cuffs and foams in three flounces at the edge of her skirt. Though she is white-blonde and has silver-blue eyes, something about the sharpness of her features reminds me of the portrait of my mother.

"Hello," I say, testing.

At the hearth, my stepmama blows out an exasperated breath. "Do you see, Lady Faye, what I must put up with?" she huffs. "A graceless hoyden! No address, no elegance." She glares at me and hisses, "Curtsy to Lady Faye, Penelope, and mind your manners."

I ignore her.

Lady Faye raises one perfect eyebrow. *She* has grace to spare, I can see. "Good afternoon, Lady Penelope," she says in a low, musical voice with just the faintest edge to it. "I am so pleased to make your acquaintance."

If I were polite and elegant, I would say the same thing back to her, but since I am a hoyden, I nod and say, "I'm not looking for a husband."

Lady Faye cocks her head. "No?" She beckons to me, and I step closer, my feet sinking into the deep carpet. "Every girl wants a husband, Penelope," she says softly, only to me. "A strong, brave man to love and cherish her and protect her from the outside world, to be a father to her children, to instruct her and counsel her and allow her to be the sweet and lovely adornment of his home."

I am about as far from *sweet* and *lovely* as any girl could be. And the very thought of a marriage like that makes me shudder.

"I want the best for my girls," Lady Faye goes on. "I want them to be happy, forever. If I choose to sponsor you, Penelope, you too will enjoy blissful happiness." She looks me up and down, and when she speaks it's louder, so my stepmother can hear. "But you will never attract a man dressed as you are, with such crude manners. You must seek to transform yourself."

"*Exactly*," Stepmama interrupts. "She will not behave in a ladylike manner, and she refuses to change that shabby dress for something more appropriate to a young miss."

"Mm, it is a very ugly dress," Lady Faye notes. "Though it suits her well enough." Then she turns to talk further with Stepmama, and I stand there stupidly, like a piece of furniture, realizing that Lady Faye has just given me a carefully phrased insult.

"Do you think there is anything to be done with her?" Stepmama asks.

"Oh, she will be drawn in, despite her intransigence," Lady Faye replies. "It is simply a matter of getting the wheels turning. Can I count on you to play the role we discussed earlier?"

My stepmother draws herself up as if she's about to sail into a sea battle. "Yes, indeed, Lady Faye. I know just what to do." She turns to me and raps out an order. "Go to your room at once, Penelope, and await me there."

With a shrug, I go.

IN MY ROOM I sit at my desk and look over the pages of writing. Maybe I got the calluses on my fingertips from holding a pen. I am beginning to think that my stepmother was lying when she said I haven't been ill, because what else could explain the strange holes where my memories should be? Perhaps I had a knock on the head?

A bustle at the door, and Stepmama barges into the room. Ah. Battle is engaged.

"You have been living in this house at my sufferance, Penelope," she begins. "You are an ungrateful girl, and far more trouble than you are worth, and you owe me much; more than you could ever repay. Your rudeness to Lady Faye forced me to this, you know."

I stand. "What *are* you talking about, Stepmama?"

She stabs a finger at me. "Your father was a duke, but he had nothing—he was hardly a proper man at all, to be sure—and he left you nothing. Despite your proud ways, and your Lady this and Lady that, you are a pauper. You cannot depend on me to support you. From now on, you must earn your keep."

I reach into my skirt pocket for my thimble and feel a

little faint when I remember that it's still missing. "Are you turning me out into the street?"

"Believe me, I have considered it. Your mother knew the streets well enough, or so I've heard."

I seize on her words. "My mother? Did you know her before she died?"

For just a moment, Stepmama falters, as if searching her memory for something that isn't there.

"Her picture is here," I persist. "Upstairs, in the long portrait gallery. Have you seen it?"

Stepmama stares blankly at me for a long moment, and then I see it—the memory slots into place behind her eyes. "Her portrait. Yes, of course," she says, and then recovers her bluster. "But that is not to the point, Penelope. Lady Faye has convinced me to let you stay, if only to repay what you owe me. You've never done a stitch of work in your life, but you will learn—oh yes, you'll learn." She looks around the room. "I have long needed a second dressing room at this end of the east wing of the house. You may leave your things here. Go down to the kitchen, and one of the servants will tell you about your new duties."

I think about arguing, insisting that the house is mine, not hers, but I don't have money or influence or lawyers. My stepmama is an implacable force, and for now I must bow to necessity.

CHAPTER

10

"THERE IT IS," THE HUNTSMAN SAYS TO SHOE AS THEY reach the crest of a hill. "The Godmother's city." After yet another day of walking, Shoe is stumbling with weariness, but he is stubborn about following the pull of Pin's thimble. Having left the forest trails at midday, Shoe and the Huntsman and the horse and the two tired trackers are on a wide dusty road; in the distance are mountains, their snowcapped peaks turning pink with the setting sun. In a valley below the mountains, the late-afternoon light flows like honey over the city.

To Shoe's surprise, it is beautiful. At the top of the valley stands a graceful castle, its white towers tall and ephemeral in the golden light. Its central tower is the tallest; high in that tower is set a huge round clock that looks to Shoe like a giant, stern face watching over the valley. The streets around the castle are wide and lined with trees, interrupted here and there by green parkland edged with grand mansions built of pink-tinged stone. A gleaming silver river snakes through the middle of the city, ending at a high waterfall. There the river drops in lacy swags straight down to a long lake that is already in shadow.

"I expected something more like the fortress," Shoe says.

"Aye, well." The Huntsman shakes his head.

Shoe looks questioningly up at him.

The Huntsman shrugs his broad shoulders. "It's more like her fortress than it looks, lad."

Shoe studies the city again. In his hand, the thimble gives a tug. Pin is in there, somewhere.

As they go down the road, the sun dips behind the mountains, twilight falls, and the lights in the city begin to come on.

"You'd better take your pack," the Huntsman says as they reach the valley floor. The city, all dark shadows and gleaming points of light, looms before them. Shoe hears, faintly, the sound of the giant clock striking the hour. The road leads straight to a gate in a high wall that surrounds the whole city. From up on the mountainside, Shoe hadn't noticed the wall, but here it is. Covered with brambles. He takes the pack from the Huntsman and slings it over his shoulder.

Two guards dressed in neat blue uniforms stand on either side of the gate; their pikes gleam bronze in the flickery light of torches in sconces.

The Huntsman gives them a competent nod, which they return, permission to enter.

Shoe stumbles past them with his head down; the trackers slink after the Huntsman's horse. In the shadow of the gate, Shoe pauses. There's something . . . the faintest sound, at the edge of hearing. A suggestion of well-oiled, whirring gears. The air tingles just a bit, as if he's passing through the thinnest icy curtain. Taking a deep breath, he steps through the gate and into the Godmother's city.

The street, paved here with cobblestones, winds up the valley. Buildings crowd its edges; graceful bridges span the river. Ahead, the castle looms. Fires burn blue at the top of its high towers. The clock on the highest tower seems alert, watching.

"Where are all the people?" Shoe asks, noticing that the streets are empty; all the doors and windows are tightly closed. At every doorway is a lighted lantern.

"Curfew after the clock strikes eight," the Huntsman says. "In most of the city, at least. It's all under strict control, lad."

The Godmother's control, Shoe guesses. She must have enormous power. The cobblestones under his feet are lined up with exact precision and are scrupulously clean, not a pothole or puddle or pile of horse manure to be seen. It even smells clean, like bleach and soap instead of woodsmoke and drains and dinners cooking. The houses that line the street, too, are whitewashed, and each one has a neat square of garden below its windows. Gardens full of flowers. Blue, Shoe guesses, and no weeds.

The main road goes over a bridge, then continues its winding way toward the castle.

As they reach a corner, the Huntsman pulls his horse to a stop. He nods at a dark alleyway. "She'll be looking for a runaway shoemaker," he says. "You'll want to keep your head down and stay to the lower city, which she doesn't watch as carefully."

Shoe looks up at him. "So you really are letting me go?"

"You're the one who chose to come here, lad," the Huntsman says.

True enough. "Will you get into trouble, not turning me over to the Godmother as you were ordered?"

The Huntsman shrugs his broad shoulders. "I've been spying for my friends in the forest, as you can likely guess. I'll go to them now, and I'll be safe enough. You, though—be careful when you start looking for your girl. She won't be in a prison or anything simple like that. She's too important."

Important because she'd tried to escape? Or for some other reason? "What does the Godmother want Pin for?" he asks. The Huntsman is right—it has to be more than a simple punishment. A whipping, or prison, or impalement on a wall of thorns would be so much easier for the Godmother to carry out than bringing Pin here.

The Huntsman shrugs. "I don't know." He leans closer and lowers his voice. "You won't have much time. If both of you come into the forest, we'll find you if we can."

Shoe nods.

The Huntsman reaches a hand toward Shoe. "Good luck to you, Shoemaker."

"Just Shoe," Shoe says. He reaches up, and the Huntsman gives his hand a firm shake. "Good luck to you, too." And he ducks into the alleyway.

THE FIRST NIGHT, it's all he can do to stagger to the darkest alley off the most twisted street, where he finds a doorway to curl up in. He falls into a deep sleep as soon as he's settled.

When he wakes up in the cold light of morning, with the echoes of the striking clock lingering in his ears, small hands are trying to tug his backpack out from under his head. Somebody else is unlacing his boots. "Go 'way," he mumbles, and sits up, as two ragged children skitter down the alley, jeering as they go.

Shivering, he creaks to his feet, stomach growling. Stupid to forget that even perfect cities like this have thieves in them, assuming he ever knew it. With a lurch, he remembers Pin's thimble. But it's still there, clutched in his hand, and he breathes a sigh of relief.

Before he does anything else, he needs something to eat. He crouches on the step and reties his bootlaces, then goes through the backpack. During his travels with the Huntsman, he shared all of the cheese with the sad-eyed trackers, and all of the gingerbread too, even though he'd wanted to save a bit of it for Pin. Sadly the pack is empty of food, but instead he finds a small pot with a cork stopper in it. Pulling out the cork, he smells something sharp and green—it's the salve that the Huntsman was putting on the trackers' backs to soothe their whip welts. He can use it on his own memories from the Godmother's fortress. "Thanks," he whispers, and hopes that the Huntsman won't meet his own punishment at the Godmother's hands for letting him go. Digging further in the backpack, he finds the bag of gold coins Pin had put there. He'll be able to buy something to eat. He puts the thimble in his coat pocket and heads out.

The streets of the much smaller lower city, where he spent the night, are dark and narrow and twisted and smell very strongly of inadequate drains. It's not under control, and the city guards in their blue uniforms stay away from it. The lower city is for the street sweepers and shovelers of night soil and the thieves and beggars and brothel-keepers. It's as if the Godmother's city needs these dregs and drabs of humanity, but it sets them aside because it doesn't want them dirtying up the place.

When he ventures onto the pristine streets of the upper city, the first thing he notices is that the castle tower marks the hours with absolute rigidity. At seven the shops open; at twelve they close for an hour. At eight, the bells will send everyone scurrying indoors to lock their houses up tight. The people he passes are well dressed and seem to have their heads cocked as if listening for the bells that regulate their day. They are all wearing varying shades of blue; they all smile stiffly and nod politely to one another as they pass. It's all too regimented. Too perfect. It makes the hair stand up on the back of his neck.

In his ragged, dirty clothes, he's a bit too noticeable, and a couple of blue-coated guards eye him, fingering their pikes as if they'd like to run him through.

After fleeing back into the lower city, Shoe steps into a shabby shop where a baker has just placed a tray of piping hot rolls in the window. "Could I have three of those?" he asks, and takes the clinking purse out of the backpack.

"Aye, to be sure," the baker says, and bends to reach for the rolls.

"Have you always lived here?" Shoe asks her.

The woman straightens. "I don't know what you mean," she says blankly.

And oh, Shoe knows that blank look—it's the look of a fortress slave who's been ripped out of her old life and given a role in whatever elaborate plan the Godmother has for this place. Are all the people in this city like that? "Never mind," he tells her. "How much for the rolls?"

"Three coppers," she says, and holds out her hand for Shoe's money. The coin he pulls out of the bag is heavy gold, as thick as his pinkie finger, and a little smaller than his palm. The baker's cheeks go pale. She stares at Shoe, looks him up and down, evidently taking in his ragged clothing, his thin, hungry face. "You must have stolen that," she whispers.

"No, I didn't steal it," Shoe says. "Well, not exactly." Pin had taken it from the Godmother's fortress.

The baker wrings her hands and backs away from the counter. "Go." She shoos him. "Take it out of here."

"But it's money," Shoe protests. He doesn't remember having money before, but he knows how this is supposed to work. "I give it to you, and you give me three hot rolls for it."

The baker leans forward. "You could buy every house on this street with that golden wagon wheel you've got there. You must have stolen it. It's dangerous. Put it away and get out of here, you thief."

"I'm not a thief," Shoe insists. Nervously he puts the coins away and leaves, hearing the baker slam and lock the door behind him.

The thimble tugs toward the upper city. Even though he doesn't have much time to find Pin and help her escape, he can't risk showing up like a blot on those perfect streets again. He needs a base, a place to start, some sort of work so he can earn money for food. A plan is starting to take shape in his mind, something he thought about during the long trudge from the ashy mountainside to the city. Pin was so sure that whatever she would find beyond the fortress walls was a way out—the Before, maybe even her real life—but he knows for certain now that it is not. There's something wrong with this city, something that begins with the Godmother, or whatever she calls herself here. And he knows he must act, quickly.

The streets closest to the river are where the merchants do their business, so he starts looking for work there, but is scorned and turned away. After a long morning of wandering, he makes his way to the street of shoemakers. At one end, the street abuts the upper city, and that's where the fine ladies and gentlemen of the grand mansions shop for their shoes. At the lower end, the cobblers and shoemakers make rough shoes for the servants and poorer classes.

Shoe starts at a shop halfway down the street. He can't sell his services as a shoemaker—that would risk drawing the Godmother's attention—but he might work as a servant. The first shoemaker he asks for work sneers and slams the shop door in his face. The second calls for her two burly sons, who chase Shoe out of the shop, scowling as he dodges their fists. The third looks shifty-eyed and points farther along the street. "You might try old Natters, down the end. Now, get along with you."

His stomach now hollow and echoing in new and interesting ways, Shoe trudges to the shoemaker's shop at the end of the street. It is a narrow building of three stories squeezed between other buildings. Compared to the pristine houses in the upper city, this house is almost aggressively dilapidated. On the ground floor there is a row of grime-coated windows made of tiny, thick panes of glass. Above it hangs a sign with the outline of a faded red shoe on it. The door is warped and covered with cracked brown paint; it groans, scraping across the floor as Shoe pushes it open and goes inside.

A hunch-shouldered old man looks up from his workbench. "Yes? What?" he asks, squinting in the dim light. He has a long face and tufted eyebrows. "What is it?"

Shoe glances around the room. On one wall is a shelf of lasts—carved wooden feet to build shoes around—all jumbled together, and on a long table are dusty rolls of leather and an overflowing bin of leather scraps for cobbling, tangled spools of heavy thread, awls and other tools, all left untidily scattered about. Shoe's hands itch to set it all right.

"You're adding decorations to the upper," Shoe says. It's very fine work the old shoemaker is doing, despite the squalor of his shop.

The old man glances down at the boot in his hands, then back at Shoe. "Ah! You know shoemaking, do you?" Shoe opens his mouth to answer, but the old man interrupts. "No, no, never mind. Forget I asked. I don't want to know. I don't want an apprentice, if that's what you're here for. The last apprentice I had disappeared, and the one before that was taken from us, and I don't have the heart for it anymore."

Shoe blinks. Where have the old man's apprentices gotten to? Did the Godmother decide she wanted them for her fortress? "Have you ever seen me before?" he ventures.

"What, you?" The old man pushes himself up from the bench—he is bent, but still very tall—and totters past Shoe to drag the shop door open wider. As the gray light spills into the room, he examines Shoe closely. "No, I've never seen you before. Now, get along with you."

Shoe grits his teeth. He's going to fail before he even gets started. "No, wait. I don't want to be your apprentice. I can work. I'm a very good worker." He puts every ounce of his honesty and sincerity into his words.

"Are you now?" the shoemaker says.

"He's very hungry, is what he is," says a piping voice. An old woman, barely taller than she is wide, half the old man's height, hobbles into the room. She's wearing a brightly striped dress, an apron made of red flannel, and has a flow- ered kerchief tied under her chin. "Just look at him, Natters. A stomach on legs, this one. Hungry, I tell you, and he'll say anything to get a bit of food into himself!"

Stooping, Natters peers at Shoe. "He does look a bit peaked, Missus."

Shoe's stomach gives a hopeless growl. "I'm not a beggar," he insists. "I can clean the windows in front. You'll have bet- ter light in here for your work if I do."

Natters and his Missus exchange a speaking glance. Shoe isn't sure what it says, but the Missus gives a decided nod.

"What's your name, young man?" she asks.

"Sh—" Shoe starts, then stops.

"Sh? What?" Natters says, cocking his head.

"Shoe," Shoe says with a shrug. He can't think of any other name to give.

"That's a bad sign, Missus," Natters says darkly.

"Hm. Maybe. Maybe not." The Missus looks Shoe up and down with sharp eyes. "I expect you eat a lot of food."

"I probably do, when I can get it," Shoe answers.

"Hah!" The old woman gives a sudden gap-toothed grin. "He'll do, Natters. We'll just have to be careful." She reaches up and grabs Shoe's arm. "Come along with me, skinnybones. You can have some dinner and then get to those windows, and then we'll see what happens."

CHAPTER 11

"Penelope, tea," my stepmama orders. She and my stepsisters are at the table eating tiny bites of toast and mushrooms. I am in the doorway, leaving the blue breakfast room after lugging the chafing dishes on trays from the kitchen. My feet hurt, and I have a blistered burn on my hand from picking up a boiling kettle, and I am tired after working until midnight polishing the silver. I woke before dawn, curled up on the kitchen hearth as close to the cooling embers as I could get for warmth.

"Now, Penelope!" Stepmama insists. "Tea!"

And it is all so . . . predictable. Stepmama playing the role assigned to her by Lady Faye, one she appears to relish very much, my stepsisters playing their roles not quite as convincingly, and me stuck in the middle of it.

Or so it would seem.

"I don't have to put up with this," I tell her, and tuck the tray under my arm.

Stepmama rears back from the table. "What?" she sputters. "What did you say?" Dulcet has paused with her teacup halfway to her lips; Precious stares with her eyebrows raised.

"I don't have to stay here," I say. "I may not have any money, but I'm not stupid, and I can certainly make my way in the world."

Stepmama lurches to her feet, bumping the table; the teacups rattle in their saucers. "You cannot leave!" she gasps, and I see a flash of what might be fright cross her face.

"Why not?" I ask. Dulcet and Precious stare as if the possibility of leaving an unhappy home is something that has never even remotely occurred to them.

"Insolent!" Stepmama sputters. "How dare you?"

"It doesn't really take that much daring," I answer, feeling very cool and collected in the face of Stepmama's outrage. She thinks things have to be a certain way, and I know that they don't.

With a shrug I leave the room, stride down the hallway, and let myself out of the front door.

The morning is bright with sunlight, the air chilly. I catch sight of the castle looming just a few streets over from Stepmama's house—no, *my* house—and a wide expanse of parkland lies across the way. I clatter down the stone steps to the road and cross it. I'll begin with a walk in the park to gather my thoughts, and then I'll decide what to do. Fortunately, I've had breakfast, so I won't have to worry about eating for a while.

Swinging the silver tray, which I brought with me by mistake, I amble along the empty, neatly raked gravel paths in the park. Every blade of grass, I realize, is exactly the same length, without a single dandelion to be seen. It's a little unnerving. Even the bushes are trimmed into smooth green spheres. My stepmother's house is rather alarmingly clean, too. Now that I've been banished belowstairs, I can see how every maid and footman is poised to swoop down on a room whenever a member of the upper family leaves it, straightening pictures, whisking away traces of dust. It's no wonder they're such a twitchy lot, my stepmother's servants.

When the clock strikes, it freezes me in my tracks. The sound rolls and echoes through the park; I look up to see that the central tower of the castle has an enormous clock set in it. It strikes nine times, each stroke a booming roar. As its echoes die away, it leaves a shuddering silence behind it. I imagine that I can hear, even from this far away, the gears of the clock turning as the long minute hand ticks into place.

Now I start seeing other people walking about, ladies in fine dresses, and men in suits, and primly dressed nannies pushing prams full of babies. Perfect, all of it. They stare as I go past in my shabby, ash-smudged black dress, carrying my tray. I am horribly out of place, a blot on the morning. No matter. I walk for a long time, until the clock strikes ten.

Strangely, by the time the last strike echoes over the city, the other walkers have left the park. It is as if they have one hour allotted for walking, and then they must go and do other things.

With a shrug, I go on my way. I am rounding a corner when two burly men wearing light-blue, lace-trimmed uniforms appear on the path before me. For some reason, seeing them makes my heart speed up. I whirl and start back the other way, and two more blue-liveried men appear. They are all wearing white wigs—they are footmen, somebody's servants. I stop. They crunch toward me on the gravel path, two before me, two behind.

"Come with us, if you please, miss," one of the men says.

I grip my tray tightly. It's not much of a weapon, but it's something. "And if I don't want to?"

"You *do* want to," the man insists.

From behind, iron-hard hands grip my elbows. I glance down. One of the hands is strangely hairy, the nails long and curved. As much a paw as a hand. Shuddering, I try to pull away, but he holds me tightly. "Lady Faye will have a word with you, miss," says the footman in a gruff voice. "If you will just come this way."

It's four against one, which means that I don't really have a choice, even with my tray. The footmen bring me to the grandest of all the grand houses along the park, the one closest to the castle that crowns the city.

"Lady Faye lives here?" I ask. "I thought she'd be living in the castle."

"No, miss," one of the footmen responds. "It's the prince who lives in the castle."

Of course. It hasn't even occurred to me until now that the city has a prince.

The footmen hustle me up the wide white stairs and inside the double front doors, and down a marble-paved hallway to a sitting room encrusted with gold.

Lady Faye is there. She is wearing a silver-blue gown that matches her eyes. "Ah, Penelope," she says, and smiles as if I have done something particularly clever.

A chill prickles up my spine. I suddenly feel as if I haven't done something clever at all, but unbearably stupid.

"Have you run away from home?" Lady Faye asks.

I glance toward the door. Two of her footmen are stationed there. "I'd hardly call it a home," I say.

"Oh, are they treating you badly?" Lady Faye asks with false concern. "Have they made you sleep in the cinders yet?"

I stare blankly at her. Something is going on. I can almost hear it, like giant wheels grinding into motion. The itchy feeling comes back. "I'm not supposed to be here," I say to myself.

"Yes you are." Lady Faye rises gracefully from her chair and glides toward me. "The more you struggle, you silly girl," she says, reaching out to touch a cold finger to my forehead, "the more tightly you'll be entangled. Now," she adds, "I would like you to meet some people. Dear friends of mine. I want you to think of them as an example."

The room is empty except for us. As I'm thinking this, the footmen turn smartly to the drawing room doors and swing them open.

"Good morning, my dear ones!" Lady Faye sweeps forward to meet the two people entering the room.

The couple—a handsome man with a neat mustache and a young woman wearing a blue visiting dress and a fashionable hat covered with feathers and lace—step into the room. They are both smiling.

"Lady Faye," the man says with a precise bow. He hands his hat and gloves to a footman. Then he takes his wife's arm again. The woman stands still. With an impatient jerk, the man pulls on her arm, and she turns her head and nods, then hands her parasol to the footman. She continues to smile, her blue eyes wide, like a doll's.

"Lord Meister, Lady Meister," Lady Faye says, "may I present Lady Penelope, a dear friend of mine."

I stare at them. The couple bow and curtsy and, still smiling, perch on one of Lady Faye's couches, which is upholstered in blue velvet. Lady Meister reaches a hand toward her head; her husband intercepts it and pulls it down to her lap again.

"Won't you join us?" Lady Faye asks me, sitting in her chair. "I shall ring for tea."

I shake my head. I'm frightened, and I don't know why. Something is wrong here.

"Lovely weather we're having," Lord Meister says. "Don't you agree, my dear wife?"

Lady Meister doesn't answer, she just keeps smiling. She reaches for her head, and again her husband pulls her hand away.

I can't look away from her smile. Then my breath catches. She is looking at me, too, straight into my eyes. As her husband's voice drones on, her smile doesn't waver.

A smile, I realize, is a horrible thing if it's held for too long.

"Excuse us just a moment, will you?" Lady Faye says brightly. Lord Meister gets up from the sofa and takes her hand, assisting her to her feet. "We would like a few words in private. Will you entertain each other while we step into the hall?"

Lady Meister doesn't answer, so I nod for both of us. Lord Meister and Lady Faye exit the drawing room.

I sit down on the couch, setting the silver tray on the floor at my feet. The polite thing to do would be to converse with Lady Meister about something inconsequential. The weather. The latest fashions. Her pretty blue parasol. I have absolutely no interest in those things, however. And Lady Meister, apparently, has no conversation. She just stares straight ahead with her doll-like blue eyes, and smiles her wide, fixed smile. Then she reaches up with her hand and plucks a long hair from her scalp. Carefully she wraps it around the end of her forefinger, making a little round nest, and then drops it to the floor. Still smiling, she reaches up and plucks another hair.

Her head, I realize with a shudder, is covered with bald patches, only partly hidden by her hat. As I watch, she pulls out another hair, then another. A pile of tiny hair-nests grows on the carpet by her foot. She doesn't blink at all. After a few long, silent minutes, I lean forward to speak in a low voice. "Are you all right, Lady Meister?"

Her head turns and her wide eyes lock onto mine. Her smile doesn't falter. She is very beautiful, and elegantly dressed, but she is not all right. I can see it in her ravaged scalp, in every taut line of her body, and in the rigidity of her face.

When she speaks, it is through the gritted teeth of her horrible smile, and her voice has the muted shriek of straining gears. "Help me," she grinds out. "Help me, help me, please help me."

My heart pounds. I lean forward and touch her knee, rigid under the soft folds of her silk dress. "How?" I ask. "What can I do?"

"Kill me," she pleads. "Let me die." Her eyes are desperate, but she is still smiling. In the silence, the only sound is her harsh breathing.

"I—" I begin, but I'm interrupted by the deep boom that rolls out from the castle clock striking the half hour.

A moment later, the drawing room door swings open.

Lady Meister's gaze is wrenched away from mine and she lurches to her feet like a puppet pulled by strings. Her husband hurries to her side. "Ah, look at the time," he babbles. He glances at the floor, no doubt seeing his wife's hair on the carpet. But he doesn't react.

I step closer to him, daring to reach out to grasp his coat sleeve. "What is the matter with her?" I whisper, too softly for Lady Faye to hear me.

For just a second, his eyes flash terror, and he flinches away. "Nothing, nothing, it's nothing," he mutters.

So he's just as desperate as his wife is; he's just better at hiding it. My hands clench. I can't help them; there's nothing I can do.

"We must be on our way." Lord Meister takes his gloves and hat from the footman who has appeared at his elbow. He puts his wife's parasol into her limp hands. She drops it, and he picks it up and shoves it into her hands again. "Come along, my dear," he says, with a stiff nod to me. They go out the door.

I pick up my tray from the floor and get to my feet.

"Lovely couple, aren't they?" Lady Faye asks, coming to stand at my side, all glittering perfection.

I shake my head. "You said they were an example."

Lady Faye gives me a chilly smile. "I believe I mentioned what happens to those who struggle, didn't I?" Without waiting for me to answer, she goes on. "Certain things are inevitable, Lady Penelope. If you simply accept that, you will find much happiness in your future."

I open my mouth to argue when Lady Faye reaches over

to tap the silver tray that I am holding. "Did you steal that from your stepmother's house?"

"What?" I start to say, still seeing Lady Meister's ravaged smile. "No, I—I mean, I didn't steal it."

"Oh dear." She shakes her head with mock sadness. "I am afraid she's going to be very unhappy with you."

LADY FAYE IS right. When the blue-jacketed footmen deposit me on Stepmama's doorstep, she hustles me upstairs, where she shoves me into a tiny attic room. The door locks behind me.

"And here you shall stay, Penelope," says Stepmama's muffled voice from the other side of the door, "until you mend your manners!"

Her footsteps fade away.

I take a deep breath and look around. A narrow bed with a thin mattress on it, but no sheets or blankets, is pushed against one wall. I stoop to peer underneath, and sure enough, there is a cracked chamber pot. High on the other wall is a narrow window; its panes are broken, and chilly air blows in from outside. On the third wall is the door, and on the fourth is a low hearth choked with ash, but no fire.

For a long time I pace, angry, and that keeps me warm. This is *my* house, I think, and Stepmama has no right to treat me like this, and *how* could I have been stupid enough to get tangled up with Lady Faye, who is, I am realizing, a lot more dangerous than she appears. She is like a knife. So far, I've only seen the lace-edged, blue-velvet sheath, but it's hiding wickedly sharp steel, of that I am sure. I don't know why she introduced me to Lady Meister. She was making some kind of point, and a warning, but I don't know what I'm supposed to be doing about it.

Outside the window, the sun tilts toward the west. When it goes down, the room grows dark. The clock strikes six, and each toll makes what's left of the window shiver in its frame. Nobody comes to bring me dinner. The room grows colder. The clock strikes seven, and then eight. The weight of grief settles over me again; to console myself I finger the silk-stitched seam along the hem of my dress. The loss feels almost physical, a yearning ache too strong for a mother I can't remember, or a father who died, I'm told, many months ago. Who is it that I miss so badly? What have I lost?

Wearily I drag the mattress from the bed—it is stuffed half with straw and half with mouse droppings—and make a kind of cocoon with it on the floor, huddling inside to keep warm.

During the night I sleep for a while, and then wake in the darkness. Slowly I climb out of my cocoon and pace the edges of the room, sliding around the bed, dragging my fingers over the cracked plaster walls. The room smells of mold and dampness and of mice. Something scrabbles in the walls, and I hope it is mice, and not rats.

It feels inevitable, my little prison, as if I've been pulled toward it ever since I woke up in the library, covered with cinders. I need to get out.

But then I'll still be in the house, and it is a prison too.

So is the city, I am starting to suspect. Maybe there's no escape from any of it. If I'm not careful, I could end up like Lady Meister. That, I think, is what Lady Faye has planned for me. At any rate, something has me in its grip, and the more I struggle against it, the more entangled I'll become.

"All right, then," I whisper to myself. I'd tried simply walking away, and had failed miserably. "I'll make them think I'm not struggling. And while I'm being oh-so-good and obedient, I'll figure out another way to get myself out of this."

HALFWAY THROUGH THE morning, I hear a step in the hallway, a key in the lock, and the door swings open.

Stepmama fills the doorway. "Well, Penelope?" she says, and folds her arms. She looks me up and down, and her nose wrinkles as if she smells something nasty.

I brush a lock of hair out of my eyes. My hand, I notice, is grubby, as is the stocking on my wrist that I'm using as a bandage. I realize that all of me is dirty. My dress is stained and its hem is growing ragged. I bite back a sharp response. "Good morning, Stepmama," I say meekly. "May I come out now?"

"Are you willing to behave appropriately?" Stepmama asks.

Appropriate behavior in this situation would be flying into a furious rage at having been treated so badly by my own stepmother. But I hold back, warily. I know this is not what she means. "Yes, Stepmama," I say.

"Hmph," Stepmama grunts. "Then you may be released. Go to the kitchen. Cook has some things for you to do."

In the kitchen, I'm put to work scrubbing pots from last night's dinner. The scalding water wets the bandage on my wrist, turns my hands red, and slops down my skirt, but I grit my teeth and keep scrubbing.

At the stove, the cook, a surly, red-faced woman with a strong accent from some faraway land, is baking. I reach for the next dirty pot and fill it with hot water from the kettle and sit for a moment, waiting for the burnt porridge encrusted on the inside to loosen. At the long table at the center of the kitchen, maids chop vegetables into symmetrical shapes, and measure flour and stir spices into sauces; there is a hearth where a spit boy keeps chicken and venison browning; an undercook pauses now and then to stir a pot of river fish stewing in butter; and there are two ovens with pots and pans of delicious smells simmering on their stove tops. I never realized before how much work happens downstairs to make a perfectly prepared dinner appear upstairs.

The cook takes a pan out of an oven and sets it on the stove top. The smell of it wafts over me. It is spicy and warm, the best thing I have ever smelled. Gingerbread. My stomach growls.

Suddenly I want the gingerbread more than I've ever wanted anything in my entire life. It must be because I missed dinner last night and still haven't been given any breakfast. "Could I have a bite of that?" I ask the cook.

The cook casts me a cross glare.

"Please?" I add, and I must look hungry and pitiful, because she breaks off a piece, puts it on a saucer, and gives it to me. I take a bite. It is warm and richly spiced, and I close my eyes, expecting it to fill me up. But it doesn't. The gingerbread makes me feel empty; its sweetness makes me long for something, but I don't know what.

Tears well up in my eyes and I blink them away—I will *not* cry—and I eat every crumb of the strangely unsatisfying gingerbread. Then I am put to work scrubbing the kitchen floor, and then Precious calls me to her room so I can iron her dresses while she scolds me for being such a trial to everyone, and then after dinner—I take a quick bite while the servants are clearing the table—there are more pots to clean. Finally, after the kitchen floor has been scrubbed again, the fires have been banked, and the servants have all cast me narrow-eyed looks as they go to their cozy beds, I curl up on the hearth to go to sleep. The air in the kitchen is chilly, and smells of the ghosts of roast chicken and a burned cake that earned an unlucky kitchen maid a slap from the surly cook. Out in the city, the clock strikes.

I have spent exactly one day behaving appropriately. I wonder how long I'm supposed to bear it.

Have they made you sleep in the cinders yet? Lady Faye's voice echoes in my head.

I shiver and edge closer to the smoldering coals. Yes, Lady Faye. They have.

CHAPTER

12

It doesn't take old Natters long to notice how extremely well made Shoe's boots are. "Where did you get 'em, lad?" he asks.

Shoe is busy cleaning each tiny pane in the front window. Getting the grime out of the edges where the glass meets the frame takes some doing. He glances down at his feet. "I made them." In his workshop in the fortress. Which he's not going to mention to this old shoemaker.

Natters is wearing a leather apron and is at his bench cutting out a vamp from a roll of cheap leather. He does it with extreme care. If he makes the whole shoe that slowly, Shoe thinks, it'll take him days. "Were you an apprentice somewhere, then?" Natters asks.

"No," Shoe answers, and wrings out the rag he's using to

clean the panes. "Not when I made these. But I must have been, before."

"But you don't remember," Natters says. Then he mutters something else under his breath that Shoe can't hear.

"What's that you said?" Shoe asks, starting on the next tiny pane.

"Never mind," Natters says. "I don't want to know."

Shoe scrubs the front windows until each tiny pane gleams. While he's working, he turns his plan over in his head. He must figure out how to get to the upper city, find Pin, and save her from the Godmother, assuming she needs saving. Knowing Pin, she's busy saving herself. He checks the thimble in his pocket, just to be sure. It's still pulling in the same direction.

"Do you have any packages that need delivering in the upper city?" he asks Natters. "Finished shoes, or anything like that?"

The old man is hunched over his workbench, still cutting the same vamp. "No," Natters says shortly. "I don't make shoes for the likes of them."

What Shoe needs is a spy, he realizes, somebody who can come and go in the upper city without being noticed. Tonight he'll sneak out into the lower city and see if he can find somebody willing to help him.

After he has swept out the shop with a mouse-chewed broom, Natters's Missus calls them to the kitchen for dinner. The house has three stories: the shop on the ground floor, the kitchen and dining table on the first floor, and the Natterses' bedroom at the top. The kitchen is dim, lit by narrow windows and guttering candles. Everything is spotlessly clean, though, every hole neatly darned, everything well repaired. It's nothing like the grubby, messy shop downstairs, which makes Shoe wonder. And it seems different from the pristine upper city. It's homey. Comfortable.

Natters's Missus has put dinner on the table. The food is simple—gristly meat, potatoes, day-old bread, bean stew with lots of salt and pepper—but there's plenty of it.

"I was right," the Missus says as she dumps the last of the stew onto Shoe's plate. "The boy can eat. Did he earn his dinner, Natters?"

"Too well," Natters grumbles, and shoots the Missus another one of his speaking looks from under his bushy eyebrows. In response, she shrugs her broad shoulders and shakes her head.

Shoe concentrates on eating as much as he can. He's taking a final bite of stew when the leftover tiredness from his long trek through the forest overtakes him. He's still holding his fork, falling asleep while sitting up at the table.

The Missus says something that he doesn't quite catch. He hears a scrape as Natters pushes his chair back from the table, then feels a hand on his shoulder. Stumbling, he follows the old shoemaker down the narrow stairs to the ground floor. He'll sleep in a tiny cubby just off the shop, Natters says. There's an old mattress in it now, and they'll clear it out properly in the morning. "Give me your coat, Shoe," Natters goes on, "and the Missus will fix it up for you."

Shoe barely gets his coat off and mutters a thank-you when he crashes onto the mattress. A blanket settles on him.

Tomorrow, Shoe thinks muzzily, as sleep comes over him. He'll start on his plan to find Pin tomorrow.

IN THE MORNING Shoe is standing in the street, wearing his freshly cleaned and mended coat and a borrowed shirt and trousers that don't fit him right, contemplating the sign hanging over the shop door. If he had some paint, he could repaint the red shoe so that people passing by would know this is a shoemaker's shop.

Not that Natters makes many shoes that Shoe can see. There are no finished shoes to display in the newly clean front window, and the old man is still working on the same pair from the day before. In the Godmother's fortress, Shoe could have made ten pairs of shoes in that time. Of course, there he'd had a particular motivation to keep up with the endless blue requisition slips.

He's about to step inside when a tall, well-dressed woman with iron-gray hair stops in front of the shop.

"Is this Natters's place?" she asks abruptly.

"Yes, it is," Shoe answers. He shoves open the warped door and moves aside. "Would you like to step in?"

The woman looks down her long nose at him; then, picking up her skirts, she sweeps past him and into the shop.

Natters looks up from his workbench with alarm. "What?" he asks, his voice quavering. "What is it?"

"I want to order some shoes, of course," the woman says. "I need four pairs, two men's, two women's, for my servants. Their measurements are here." She holds out a piece of paper.

Natters just stares at her, gripping the hammer he's been using.

"Well, man?" the woman says. "I've heard Natters makes fine shoes at a good price; can you do these for me?"

Shoe steps up and takes the paper. "Yes, he can do them," he answers for Natters. "When do you want them finished?"

"I suppose you'll need a day," she sniffs. "Not tomorrow, then, but the day after. All right?"

At the bench, Natters gives a wide-eyed nod.

"Good," the woman says briskly, and drops some coins onto the workbench, then turns and strides out of the shop.

The door closes behind her. For a long moment there is only silence and swirls of dust settling.

Natters sighs. "I suppose I'd better get started, then." He gives a few coins to Shoe and sends him out for a roll of leather. The street is at the end of the river, the farthest from the upper city, and its air is thick with the foul smell of the tannery. While he's out, Shoe gets some paint, and he keeps a coin for himself, too. When he returns, Natters is studying the page of measurements and muttering under his breath.

"Just put it here," he says to Shoe, who sets the roll of leather on the bench.

Then the Missus calls them for lunch. Shoe tells her about the customer, the order for four pairs of shoes.

"She said she heard that Natters makes fine shoes," Natters says direly.

"*Did* she now," the Missus says, and gives Natters one of those looks, along with a frown.

"She wants them the day after tomorrow," Natters goes on.

"You won't finish them?" the Missus asks.

"Better not to," Natters says, and shoots a glare at Shoe.

He blinks. Has he done something wrong? Wouldn't a shoemaker *want* to make shoes and get paid for it?

After lunch, Natters goes back to his bench to brood and stare at the page of measurements. Shoe changes into his own freshly mended shirt and trousers, and feeds the goat and the chickens that the Missus keeps in the tiny yard behind the house. Then he has a wash at the pump, and puts some of the Huntsman's salve onto his souvenirs from his time at the post. To his surprise, the welts are almost healed.

Then he takes the shop door off its hinges, borrows a plane from a neighbor, and planes the warp out of the wood so the door will hang straight. It's another thing that he doesn't remember doing before, but that his body knows how to do. But he can't think about what that means.

Shoe, do you remember anything from the Before? Pin had asked him back at the Godmother's fortress.

No, he'd told her. *Just the Now.*

And that's the way it has to be. No Before, no After, just the Now, until he finds Pin and they escape the Godmother for good.

That night, Shoe goes down to his cubby after dinner, but as soon as he hears silence from upstairs, he unlocks the shop door, eases it open, and slips out into the dark night. He doesn't remember a city, but he must have lived in one in the time Before, because he knows how to keep to the dark edges of the streets and pause before turning a corner to listen for approaching feet. He keeps a grip on Pin's thimble just in case there are pickpockets about. The curfew of the upper city is definitely not in effect here, maybe because it's too far from the sound of the castle clock striking. People pass like shadows, some of them drunk and trying to stifle their laughter, others hurrying on mysterious errands.

On one corner Shoe finds a tavern. There's no sign in front, and shutters cover the windows, but a little light leaks out and he can hear the murmur of talking from inside and now and then the muffled clink of a glass. He goes down two steps and enters. The room is smoky from a fire in an ash-choked hearth and crowded with shabbily dressed men and women who turn to look at Shoe as he walks by. They watch him warily, out of the corners of their eyes as they return to their conversations.

He finds a place at a rickety table shoved up against a wall spotted with mold.

"What'll it be, handsome stranger?" asks a boy his own

age with a rag, a tray, and a pert grin.

Shoe blinks. "Um, bread and cheese, please." He leans closer and lowers his voice. "And somebody who can run me an errand in the upper city, if you know anyone like that." He pushes a coin across the tabletop.

The tavern boy regards the coin for a moment. "A simple errand?" he asks, and cocks an eyebrow. "Or something more complicated?"

"It's probably not simple," Shoe admits.

"Right!" The boy snatches up the coin and bobs away. A short time later, he brings a battered plate with a toasted cheese sandwich on it, and a cup of foul-smelling ale that Shoe didn't order. "That's from me," he says, and gives Shoe a wink.

Shoe gulps and stares at the plate. He's not used to this kind of attention, not from girls, or from boys either.

"That's a very pretty red you're turning," the tavern boy says, and goes off grinning. He's forgotten about the rest of the order, Shoe guesses, but as he's taking a bite of his bread and cheese, a filthy, wild-haired, humpbacked old man approaches his table.

"Greetings, Your Lor'ship," the old man says, bowing. "I'm Spanner, and I hear you're looking for help with something?"

Shoe nods. "I'm Shoe," he says, "and I'm not a lordship of any kind." Spanner, he notices, is wearing an oddly hairy black suit.

Spanner plops down at the table, looks at Shoe's half-eaten food, and raises his eyebrows.

"Help yourself," Shoe says.

"Don't mind if I do," Spanner says, picking up the bread and cheese and stuffing the whole thing in his mouth. His suit, Shoe realizes, is made of rat skins stitched together, fur-side out. He's a ratcatcher. With his furry suit, his long, twitchy nose, and his small, close-set eyes, Spanner looks a lot like his own prey.

Spanner notices Shoe's interest. "If you wants to catch rats, young gen'leman," he says through a spray of crumbs, "you got to think like 'em, see? Now what is it you're wanting from old Spanner?"

"I'm trying to find someone," Shoe answers. "I need you to look for her in the upper city. Can you do it without getting caught?"

Spanner swallows and then shrugs. "Things is pretty tight up there right now. Talk of arrests and such, and extra viggle-lance."

Shoe waits a beat and then figures it out. "Vigilance, you mean?"

Spanner touches his nose. "That's it, spot on! Vigglance. Lots of footmen about, lots of watching. Trouble's brewing."

"Right." Shoe thinks of the gold coins he's got hidden away in his cubby. "I can make it worth your while."

"Can you now!" Spanner grins, revealing a gap where his front teeth should be, but Shoe catches a glimpse of wariness in the ratcatcher's sharp eyes. "Where there's people, there's rats, in the upper city too, even though them that lives there don't like it known. I comes and goes as I please, catching rats. I can find your someone for you."

"Her name's Pin," Shoe says. "She's a girl about the same age as I am, and just a bit shorter." He goes on to describe Pin, though the real Pin isn't someone who can be summed up in a simple physical description. "But be careful," he warns the ratcatcher. "I think the Godmother brought her here."

"Shhh, shhh," Spanner hisses, and hunches his shoulders. "You don't want to be talking too much about her." He glances nervously around. "So your girl Pin is important, you're saying?"

Shoe nods. That's what the Huntsman had said, too. Pin has been chosen by the Godmother for a *special fate*, he'd called it. Something bad.

"I follow what you're asking, Shoe, right enough," Spanner whispers. "I'll keep my eyes open for your girl. If she's here, I'll find out."

CHAPTER 13

Behaving appropriately is proving more difficult than I thought.

I am locked up in my attic prison again, this time for snapping at Dulcet when she ordered me to bring a fresh pot of tea to the upstairs sewing room. It was my stepsisters' hour for needlework. They were both working on their trousseaus, the fine linens and underclothes and special nightgowns they'd wear when they were married. Dulcet was sewing lace onto a dainty square handkerchief, the sort of thing that would be completely useless if you actually had to blow your nose into it. Precious was embroidering blue rosebuds around the hem of a silk peignoir. She explained that a peignoir is a light robe to wear when your maid is brushing out your hair in the evenings.

As I brought the tea in, Dulcet set aside the lacy handkerchief and rubbed her eyes; then she poured herself a cup of tea and took a sip. "This is cold, Pen," she said, setting down her cup with a sniff.

"It was hot when I left the kitchen with it," I told her.

"Don't talk back," Precious added, sticking her needle into a pincushion.

"I'm not talking back," I said.

"Yes you are," Dulcet said.

I was about to insist that I wasn't when my stepmother bustled into the room, her corsets creaking. "Ah, tea," she said, sitting with a sigh on a plump sofa covered with blue silk. "Just the thing. Pour me a cup, Dulcie dear."

"It's cold, Mama," Dulcet said with a pout, "and Pen refuses to fetch us some more."

"I'm not refusing," I put in, "I'm pointing out that the kitchen is three floors down and on the other side of the house, and the pot was hot when I left it. If you're going to drink tea in this room, Dulcie, you'll have to drink it cold."

On the sofa, my stepmama puffed up her chest and put on her look of outrage. "Really, Penelope. So ill-mannered. Go at once and bring us some hot tea."

"If you want it that much," I said, "you should go and fetch it yourself."

At that, Stepmama heaved herself from the sofa and raised her hand as if she was about to strike me. I took a stumbling step back, my heart pounding.

She lurched toward me, and then she stopped. Her hand dropped to her side. Dulcet and Precious were staring with their mouths open. Stepmama had never threatened to hit me before. "You deserve to be slapped for your insolence," she said in a strangled voice. "Now go fetch the tea as you are bid."

I took the teapot down to the busy kitchen, washed it out, filled it with hot water from the kettle and added fresh leaves, put it on a tray, and made my way back up three flights of stairs toward the other wing of the house. In a hallway, I came upon a strange, wild-haired man on his knees, examining what looked like a crack in the wainscoting. He was wearing a suit made of . . .

I stopped and stared. "Is that rat fur?" I asked him, propping the tea tray on my hip.

The man grinned up at me; he was missing his two front teeth. "It is, missy. A ratcatcher, I am. Catching rats where I can find 'em." He gave the wall a rap with his knuckles and looked me up and down. "Your name wouldn't happen to be Pin, would it?"

"No," I said, taken aback. "It's Penelope. *Lady* Penelope." Though no one would know it to look at me.

"Ah!" the ratcatcher said, and, still on his knees, he bowed deeply.

I gave him a nod and went along to the sewing room with my tray and teapot.

Dulcet poured herself a cup and took a sip. "It's cold!" she complained predictably.

"Lukewarm," I corrected, "and it's only to be expected."

Stepmama grabbed me by the arm, marched me up to the attic, and locked me in. "Such disobedience, Penelope!" she scolded. "Such willfulness! You will stay here until you can remember your proper place in this household."

I stay in my tiny prison all the rest of the day. The time passes slowly, measured out in the strikes of the castle clock. Remember my proper place, Stepmama said. My place, I suppose, is to be *good* and *nice* in some way that I'm not. But from the moment I woke up in the cinders, nothing about this place has seemed at all *proper* to me. I wonder what it is that I'm caught up in. No, that we're all caught up in—me, and the servants, and Lady Meister, with her horrible bald patches, and even my stepsister Dulcet, who is not supposed to sing aloud. Maybe everyone in the city is involved.

But I refuse to be part of it. I will not let my choices be taken away from me.

I should be tired, but my new determination makes it impossible to sleep. I want to be up, doing something, but all I can do is pace my prison as the hours pass, marked by the booms of the castle clock.

In the morning, nobody comes for a long time. I'm beginning to think rather desperately that they've forgotten me, when I hear the key at the lock. Anna, prim and neat in a freshly ironed uniform, opens the door. "You're to come downstairs, Lady Pen," she says.

Getting to my feet, I study her for a long moment. She

casts down her eyes and folds her hands in front of her.

"Anna," I test, to see if she is as obedient as she seems. "Do you have any holes in your memory?"

She flicks up a frightened glance at me, but doesn't answer.

"You do," I say for her. "So do I. I can't remember anything before that morning when you found me sleeping in the hearth."

"Shhh," she says. "We can't talk about it."

"We *must* talk about it," I insist. "Do you know what is happening?"

She shakes her head. Nervously she checks over her shoulder, then steps closer. "People disappear," she whispers. "They are here, and then they're gone, killed maybe, or taken somewhere. Not many of us notice, and most are too afraid to speak up about it."

"Lady Faye," I suggest. "She has some sort of plan."

Anna nods.

"What is she, exactly?" I press. "What does she want?" Because Lady Faye must have enormous power, to rigidly control so many people, for whatever purpose.

"We don't know," Anna says, shaking her head. "She's nothing to do with us—with the servants, that is. We try not to do anything to catch her attention."

Well, for me it's a bit late for that.

"We have to fight it," I tell her.

She stares at me, as if the possibility of resistance hasn't occurred to her before this. "We can't be talking about this, Lady Pen," she whispers, checking over her shoulder again. "You must come downstairs, as you are ordered."

I nod, understanding. "Can I wash up first?" I ask. My dress is in a state, and I don't smell very good, even to my own nose. My hair is a tangled, greasy mess. "And can I have something to eat?" After going without much dinner and with no breakfast at all, I am rather ragingly hungry.

"No, I'm sorry, my lady," Anna answers, all proper again, keeping her eyes lowered. "They want you in the drawing room at once."

Feeling quite certain that I haven't learned my place in the household, and determined to fight against whatever is being planned for me, I follow Anna downstairs. My step-mama is in the drawing room with my stepsisters. I catch my breath. Lady Faye stands by the mantel, all finely carved grace in her signature ice-blue velvet; she gives me an edged smile as I come into the room. All I can do is stare back at her. She is the power here. How can I resist her? What can I *do*?

My stepmama is wearing a new dress of dark-blue bombazine trimmed with sky-blue ribbons that clash with her red face. "You're a very lucky girl, Penelope," she says. "Lady Faye has offered to give you another chance, and of course I could not refuse such a request. You will receive a young gentleman suitor in one hour's time."

"But first she must be transformed," Lady Faye says.

"Wait," I put in. "A gentleman? A suitor?"

"Oh, transformed to be sure," Stepmama agrees, fawning on Lady Faye, ignoring my questions. "She cannot receive her future husband looking like that." She wrinkles her nose. "You look frightful, Penelope."

"I can hardly help it," I snap. I've been locked up in the attic for a day and a night and working in the kitchen before that.

"Really, you should be ashamed," my stepmama says. She seems very tightly wound.

By the mantel, Lady Faye is smiling sharply as she watches us. "Precious," she says, "can I leave Penelope's transformation up to you?"

My stepsister turns pink at the attention. Then she looks dubiously at me. "I hope so, Lady Faye."

"It may seem an impossible task," Lady Faye says, "but you must try to make her presentable, at the very least."

"I don't want a husband," I put in, but it's as if I haven't spoken.

As Precious pulls me toward the door, Stepmama follows; in the doorway she grabs me, her fingers digging into my arm. "Lady Faye has chosen you, Penelope," she hisses through a fixed smile. "We cannot risk her disapproval. You simply *must* behave yourself."

With that, I am whisked up to Precious's room to be transformed while Stepmama, Dulcet, and Lady Faye wait in the drawing room.

If there is one thing Precious understands, it is fashion. She knows the very latest dress patterns and is always impeccably turned out.

"You *are* lucky," she says, closing the door to her room, which is, surprisingly, not blue, but decorated in shades of pink and green. The colors shouldn't go well together, but somehow they do, because it is Precious who combined them. "Lady Faye brought you a dress, Pen." She goes to the bed where a large, square box is sitting on the pink-and-green striped silk coverlet. "No one knows where she gets her clothes, but they are exquisite, far finer than any seamstress in the city could produce." She opens the box to reveal a dress nestled in rustling silver paper.

It is a simple tea dress with a low neckline and puffed sleeves, just right for an unmarried young girl like me. It is made of silk the lambent blue green of the sky just after sunset. I hold it up to myself and look in the mirror.

"I would kill for a dress like that," Precious murmurs at my shoulder, and I realize that she is at least partly serious. She points to a screen in the corner. "Take off those filthy clothes," she orders.

For a moment I consider my options. I could try running away again, but I doubt I'd get any further than I did last time. I could refuse to get ready for the suitor, whoever he is, but I am certain that Lady Faye has brought her footmen along. They'd probably enjoy stripping me naked and stuffing me into the dress.

Frowning, I go behind the screen, where I peel my black dress from my skin and unlace the shoes that pinch my toes. There's a knock on the door and Anna and two other maids carry in a copper bathtub and can after can of hot water. They troop out again, and Precious orders me to get into the steaming tub. The hot, scented water feels so good as I sink into it up to my neck and then duck my head. Taking the makeshift bandage off my wrist, I find that the mysterious gash has healed into a puckered white scar. I wash with lavender soap and scrub my hair, and the water turns brownish gray. I can't even remember the last time I had a bath.

I really can't; it's alarming, yet another hole in my memory. But Precious is impatient, and I don't have time to think about it.

"Stand," she orders, and as I do she heaves up a can of chilly water and dumps it over my head to rinse me off.

"Brrr," I complain. "It's cold."

"Lukewarm," Precious taunts. "It had to come all the way from the kitchen." Then she gives me a towel the size of a bedsheet and I dry off and wrap it around myself while she sits me down before her dressing table. It is covered with pots of color and tint and bottles of perfume.

"You have lovely long eyelashes, Pen," she murmurs, inspecting me in the mirror. She hands me a pot of cream. "Here, rub this into your hands so they don't look so chapped." She inspects me further. "Your hair is awful."

I look at myself. It is as if somebody hacked my hair off

short, not caring what it would look like after. As I rub in the hand cream, Precious pulls some scissors out of a drawer and trims the ends of my hair, then brushes and shapes it with her fingers. It curls as it dries, and she gives a brief nod of approval. Then she gives me silk stockings and slippers that look like they'll fit my feet as if they were made for me, and a petticoat. It has lace sewn along its hem; the stitches, I notice, are no bigger than a grain of sand.

She goes to her wardrobe and pulls out a corset. "I won't wear that," I tell her.

"You'll have to," Precious replies briefly, "to fit into this dress."

Unfortunately, she is right. The dress fits only with the corset squeezing me into the right shape. I get it on and Precious laces it tightly.

I look down at my plumped-up breasts. "They look like fruit laid out on a tray."

Precious gives a surprised snort of laughter. As I turn to her, grinning, suddenly liking her quite a lot, I see her remember her stepsister role. She turns the unladylike snort into a disdainful sniff.

"And now the dress," she says reverently. She helps me climb into the dress and buttons it up my back. There are shoes, too, dainty slippers the same blue green as the dress. I put them on and we both stand, looking at me in the mirror.

I hardly recognize the girl—no, the young woman— reflecting back at me. She looks older and taller and very proud. I hate to be so fashionably blue, but the color of the dress suits me exactly; it sets off my dark hair and turns my skin ivory smooth, and even makes the shadows under my eyes look interesting and alluring, and not like simple exhaustion. Not pretty, but not bad, either. "It's all right, isn't it?" I ask a little breathlessly.

Precious's eyes widen. "Surprisingly so," she says. She leans over her dressing table and puts a little red from a pot on her pinkie finger, then dabs the color on my lips. Then she rummages in a box of jewelry and finds a string of maidenly pearls, which she fastens around my neck. "There," she says, with an approving nod. "You're actually quite presentable, Pen."

I take this as an enormous compliment. "Thank you, Precious," I say seriously. "You could set up a business doing transformations like this. You're wonderful at it."

Her eyes go wide with shock. "What a thing to say! Me running a business!" She shakes her head. "It's no wonder you get yourself into such terrible trouble, Pen, thinking such improper thoughts."

With a shrug I follow her down to the blue drawing room. The potential husband is already there, sitting on the sofa where he's been drinking lukewarm tea with my stepmama and Dulcet, who is saying something about a fancy ball at the castle. Lady Faye is still stationed by the mantel, watching over all. They look up as I come in.

"Penelope," my stepmama says, coming to the doorway and taking me by the hand, then dragging me to the sofa, where the man is getting to his feet. "This is Sir Edward Poach." She turns to him. "Sir Edward, may I present my stepdaughter, Lady Penelope." She digs her fingernails into my palm—a warning—and then puts my hand into his.

He is at least twenty years older than I am. His lips are wet; as he looks me up and down, he licks them with a tongue like raw liver and they become even wetter. His hand is damp and fleshy.

"Lady Penelope," he says, and leans closer to examine my face. His breath smells like he's been chewing anise seeds. He doesn't let go of my hand. He looks as if he wants to bury his face in my cleavage, what there is of it. "I am pleased—ah, most pleased to make the acquaintance of such a lovely, ah, young girl."

He is horrible. Lady Faye knows he is horrible. What I *should* do is smile and make polite conversation with Sir Edward Poach. But I can't. I open my mouth to proclaim that I will absolutely not contemplate marrying such a man.

Lady Faye watches me with a keen glint in her eyes as if she knows exactly what I am thinking.

My mouth snaps closed again. She *wants* me to make a scene. Why? She must have something to gain from it.

All right, then. I'll try fighting a different way. I'll be a good girl and see what happens. "Won't you sit down, Sir Edward?" I ask sweetly, and, sweeping my wide skirts aside, I seat myself on a sofa.

Smiling lasciviously, Sir Edward sits close beside me; his leg presses against mine.

"Can I offer you more tea, Sir Edward?" Stepmama asks. She pours out and goes through the politenesses of *one lump or two?* and *would you like a slice of lemon?* As she speaks, Sir Edward's eyes crawl up and down me again. It doesn't matter that I'm wearing an exquisitely stitched dress, I might just as well be naked.

"You are simply delightful," Sir Edward says, grasping my wrist with his sweaty hand.

Ugh. Testing, I try to pull away, but he grips me tightly. "More tea?" I offer.

He drags his eyes away from my cleavage. "Ah, no," he says. "Perhaps you will allow me to say, Lady Penelope, how very eager I am to announce our engagement."

What? "But you haven't proposed to me yet."

"That's just a formality," my stepmother says tightly.

"How exciting," Dulcet says in a high voice. "To be getting married!"

Feeling trapped, I look around the room. On the sofa across from me sit my two stepsisters, their faces fixed in masks of politeness. Stepmother glares at me from a chair next to the tea table. Lady Faye still stands at the mantel, watching me with a faint smile on her pale face.

Oh, I see. She wants me to feel trapped. She wants me to know that, like Lady Meister, there is nothing I can do to escape from whatever she has planned for me. I can't let it happen.

Lady Faye knows exactly what I'm about to do, but I can't help it. I do it anyway. I wrench my hand away from Sir Edward and wipe it on my skirt. "I am not marrying this man," I announce.

Sir Edward sits back blinking, his wet mouth open wide with surprise. "What?" he stutters. "Wh-what?"

"But Pen, you must," Dulcet says from the sofa.

"I don't even know him," I say.

"You don't have to know him," Precious puts in, "you just have to marry him."

"No!" I insist.

My stepmama goes red, and then blotchy white. "Penel-ope," she snarls. Then she grabs me by the arm and pulls me from the room, dragging me down the carpeted hallways to the narrow stairs that lead up to the attic, steaming and hissing like a teakettle all the while. We get to the prison room and, still gripping me, she draws back her hand and gives me a bone-rattling slap across the face. My head snaps back and black spots dance across my vision.

"How—how *dare* you," Stepmama pants. She slaps me again, and then, as my head whirls and the tiny room spins around me, she claws the pearls from my neck and grips the collar of my blue dress with both hands and rips it down the seam in the middle, until I am left stunned and shaking in a few rags of silk and a petticoat and Precious's corset.

Stepmama draws herself up in the doorway. Her hair has come loose, and she is gasping for breath. "You have no idea what you have done, you stupid, stupid girl." She takes a breath to say more, then puts her hand to her chest and goes even paler. Taking a lurching step backward, she slams the door, and I hear the key in the lock.

Shivering, I sink to the floor.

I have been too slow, too stupid. I should have realized that Lady Faye is making her point again. *Do you see what happens when you resist?*

I am in trouble—far, far more trouble than I realized before.

14

THE SUN IS SETTING, THE MISSUS IS ABOUT TO CALL THEM for dinner, and the gray-haired customer wants her servants' shoes ready by the next morning. Most shoemakers wouldn't have any trouble getting the shoes made, but Natters has spent the day dithering about which leather to use, and then he can't find the paper with the measurements on it, and then he finds the paper and loses his favorite awl among the clutter on his workbench.

"Do you want me to straighten it up?" Shoe asks. In the Godmother's fortress, he always kept his work area clean, the tools neatly racked. Seeing Natters's disorder makes him feel twitchy.

"No, I don't," Natters snaps. "And you don't need to be staying so busy, either."

Shoe has been sweeping the front step, airing out the shop. During the morning, he cleaned out his cubby, and then he sanded the sign and repainted the red shoe and hung the sign back over the door again. Something about the work is satisfying; he's learning about himself that he likes order and for things to be clean and in their proper places. "I work for you," Shoe protests. "This is what I'm supposed to be doing."

A dark mutter. "Go and see if the Missus has anything for you to do."

The Missus has been scrubbing the kitchen floor, so she has Shoe move the table and chairs back in, and then they have dinner. Natters picks silently at his food, and the Missus casts him worried glances and then gives Shoe another cup full of goat milk and the rest of the boiled potatoes to eat.

After dinner, Shoe says good night to them and goes down to his cubby, where he waits until the kitchen floor overhead stops creaking, which means Natters and his Missus have gone up to the third floor to bed.

Stealthily, Shoe creeps into the workshop and lights a candle. At Natters's workbench, he sorts among the scraps of leather and jumble of tools until he finds the paper with the measurements on them. Making the servants' shoes shouldn't take very long.

He sets to work, choosing a last for each shoe, then cutting out the leather and stitching it. It feels good to be doing his shoemaking work again; it's as if his hands have missed the old, familiar movements.

While the glue on the soles is drying, he slips out the door and through the shadowy streets to the tavern. The boy with the tray gives him a wink and a grin, and then nods toward a table in the back where Spanner the ratcatcher is hunched over a tankard.

Shoe slides onto the bench across the table from him. "Did you find her?" he asks.

"Good evening to you, too," Spanner says, then takes a long drink of ale. He sets down the tankard and wipes foam off his upper lip. "I b'lieve I did, Shoe. I b'lieve so."

It's what Shoe was hoping, but to hear that Pin is actually here, in the city, makes his heart start to pound. "Is she all right? Where is she? Did you talk to her?"

"I think it was her." Spanner leans across the table and lowers his voice. His breath smells of ale and of the garlic he must have had with his dinner. "She looked like what you said, tall with the dark hair and the gray eyes. But she says her name isn't Pin, it's Penelope. *Lady* Penelope."

Shoe frowns. "That can't be right."

"Could be she's hiding?" the ratcatcher asks. "Pen sounds like Pin."

"Maybe," Shoe says, but he doesn't really think so. It doesn't seem like something Pin would do, hide under another name. "What else about her?"

"Well, Yer Shoeship, she's Lady Penelope, like I said, and I put out the word with them that's got their eyes open about such things, and they put me on to her."

Them that's got their eyes open. "You mean you're a spy? And there are more spies in the city like you?" Shoe asks.

Spanner puts a finger alongside his nose and gives Shoe a meaningful nod. "Them that knows."

Shoe leans forward, across the table. Maybe Spanner is like the Huntsman, a rebel. "Are you fighting the God-mother?"

"Not much we can do, is there?" Spanner coughs and spits on the filthy floor.

"I don't know," Shoe whispers. Maybe there isn't. There's only one thing he has to do here, anyway. "What about Pin?"

"Your girl lives in a fine, great house up by the castle," Spanner answers. "Very rich place, the house that she's living in. Very fancy."

So Pin—or Penelope, if that's her name now—is a fine lady. That would worry him, except he knows Pin, and she won't care if she's a lady and he's a simple Shoe. He puts his hand into his coat pocket and grips the thimble. It doesn't pull anymore. Maybe he and Pen have been apart for too long.

"Rats, though," Spanner continues.

Shoe blinks. "What?"

"It's a fine house, but it's still got rats in the walls."

"So you can go back again," Shoe realizes. "Will you take a message to her for me?"

"That I will, Shoe," Spanner says with his gap-toothed grin. "That I will."

AFTER SHOE HAS given Spanner his message for Pin, he hurries through the dark streets to Natters's shop. For the rest of the night, he works on the shoes, finishing just before dawn, when he falls into bed in his cubby and drops straight into sleep.

He wakes a short time later when the Missus calls down the stairs that breakfast is ready. To wash off the sleep that is clinging to him, he goes behind the house and sticks his head under the pump, then eats breakfast and follows Natters back down to the shop.

At the sight of the four finished pairs of shoes lined up on his workbench, Natters freezes. He blinks twice, glances aside at Shoe, and then, without saying a word, goes to the bench and starts rummaging around in the tools and scraps of leather.

With a shrug, Shoe goes to prop the door wide so customers will know they're open and fetches the broom so he can sweep the front step. Then he runs a few errands for the Missus. As he comes into the shop again, he sees that the gray-haired woman has come to collect her order. She is holding up one of the shoes, inspecting it, examining the sole.

"These are very fine," she says. "You do exceptionally good work, Natters. You deserve more business; I shall spread the word."

"No!" Natters blurts. "It wasn't me. I didn't make the shoes." He doesn't look at Shoe, who knows that Natters knows he is a shoemaker and that he must have done it. "It was . . . it was elves. Must have been. Elves coming into the shop at night and making up the shoes. Here, I'll ask my servant." He glances aside at Shoe. "Did you see any elves in the shop, Shoe, or were you sound asleep in your cubby?"

"Um, I didn't see any elves," Shoe says slowly. He shoots Natters a *what are you talking about* look, and Natters lowers his bristly eyebrows and gives a tiny shake of his head.

Shoe keeps quiet.

"Still, it must have been elves," Natters says. "There's no other explanation for it."

"Elves!" exclaims the woman. "From the stories I've heard, you are a lucky shoemaker to have elves working in your shop." She places a few more coins on the workbench. "I shall certainly spread the word about *that*." With a last nod to Natters, she sweeps out of the shop.

When the door closes behind her, Natters puts his head in his hands. "Elves," he mutters to himself. "That was the best you could come up with? Elves?"

Shoe braces himself because he knows Natters will be angry with him. "I did something wrong, Natters," he begins, "but I'm not sure what. Whatever it was, I'm sorry about it."

Natters sighs. "I used to have a shop at the upper end of this street, you know. I was an excellent shoemaker." He glances up at Shoe from under his bushy eyebrows. "Not as skilled as you are, Shoe, judging by the shoes you made last night, but I was good. I used the finest leathers, and I was paid in gold, and I had the best apprentices. You see where this is going, lad?"

Shoe gulps. All of a sudden he does, and it makes his blood run cold. "The Godmother."

Natters nods sadly. "She took them. My apprentices." He sighs. "The apprentices were good lads and they were as dear to the Missus and me as our own sons would have been. First we lost Jory. He just disappeared one day, gone without a trace. The Missus and me were the only ones who noticed. Nobody else even remembered him. After that I trained up another apprentice—Jo, that was—and he went, too. I think she was using me to train them up, and she took them when they were ready."

Shoe thinks back to the other Shoemaker in the Godmother's fortress, the one who had gone mad after making sets of twelve dancing slippers for days and days without end. "Was he—" His voice is rough, and he clears his throat. "Was one of them a bit older than I am? Brown hair and a nose that looked like it had been broken a couple of times, and a missing tooth here?" He taps one of his front teeth to show Natters which one.

"Yes. That's him. Jo. He looked like a rough sort, but he made a fine shoemaker." Natters rubs his eyes. "I suppose he was with you in that place?"

Shoe nods. "So you know about it. The fortress."

"Yes, we know. Or we guess, at any rate." He sighs. "Did you know him, then?"

"Not really," Shoe says. "We weren't . . ." It is hard to describe living in the Godmother's fortress. "We didn't have names, and we weren't allowed to talk, and we didn't have anything to talk about, anyway. We were only supposed to work." Pin had changed all that for him, but before her he'd been a good and obedient Shoemaker. Except for the dogskin slippers. He'd done that right after the other Shoemaker – Jo—had been taken away. It had only been a tiny rebellion, but he'd paid for it at the post.

"You escaped, did you?" Natters asks. At Shoe's nod, he goes on. "The Missus figured it out—where you came from. And now you see why we didn't have the windows cleaned or the sign repainted?"

Shoe nods. "You don't want to draw the Godmother's attention."

"Right." There is a long silence. Absently Natters lines up the tools on his workbench, then starts sorting scraps of leather into neat piles. "Most people don't realize what it means to be caught up in it, as we are." He falls silent again.

Shoe has his own ideas about what the Godmother is up to, but he wants to hear what Natters has to say about it. "Caught up in what?" he prompts. "What, exactly, is going on?"

Natters shakes his head and sighs.

Shoe steps closer. "Tell me," he insists.

For a long moment Natters regards him from under his bushy eyebrows, as if gauging how far Shoe can be trusted.

"No, lad," he says at last. "We don't have the heart for it any-more, me and the Missus."

Shoe shakes his head, not accepting Natters's refusal to say more. "There's a girl who helped me escape from the Godmother's fortress. Her name is Pin and she's here in the city. I think she's important, somehow, to whatever the God-mother is planning."

"Then you want to stay away from her, Shoe," Natters says, frowning.

"I can't," Shoe says. "I have to help her get out."

Natters lurches to his feet. "Don't be stupid, lad. You can't help her. You could go in and try, but you'll only draw the Godmother's notice, and then you'll be killed or broken, or you'll disappear without a trace like my other apprentices."

Shoe gives a stubborn shake of his head. He puts his hand in his coat pocket and closes it around Pin's thimble. It warms at his touch. "I don't care what happens to me," he says. "Pin saved me. Now I have to save her."

CHAPTER

15

PRECIOUS HAS KNOTTED THE LACES OF THE CORSET SO tightly that I can't breathe. They are tied at my back and I can't unknot them and I can't get any air into my lungs.

Tears run down my face, stinging where my stepmother hit me. I gasp for a breath, and then another, and scrabble at the corset laces. *It will not come off.*

"Stop it," I gasp and try to take a deep breath to calm myself. The corset cuts into my ribs. "*Stop. It,*" I grind out, and with an effort of will I push all the air out of my lungs. It's enough to loosen the laces in the back, and I get my fingers under the knot and with a vicious jerk I break it, and the corset loosens, an enormous relief. I take a deep, shuddering breath. With shaking fingers I unlace the corset and fling it away from me, into the corner of my tiny prison room.

I sit on the bed against the wall and draw up my knees and wrap the shreds of my silk dress around me. I use the snowy white petticoat to wipe the tears off my face. With my fingers I feel the place where Stepmama hit me. A bruise is rising on my cheek; it feels sore and swollen. My head is pounding from the blows, and from the crying.

"What now, Pen?" I whisper to myself. I thought myself so clever, pitting myself against Lady Faye, but I am not winning this contest. She was right, and she is still right—the more I struggle, the worse it gets.

I rest my head on my knees and contemplate the wall of my prison. The plaster is cracked. Black mold is crusted where the walls meet the floor. I haven't eaten anything since the scrap of bread and cheese I had last night. The wind hisses through the broken window. It's going to be a cold, hungry night.

I am so alone.

Tears start leaking from my eyes again, running down my cheeks and soaking into the petticoat. For a while I let myself cry.

At last I run out of tears, and I wipe my face again with my damp petticoat and lift my head. I have to get out of here.

All right. I have a shredded silk dress. That's something. Silk is a strong material, and if I could squeeze myself out the attic window, I might be able to use it as a rope to lower myself to the roof. From there I could climb to the ground.

Or fall to my death on the cobblestoned street.

I am wearing only a petticoat.

If I manage to get out the window and down to the street without falling, I will be practically naked, and I can't go running through the streets without any clothes on. If things get desperate enough, though, I might consider it.

I also have two silk stockings. I'd have to use them as part of the rope.

And, one of my shoes fell off as I was being dragged by my stepmother to the attic.

So that is all I have. One shoe.

It is a good shoe. Well made, and it fits me perfectly.

But a single shoe can't save me.

IN THE MORNING there is the sound of the key at the lock, and the door swings open. I sit on the bed and pull my legs up so the petticoat I'm wearing will hide my naked front.

It is Anna with my ragged black dress over her arm and my toe-pinching shoes in her hands. Her sympathetic gaze lingers on my face. During the night, the bruise from my stepmother's blow moved to my left eye, which is swollen shut. "Am I—" I have to stop and cough to clear my throat. "Am I being let out?"

"We're not supposed to speak to you. I'm only to tell you to put your clothes on and go to the kitchen." Anna hands me the dress and the shoes and then hurries from the doorway.

Stiffly I get to my feet. I button my ragged black mourning dress, then lace my ill-fitting shoes. I keep the one shoe, putting it in my pocket.

I make my way to the kitchen; the shoe in my pocket bumps against my leg as I walk, as a reminder. The cook gives me some leftover eggs and toast from breakfast, and when I finish gulping them down like the starving thing that I am, she puts me to work scrubbing out pots. The cooks and servants look carefully away from me, and they speak in hushed voices. They seem frightened, as if something terrible is about to happen.

Or maybe it already has.

Lady Meister, I hear a maid whisper. *Yes, it's true. She—* The maid glances aside at me and then falls silent.

I feel a chill in my stomach. What? What is true?

In the afternoon, I am lugging cans of bathwater up to Dulcet's room—she doesn't speak to me, either, just pretends I am not there—when I meet the ratcatcher. It seems like such a long time ago that I saw him before, but it was only yesterday.

He is poking his long nose into a hole in a dark corner of the hallway; he pulls it out as I pass. "Greetings, Lady Penelope," he says, with his gap-toothed grin.

I set down the heavy cans of water and rub my tired arms. "Hello," I say. "More rats?"

He shakes his shaggy head. "No, miss. Message for you."

I blink my one good eye. "For me?" I don't actually know

anyone else in the city—at least, not that I can remember.

"From Shoe," the ratcatcher says.

"A shoe?" It doesn't make any sense. I pull the one perfect shoe from my pocket and inspect it. The stitching along the sole is almost invisible; the shoemaker who made this is an expert craftsman. "I have a message from a shoe?" I repeat.

"No, Your Ladyship." He lowers his voice. "From your young man."

I shake my head. "I don't have any young man."

"Shoe," the ratcatcher insists. "Nice-looking chap, yellow hair?"

"I don't know anybody like that," I say, putting the shoe back into my pocket.

"Well, he knows you, Your Ladyship," he says, and taps his nose. He opens his mouth to say something else—to deliver his message, I guess—when a door down the hallway slams open.

Dulcet's head pokes out. "Bring the water at once," she orders.

The ratcatcher's mouth snaps shut.

"What message?" I whisper, as I heave up the cans of water.

His nose twitches and he blinks quickly.

With a sigh, I start down the hallway toward Dulcet's room.

"*Thimble*," the ratcatcher hisses after me.

I stumble. Water from the cans sloshes on the floor.

When I look around, the ratcatcher is scurrying around the corner and away.

Thimble? What does this Shoe person know about my missing thimble?

I DON'T HAVE time to think about the message, because I am kept hard at work without any break for a midday meal. The cook scolds, the servants pretend they can't see me, and I go wearily from task to task, my face aching, my fingers cold, my stomach empty.

This is all part of Lady Faye's plan for me, I surmise as I slop soapy water over the back doorstep and bend to scrub at it with a bristly brush. I am at my absolute lowest now. There is no escape; I have no choices left.

Late in the afternoon, an undercook sends me to the market for potatoes. I don't remember the market, but my feet find the way. The air is cold, and as twilight falls, it gets colder, and I wrap my arms around myself as I go along the wide, well-lit streets to the grand square at the center of the city where the market is set up. The castle clock is about to strike six, and I have to hurry to find a shopkeeper willing to sell me a burlap sack full of potatoes before all of the shutters are closed and the stalls taken down. It is awkward to carry. I try wrapping my arms around the sack, but then it's hard to walk, so I heave it up over my shoulder and trudge along that way. As the clock is striking six I am rounding a corner when somebody runs into me on my swollen-shut-eye side.

The sack falls to the street, bursts open, and potatoes go rolling away in every direction.

"Oh, curse it," I say to the person who bumped into me. "Can't you watch where you're going?"

He is a tall man wearing a leather cloak down to his ankles; a wide-brimmed hat hides his face. "I do beg your pardon," he says politely, and I catch a glimpse of a well-shaped mouth that curves into an easy smile. He has two dogs at his heels, tall black and tan hounds with long ears and wagging tails, and he holds up his hand, keeping them in place.

I am hungry and exhausted and cold and I don't have time for pretty politeness. "I'll give you my pardon," I say crossly, "if you'll help me pick the dratted things up." I shove the sack into his hands and go down on my knees, grabbing after the potatoes. Most men would stalk away at being spoken to so sharply by someone who appears to be a servant girl, but he holds the sack while I put the potatoes in. One of his dogs fetches a potato and brings it to me, holding it gently in its mouth.

"Drop it, Blue," the man orders, and the dog obediently drops the potato into my hand.

I wipe the slobber off it with my sleeve and put the potato into the sack. "That's all of them," I say.

The man leans down to help me to my feet.

I feel his hand on mine, and then black spots are swimming before my eyes and the ground feels very far away, and I am falling—and his arm, strong and warm, comes around my shoulders to steady me.

"Are you all right?" he asks. His voice is deep and rich, like melted chocolate.

Mmm, chocolate. I am so very hungry. "Obviously I am not," I snap. "Just give me the sack and I'll be on my way."

He doesn't hand over the sack of potatoes. He bends closer to peer into my face, and I get a glimpse of very bright blue eyes in a face of chiseled handsomeness, and a swoop of curly black hair parted on the side. "You're unwell," he says, and the concern in his eyes is genuine. "I think you'd better come with me." He takes my arm, and leads me along. It is very unlike me, but I am too limp to resist. We go down the street, turn a corner, and he brings me into a warm, well-lighted, cozy room. A tea shop, I realize.

With great courtesy he leads me to a table and pulls back a chair, and I fall into it. "Tea," he says to the waiter who hurries up to him. "And a tray of pastries, and perhaps some strawberries."

"Yes, sir," the waiter says with a crisp bow, and turns to hurry away.

"And chocolate, if you please," I call after him.

At that the man turns his charming smile on me, and it's the first time anyone has smiled at me in the longest time—so long that I can't even remember the last time. He sits down at the table opposite me and, strangely, leaves his hat on, as if he doesn't want anyone in the shop to notice him. His face is shadowed, but I can see him well enough. He is young, maybe a few years older than I am. And he is very well dressed. That, with the impeccable manners, tells me that he's quite at home here in the neighborhood nearest the castle.

He is studying my face. "You speak like a lady," he says quietly in his velvety voice, "and you carry yourself like one, but you look like a famished, ill-treated scullery maid. Which are you?"

A sharp reply comes to my lips but I bite it back, and instead I shrug wearily.

The man gives a charming smile. "You are a mystery, then."

I think what he means is that I'm some sort of romantic mystery woman, when there's nothing at all romantic about sleeping in the cinders of the kitchen hearth, or lugging five cans of hot water up four flights of stairs to Dulcet's bedroom and being scolded because her bath is only lukewarm, or scrubbing an entire five-course dinner's worth of pots until the skin of my hands is chapped and red. "I suppose I am," I say noncommittally. I am a mystery to myself, anyway.

The waiter delivers a pot of tea and a tray of gorgeous pastries, some of them oozing chocolate.

Seeing the food makes me brighten. "Well, I *am* famished," I add, and I scoop up a strawberry, drag it through a bowl of whipped cream, and pop it into my mouth. It is sweet and tart at the same time, delicious. I follow it up with a bite-size muffin. There's gingerbread, too. My hand hovers, ready to choose it, but for some reason I don't want to, so I take a little chocolate roll instead. "You may pour me a cup of tea," I say through my mouthful. He does so, and I take a long drink.

His dogs are lying under the table, their muzzles on the floor with their long ears puddled about them; their brown eyes look up beseechingly. "They're very good dogs," I say, bending to pat their heads. "Do they go with you everywhere?"

His face softens as he looks down at them, and this time his smile is different, not as practiced. "They do. I breed them. This is Blue," he says, nudging one with the toe of his boot, "and the other is Bunny."

I start to make a joke about the names—really, what kind of person calls his dog Bunny?—and for the first time I look him full in the eyes, and something very strange happens.

It is as if a gear has engaged, and I feel completely enmeshed in his gaze. I can't look away. The same thing, evidently, has happened to him. His blue eyes widen.

"Who are you?" he whispers, and his voice is not velvet, but rough.

At the question, a wave of sudden sadness washes over me. I reach into my dress pocket so habitually—to take comfort from my missing thimble—and realize that I've lost my perfect shoe. It must have fallen from my pocket somewhere in the marketplace, maybe when I bent to pick up the spilled potatoes.

Shoe, thimble, all the things I want to remember but

don't—too much has been lost. Who am I? I am nothing. The more I fight, the more tightly I am bound. All my choices are being taken away from me. It is enough to break me, at last. I feel tears welling up, and I blink them back.

His fingers graze my cheek, tender along the bruise where my stepmother struck me. "You burn so brightly," he says. "You are like a flame, my mystery girl. You must tell me who you are."

I am no flame. All my fire has burned away, leaving only ash. "I don't know who I am," I whisper.

He leans closer. "Just tell me your name."

My name. Trembling, I shake my head.

"Please." His voice is urgent.

I wish I could tell him.

But I can't. Something about this is wrong; I can *feel* it. It's too sudden.

Come on, Pen. *Think.* "Do you know Lady Faye?" I blurt out.

"Of course. Have you met her?"

I ignore his question. "Did she send you here? Did she tell you to find me?" Is this another one of her traps?

"No," he says slowly. "I think we were meant to meet. Don't you feel it too?"

Yes. No. I don't know. I am light-headed from hunger and exhaustion and I don't know what I'm supposed to do, or how to do what I'm not supposed to do.

The only thing I can think of is to run.

I push away from the table and stumble toward the door.

Behind me, he gets to his feet; one of his dogs barks. "Wait!" he calls after me.

But too late. I slip out the door and into the street, where it is dark and I can make my escape.

When I get home, I am immediately sent to my attic prison without any dinner, as punishment for forgetting the potatoes. Exhausted, I curl on the lumpy mattress and wrap my arms around myself, ready to fall asleep at once.

But I can't stop thinking about him. The velvet-voiced young man in the tea shop, who asks me questions that I cannot answer.

CHAPTER

16

MORE CUSTOMERS HAVE COME TO THE SHOP TO ORDER shoes made especially for them by elves. There is going to be a ball at the castle, they say, and everyone wants dancing slippers to match their ball gowns. Those that wear these wonderful elf-made shoes, it is said, will never get a blister on a heel or feel a pinched toe or have sore feet, not even if they dance until the clock strikes midnight.

Grimly, Natters takes their orders and their coins, glares at Shoe, and goes upstairs to dinner and bed, leaving Shoe to work late into the night by candlelight.

Shoe is stitching a seam along the edge of a slipper-sole when he hears a *tap-tap-tap* at the shop door. He puts out the candle and holds his breath.

Tap-tap-tap, and then another louder *tap-tap*.

In the near-darkness, Shoe feels his way across the shop to the door, where he stands, the silence pressing against his ears.

"Yer Lor'ship," comes a muffled voice from outside.

Spanner. Quickly Shoe goes back to the workbench and relights the candle, then unlocks the door and pulls the rat-catcher into the shop. "What's the matter?" he whispers.

Spanner smells of sweat and of something rancid that might be dead rat. He shakes his wild-haired head. "Your girl, Pin," he answers. "She's in a pile of trouble."

Shoe nods. "I know she is. I'm trying to figure a way to get her out of it." He doesn't have much time left, either. He's caught enough whispers from the people on Shoemaker Street to know that Spanner is right. Trouble is coming.

"Your Pin is living in that big house right enough," Spanner goes on. "But she's not a fine lady like I thought. Them other fine ladies that live there, they're treating her bad, like."

In his chest, Shoe's heart gives a lurch. "Bad how?"

"Somebody's laid hands on her," Spanner says with a frown. "That stepmother of hers I guess. Her face is all swelled up. An' I didn't notice before 'cos I doesn't usually notice such things as that, but her dress isn't so fine, neither, and she looks half starved." He rubs his nose. "I know that look, I does."

"I know it too," Shoe says darkly. "I should have tried to get her out before this."

"Nothing you can do about it, Shoe," Spanner says.

"There's no getting into that house for you, and the servants isn't talking. Most of 'em wouldn't be no help anyway."

"I'll figure out a way," Shoe says. He reaches out and grasps Spanner's hunched shoulder. "Thanks for your help with this. I'll return the favor any time you say."

"Aye, I know you will," Spanner says.

"And, look." He suspects that Spanner is an important person in the city's network of people who are aware of the Godmother's power. "Put out the word with *them that knows.* That trouble you're waiting for. It's coming soon."

"Right-o," Spanner says with a nod. "Will do."

Shoe gives him a handful of coins from Natters's workbench and opens the door so the ratcatcher can slip out into the night, then he locks the door again. Worried, he paces. When he grips Pin's thimble, he can almost feel it, like a low thunder at the edge of his hearing. He *has* to get Pin out of whatever she's tangled up in. It may already be too late.

After a while, he goes back to work at the bench, steadying his shaking hands so he can make shoes so fine only elves could have crafted them.

In the morning, Natters shakes him awake from where he's fallen asleep with his head on the workbench.

"The shoes are finished," Shoe says, his voice creaky.

"I can see that well enough," Natters says. "Come and have some breakfast."

Yawning, Shoe follows him up to the kitchen, where the Missus puts bowls of porridge on the table before them.

"There's bacon and egg to come," she says in her piping voice. "Eat up."

By the time he's drunk a cup of tea and eaten half a bowl of the porridge with goat milk, Shoe has woken up enough to put two thoughts together in his head. "Natters," he says, setting down his spoon. "Missus Natters. There's something that I have to do."

At the table, Natters nods; the Missus gets up from her chair and goes to lean against him; he puts an arm around her wide hips.

Shoe rubs his eyes, weary. What he's planning will put them in danger; it'll draw attention that they don't want, and it might break their hearts, too. How can he consider doing such a thing?

"Go on, lad," Natters prompts.

"No, I can't," Shoe mutters to himself. "I'll figure out another way to do it."

"Your girl," the Missus puts in unexpectedly. "Pin's her name?"

Shoe looks up. "Yes. Pin."

"How long did you know her before she got caught up in this?" the Missus asks. Her bright eyes are sharp.

With a shock, Shoe realizes that he and Pin were together for only a few days. He's been working here in the shop for longer than that. "Not very long," he admits. "But she saved me. We escaped together. She knows me, and I know her better than I've ever known anyone." Which is true, as far as he can remember, because his Before is still lost to him. "She's brave, and smart, and sharp, and she's beautiful too, and she laughs at irony." And then he adds, "If there's ever an expected thing to do, she'll do the opposite."

"Does she love you?" the Missus asks.

Shoe rests his elbows on the table and puts his head in his hands. "Maybe," he says, his voice muffled. "Probably not. I don't know."

There is a silence. When he looks up, the Missus has gone back to her seat and she and Natters are having one of their conversations where neither of them says anything.

After a moment, Natters gives a resigned shrug. "All right, Missus, if you think so."

"I do," the Missus says, and gives a satisfied nod. "We'll do what we can to help you, Shoe. What is it you're planning?"

"I have to get into the house where Pin is living and try to get her out of there. But the Godmother has plans for her, so it might be dangerous." Shoe pauses. The Missus gives an impatient nod, and so he goes on. "This is what I'm thinking. Natters, you're the most famous shoemaker in the city right now. The orders are coming in faster than we can fill them."

"It's the prince's ball up at the castle," Natters puts in.

"Right." Shoe nods. "There are fine ladies living at the house where Pin is, and they'll probably be invited to this ball, and they'll want the best, elf-made dancing shoes." He'll try to keep Natters out of it if he can. "If I tell them I'm taking orders for your shop—"

"—They'll not let you in the door," Natters interrupts.

"They might," Shoe argues.

"Natters is right," the Missus puts in. "They won't let a servant in to see the ladies. He's the shop owner; it'll have to be him that gets you in."

CHAPTER

WHILE I SCRUB POTS IN THE LATE-AFTERNOON KITCHEN, I think about the tea shop man. I only caught glimpses of his face, but I'd know him again if I saw him. I'd recognize his chocolate-smooth voice and easy smile.

I wonder if he is thinking about me, the snappish girl with the bag of potatoes and the black eye and the enormous appetite for pastries.

Oh, he probably isn't. He's handsome and obviously rich; it's likely enough he's got beautiful girls like Dulcet and Precious flinging themselves at him. Why would he look twice at a wretch like me?

But I am his mystery girl. We shared something, there in the tea shop. Maybe he *is* thinking about me.

"Pen," a housemaid interrupts.

I look up. "Yes?" It's Anna.

She holds out a bucket with a brush and a rag in it and a jar of brass polish. "I've got the table to set for dinner. Would you do the hearth in the downstairs blue drawing room?"

"Yes, all right." I set down my scrubbing brush and dry my chapped, reddened hands on my increasingly stained and ragged dress. Taking the bucket, I trudge up the stairs from the kitchen and down the hallway.

I go into the drawing room. My stepsisters are there with two other people, tradesmen of some kind, I guess, a tall, bent old man wearing a leather apron, and a boy about my age holding a wooden toolbox; he's the old man's servant, evidently.

As I come into the door, the younger one gives a start and his eyes widen. He stares at me as I cross the room to the hearth. Giving him a little frown, I set down the bucket and go to my knees, pulling the grate out of the ashes.

"No, no, Dulcie," Precious is saying patiently. "You can't wear brown slippers with a blue dress to the prince's ball. Hm." She pauses. "Silver would be lovely, though." She looks at the tall old man, who is holding a set of metal calipers and a measuring tape. "Can the elves who work in your shop do them in silver, Shoemaker?"

"Yes," the old shoemaker says. "They can."

Keeping my head down, I get on with my work, scrubbing the ash from the grate, then using the rag to apply the brass polish. Behind me, the shoemaker is slowly measuring each of Dulcet's stocking-clad feet, and then Precious's. I polish the brass grate until it shines, and then I gather up my brush and my rag and my bucket and leave the room.

The shoemaker's servant follows me into the hallway.

"Pin," he whispers.

I stop and turn. He is about my height, slim and straight. He's got one of those thin-skinned faces that show every blush. Something about that bothers me, though he's quite good-looking, too. "You're mistaken," I tell him. "My name is Penelope."

He frowns. His green eyes are very serious. "You don't remember me."

"I have never seen you before in my life," I say. The bucket is heavy, and I set it on the floor between us.

"Yes you have."

"No I haven't," I insist. Talking to him is making my head hurt, and that makes me snappish. "And I didn't like you staring at me like that, either."

"Pin, it's me," the young man says, a hint of desperation in his voice. "Shoe. Do you really not remember?"

"Oh, you're *Shoe*?" I say. "You're the one who sent the message with the ratcatcher." I narrow my eyes, suspicious. "What do you know about my thimble?"

"You don't remember," the young man named Shoe mutters, as if talking to himself. His face has gone rather alarmingly pale.

"I don't remember a lot of things," I say impatiently. "Now, what about the thimble?"

He blinks. "I've got it here." He puts his hand into his coat pocket and brings out my thimble.

"Where did you get that?" I ask, and reach out to take it from him.

He closes his hand around it. "You gave it to me, Pin," he says seriously.

"Pen," I correct. "Penelope. *Lady* Penelope, actually. And I didn't. You must have stolen it." It's the only explanation, because I never would have given my thimble away to anyone.

"No, I—" There is the sound of a door opening from down the hallway, and he lowers his voice. "Pin, you have to get out of this house," he says urgently.

Well, I know that perfectly well. But what has it to do with him? "I think you should give me the thimble—*my* thimble—and go away," I say.

"Will you come with me now?" he asks, holding out his hand.

"No," I say, and take a step away. He tries to follow and trips over the bucket I'd put down between us, lurching into me; we both stagger back until I bump into the wall, and he bumps into me. We stand there nose to nose for a moment, panting. I feel the length of his body, pressed against mine.

"Pin," he breathes.

"Pen," I tell him.

"Pin," he repeats.

"Oh, you are stubborn, aren't you?" I say.

As an answer, he leans closer and his lips brush against mine. A kiss. I am so surprised by it that I can't move. The kiss deepens. My lips tingle and warmth spreads through me, and I savor it, the touch of another person when I've been alone for so, so long. I close my eyes. Somehow my arms have gotten around his neck and I am kissing him back.

At that moment a door slams, and I look over Shoe's shoulder to see my stepmother coming down the hallway in full sail.

"Oh, curse it," I mutter, and shove him away from me. He stumbles back and trips over the bucket again, landing sprawled on the floor before Stepmama.

"What are you doing?" she shrills. "Penelope!"

Shoe's face is scarlet, and he scrambles to his feet.

"You *slut*," Stepmama says, kicking the bucket aside and bearing down on me. "Carrying on in the hallway with a"— she looks Shoe up and down, sees his raggedly cut hair and his shapeless coat—"with a common servant. I might have expected it!" She raises her hand to strike.

Shoe steps in front of me, holding up his arm to block the blow.

Stepmama's face turns red and she looks as if she might explode.

Then the shoemaker pokes his head from the drawing room.

Stepmama lowers her hand quickly and draws herself up, but continues to glare past Shoe at me.

It's all I can do to lean against the wall and try to catch my breath.

"Shoe," the old shoemaker says, "I'm finished with the measurements. Come along now."

Shoe has gone pale again. He turns to me. "I'm very sorry," he blurts, backing away, and he takes the wooden toolbox from the shoemaker and they go down the hallway and out of the house.

I, of course, am given the usual punishment.

Only tonight, as I curl on the mattress of my prison room, my cheek throbbing with a new bruise, faint with hunger and aching with weariness, I think about Shoe, a mystery himself, who stole my thimble and who calls me by the wrong name and who is so sure he knows me, even though I am absolutely certain that he does not.

And as I am falling asleep, my thoughts drift to the velvet-voiced tea shop man. I feel the gentle touch of his fingers on my face. I want to see him again. Somehow I know that I will. Our next meeting has a kind of inevitability about it.

CHAPTER

18

As soon as they come out of the fine mansion, Shoe
opens his mouth to tell Natters what happened in the hallway
with Pin.

"Not here," Natters interrupts, with a glance around the
busy street, wary of listening ears. "Not until we're back at the
shop."

Shoe walks with him in frozen silence along the wide,
well-patrolled, well-lit streets and graceful bridges of the
upper city, past the market square, and into the winding,
darkening streets of the lower city, where the river smells like
dead fish and open drains.

All the way, he's cursing himself. Pin is in trouble and
it's his fault, and now he's made her trouble even worse, very
likely, and she thinks he's a thief and—and he kissed her and

she probably hadn't liked that at all—and she will never trust him to help her get away, not after this.

At the shop, Natters hustles Shoe inside, and then locks the door behind them.

"She's—" Shoe starts.

"Wait," Natters interrupts. "The Missus'll want to hear it, too."

They go up to the kitchen. It is fragrant with the smell of bean soup on the stove and of freshly baked bread, and it's warmly lit by candles and a coal fire in the hearth.

Natters points to the table and Shoe sits and drops his head into his hands.

After a moment, the Missus sets a cup of hot tea before him and she and Natters take their places at the table.

"Well?" the Missus prompts.

"I can't believe how stupid I am," Shoe mutters.

"What is it, lad?" Natters says with surprising gentleness. "She was Pin, wasn't she?"

Shoe looks despairingly across the table at them. "She doesn't remember me. She doesn't remember any of it," he says, his voice rough. "The Godmother must've used her magic to take all of her memories away. The fortress, the wall and the thorns, the forest, all of it."

Natter and the Missus nod, as if this isn't unexpected. "So she's not your Pin," the Missus says.

"She was never *my* Pin," Shoe says. "Now she's Lady Penelope, she says." He curses himself again, and presses the heels of his hands over his eyes. In the darkness there he sees her again, her pale face bruised, her eyes sharp and suspicious, and smudged with weariness, too. And she wore shoes that looked like they didn't fit her very well; it'd been the first thing he'd noticed. He takes a shuddering breath and then opens his eyes. "She doesn't remember me at all. She—" He takes the thimble out of his pocket and sets it on the table. It glows warmly in the candlelight. "She remembers this."

"A thimble," says the Missus, with a meaningful look at Natters.

"No matter," Natters says to her. "The girl's forgotten him. Shoe is well out of it now."

No. He's not. Shoe stares at the thimble. He takes another deep breath and wraps his hands around his mug of tea.

Oh, you are stubborn, aren't you, she had said to him.

True enough, he is. He takes a sip of the hot tea and it burns a trail down to his stomach. Even if she doesn't remember it, she's still herself; she's still Pin. Nothing has changed. He has to get her out.

AFTER BEAN SOUP and bread for dinner, Shoe drags himself down to the shop. All night he and Natters work on their long list of orders for shoes made by elves, dancing slippers, mostly, for the prince's ball at the castle. Shoe tries to think of how he's going to get Pin—Lady Penelope—out of the fine house she's imprisoned in, but he's gone too many nights without sleep, and his thoughts are fuzzy.

After Natters has nudged him awake for the third time because he's fallen sound asleep sitting up, he goes to his cubby, where he collapses into bed.

In the morning his head is clearer and he knows exactly what he's going to do. At breakfast, he tells Natters and his Missus that he has a plan.

Natters shakes his head, gloomy. "I'm telling you, Shoe," he says. "You're better staying out of it."

"I'm already in it," Shoe says. "Whatever it is." He bends his head and rubs his eyes, still tired. "Natters, I have to know. What am I fighting against?"

Natters shakes his head. "Fighting, he calls it," he mutters grimly. "You can't fight it, lad."

"Is it some kind of magic?" Shoe asks, stubborn.

Natters shakes his head. There is a long moment of silence. Faintly, in the distance, Shoe hears the castle clock striking eight. Past time to open the shop.

"Story, we call it," the Missus says unexpectedly.

"No, Missus," Natters protests.

She reaches across the scuffed wooden table and pats Natters's hand. "We can't keep quiet any longer. It is time to act."

The Missus is small and stout and she wears a flowered kerchief over her graying hair, but to Shoe she suddenly looks wise and strong, and in her eyes he can see her sorrow for their lost apprentices. She folds her arms and nods at him. "Story."

"It's the Godmother's magic?" Shoe asks.

"It's much more powerful than that," the Missus says.

"What is it, then?" he asks. "How does it work?"

Natters and his Missus exchange one of their looks. She nods at him to speak. Natters sighs. "You know stories, right? Ordinary ones. They have a kind of shape to them."

Shoe nods. "Beginnings, middles, and ends, you mean?"

"Yes." Natters raises his empty cup and the Missus pushes herself from her chair and goes to fetch him more tea. "It's well enough when an ordinary story is told. Happy endings and the like. But what if . . ." He trails off.

The Missus sets the teapot on the table. "Help yourself, Natters," she says, nudging the sugar bowl closer to him. Settling herself in her chair, she nods at Shoe. "What if the stories aren't told? What if they're lived? What if you were forced to live your life in the shape of a story that is not your own, with no choice about who you are and where you're going?"

Shoe thinks about this. His life doesn't really have any story to it at all. He can't remember its beginning, before his enslavement in the Godmother's fortress. Maybe this is its middle. And he doesn't want to think much about an ending.

The Missus pours herself more tea. "What we think happened is that—at the beginning"—she gives Shoe a meaningful look—"at the beginning of it all the Godmother used the stories to give herself more power. There was a kind of dark witch who thwarted her, so the stories couldn't take over. But then something changed."

"A plot twist," Shoe puts in.

"That's the idea," the Missus approves. "The stories have a kind of power in themselves, and as they were told and retold they grew too powerful. They became Story; they became real. The witch tried to fight Story and was killed. Story uses the Godmother, now, to achieve its endings. Story warps the world around it, forcing people into the shape of it."

Shoe frowns. "Pin's stuck in a living Story, is that what you're saying?"

The Missus gives a grim nod.

"And there's no way to get her out?"

"The wheels turn, Shoe," Natters says. "Story is a meat grinder. Those who are caught up in it are ground down and put to use. One way or another, it uses all of us; we all serve it whether we like it or not, whether we know it or not. Not even the Godmother can truly control it." He shakes his head. "There's no escaping it."

"In the Godmother's fortress we were outside Story," Shoe corrects.

Natters shrugs his narrow shoulders. "Maybe you were. Or maybe you helped it turn, making the shoes, and all the rest of it."

"Maybe," Shoe agrees, thinking of all the slaves in the Godmother's fortress, spinning away like tiny gears in a giant machine.

"At any rate, you're a shoemaker, Shoe," Natters adds. "There's no other place in Story for the likes of you. If you try to change it, it'll grind you up and spit you out, and there's nothing you can do about it."

"I have to try to get Pin out," Shoe insists.

Natters shakes his head sadly.

"What are you thinking, sneak into her house and spirit her away?" the Missus asks.

Shoe nods. "The prince's ball is tomorrow night. I'm guessing her stepmother will be invited to it. It's the only chance I'll have to get in there." And this time he'll give her the thimble, to convince her to come. He leans forward, elbows on the table. "And then we'll have to get out of the city somehow." He's seen the bramble-covered city walls and the guarded gates. "It'll be tricky."

"You'll go down the river, of course," the Missus says.

"But there's the waterfall," Shoe says, remembering the view of the city he had with the Huntsman.

"There's a way down," the Missus says. "A path. It's a bit slippery, but it's not so bad if you've got good sturdy shoes. We can have a boat ready at the bottom."

Shoe blinks. "We? You and Natters?" It's too much to ask of them.

The Missus shakes her head. "There aren't many of us, but my Natters and I are not the only ones in the city who notice that the wheels are turning."

"What wheels?" Shoe interrupts.

"The story is told and retold, didn't I say?" the Missus answers. "It ends, and then it begins again. Every time the

Godmother finds new people for it to grind up and reshape. The main characters change, but the rest of us stay here, playing our parts." She nods wisely. "Now, Shoe, Natters has given you the dark truth of what you're caught up in, and there is little hope, but it's clear this girl is important to Story. We will do whatever we can to disrupt it."

"Who is the *we* exactly?" he asks.

The Missus nods again, and he sees not just wisdom, but hidden power, too. "We who know what we have lost to Story. There aren't many of us. Your friend the ratcatcher is one. Another is a street sweeper who watches the castle for us, a few maids and footmen in some fine houses, one or two of the lords and ladies living in those fine houses. We secret few know that the Godmother used her magic to rip us out of our lives. She takes the very best craftspeople for her fortress, and the rest of us, along with the lords and ladies and the important ones, she brings here, to her city."

"You remember, then?" Shoe interrupts. "Your life Before?"

Natters shakes his head, and the Missus answers for him. "No, we don't remember. Her magic is too strong for that. But we know about the Before; we know how much we've lost. We can sense the turnings of Story's wheel. We haven't resisted before, but now, perhaps, it is time."

"You said it's impossible," Shoe says. Natters had made it very clear about the crushing and grinding and the hopelessness of it all.

"Maybe it is," the Missus says, with a shrug of her broad shoulders. "But this time we will fight it."

"Sand in the gears," Natters puts in.

The Missus holds out her knobbed, age-spotted hand to her husband—and he takes it in his. "That is why we will help you, too."

"Thank you," Shoe says. Story sounds huge and unstoppable, but maybe they will find a way to escape it. Once they're outside the city he might be able to find the Huntsman and his band of rebels. "I have a lot of gold coins that you can have," he remembers. "Can you get us supplies?"

"Leave that to me," the Missus says.

They discuss the other arrangements to be made, the path and the boat, and the rest of it.

"And you think she'll come with you?" Natters asks, his voice doubtful.

"I hope so." He takes the thimble out of his pocket. "This will help, I think."

Then Shoe goes down to the workroom to spend the day sweeping the front step and helping Natters match the elven-made shoes with the people who come into the shop to pay for them. He goes out to the tavern and leaves a message for Spanner with the flirtatious tavern boy, and, blushing, comes back home. The Missus reports that a boat has been found and is to be packed with supplies. By tomorrow night, all will be ready.

That night after dinner he goes down to the shop again

and lights a candle. He remembers Pin's measurements exactly. He chooses the finest, most supple leather and softest sable for a lining; he cuts carefully and stitches soundly. He makes her a good, sturdy, warm pair of boots. They are boots for climbing down a slippery waterfall path, for walking long distances, boots for running while being chased by trackers.

Boots for her escape from Story.

19

My stepsisters and stepmother have been invited to the prince's ball at the castle. They spend the entire day getting ready. I am run ragged lugging bathwater and washing silk stockings and hanging them up to dry, and ironing acres of petticoats with lace trim, and fetching restorative cups of tea that had better not be lukewarm, or I'll get my ears boxed for it.

Wearing silk robes—peignoirs, maybe—over their petticoats and corsets, they have a light supper that I bring to them on a tray. They eat most of it, so I am left only a few leftover crusts, which I gulp down as I carry the tray to the kitchen. Then I hurry back upstairs to watch them finish getting ready.

The dresses were made by the finest dressmaker in the

city and must have cost their weight in gold, or maybe more.

Dulcie puts on hers first—it is a confection of sky-blue silk cut very low to reveal her corset-plumped breasts. It has an overskirt of lace and a bodice stitched with seed pearls, and there are shoes of silver leather fetched from the shoemaker's shop by a footman earlier in the day. Precious fusses around her, adding an ostrich feather to her piled-high blonde hair, changing her pearl necklace for a sapphire one.

"Pen, fetch my new gloves," Dulcet orders.

I go to the closet to get them, handing her the box. She wrinkles her nose at me and makes a shooing motion with her hands. "Go stand over there, out of the way."

I consider giving an elaborate curtsy, but I suspect the irony of it would be lost on her.

After Dulcet has pulled on the elbow-length white kid-skin gloves and fastened their mother-of-pearl buttons, it is Precious's turn. Her dress is more modestly cut at the neck-line—she doesn't have as much cleavage to show off as her sister does—but the skirt and bodice are an elaborate swathe of midnight-blue velvet. The overskirt is sheer net covered with gleaming crystals that must have taken the poor seam-stress who stitched them days to finish. The effect of the crystals over the dark velvet is of a midnight sky studded with stars. Precious's gloves are the same midnight blue—a daring choice—and she wears no jewelry around her neck, but dia-mond pins glint in her sleekly braided brown hair.

They link arms and stand admiring themselves in the

gilded mirror. They are both stunning. "Prince Cornelius will surely choose one of us, Dulcie, don't you think?" Precious asks.

Dulcet gives a self-satisfied nod. "I do think so, Precious."

Oh, so I see now what they're up to. They both want a husband, and they've got their eye on the prince. I know that a prince lives in the castle, of course, but I can't remember ever seeing him before, and I've never thought about him as a real person who might end up marrying one of my stepsisters. Wouldn't *that* please Stepmama, if Dulcie or Precious ensnares a prince!

Still, I can't help admiring their reflections in the mirror.

I catch a glimpse of myself there, too. Compared to them, I am a drab, ragged blot. My hair is tangled and dirty, I am too thin from being sent to the attic without any supper, the bruise on my cheek has turned a lovely greenish-purple color, and one of my eyes is still swollen from my stepmama's latest fit of fury.

"Stop staring, you stupid girl," Dulcet says to me.

I blink. "You both look beautiful," I say truthfully. They preen for a moment, and then I add, "It's too bad you don't have tempers to match."

Unfortunately my stepmama, coming into the room, hears the end of this comment. She scolds for a moment, but she is too pleased with her daughters' turnouts to pay any more attention to dirty, ragged me.

"Oh, girls," she says, and clasps her hands on her wide

bosom. They both pose and turn so she can appreciate the entirety of their splendor. Stepmama is handsome in rich blue silk with a dangerously wide skirt. All the blue, I realize, is a tribute to Lady Faye. Perhaps they are so excited about the ball because she has promised one of them the prince.

It is almost time; they can't risk being late. In a flurry, they put on their wraps and mince out to the street, where a carriage is waiting for them. Stepmama's dress has a train, so I have to lurch behind her with the extra fabric bundled in my arms so it won't drag on the steps or the cobbled street, and then kneel on the carriage floor arranging the train while she settles herself in her seat. I am scolded again and sent for hot bricks to warm their feet, and then I am sent running to Step-mama's dressing room to fetch another shawl, and at last the carriage door is latched and the coachman shakes the reins and they are off to the prince's ball.

I stand in the darkened street watching them go. The streets of the upper city, usually quiet at night, are teeming with people; in the distance I hear shouting and laughter, and then the unexpected sound of glass breaking. On a nearby street, a line of carriages trundles toward the castle; the horses' hooves clop loudly on the cobblestones. Beyond the house, only a few streets away, stands the castle. Its tall white towers are aglow as brilliant blue lights beam from their tops. The clock in the central tower is lit from within, and shines over the city like a stern, always-watching face. The clock weighs heavily on me, looming more than it should, really. For just a moment, I feel like a tiny clockwork girl, enmeshed in gears so huge I can't even see them, I only know that they are there, grinding on toward some unknown end.

As I watch, a heavy fog creeps up the street. It flows around the houses, turning the lanterns into muffled glows. The fog swathes the castle; it wraps smoky tendrils around the slender towers. It flows around my ankles and washes like an incoming tide up to the doorstep. The fog should smell dank, like the river, but it reminds me of pine trees and ferns, a fresh, green smell. Perhaps it has come from the forest outside the city.

Despite the fog, the sky above the castle stays clear and spangled with stars.

With ringing booms, the clock strikes the hour. At the sound, the mist swirls as if disturbed. The last strike fades away. Eight o'clock. Time for the prince's ball to begin.

The fog thickens again. My stepmama and stepsisters won't be home until after midnight. This might be the only time for me to escape, if I still dare it.

As if summoned by the thought, heavy footsteps echo on the cobblestoned street as the fog parts and two sturdy men dressed in light-blue livery—Lady Faye's footmen—emerge. They both stare insolently as they pass into the fog . . . and their footsteps stop. They are there, waiting. Guards.

Like the little clockwork girl that I am, I turn and, wading through the fog, climb the front steps and go into the house. It is dark and empty. All the servants have been given the night off. I stand in the front hallway for a moment, feeling strangely bereft.

Would I go to the ball if I could? Almost everyone from the upper city was invited; my tea shop man is probably there, too. Maybe he will dance with Dulcet or Precious. And Lord Meister and his horribly smiling wife; surely they will attend. I am a lady, the daughter of a duke, and I should have been invited, too. Perhaps I was. . . . Perhaps I never saw the invitation.

The shoemaker's servant, Shoe, won't be there, I am certain. I don't think servant-thieves get invitations from princes.

I don't even know why I'm thinking of him. With a weary sigh, I make my way through the silent house to the kitchen. It is dark except for a few embers in the hearth. It smells like the ghost of gingerbread. Now I really do feel unhappy.

"Don't you dare cry, Pen," I tell myself in a quavery voice.

I sit down on the hearthstones. My feet are tired and sore in their pinched shoes. Slowly I unlace them and take them off. I remember that I don't have the shoe in my pocket anymore, the one perfectly fitting shoe from the outfit I was given to meet my horrible suitor in.

I lie down on the hearth, getting as close to the warm embers as I can. "What did you do with your shoe, Pen?" I ask myself wearily.

Before I can answer, I am asleep.

CHAPTER

20

WHEN I WAKE UP, LADY FAYE IS THERE.

She is sitting in a straight-backed chair beside the hearth; she is splendid in a ball gown—ice blue, of course—and a necklace of diamonds as big as knucklebones. She glimmers with a cold light as if lit from within. If I was a blot next to my stepsisters, I am a mere smudge next to her.

I groan and sit up, rubbing the sleep out of my eyes. "Somehow I knew you would come here tonight," I say.

"It does have a certain . . . shall we say . . . inevitability about it?" she answers. Then she gives me an almost benevolent look. "You've been having an awfully bad time, haven't you, Penelope? Isn't there anything I can do for you?"

It is a tiny kindness, and certainly one with other motives, but it makes a lump of sadness rise in my throat so that I can't speak. I shake my head. I will not ask her for anything.

"Mmm." She pulls something out of a pocket in her skirt and slips it onto her finger. It glints in the dim light of the fire.

It is a silver thimble, the twin of my missing thimble, the thimble that Shoe stole from me. As I stare, she taps it against her pearly-white teeth, thinking. "In some ways you are very like your mother," she says unexpectedly.

"My mother?" I manage to croak. I have no memory of my mother, apart from the painting of her in the long gallery at the top of the house.

"Oh yes. And you are not at all like her in other ways." She is silent for a moment. "Sometimes I miss her, you know. Her whole purpose was to thwart me, but we were good friends at one time, your mother and I."

"I suppose my purpose is to thwart you too," I say, but I really have no idea what she is talking about.

Lady Faye smiles, and now the smile has an edge. "You can be a bit of a trial, my dear," she says condescendingly, "but you're not exactly a challenge." She waves her hand, changing the subject; the thimble gleams on her finger. "Now. On your feet. The clock struck ten while you were asleep. It is time to get you ready for the ball."

I stay where I am in the cinders. "I don't want to go to the ball," I say.

"Yes," she says, almost gently. "You do."

The wheels groan into motion. I can almost feel the house shaking as they turn. I really am caught up in it, something much bigger than I am. I am only one person, and I cannot resist the pull. I am so tired of not knowing who I am. So tired of resisting. Tonight—just for tonight—I will let it sweep me away.

Because I *do* want to go to the ball. I want to find my tea shop man and see him smile at me and then dance with him until midnight, and then I want—well, I don't know what I want, but it's anything but staying here to be slapped and scorned and locked up in a freezing attic.

I hold out for another lurching turn of the wheel, and then I give in. "All right." I get to my feet. "Send me to the ball if you have to."

"Such grace!" Lady Faye snipes, but she is clearly pleased. "But I suppose that is part of your appeal, isn't it?" She gets to her feet too, and shakes out her skirts. "We must hurry. We shall go to my house for your transformation, and then you shall make your entrance. Come along!"

AT HER HOUSE Lady Faye brings me to a dressing room of gold and blue, glimmering with candlelight, as exquisite as a jewel box. She seems excited, her movements brisk. "Out of that foul dress, my dear," she orders. A clap of her hands, and a troop of mouse-like maids clad in light-blue uniforms scurries into the room. In a twinkling I am bathed and dried, standing naked and perfumed in the center of the room. The maids hurry out the door with their eyes lowered.

Lady Faye paces around me. The thimble is on her finger

again. She examines me from head to toe.

I raise my chin and keep still under her critical gaze.

"You'll have to wear gloves to cover your hands," she says. I look down at my hands, and yes, they are reddened and chapped from scrubbing pots and kitchen floors and grates, and it's not something any lotion can fix. Also there's the livid scar on my wrist from the wound I don't remember getting.

She touches my shoulder with the thimble. It is bitterly cold against my skin. She drags the thimble along my collarbone as if she is measuring me, and it leaves a trail of ice behind it. I control a shiver. Then she reaches out and taps the thimble against my cheekbone, right where the bruise is worst.

"This I cannot fix," she murmurs. "Stupid woman, leaving bruises where they can be seen."

I blink.

"Your stepmother," Lady Faye explains. "Instead of striking your face, she should have had you whipped where the marks wouldn't show." She gives a delicate shrug. "But she is a crude, intemperate woman."

Her words leave me colder than the thimble's touch.

"You will have to be masked," Lady Faye decides. Her voice turns satisfied. "Yes, that will do. The Mysterious Stranger arrives late at the ball. All turn to watch her enter. It will be perfect." She paces around me again, muttering, and her measuring gaze darts up and down my body. The air tightens and tingles; the walls close in around us. All but two of the candles flicker out; shadows crouch at the edges of the room.

I find that I am gasping for breath as if I've been running. Every inch of my bare skin prickles with excitement.

"The flame, I think," Lady Faye murmurs. "Oh, you will burn brightly tonight, my dear." Her hand swoops up. In the dim room, her thimble throbs with an icy glow. Around she paces, and the cold touch of the thimble slashes across my shoulders, between my breasts, down the long length of my legs.

"Close your eyes," she hisses, and sweeps around me again. The thimble flares with a brilliant light, and I clench my eyes shut. She rests the thimble against my bruised face, pressing it against my cheekbone.

"Do not move," Lady Faye whispers, and I can hear the tension in her voice.

I take a dragging breath, and then there is no air at all in the room. My eyes pop open, but see only darkness.

All at once I am hit by a blow that strikes my entire body at once as if I am a fly trapped between two closing hands. Freezing silk slithers against my skin. I give an undignified squeak, and then the pressure goes away and I am left wavering at the center of the room, trying to find my balance.

Lady Faye is panting. With shaking hands, she lights a few candles.

As the room brightens I steady myself, then realize that I have something covering my face; I can see a mask at the edges of my vision. I look down, and I'm not naked any longer.

Moving with less grace than usual, Lady Faye goes to a corner and drags out a mirror covered with a velvet cloth; she pulls the cloth away and lets it fall to the ground.

"Look," she orders.

I step closer to see myself in the mirror.

She said *flame*, and that is what I am. The dress is deceptively simple, a plain bodice that leaves my shoulders bare and then flares into a swirling skirt. But every stitch of it is exquisite, and is fitted to the lines of my body with such perfection that I appear tall, proud, graceful.

And the color. At the hem is the faintest hint of ashy gray, but the rest is flowing silk the color of living flame. I burn against the shadowed walls of the dressing room. I turn and the skirt swirls with vermilion and gold and the brilliant crimson of glowing embers. The air shimmers around me as if with the heat of fire.

The heels of the shoes are impossibly high, but they fit so well that they make my feet forget the weariness of an endless day of work and long to dance all night. They are aflame with hints of ruby and fire opal—and the rest is as clear as glass.

Around my neck are more fire opals, each burning with its own flame. My gloves are of gray silk fastened with tiny fire-opal buttons. And I wear a mask of gray silk that covers my bruises and makes my face beautiful and mysterious at once.

I become aware that Lady Faye is standing at my shoulder regarding my reflection. She gives me a smug smile. "You are transformed, Penelope."

I have to admit that I am. It is just a dress, I tell myself. It's just jewels and gloves and well-made shoes. But it feels like more than that. It feels like power.

"You are ready," she goes on. She gives me one last approving look. "Come along. It is time to go to the ball."

CHAPTER

THE MISSUS HAS USED HER CONNECTIONS IN THE CITY TO find black trousers for Shoe and a dark gray sweater and a black knitted cap to cover his light-colored hair, all for blending into the shadows of the night. In a small pack he has candles, rope, a hooded black cloak, and the boots he made for Pin. In his pocket he has the thimble.

Three times Natters has described where he'll find the boat and reminded him to be extra careful when they get to the last part of the path where the spray from the waterfall makes the rocks particularly slippery.

"I'll be careful," Shoe promises. "You're sure you'll both be all right? You won't get into trouble for helping me?"

"We'll weather it," the Missus assures him.

"You're just a runaway servant," Natters adds. "We had

no idea what you were up to."

And finally it is time to go.

They stand in the darkened shop; Natters has his arm over the Missus's shoulder, and she leans into him. "Be careful, lad," Natters says.

"I will," Shoe says. "I'll send word somehow. I mean, if you don't hear from me, you'll know . . ."

"Best not to speak of that," Natters says gruffly.

Suddenly Shoe feels desperately sad to be leaving them, this old, lonely couple who have shown him nothing but kindness. "Thank you," he says, his voice rough, and then the Missus is pulling his head down for a kiss and Natters is giving him a hug, and they push him out of the shop into the darkened street, and he hears the lock click closed behind him.

Shoe takes a deep breath, settling himself. He has a plan for getting Pin out, and the time to start it is now.

The streets of the lower city are busier than usual at this time of night. He keeps to the side streets and the shadows, and nobody gives him any trouble.

As he approaches the upper city a thick white fog rises, and soon he is surrounded, the fog opening up before him and swirling closed behind him. There are people on the streets here, too, and he hears drunken singing and running feet, and once a shrill scream that freezes him in his tracks until it turns into a shriek of laughter. The curfew must be suspended because of the prince's ball. And everywhere is the fog. One of the arched bridges over the river is free of it, and as he crests it he looks back and has a view of the entire city laid out below him, and beyond it the depthless black that is the surrounding forest. The fog is flowing over the walls of the city, filling the streets, muffling the buildings. It smells of the wind in the pine trees and of ferns and rain; it is as if the forest has invaded the city for the night. It is a kind of promise, the fog, that Story does not see all. This is a fog for hiding and sneaking in, for two people to find their way to a boat waiting for them at the bottom of a waterfall.

Shoe reaches the other side of the bridge, plunging into the fog again, hurrying with quiet footsteps until he reaches his destination.

Earlier he'd left a message for Spanner with the teasing boy at the tavern, and he finds the ratcatcher right where he expects to, in a clump of bushes at the edge of the park across the street from the huge house where Pen is living.

"Spanner," he whispers.

"Greetings, Yer Lor'ship," he hears, and the fog swirls aside and he sees the ratcatcher's twitchy long nose and gap-toothed grin.

"Are they all gone?" Shoe asks.

"Aye, and your girl Pin is gone, too," Spanner answers.

Pin gone? He was expecting to find her here, left behind while her stepmother and stepsisters are away at the fancy ball.

"Not to worry," Spanner says, tapping his nose. "I followed.

And then I came back to tell you, right?"

He is interrupted by the first boom of the clock striking. The sound of it is so loud as it rolls out from the castle, Shoe finds his shoulders hunching. It's far louder here than in the lower city. He glances up and sees, a few streets over, the pale, broad face of the clock looming above the fog. The bells toll their number and at last the echoes fade away. Eleven o'clock. It's getting late.

Spanner is cleaning out his ear with a finger. "Noisy, that," he comments. "Right, Shoe, as I were saying. There were watchers here earlier, footmen, like, but they've gone away. Then the girl Pin came out the door with . . ." He lowers his voice. "Well, you know who. With her."

Shoe feels a shiver of worry. The wheels of Story are turning and the Godmother has Pin under her eye. He'll have to be quick and clever to get her out. But he's got the thimble and Pin's boots in his pack. His plan could still work.

"Off they go to another house," Spanner goes on. "I waits a bit to see if they'll come out again, and they do, don't they? Only your Pin is dressed as a lady as fine as can be, and they both get into a carriage the color of a pumpkin, and off they go." He points toward the castle. "To the ball."

"Pin is at the prince's ball?" Shoe repeats blankly. This was not part of the plan.

"That's what I'm saying," Spanner says.

"All right," Shoe mutters, turning over the possibilities in his mind. He could come back and try another night, but something about this night feels wound tensely tight, the gears about to click into place so the wheels can turn and bear away all before them—but not turning yet. If he waits, he knows it'll be too late.

"Yer going up there?" Spanner asks, nodding toward the castle.

"I am," Shoe says. "You should go back to the lower city." As the old ratcatcher turns away, Shoe grabs his shoulder. "And be careful. Tell *them that knows* to keep their heads down. It could be bad."

"Be careful yourself, Shoe," Spanner says with a nod, and disappears into the fog.

CHAPTER

22

AT THE STROKE OF ELEVEN, I ENTER THE BALLROOM. IT IS an immense, high-ceilinged room lit brilliantly with hundreds of candles that are reflected a thousand times in mirrors with gilded frames. At one end of the room is a row of glass doors leading out to a stone terrace; at the other is a small orchestra on a dais. As the clock strikes, the loud tones filling every crack and corner of the room, the music pauses and the dancers whirl to a stop. The men are dressed in black or gray or very dark blue; the women are in every shade of fashionable blue, with here and there a daring green or a vibrant purple.

In the carriage, Lady Faye gave me a wrap to wear into the ballroom. It is made of the lightest silver-gray material and surrounds me from head to toe like a swirl of smoke. I pause in the wide doorway, the Mysterious Stranger, while everyone in the ballroom stares at me. The bells toll nine, ten, eleven, and Lady Faye plucks away the wrap. I hear gasps as the other guests see me and the last echoes of the bells fade.

I have to admit that it's a wonderful moment.

"You have a keen sense of the dramatic entrance," I whisper over my shoulder to Lady Faye.

"You will enjoy yourself tonight, Penelope," she says, and it sounds a little like an order. "Especially after I introduce you to the prince."

The one I really want to look for is my tea shop man, but I suppose the prince will do for now.

The music has started up again, but the dancing couples watch us as we parade along the edge of the ballroom to a knot of people clustered around one tall young man.

It's him. Tall, black-haired, with brilliantly blue eyes. He is all in black with a red sash and some sort of gold circlet on his head. My breath comes quick. He sees me at the same moment and frowns, maybe feeling the same pull toward me that I feel toward him.

As Lady Faye and I reach him, the crowd melts away. To my astonishment, Lady Faye bends into a graceful curtsy. "Your Highness," she says, and straightens.

"*Highness?*" I whisper. The circlet he's wearing is a *crown*. "He's the prince?" Lady Faye nudges me, and I add my own much less graceful curtsy.

"Your Highness, may I present my goddaughter?" Lady Faye takes my hand and leads me closer. "Tonight she is incognito; you may call her Lady Ash."

Behind my mask, I roll my eyes.

Catching me at it, the prince—my tea shop man—raises his eyebrows.

"Goddaughter," Lady Faye goes on, putting my hand into his, "this is Prince Cornelius."

I press my lips together to keep from laughing. *Cornelius.* What an unfortunate name.

The prince does the expected, polite thing. "Lady Ash, would you honor me with a dance?" he asks, and gives my hand the faintest squeeze.

I nod in a way that I hope looks mysteriously enigmatic. Or maybe enigmatically mysterious.

He leads me out onto the dance floor, and the other dancers make space for us. He whirls me around. I don't remember learning to dance, but my feet and body know exactly what to do.

"I suppose it was inevitable," I say to him.

At the sound of my voice, he stumbles ever so slightly, and then his hand is steady at the small of my back again. His blue eyes go serious as he examines my face, what he can see of it behind the mask. "Is it really you?" he asks.

"I am most definitely me," I answer, and I flash him a quick grin. Suddenly I'm filled with fizzing excitement just to be here in this glorious ballroom instead of getting the kitchen hearth all wet with tears. Lady Faye was right—I am going to have a wonderful time tonight.

The corner of his mouth quirks up with his easy smile. "I think I may have met you before, Lady Ash," he says in his velvet voice.

"I've met you too," I answer. "What did you do with my potatoes?"

"Your—?" And then he laughs. "Oh, those. I hope you didn't get into trouble for that."

"I was sent to bed without my supper," I say.

He laughs as if I have told a joke and whirls us into a spin.

"I really was," I tell him as my skirt wraps around my legs and flares out again.

His beautiful mouth stops smiling. "I'm sorry." He slows us. The music has slowed, too, and we are closer now, my hip against his, my gloved hand resting on his broad shoulder.

"It's not your fault," I say. "And I'd had lovely pastries to eat, so I didn't miss my dinner too much."

The other dancers stare; I have a feeling he's paying too much attention to me, that one dance is polite and two dances is interest, and why is Prince Cornelius smiling so warmly at this mysteriously masked woman?

"You're even prettier," he says, "when you're not covered with cinders."

"I sleep in the hearth," I admit. "Also, I am not pretty." Both things are perfectly true.

"No, you're not pretty," he agrees. "You're beautiful."

I roll my eyes. "Surely you can do better than that."

He whirls me around again, then bends to whisper into my ear. "You're not making this easy."

"It's not supposed to be easy," I whisper back.

He smiles down at me. "With most girls it is. Instantaneous, even."

I shrug. "I suppose it is easy for someone like you. But you'll find it difficult to charm me with just that smile of yours. I want more."

He is silent for a few moments. The music of the waltz wafts around us. When he speaks again, his voice has changed, as if he's speaking half to himself and half to me. "You're right, I think." He gazes down at me. "It shouldn't be easy, or instant. It should be more than that." For just a moment, as I look up into his eyes, there in the midst of the ballroom, it is as if I can see past the smiling, handsome surface of him, and I'm almost surprised to glimpse a real person there, a young man not so much older than I am, who is, perhaps, not as sure of himself and his charm as he seems to be.

He blinks. "You're a very strange girl."

Oh, if he only knew. I nod.

And then he smiles, and he has put the princely mask on again. I suppose he's more comfortable wearing it. "I would like to see you again after tonight."

Instead of answering, I give him the smile of enigmatic mystery.

"Will you tell me your name?" he asks.

"I'd rather hear about your name," I say. "Cornelius." I say it again, drawing out the syllables. *"Cor-neeeeel-yus."*

"I know, it's terrible, isn't it? I'm named after my great-uncle." He bends closer, and lowers his voice, and it is like chocolate again, warm and smooth. "My friends call me Cor."

I look up at him. "What should I call you?"

"I think you should never call me Cornelius," he answers. He smiles. "Tell me your name."

Suddenly the ballroom is too hot and crowded, and I can feel the wheels turning again, pulling me along somewhere faster than I want to go. "I—I'll tell you later," I say breathlessly, trying to resist. As we spin, I catch a glimpse of the glass doors leading out to the terrace. "At midnight. Meet me outside at midnight, all right?"

He agrees. The terrace. Midnight.

CHAPTER

23

SHOE IS GLAD OF HIS DARK CLOTHING AS HE PADS UP THE streets to the castle and finds an unguarded delivery entrance that leads to a storeroom. Through that he discovers some narrow stairs that take him to a passageway which connects the servants' quarters to the public rooms of the castle. Most of those rooms are empty and dark; the servants are all either in the kitchens or helping with the ball. He feels as if he's backstage at a theater, skulking around in the dark margins while real life is happening under the lights in front of a rapt audience.

Maybe that's what the castle is: a stage, where the most important parts of Story are meant to play out.

He is a shadow as he slips closer to the ballroom, following the sounds of distant music and tinkling laughter. As he is crossing what looks like a drawing room, lit only by a lamp turned low, a servant wearing the prince's red livery and a white wig comes in another door. Shoe freezes; his heart pounds; he is caught. He knows he looks like a thief, dressed in dark colors with a pack on his back. But the servant's gaze passes over him as if he doesn't exist; the man picks up the lamp, then turns and carries it out the door.

Shoe stands frozen in the middle of the dark room. The servant had looked right at him. "That was a strange piece of luck," Shoe whispers to himself, and goes on.

Quietly he sneaks from room to room until he goes into a library and finds a door half hidden behind a heavy velvet curtain. He puts his ear to the door. On the other side is the sound of music and talking. Crouching, he reaches up to slowly turn the knob and crack the door open. The sounds grow louder; he smells flowers and perfume and the faintest tinge of sweat. He peers out. At first a woman's wide skirt is blocking his view, but after a minute or two she shifts to the side, and he can see the entire ballroom. He blinks at the brightness.

He sees Pin immediately. All the others are burned-out cinders, but she is a flame. She is wearing a mask and dancing with a tall young man with curly black hair. Shoe ignores him; he can see only Pin. The air practically shimmers around her; she is all quick energy and joy, and he sees the flash of her wicked grin.

Seeing her again makes his heart lift the same way it

always does when he sees her. He feels a stab of despair, too. She is entangled so tightly in Story, and it is late, very late. How can he possibly get her out of it? She looks happy, twirling around on the dance floor with her young man. What if she doesn't want to escape?

No, he knows Pin. She is so uniquely herself—she can't live according to the mechanical will of Story.

"Well, this is an unexpected twist," comes a cold, clear voice from behind him. A light flares, a lamp being lit.

He whirls, still crouching, his heart pounding, ready to flee.

It's her. A spasm of fright seizes his whole body; he knows what a rabbit must feel like when staring into the jaws of a wolf.

The Godmother is dressed all in icy blue. The last time he saw her was when he went to the post. She was wearing blue that day, too.

She glides closer, reaches past him, and closes the door that was opened onto the ballroom. The room falls silent.

"It's the young Shoemaker, isn't it?" the Godmother asks. She reaches down with a pale, long-fingered hand, pulls the knitted cap off his head, and tosses it aside. "Yes, it is. How very interesting to find you here. I think one of my Huntsmen has some explaining to do."

He's trapped. He could try escaping through the door behind him and into the ballroom, but he knows he won't get far going that way dressed as a thief. But he's not going to cower on his knees, either. He grits his teeth, gets a grip on his fear, and climbs to his feet.

The Godmother is regarding him with a sharp smile lurking at the corners of her mouth. She taps her teeth with her fingernail. No, with a thimble. He remembers Pin's thimble and stops himself from reaching into his pocket to be sure it's still there.

"What *are* you doing here, Shoemaker?" she asks.

"I'm here for Pin," he answers, trying to keep his voice steady.

"Mm. I think you're not here at all," she says. "You are not part of this. I advise you to scurry away at once or something nasty might happen to you."

He shakes his head, stubborn. "I'm not leaving unless Pin comes with me."

Tap-tap, thimble against teeth. "Did you know that there's a post here in the city? It's in the marketplace. I don't have to use it very often, but it makes an excellent deterrent to crime and other such things." *Tap-tap*. "I'd hate to see you at the post again, Shoemaker. I'm not sure you'd survive it a second time."

"It's a risk I'm willing to take," he says unsteadily.

"Oh, I'm sure." She gives a low laugh. "So pale. Are you frightened?"

He had been, but suddenly he has become furious. "No," he bites out. "I'm going to stop you. I'm going to stop Story from turning."

She laughs again, the tinkling sound of breaking icicles. "What are you going to do, boy? Heroically make shoes? No, there is nothing you can do to stop this. In fact, the ending of your sordid little story is approaching rather quickly."

He tenses as she steps closer. She raises her thimbled finger, brings her hand close to his face, and brushes aside a lock of his ragged hair. His heart is slamming in his chest and his every nerve is trembling with the urge to flee. He tries to take a step back, but he is frozen in place. She touches his forehead with the thimble; it flares with icy cold.

The *thimble*, he realizes in a terrified flash. It's how she takes away memories, how she forces people to do her bidding. She's going to make him forget Pin.

Then the Godmother gives an edged smile and draws back her hand. "Wait," she says softly, and cocks her head as if something has just occurred to her. "I believe I can come up with a better twist than that. Yes, I think so. It will be entertaining, and it will all lead to the same thing in the end." Briskly pulling the thimble from her finger, she nods at the door. "Penelope will be meeting the prince on the terrace at midnight. You will find her there very soon, alone, waiting for him." She steps aside, giving him a clear path out of the room.

Released from her spell, he's taken two quick steps toward the door before his brain catches up to what she's said. "Why are you telling me this?"

"I want you to see how little you matter, you silly boy.

Penelope has absolutely no memory of you. She will never choose you. She is meant for other, bigger things, not a nameless, pastless Shoemaker. There is nothing you can do to change what will happen here tonight. You can try. But you will fail." Her smile sharpens. "And you know what is waiting for you when you do."

The post.

And the wheels of Story, grinding toward its inevitable ending. He can't stop them from turning, he will only be crushed. In that grim thought he glimpses a fleeting truth. "You're just as caught up in it as the rest of us," he realizes.

The Godmother flinches, just the faintest flicker of a flinch, but he sees it.

Then she is all coldly controlled fury, her smile the glint and slash of a blade. "Very soon you will die a bloody and bitter death, Shoemaker," she hisses. "And as you die, you will understand that your life was such a tiny thing that no one will even notice you are gone." She turns on her heel and sweeps from the room, leaving Shoe in the darkness.

CHAPTER

24

THE DANCE ENDS AND MY TEA SHOP MAN TAKES MY HAND.
"I will return you to your godmother now, Lady Ash," he says
formally.

"Thank you, Prince Cornelius," I say. I see him wince
just a little as I say his name.

As the prince and I leave the dance floor, Lady Faye is
returning to the ballroom from a hallway. She seems flustered, if such a thing is possible, her ice-blue eyes burning
with something that looks like fury. Seeing me approaching
with the prince, she puts on a glittering smile. "You enjoyed
the dance, Lady Ash?" she asks me.

"Oh, immensely," I answer. "He didn't step on my toes
even once."

The prince gives me his charming smile. "If only I were

half as graceful as my partner."

At that, I see Lady Faye give a little nod as if the prince's courtly words have reassured her.

The prince bows. "Enjoy the rest of your evening, Lady Ash." As he raises his head, he whispers, "Until midnight."

I swallow down the flutter in my stomach and nod. He bows once more to Lady Faye and rejoins the cluster of his friends and courtiers while Lady Faye takes my arm and leads me away. "You made quite an impression," she says, a smug tone in her voice.

"So did he," I answer.

And then we are standing before my stepmother, who is resplendent in blue and flanked by blondly brilliant Dulcet and midnight dark Precious.

"Lady Faye," Stepmama fawns. "And your mysterious and lovely companion. Three dances with the prince! It will give us something to talk about for weeks." She gives me an ingratiating nod. "Manners, girls," she hisses through a fixed smile, and my stepsisters sweep into graceful curtsies, though I can see the jealousy rising off them in waves.

"This is my goddaughter," Lady Faye begins. She's about to introduce me again as Lady Ash.

"Hello Precious," I interrupt. "Dulcie. Your hair is coming down in the back." I give them my brightest smile.

They recognize my voice at once. Their eyes go wide and their mouths drop open; Stepmama's face turns bright red. "*Penelope?*" she hisses.

It is almost as wonderful a moment as my grand entrance.

Lady Faye steps back, as if to watch the fun.

"So pleasant to see you this evening," I say, and give them a wink from behind my mask.

Stepmama's face has pale blotches on it now, and all of her teeth are bared in a smile. Her bosom swells, and I see her hand clench into a fist—but she is in a ballroom, and she doesn't forget herself. "May I speak to you for a moment, Lady Faye?" she asks in a choked voice. Lady Faye gives a graceful nod, and they step away from my stepsisters and me.

Precious is staring at my dress. "That is the most gorgeous thing I've ever seen," she breathes.

"Isn't it nice?" I turn my hips, making the skirt swirl around my ankles. "It fits perfectly."

"I would kill for a dress like that," she says, and this time I know she means it.

"The fashion won't be blue anymore, will it, Precious?" Dulcet asks.

Precious looks me up and down again. "No," she says shortly. "Embers."

Dulcet gives a little sigh. "I look terrible in orange."

I can't help but laugh at that. Poor Dulcie! Maybe it's the thrill of the evening, but suddenly I like everybody in the room, even them. I reach out to pat her gloved hand, and she and Precious smile tentatively back at me. It's a quick, unexpected moment of sisterly kinship. Then I decide to show them how comfortable I am moving in such an exalted social circle. I survey the ballroom. "I expected to see my friends Lord and Lady Meister here this evening."

Precious stares. "Who?"

"Lord and Lady Meister," I repeat.

Dulcet steps closer and grips my arm. She casts a nervous glance at Stepmama and Lady Faye, who are deep in conversation. "Do not say those names," she whispers.

"What?" I say blankly. "Why ever not?"

Precious steps closer. "She hasn't heard, Dulcie, it's obvious."

"Shh, I'll tell you," Dulcet says, and we put our heads together to hear Dulcie's whispers over the music and talking. "Lady Meister is dead, Pen," she says. I can see her gloved hands twisting nervously together. "She fell from a balcony and died."

"It was an accident," Precious adds.

A horrible sinking feeling settles in my stomach. Fell from a balcony? "No," I say slowly, seeing again Lady Meister's fixed smile and hearing her desperate pleas: *kill me, please kill me.* "She didn't fall. She jumped."

Dulcet and Precious stare at me in shock, and I sense the outline of some grim secret, something always present yet never spoken of. Suddenly the ballroom seems gaudy and overbright and thick with the stench of heavy perfume and sweat; the laughter is too shrill and the music too loud. I feel certain that I shouldn't be here; I don't belong here; I have to leave. I am looking frantically for a doorway—for an escape—when I feel a cool draft, and Lady Faye is at my shoulder.

"My dear Penelope, it is nearly midnight," she says. "Don't you have someplace you're supposed to be?" She touches my shoulder, and I see the glitter of her thimble on her finger. It strokes icy cold against my skin.

I catch my breath and feel the pull of something huge and inevitable.

Yes.

Midnight.

I don't want to be late.

WHEN I GO OUT TO THE TERRACE IT IS NOT YET TIME FOR my meeting with the prince, and I am glad of it, for I need some fresh air to clear my head. I close the glass doors behind me, shutting away the sound of the ball and the heavy scent of sweat barely covered by perfume. My stepsisters had said something upsetting, hadn't they? I rub my temples. Nothing. It was nothing. The evening has been a whirl of fizzing excitement, but as midnight approaches I feel wound tighter and tighter, as if something awful is about to happen, even though I know it's more likely to be something wonderful.

The terrace is a wide stretch of smooth stone with two steps at its edge leading down into a garden. I pace across the stones to the steps and look out. I untie the mask and take it off, letting it fall to the stones; there's no point in disguise anymore. The chilly air feels good against my bare face. Tendrils of fog twist along the garden path, but above, the sky is crystalline. The huge clock face in the castle's central tower looms at my back like a full moon. Its hands have almost come together, pointing straight up. Just a minute or two and it will be midnight.

There is a rustling in the bushes, and a shadowy shape steps onto the path. For a moment I think it might be Prince Cornelius, but as the shape steps closer I see that it is the shoemaker's servant. He is dressed all in stealthy black and gray, but his fair hair gives him away. He looks up at me, two steps above him.

"You again," I say.

"Yes, it's me," he answers.

"What do you want, thimble thief?"

He takes a shaky breath and I realize that he's wound even more tightly than I am. "I know you don't remember any of it, Pin, but can't you feel the wheels turning? You're caught in Story, and it's going to pull you into a terrible ending."

I blink. I have felt the wheels, and I do feel the pull. But somehow it doesn't seem to matter. I feel as if I'm standing beside myself, separate from what is happening. "It's not so terrible," I find myself telling him. "If it happens the way it's supposed to, I get to marry the prince, and I like him well enough. That is what I want."

"No you don't," he says.

"Oh really," I say. "What do I want, then? You?" Despite myself I can't help but think of the feel of his lips against mine in the bare moment we had in the hallway before Stepmama caught us. I suppose it's because his is the only kiss I can remember.

"You probably don't want me," he says steadily. "You don't have to want anybody, and if you did you should at least get to choose. I know you, Pin—" He opens his mouth to go on when I hear the gears in the enormous castle clock turn and a heavy clicking of the hands into place. The first strike of midnight rolls out with a heavy *boom* that makes the ground tremble under my feet.

At the sound, I click into place, too. I know exactly what I am going to say.

Shoe goes as pale as chalk. "Pin—" he starts again.

"My name is Penelope," I remind him. "You don't know me at all, and I certainly don't know you."

Boom comes the second strike.

Shoe comes closer so he's just one step below me; before I can pull away, he grabs my wrist. As the third *boom* rings out, he reaches out and roughly strips the glove from my hand; fire-opal buttons pop off and go rattling away over the veranda stones. I try to jerk my hand back, but he holds it tightly.

A fourth ringing *boom* rolls out from the clock over our heads.

He turns my hand and runs shaking fingers over the livid

scar on the inside of my wrist. "I know how you got this," he says, his voice urgent. "We were escaping—"

A fifth *boom* drowns him out.

"—from the Godmother's fortress," he goes on. "You were climbing the wall and thorns slashed your wrist. It's how the trackers were able to follow us."

"I don't believe you," I say, and try to jerk away again. I don't like this story he's telling me. "It didn't happen."

"Pin," he says, "we almost escaped once; we can try again."

The sixth *boom*, and he flinches, but he still doesn't let me go. I am trembling now, my heart pounding. He's wearing a pack, I realize. He's ready to escape, and he wants me to go now. "No," I say.

Relentless, the clock strikes again. Seven.

"We're almost out of time," he says desperately.

"No!" I insist, and jerk away from him.

He releases my hand and I stumble backward, trip over the step, and land sprawling on the terrace.

Boom comes the eighth strike.

I sit up, the skirt of my dress billowing around me.

A slim shadow, Shoe is quick to leap the last step to crouch beside me. He touches the flaming silk. "Where did you get this?" he asks.

The question shakes me; it is so unexpected. "What?"

The clock strikes again—*boom*. Nine.

Shoe's face is intent. "Where did you get the dress? No

seamstress in the city could stitch a dress like this, Pin. *Who made this dress?"*

"It was a gift—" I begin, but I am interrupted by the roaring *boom* of the tenth strike. "From Lady Faye," I finish, as the echoes ring around us.

"The Godmother," he corrects. "You're wearing a dress made by the Godmother's seamstresses," he says. "That's irony for you, Pin."

"What?" I say.

"Never mind." He shakes his head. "Please come with me. This is the only chance we'll have." His voice turns ragged. "I won't be able to ask again."

The eleventh strike. *Boom.*

Shaking off Shoe's help, I climb to my feet, brushing a lock of hair out of my eyes, arranging my skirts. He waits, pale down to his lips.

"No," I say.

Shoe flinches as if I've hit him.

The clock strikes twelve. The triumphant sound rolls over us and out over the city. I find myself trembling, as if the ground is moving under my feet.

Shoe steadies me and then he takes my hand; no, he puts something into my palm that feels small and round, like an acorn, and closes my fingers around it. He bends to kiss my clenched fist. Then he steps back and slips away.

My ears ring in the sudden silence.

CHAPTER
26

From the shadows, Shoe watches as Pin looks down and sees that he's given her the thimble. She holds it up, inspecting it.

He knows he should run, to try to get away before the Godmother has him captured and taken to the post for his bitter ending, but he has to see what happens next.

He gives a wry shake of his head. That was part of Story's power, wasn't it? People always wanted to find out what happens next.

But Pin's got the thimble, and the thimble holds some kind of magic. Maybe she can use its power to resist the pull of Story.

The glass door leading out to the wide stone area cracks open. "Lady Ash?" calls a low voice.

Pin's head jerks up. With a frown, she clenches the thimble in her bare hand.

The tall man she was dancing with before crosses the stones to her. The prince, Shoe assumes. "You've lost your glove," he says to her, and takes her fist in his hand.

She shivers at the touch. But she holds on to the thimble.

Shoe steps closer, out of the darkness.

Neither the prince nor Pin notices; it's as if they are caught up in an inevitable scene, intent on acting their parts in service to Story. The thimble is not working, he thinks, with a cold shiver.

"Are you going to tell me your name now?" the prince asks.

When Pin speaks, her voice is uncharacteristically hesitant. "Ye-es. Um. No. What is happening here, exactly?"

The prince shakes his head, looking suddenly less sure of himself. "I think, perhaps, I am falling in love with you."

Shoe is close enough to them now that he could reach out and touch Pin's bare shoulder. "No you're not," he whispers. It's Story at work, not true love.

The prince looks up, straight at Shoe, but his face doesn't change; he doesn't even see him there not two paces away; he doesn't hear Shoe's words. It's just like the servant in the drawing room, Shoe realizes. Story is forcing things onward, and the Godmother was right—he doesn't have a part to play. He has no more substance here than a shadow and can only watch as the scene unfolds. He feels a sharp stab of despair.

The prince strokes Pin's hand and murmurs, "May I kiss you?"

She gazes up at him, her face quizzical. "I suppose so," she says, and tips her head back. Her lips part.

The prince puts his hands on Pin's bare shoulders, brings his face down to hers, and kisses her.

"Well, that's it," Shoe mutters to himself. "It's all over after this."

Pin reaches up and twines her arms around the prince's neck, deepening the kiss, as if she's seeking something. Then she turns her face away. "No," she says with a puzzled frown. "That wasn't the same at all." The prince, his eyes closed, bends his head to place gentle kisses down her neck.

"The thimble," Shoe whispers, the merest breath of a reminder.

She doesn't look at him when he speaks. But raising her clenched fist—at last—she takes the thimble and slips it onto her finger. She blinks and shakes her head.

She looks over the prince's shoulder, straight at Shoe, as if realizing he's still here. "This is entirely your fault," she whispers.

What? He stares.

"You shouldn't have kissed me."

Their kiss in the hallway, she means. "You kissed me back, Pin," he reminds her.

She gives a huff of irritation and pulls away from the prince. "Let me go," she tells him. But his hands hold her shoulders, keeping her close to him. Suddenly she wrenches herself out of his grip, and as she steps back, the heel of her shoe catches in her hem. There is a tearing sound. "Oh, bother this dress," Pin says, and stumbles.

"Lady," the prince says, stepping after her. "Tell me your name."

She jerks away from him. "No—" she blurts. "I have to go." She looks past the prince, shooting Shoe a special glare. "I have to, um, be home by midnight. I'm late." The torn edge of her skirt tangles around her legs and the shoe twists off of her left foot. "Oh, curse it." Hopping, she yanks her dress up to her knees. "Don't follow me, either one of you." She jumps the two steps down and into the garden and flees, hop-stepping on one shoe and one stocking-clad foot. The fog closes around her and she is gone, leaving one jeweled high-heeled shoe on the stones behind her.

"Either one?" the prince says aloud, blinking and shaking his head as if waking up after a long sleep. He turns and sees Shoe. "Where did you come from?" His eyes widen as he takes in Shoe's dark clothes and pack. "Thief!"

"No, wait," Shoe says, backing away.

"Guards!" the prince shouts. In response, the glass doors leading to the ballroom crash open. Four castle guards in red uniforms burst outside. "Catch him!" the prince orders, and points.

Shoe makes it three steps into the garden before two of the guards bring him down hard on the gravel path. He struggles against their grip, but iron-hard hands drag him to his feet and wrench his arms behind his back. He catches a glimpse of the prince bending to pick up Pin's lost shoe.

"To the prison, Your Highness?" one of the guards asks him.

"No!" Shoe twists, and a guard elbows him hard in the stomach. He gasps for breath, but keeps struggling. From there it'll be straight to the post and the bloody, lonely death the Godmother has planned for him.

The prince is examining Pin's shoe. He glances aside at the guards. "Yes, of course the prison," he says, and turns to go back into the castle.

"No—wait," Shoe says, and desperation wrenches the next words out of him. "I know her name!" The moment he says it, he regrets it.

The prince freezes. "What?" He turns. "Hold," he says to the guards, and paces toward Shoe.

He swallows down his fear and goes still in the guards' iron grip. The prince is taller than he is, so Shoe has to tip his head back to meet his eyes. "I know who she is," he says.

"What is her name?" the prince asks. He rests his hand on Shoe's neck where it meets his shoulder and gives a threatening squeeze. "Tell me now."

From the corner of his eye, Shoe glimpses a figure in blue at the ballroom doors. He shakes his head. "Not here."

The figure steps outside, her skirts swirling. The Godmother.

Shoe lowers his head. "I'll tell you everything," he promises, knowing himself for a coward, hating the feel of the words in his mouth. "Just don't let her have me."

A frown creases the prince's forehead. "What?"

"Did she leave her shoe behind?" the Godmother asks as she approaches.

At the sound of her voice, Shoe shudders. "*Please*," he grates out, and then she is there.

"Ah, I see she did. And you've got it. Well done!" The Godmother bestows a smile on the prince, who nods. She turns her ice-cold eyes on Shoe, and he reads triumph there. "And I see you've caught a thief, as well." She reaches out to tap Shoe's cheek with a finger as cold as marble; he flinches away from her touch. "Let me have him, will you, Your Highness?" she asks. "I think he needs to be made an example of."

The prince frowns.

Shoe closes his eyes. It's all over; he's as good as dead.

"Lady Faye, I thank you for your offer of assistance," the prince says politely. "But I don't wish to trouble you. I will deal with this."

Shoe's eyes pop open. The Godmother is staring at him with icy hatred.

"Guardsman, if you would be sure Lady Faye returns safely to the ballroom?" the prince says. One of the guards bows and holds out his arm to the Godmother.

Her nostrils flare and then, ignoring the guard, she whirls and stalks back into the castle.

The guards haven't let Shoe's arms go; he's not out of this yet.

"Talk," the prince orders.

Shoe shakes his head. "Not here, I told you. Someplace quiet."

One of the guards cuffs him on the side of the head. "You refer to your prince as 'Your Highness,' boy."

"Someplace with no guards, *Your Highness*," Shoe adds, shaking off the blow.

A hint of a smile lights the prince's eyes. "Yes, all right," he agrees. He is still holding Pin's shoe; he taps it absently against his leg. He addresses the guards holding Shoe. "I have to be present until the ball ends. Take him to my chambers and stand guard outside the door until I get there."

"Yes, Your Highness," the guards holding Shoe say.

The prince goes back to the ball.

Shoe goes to stew for a few hours in the juices of his own self-loathing.

As ordered, the guards lock Shoe into the prince's chambers.

It is a surprisingly nonprincely room, at least as Shoe thinks of princes. It is huge and cavernous, but there is no gilding in sight, no velvets or silks, just a massive four-poster bed made of some dark and heavy wood and hung with ancient-looking embroidered cloth. There are comfortable chairs and a low table stacked with books with scraps of paper left in them to mark where the prince has left off reading. The prince must be a sporting man as well as a scholarly one, because there are a pair of gaiters hung by the fire to dry and two long-eared hunting dogs by the hearth. Both dogs come to Shoe as he's shoved into the room, their tails wagging.

He pets them absently. For a while he paces, working off the energy of his abandoned flight and the confrontation with the Godmother, and enumerating to himself his many faults and failures, starting with cowardice and including stupidity and blindness, not to mention cowardly blind stupidity. He can't help think of Pin, too. The dress, yes, but even more the curve of her breasts, her quick, graceful movements. The silken skin of her shoulders. He'd longed to run his hands over that silk, and trace the line of her collarbone with his fingers, and kiss his way up her neck . . .

"Stop it," he mutters roughly to himself. It wasn't fair to her—she didn't even know him anymore.

He paces some more, until a wave of exhaustion knocks him over and he takes off the pack and sprawls on one of the comfortable chairs.

When the prince comes in, he can barely muster the energy to sit up.

"Stay there," the prince orders. The dogs wag over to him, and he greets them and sends them back to their bed on the hearth. He sighs and takes the golden circlet off his head and tosses it into a drawer in a massive wardrobe that takes up one full wall of the room.

Then he pulls off his boots—well made, Shoe notes, though he could do better—and tosses them into the wardrobe too, and unbuttons the top of his tunic. In his socks, he comes to stand before Shoe's chair.

"Thank you," Shoe says, getting wearily to his feet.

The prince raises his eyebrows.

"For not letting her have me," Shoe explains.

"I didn't do it for you," the prince says briefly. "I don't like the post."

"I don't either," Shoe agrees wholeheartedly. "Why don't you have it taken down?"

The prince rubs his forehead as if it aches. "I—I don't know." Then he frowns at Shoe. "Who are you?"

"I'm a shoemaker. My name is Shoe."

"A shoemaker. Named . . . Shoe," the prince repeats slowly, and shakes his head. "What exactly is going on, Shoe? And no more delays or deals. Just the truth." He looks tired, but there is steel in his voice.

Shoe can tell from the room that the prince is no idiot and has figured out that this is not just about him and Pin. "How much of it do you want to know?" he asks.

"From the beginning." The prince goes to lean against the mantel by the hearth. "Speak," he orders.

Shoe sits and puts his elbows on his knees. "Pin and I—"

"Pin is her name?" the prince interrupts.

"Yes," Shoe answers. "Well, no. Not really. We were slaves in the Godmother's fortress. You know her as Lady Faye," he adds. The prince raises his eyebrows, and Shoe goes on. "Pin was a Seamstress and I was the Shoemaker."

He tells the whole story, describing the fortress and the slaves, and his escape with Pin over the wall and into the forest, and her thimble—skipping the part about their kiss. Then he goes on to explain about Pin's capture by the Godmother and his by the Huntsman—not mentioning the Huntsman's rebels hiding in the forest—and his journey to the city and attempts to find Pin and help her escape. "She doesn't remember any of it," Shoe says bleakly. "The Godmother took it all away." Then he tells about Pin's role in Story, about her awful stepmother and stepsisters and how he'd gone with Natters to get into the house—skipping the part about the second kiss—and how he'd come to the castle to ask Pin to leave the city with him.

"You're in love with Pin," the prince observes.

Shoe's voice is hoarse from the telling. "Yes," he says shortly.

"But she doesn't remember you. And I seem to be falling in love with her myself." The prince half smiles, as if thinking of Pin. "She is quite extraordinary, isn't she? She sees right inside you. What is her name now?"

"Penelope," Shoe says, giving it all away. After all this, he feels certain the prince isn't going to hand him over to the Godmother, not if he can help it. "Lady Penelope. She lives in a house two streets away from here. That's probably where she's gone."

"Thank you," the prince says.

Shoe puts his head in his hands. "I shouldn't have told you," he confesses. "It's the worst kind of betrayal of her. I did it because I'm afraid of the post."

"You've experienced it before?" the prince asks. "At the fortress you told me about?"

Shoe can't find the words. He nods.

"Don't blame yourself too much," the prince says morosely. "I behaved just as badly."

Shoe looks up. Standing there in his socks, without his crown and without his mask of formal nobility in place, the prince looks like a much more ordinary person, one who might make the same mistakes as a shoemaker.

"I tried to charm her when I should have been getting to know her better," the prince explains. He looks down at his hands, and Shoe realizes that the prince isn't that much older than he himself seems to be, maybe twenty or twenty-one. "Trying to force her to stay. She ran away from me."

"From me too," Shoe puts in.

The prince gives a wry smile. "Yes, from both of us." He moves from the mantel and settles into one of the other comfortable chairs. One of the dogs comes over and puts its head on his knee, and he strokes its long ears. "Now, tell me about Story," he orders.

Shoe tells him what he knows, how the workers in the Godmother's fortress are slaves to Story, and then what Natters and the Missus told him about the relentless turn of the gears and wheels of Story, how it is impossible to escape, that they are all about to be ground up and reshaped and forced into an ending that none of them—except the Godmother—wants.

The prince nods and rubs his forehead again. "Yes," he says, as if approving of Shoe's recitation. "It's not anything I could put my finger on, but I have long suspected that something in this city was not right."

Shoe knows the prince isn't going to like this next bit. "You're caught up in it too," he explains. "You're meant to be Pin's ending. But Story hasn't given her any choice about it, or you either. It wants to force you together."

When he stops speaking, the prince gets up and crosses to another table, where he pours something into a cup and brings it to Shoe.

Shoe takes a sip. It's wine, which he doesn't remember ever tasting before. It is rich and heavy on his tongue, and it soothes his raw throat as he swallows it down.

The prince has poured his own cup and settles in his chair again. "You've admitted that Penelope doesn't love you." His finger rubs the side of the glass. "And you presume that I don't really love her either, that all I feel for her is due to us being caught up in Story."

Shoe feels a flush prickle on his cheeks. "It probably is," he says stubbornly.

So far the prince has been surprisingly open. But now the walls go up. "Maybe it is," he says with some coldness. "And maybe it isn't."

They immediately fall silent. Shoe drinks more wine and begins to feel sleep creeping over him.

On the other chair, the prince eyes him closely, and pronounces, "You'll take me to Penelope in the morning."

Shoe considers the possibility of saying no. He doesn't really have much choice. "All right," he agrees. "I will. But we can't tell her what to do. She must decide for herself."

CHAPTER

27

THE PRINCE'S BALL HAS CHANGED EVERYTHING.

In the morning I wake up in my stepmama's house—my house—in one of the many guest bedrooms on the second floor. I claimed the room last night when I came home all flustered from the ball. I didn't see my stepmother or stepsisters, I simply found the room, took off my ragged ball dress, climbed into the chilly bed, and went to sleep with the thimble under my pillow. I didn't want to think about the clock striking or how handsome Prince Cornelius had looked in the dim light of the terrace or how his kiss hadn't been quite the same as . . .

Well, as the only other kiss I can remember.

I reach under my pillow and pull out the thimble. It is the only thing I *do* remember clearly. It is simple, silver, entwined with roses and brambles, without a fleck of tarnish. It feels heavier than it should, as if it's more solid than anything in this city. It's a rock of security in the midst of a roaring river. I fold my fingers around it.

Shoe had it.

I'm not sure what to think about him.

As the castle clock struck midnight, he'd told me . . .

. . . things I didn't want to believe.

I turn my wrist, examining the scar there. It is jagged, pale; it looks as if I might have been stabbed by a thorn, as he said.

If I am this Pin—if I *was* this Pin, before—maybe that explains all the holes in my memory. But who was I before that? Who am I now? The questions threaten to sweep me away. Darkness edges my vision; nothingness looms behind me.

"It's all right," I tell myself in a trembling whisper. "It'll be all right." My voice sounds tiny and frightened. The Nothing threatens to overwhelm me.

I wrap both hands around the thimble, and hold on.

The thimble is heavy and solid, and the room becomes real around me again. Its walls are painted blue. The coverlet on the bed is edged with lace. There's a fire in the hearth— this is an excellent sign; it means the servants have been told I am here. It means Stepmama knows I'm here and hasn't had me dragged in disgrace up to my attic prison. I take a deep breath, steadying myself. I expect they don't know what to do with me.

I push back the covers and climb out of the bed and see an even better sign. While I was sleeping, a maid has brought me something to wear. They've unpacked a box of my clothes from the attic, because there is a clean black silk dress and underclothes and stockings. But there are no shoes. I left my other toe-pinching ones at Lady Faye's house last night, I remember.

Lukewarm water is in a bowl, and there's a fresh towel, so I have a quick wash and put on the dress and stockings and put the thimble into my pocket. The dress doesn't fit me quite properly. I'm thinner than I used to be thanks to the usual punishments. A good breakfast will help with that.

Before going down to the breakfast room, though, I go upstairs to the long portrait gallery. Its windows only face the afternoon sun, and it is morning, so the room is dim, like a cave, and dusty. I pad along in my stockinged feet to the end, to the picture of my mother.

There she is, hiding away in the shadowed forest, smiling her secret smile, the thimble bright against her dark skirt.

"I found the thimble," I tell her. "Even though it seems I've lost everything else."

As I stand there in the dim room with sparkling motes of dust floating around me, looking into my mother's painted face, I slip the thimble onto my finger.

A flash of memory slams into me.

My mother—her real self, not a painting—in a hurry, tying her hair back into a long braid. She is dressed all in black and her face is sharp and pale with worry. Snow whirls around us. My hands are cold—I remember the bite of frost and feel again the searing warmth of the thimble as she places it in my palm and curls my fingers around it.

Never lose this, she says.

Then she looks over her shoulder and turns away.

I reach after the memory with trembling fingers— *Mother!*—but it is gone. I blink and I am standing on shaking legs in the picture gallery.

My mother's painted face regards me with the same ironic smile.

"I didn't lose it," I tell her. "I only lost myself. And you."

My mother. What was it that Lady Faye had said about her?

. . . *we were good friends at one time, your mother and I.*

But then my mother had . . . thwarted her, Lady Faye had said. Who *was* my mother?

I gaze at the thimble in my palm. It's such a strange thing for me to have, really. A strange thing for my mother to give me. A thimble represents all that is ladylike and pure and unspotted with blood, unmarked by the painful pricks of a needle. If I think of a perfect lady, she has her head demurely bent over an embroidery frame, with the thimble on her finger, maybe biting her lip with concentration as she stitches. I am nothing like that; I am no seamstress. Neither, I am certain, was my mother. Yet the thimble she gave me is a thing of power.

I think it means that I must try to be like her. I don't know who I was, or who I am, but I can try to thwart whatever Lady Faye is trying to achieve.

Of course, I haven't any idea how to go about doing that. All I know is that she wants me for something, and I cannot let her have me.

Pondering what I'm going to do next, I head for the breakfast room. On the way, I pass a maid, who bobs a curtsy. Oh yes, things have changed. All because of a pretty dress and three dances with a handsome prince.

I pause outside the door. Time to face the wild animals.

I go in. It is past eight o'clock, so Stepmama, Dulcet, and Precious are already at the table. Clearly they've been staring at the door waiting for me, because as I come in they paste wide and welcoming smiles on their faces.

"Good morning," I say, and go to the sideboard. I am famished, and there is poached egg and toast with a delicious-smelling herbed butter sauce that a kitchen maid probably had to stir over the stove for an hour, and bacon and more toast. My plate loaded, I go to the table.

"Pass the jam, would you, Dulcie?" I ask through a mouthful of egg.

With a clatter, Dulcet drops her fork and grabs for the jam pot.

"Ta," I say. In stunned silence, they let me eat for a while. I enjoy every bite of my breakfast.

"Well!" my stepmama exclaims after the sight of me

eating has obviously gotten to be too much for her. "Girls!" She means me, too. "The ball last night. Quite an affair. Dulcet and Precious, you acquitted yourselves well enough." She turns a gimlet gaze on me. "But you, Penelope. To have earned such favor from Lady Faye. It is no wonder the prince paid you such marked attention."

"The dress was magnificent," Precious puts in, envy dripping from her voice.

"Precious!" Stepmama scolds.

"Well, it was," Precious says with an elegant shrug.

"None of it had anything to do with the dress," I say, and eat another bite of toast piled with jam. "The prince would have danced with me if I'd been wearing rags and no mask." I wash down the toast with a drink of tea. "It's almost as if we were meant to be together."

Stepmama's eyes widen. I can see that she's contemplating having to call me *Your Highness* or *Princess Penelope.*

I take pity on her. "The prince doesn't know my name, and he doesn't know where I live."

My stepmama blinks. "Doesn't he?"

Suddenly I feel adrift, and grip the edge of the table to steady myself. I long for my connection to the prince to be real, not because he is handsome or because of his deep, molten-chocolate voice, but because I caught a glimpse of him—the *true* him—when I looked into his eyes.

But this might be my one chance to escape from the city. I can't risk it on a mere glimpse. And despite our attraction to each other, he doesn't know me—not really. "He has no idea who I am," I tell Stepmama. I don't mention that I don't know who I am, either.

I can see her calculating whether that means she can lock me up in the attic again.

I slide my hand into my pocket and feel the reassuring warmth of my thimble. "I'm leaving," I say, before Stepmama can decide what to do with me.

"What?"

"I'm packing some things in a knapsack, and I am leaving. Not just the house, but the city. You'll probably never see me again."

"But Pen—" Dulcet puts in.

"I'll need a warm coat," I interrupt. "I think there's one in the attic. Can you find it for me, Precious?"

My stepsister nods dumbly.

"And some boots." I slide my stockinged foot from under the table and waggle it at them. "Somehow I've lost all my shoes."

"But—" Stepmama puts in. Her face is starting to turn an alarming red. She wants to protest.

"*Mama*," Dulcet hisses. Then she gives me a false smile.

Precious is more blunt. "Mama, if she is gone the prince will still be available."

The red recedes. My stepmama draws herself up. "Well then!" She looks around for a servant to give orders to. "You, boy," she snaps at a footman who has just come into the room.

His eyes are wide. "He's here," he blurts out. "The prince, ma'am. He's asked to see all the ladies of the house. He's in the blue drawing room."

Stepmama surges to her feet. "You say he doesn't know your name or where you live?" she asks me.

I nod and eat a bite of bacon. I slide my other hand into my pocket and grip my thimble—for strength. I can feel an urgency, the larger force trying to bring me and Prince Cornelius together. The wheels must be turning. Instead of responding to the pull, I distract myself by thinking about bacon. Mmm. Nice and crispy, just the way I like it.

"Dulcet, Precious," Stepmama says. "That means he's here for one of you. Come along, girls." Daintily Dulcet wipes butter off her fingers and gets to her feet as Precious stands and primps the lace at her collar. "If you are leaving, Penelope," Stepmama says grandly, "then you had better go."

"Good-bye," I say, giving her a wicked grin.

With a sniff, Stepmama sails out the door. Dulcet and Precious pause in the doorway. "You're really going away, Pen?" Dulcet asks.

"Yes, I am," I say. If I'm caught up in something, the only thing to do is escape it, and that means leaving the city. My thimble will help me avoid Lady Faye's footmen, I hope.

"Well, good-bye," Precious says.

"Good-bye," Dulcet echoes.

We regard one another for a moment, awkwardly silent.

"We wish . . . ," Dulcet begins.

"We wish we could have been better sisters to you," Precious finishes.

I pause, then give them a wry smile. "I wish everyone could hear you sing, Dulcie," I say, "and that you could dress every woman in the city, Precious. But I don't think you've had much of a choice."

"Girls!" comes Stepmama's shrill voice.

Dulcet gives me a quick smile in return, and Precious shakes her head, and they hurry out.

I stay and finish my breakfast quickly. The prince doesn't know I'm here, so I don't need to run off without any shoes on. Maybe Dulcet has a pair of boots I can borrow. They might fit if I wore two pairs of socks.

The footman appears at the door again. "I'm sorry, Lady Pen," he says with a bow. "The prince asks for you especially. You're to come to the blue drawing room at once."

My bite of toast and jam turns to ashes in my mouth. Caught up again. I ponder the possibility of making a run for it. But no. Lady Faye will have planned for that. Slowly I stand and brush the toast crumbs from the front of my dress, check my pocket for my thimble, and follow the footman upstairs. Four big men in red uniforms are waiting outside the drawing room door. The prince's bodyguards, I guess.

I give them a nod and walk into the room.

The first person I notice is Shoe—turning up again where he shouldn't be. I catch him casting me one quick glance, and then staring down at the floor with his hands shoved in his pockets. Maybe he thinks I won't pay him any attention if he keeps quiet.

Stepmama, looking blotchy, is sitting on a spindly chair almost hidden by the spread of her wide skirts. Dulcet stands at her shoulder, Precious next to her.

The prince is standing in the middle of the room holding a box. His long-eared, sad-eyed dogs are lying on the floor by his feet. His curly black hair is neatly combed and he is wearing practical riding clothes, a sheathed knife at his belt, and a long leather coat lined with fleece that makes his shoulders look very broad.

Beside him, Shoe, still in the dark clothes he was wearing the night before, with the same pack on his back, looks rumpled and a little tired.

I narrow my eyes. "You again," I say to Shoe.

For some reason it makes me happy to see him flush. "Me again," he mumbles.

Then I realize what must have happened. "You told the prince where to find me," I accuse.

Shoe's face goes even redder, with shame, I assume. Even his ears, from what I can see of them through his shaggy hair, are red. He stares stubbornly down at the carpet.

"He had to do it," the prince interrupts. He gives me his most charming smile. "Good morning, Lady Penelope." From their spots on the floor by his feet, his dogs wag their tails.

"Yes, good morning," I snap back. He should know better than to try that smile on me.

"I believe you lost something last night." The prince opens the box and pulls out a shoe studded with jewels, the one that twisted from my foot as I was fleeing the castle.

"I have no idea what you're talking about," I lie. I'm not going to make this easy for him.

"I think you do. Will you try it on?" He gives a little bow and gestures toward a chair that faces him.

I think about saying no, but there isn't any point. Now that it's started, the scene will play out, no matter how hard I struggle. "If I have to," I mutter. I go to the chair, sit gracelessly down, and stick out my foot.

"It is the only way I can be certain you are Lady Ash," the prince says.

"You know very well that I am," I say.

He is about to go to his knees before me, when Shoe stops him. "Cor," he says firmly, and that surprises me, that Shoe knows to call Prince Cornelius by the name his friends use. "Let me do it."

The prince blinks. "What?"

"I'm a shoemaker," Shoe says. "I can see if the shoe really fits her."

"Oh. Yes," the prince says blankly, and I wonder if he can feel the sudden halt and stutter of the thing we are caught up in. He shakes his head, refocusing. "Yes, of course," he says, and hands the shoe to Shoe. "If you will."

Setting down his pack, Shoe comes to me and kneels before my chair. He keeps his head lowered so I can't see his face, just the top of his hair. "I shouldn't have told him your name," he whispers.

"It was a snaky thing to do, Shoe," I tell him.

He nods. "I know it was." He looks up, and his eyes are very green in the blue room. "I'm sorry, Pin."

I shrug. "Prince Cornelius would have found me anyway. One way or another."

He nods. "Give me your foot."

I stick my foot out and he takes it. His voice was gruff, but his hands are gentle. As he is sliding on the shoe, there is a flurry at the door. It is behind me, so I don't see who it is, but I see Shoe look up and past me. His face goes deathly pale.

I turn to look, and Lady Faye sweeps triumphantly into the room. She takes in the scene—me in the chair, Shoe on his knees holding my foot and the shoe. Her eyes turn the incandescent blue of the coldest ice, and she stares furiously at Shoe. "You," she hisses. "You are *not* supposed to be here."

Shoe looks frozen in place. I shove my foot the rest of the way into the shoe and stand up, steadying myself on his shoulder. "Yes," I say. "He does keep turning up in the strangest places, doesn't he?" With my knee I nudge Shoe's arm, and he climbs stiffly to his feet so that we are standing shoulder to shoulder.

"Lady Faye! How lovely to see you!" Precious says suddenly, and elbows Stepmama, who surges from her chair and turns the invasion into a drawing room visit, performing the social necessities flanked by my stepsisters and assisted by the prince, who is giving Lady Faye a warm smile and coming forward to greet her. Their combined force of personality is sufficient to the task; they draw Lady Faye farther into the room.

As she passes I can feel the tension in Shoe's body, and it's clear from her fury and his reaction to it that they have some history together. It's likely Shoe hasn't come off the better for it, either. It all has something to do with this huge, relentless thing that has ensnared me. *Story* is what Shoe called it. *This* is the thing that I must thwart. I know that Lady Faye is the Godmother and is involved in it somehow, and it's obvious that Shoe is too, and the prince. And though I don't know their roles exactly, I do know that, despite everything, Shoe is not my enemy.

I brush the back of my hand against Shoe's and feel him flinch. I put my other hand into my pocket. My mother's thimble is there, and it warms at my touch; I slide my first finger into it.

"Don't worry, Shoe," I breathe.

He glances aside at me. I give him a quick grin, and his eyes widen.

In the center of the room, Lady Faye is glaring at us, ignoring Stepmama's polite entreaties—*Tea? A chair by the fire? Perhaps a bite to eat?*

"Never mind all that," Lady Faye says, and waves a hand at Stepmama as if brushing away a fly. She takes a step toward me and Shoe. She has her other hand clenched, and I see a bit of frozen light leaking out from between her fingers.

"She has a thimble," Shoe whispers.

I answer with the faintest of nods. Inside my pocket, my mother's thimble burns on my own finger.

"We'll keep this polite," I say. "Why have you come here, Lady Faye? I don't think you were invited."

She seethes with cold fury. Her nostrils flare and her eyes spark. "Take off the shoe, you stupid girl. Take it off, now! The prince puts it on your foot and realizes that he loves you. It is inevitable. *It must happen.* The *prince*, not this meddling fool." She jabs a finger at Shoe.

"No, I don't think so," I say.

"I will not be thwarted. Give the shoe to the prince at once," she orders.

I give her my most evil grin. "The shoe stays with me." To my surprise, I feel Shoe's hand take mine in a steady, reassuring grip. A source of strength. "Lady Faye," I say. "You are in my house. My stepmama is here, and my sisters." Dulcet and Precious nod, showing that they are with me, and after a nudge from Dulcie, Stepmama blinks. I can see her reconsidering her loyalty, unsure of what to do. "Prince Cornelius is here too, armed with a knife and two ferocious dogs." I glance at Blue and Bunny; both dogs are cowering behind the prince's legs with their tails lowered. "In addition," I add, "four of the prince's bodyguards are outside the door. You can do nothing to us here."

She bares her teeth. "Oh, can't I?" She takes a sweeping

turn around the room, her chin raised, her silken skirts rustling and hissing about her; the prince and my stepmama and stepsisters flinch away. The cups from stepmama's tea set rattle in their saucers and the dogs whine. Shoe stays steadily at my side. Lady Faye takes another turn, and the gathering magic crackles around her. "You, prince," she beckons. Her raised hand glows blue with the power of her thimble.

Before Prince Cornelius can respond, I step forward to intercept her. "And," I add, "I am not defenseless." I draw my hand out of my skirt and hold it up. The shimmer of warm, fire-colored light spills around us.

Seeing my thimble, she recoils. "Ah," she gasps, as if she's been slapped. "You had it all along."

"No," I say. "But I have it now, and I am strong enough to use it."

"You stupid girl," she spits. "You don't understand." She grips her own thimble until the skin stretches tightly over her knuckles. "You have no idea what you're dealing with. And yet you would set yourself up as my antagonist, would you?"

"Apparently it's an inherited position," I answer.

"Inherited position," she sneers. "You are nothing compared to your mother. Nothing."

I give a shrug that I hope seems confident. "Nevertheless, you can see very well that I am in a place of strength. There is nothing you can do to us here."

Lady Faye, still panting with rage, looks around the room, calculates, and gives a narrow-eyed nod. The light from her thimble flickers out. Then she steps closer, speaking only to me. "All right. I will go. But Story is not finished with you yet." She raises her voice. "It is not finished with any of us. Story will have its ending." She glances aside at Shoe. Her voice drips with venom. "And the special ending I promised still awaits you, Shoemaker."

Well, that is quite enough of that. It is time for my step-mother to be a hero. "Stepmama," I say loudly. "Please show Lady Faye to the door."

Dulcet and Precious at her side, Stepmama collects her-self, eyes me and then Lady Faye, and makes her choice. She sails into battle, all flags flying. "Lady Faye!" she trills. "Do come again soon." The three of them usher Lady Faye out of the room.

When the door closes behind them, I leave the thimble in my pocket, draw my hand from Shoe's, and flop down on the couch. "Phew." I inspect my finger. The thimble burned when I was facing down Lady Faye, hot enough to scorch, but the tip of my finger isn't even pink.

"That was a bit tricky," the prince says from over by the window. He parts the curtain, looking out. Watching for Lady Faye to leave, I assume.

"A bit," I agree. A vast understatement. With my toe I push the high-heeled shoe off my other foot; it falls to the carpet with a thud.

Shoe is standing, still staring at the door as if he can't believe Lady Faye is gone.

"What did you do to make her dislike you so much?" I ask him.

"I, um . . . ," he says blankly, as if he's busy thinking about something else.

"You have this bad habit of turning up places where you're not supposed to be," I say.

He turns and focuses on me, all grim intensity. "Yes, that's it. Pin, we have to—"

"She's gone," the prince interrupts, looking out the window again. "But I can see four of her footmen from here, and no doubt there are more of them lurking about."

"She's not done with us yet," I say, sitting up.

"No." Leaving the window, the prince crosses the room, Blue and Bunny at his heels. "Go lie down, you ferocious creatures," he says, pointing at the floor. When they do, he sits beside me on the couch. "It is no secret that Lady Faye is the true power in this city." He glances over at Shoe. "If she's got a punishment in mind for you, Shoe, she'll get you eventually, and you too, Lady Penelope. There's nothing I can do about it." He looks steadily at me. "The only way I can protect you is to marry you."

"No," I say. "That's exactly what Lady Faye wants. It's the last thing we should do. And even if we did, it would still leave Shoe," I point out. "What does she want to do to you, anyway?" I ask him.

Shoe shakes his head and doesn't answer.

"Hm." There is a long silence. "Why is Lady Faye doing this?" I ask suddenly.

Prince Cornelius shrugs his broad shoulders. "Power?"

"Yes, but how?" I push. "The endings are always the same. How does that give her power?"

"She's caught up in it too," Shoe puts in unexpectedly.

I blink. "Lady Faye, you mean? The Godmother?"

He nods.

"So," I say slowly, thinking it through. "It's not Lady Faye who wants power. Story gains power by forcing these endings. *Happily ever after* endings," I add with a grimace. "Boring endings. They're all the same." I get up from the couch, pace a few steps, and then go on. "It's wearing a rut. Every time Story's wheel turns, it gains more power. Lady Faye is just serving its will."

Prince Cor is staring intently at me. "I think you're right, Lady Penelope."

"What can we do to stop it?" I ask. "It doesn't feel like anything we've done has broken its power."

"No," the prince says.

"Story will have its ending," Shoe says, reminding us of Lady Faye's words.

I feel a moment of despair. "We want to thwart it, but it's so powerful. How can we know that we aren't just doing what Story wants us to do? How can we know if we're acting out our own will?" I look to the prince. "At the ball, at midnight, I tried to get away, remember? I thought I was escaping from the thing I was caught up in. But Story meant that to happen—when I lost my shoe and you found it and then came here to try it on me. That was all Story." I shudder, thinking of how close to an ending we just came, and I didn't even realize it.

"Some people are resisting it," Shoe says.

"You, for example," I say, as I begin to understand. For when he took the shoe from the prince and put it on my foot, he saved me from that ending. No wonder Lady Faye had been so furious.

He looks away. "You do the unexpected thing too, Pin."

I wonder what it will mean for Story if it can force somebody like me—the daughter of the woman who thwarted the Godmother, the bearer of a magic thimble—into one of its prescribed endings. If I can't resist it, maybe nobody can.

"What are we going to do?" Prince Cornelius asks. His dog Bunny whines and he leans down to pat her head. "Shhh," he murmurs.

I frown, becoming more impatient. "We have to do something. We must. If we don't, we'll just get caught up again. We'll have to act, and hope that we're not falling into Story's rut when we do. I am quite strongly set against playing a part in any ending that I don't choose for myself." I nod, deciding. "It's clear that I have to leave the city at once, and Shoe should come too. We can't let Lady Faye get her hands on him."

Shoe looks grim again. "Yes." He turns to the prince. "Cor, will you help us escape?"

The prince nods. "I could, but it won't be easy. She calls her men *footmen*, but they are really armed guardsmen, and there are a lot of them." He shakes his head. "I could call up my own guard to fight them off, but I'm not sure they can manage it. And she'll have all the gates that lead out of the city watched and her men ready to pursue."

"I've got a boat," Shoe says. "If you can get us to it, Cor." He explains about the shoemaker friend and his Missus and the boat hidden at the bottom of the waterfall and the supplies and how being on the river will throw off the trackers. All of his careful preparations. "Oh," he adds, remembering something else. He crosses the room to where he left his pack, crouches to dig through it, and pulls out a pair of boots, which he brings to me. "They're for you."

They're beautiful, sturdy boots lined with warm fur. I slide one of them onto my foot. "You made these," I say to him.

"Yes," Shoe says.

"Your preparations are all well considered, Shoe," the prince puts in. "Except there's one more thing. Lady Penelope, I want to come with you."

I look up from tying the laces of my new boots. When I meet his keen blue eyes, my breath catches. *Should* he come? Or is that Story forcing us together? "I'm not sure that's a good idea, Prince Cornelius," I say slowly. I stand up and stomp my feet on the floor to test the fit of my boots. Perfect.

This time he doesn't bother using the smile on me. "Call me Cor, won't you, Lady Penelope?" He gets to his feet; then he glances at Shoe and lowers his voice, though I know Shoe can overhear what he's saying. "I think we need to find out what happens when you and I are not caught up in Story." He holds out his hand to me. "I want to test how strong our feelings for each other really are. No false smiles, no masks, no prince and mysterious Lady Ash, just us."

I step closer and take his hand. It's big and warm and it makes me feel safe. To me, he's a lot more charming when he's not trying to be charming. The irony of that makes me smile.

His eyes light with hope. "So you think it's worth trying?"

Oh, I still feel that inexorable pull toward him; I can see he feels it too, and it makes me mistrust any connection we share. "We-ell . . . ," I begin.

I have seen the surface of him—the princely mask he wears for whatever reason—but I have caught only glimpses of the rest of him. He is intelligent and truly noble, I think, and he was unexpectedly kind to the snappish servant girl who dropped her bag of potatoes, and I have seen such gentleness in the way he treats his dogs. And I like the way he left this choice up to me.

I give a decided nod. I do want to discover who Cor really is, instead of who Story wants him to be. "Yes," I say to him. "It's worth a try. And you can call me Pen." I gaze up into his intensely blue eyes. He smiles down at me, and it's a different, truer smile than the ones he wielded before. I like it.

After a few moments I turn to thank Shoe for the perfect boots, but he is carefully looking away from Cor, and me, apparently finding something infinitely fascinating about the wallpaper beside the door.

PART
THREE

CHAPTER

28

As night falls, the fog rolls out of the forest again, flowing over the wall and through the streets of the city like a white river, cresting at the rooftops, smelling of pine and fern, and of snow. Out of the fog rise the slender white towers of the castle; on the central tower the clock's face is wide and watchful. The streets are swarming with the Godmother's footmen. Some of those footmen, Shoe knows, have naked tails, some have twitching, furry ears, some have the snouts of pigs; some of them are wearing blue uniforms, some wear nothing but their own fur; they are all armed with short, wickedly sharp knives. The prince's red-coated guards come out to meet them, and they clash and struggle and are separated by the fog only to come together again. The night echoes with screams and shouts, the sounds of glass breaking and running footsteps, and over it all the clock tolling cease-lessly, roaring booms that shake the ground.

Prince Cor had wanted to wait a day or two before fleeing so he could assemble a few guards and pack his things, and take the dogs back to the castle.

"No," Shoe says. He feels a knot of urgency tighten in his chest. "She'll be after us. We have to go *now*."

"He's right," Pin says, and, leaving the dogs with Pin's stepmother, they go.

They are three swift shadows passing through the fog. The prince knows the streets well—he often walked the city with his dogs just before curfew, wearing a wide-brimmed hat and cloak to avoid being noticed. They evade the rov-ing bands of footmen and reach the place where the river hurls itself over a cliff to slam into a lake far below. The steep path down to the lake is dark, slicked with ice, and slithering with fog. Freezing spray from the waterfall blows over them, and all three are soaked and shivering by the time they find themselves standing on a pebbly beach surrounded by cliffs; they've reached the lake by the only accessible path. From overhead they hear the continued booming of the clock. The sound echoes, as if it is seeking them.

"It should be over here," Shoe says, and sure enough they find a boat pulled up on the shore. It is a long, slender boat with supplies in packs; there are oars in the middle and a til-ler at the stern. They leap in and Cor goes straight to the oars and rows them silently into the darkness of the long lake.

SHOE SPENDS THE entire night crouched in the bow of the boat, his ears pricked for the sound of pursuit, tense with alarm and the absolute certainty that the Godmother's blue-coated footmen are going to catch them. But there's only so long that fear can grip; eventually it lets go. The sound of the clock recedes into the distance; the river turns and the city disappears, and all is silent, the river carrying them faster now, the forested banks sliding past dark and quiet. The pounding of his heart slows and the cold air creeps in. He wraps his arms around himself, shivering. As the dawn lightens the sky to the east, Shoe feels the lack of sleep catching up to him.

Pin and Cor are tired too, he can see; their faces look gray in the early morning light and their eyes are shadowed. Pin has the tiller and is keeping the boat in the middle of the river's current. Cor is at the center of the boat; he's been rowing to speed them along, but is resting now, the oars pulled up, dripping.

Pin is wearing the warm hooded cloak he'd brought for her in his pack. She looks back at the smooth surface of the river marked by the line of their wake. When she speaks, her voice sounds thin, weary. "I think we've done it. We've gotten away."

The knot of urgency tightens in Shoe's chest again. "No we haven't."

Cor glances over his shoulder at Shoe, his eyebrows raised.

"They're coming," Shoe tells them. He is certain of that.

"It's just her footmen," Pen protests.

She doesn't remember the Godmother's fortress, Shoe reminds himself, and the snakelike Overseer or the cruel pig-snouted, goat-footed, wolf-eared guards.

Cor pulls the oars in farther and rolls his shoulders, loosening muscles tired from rowing. "They have to stop to rest sometime," he says. "We can easily stay ahead of them."

Shoe shakes his head.

"You've fled from them before," Pin observes.

"So have you, Pin," Shoe says. "They are the guards at her fortress. Most of them aren't true men. She makes them out of animals, using her thimble, I think, but they don't turn all the way. They still have snouts or tails or scales." He pauses to think. "But her trackers are different. Those were men that she turned partly into hounds, maybe as a punishment." He remembers the Huntsman's sadness that the trackers hadn't been given tails when they'd been changed. "The trackers are intelligent, and they have very keen noses. She has Huntsmen too, and they're men."

"We will head for East Oria, the capital city," Cor says firmly. "My mother, the queen, is there. A few animal-men armed with knives will be no match for her armies."

Shoe blinks. It's the first time he's considered what might lie beyond the reach of Story. But of course there's something else to the world. The people of the city, and the slaves in the fortress—they were all taken from somewhere. But that doesn't mean Cor's memories of East Oria and a queen are true.

"How far is East Oria from here?" Pin asks.

"I . . . I do not know," Cor answers slowly, frowning.

Shoe nods to himself. The Godmother's city won't be on any map.

Cor's face brightens. "I do know that East Oria is on the coast. Certainly downstream from here. We can head that direction and go from there. It can't be too far." He inspects the blisters that he's gotten from rowing. "At any rate, we'll have to leave the river soon; I don't know how long it'll take us to get through the forest, but we've got supplies enough, and we shouldn't have any trouble staying ahead of the God-mother's footmen."

"We'll never make it," Shoe tells them.

"Of course we will," Cor says.

"No, we won't," Shoe insists.

"We have a head start," Cor says with some stiffness. He's not used to being contradicted. "They can't catch us now."

Another twist in the urgency knot. Shoe takes a deep breath, and repeats his warnings, sterner this time. "She'll order the footmen to come after us—she probably already has—and they'll do it without stopping to eat or sleep. They won't stop until they've caught us, or they've killed them-selves trying. And then more will come."

Pin is staring at him. "We can't get away, is that what you're saying?"

Shoe doesn't meet her eyes. "They are coming. That's all I know." And there's more. "Cor," he adds hesitantly, "the Godmother used her magic to bring everyone to the city to play a role in Story. They've all been taken away from somewhere else, and their memories erased. She must have brought you there, too." He braces himself for Cor's inevitable anger. "It's possible there's no such place as East Oria, there's no queen, and you're not a prince."

The boat rocks as Cor straightens and then draws a deep breath to protest. Then he lets it out. "I—" He shakes his head. "I am certain you are wrong. My memories are too clear."

"Still, it means we can't be absolutely sure of what's out there," Pin says wearily. "It's hopeless. Why did we even bother to escape, if there's no escape?"

Shoe offers the only hope he has. "We might find some help. The Huntsman who brought me to the city told me that he and some other rebels have a hiding place in the forest."

"Rebels?" Pin asks.

"People who have escaped from Story," Shoe tells her, "and are fighting it. We could join them."

"You're sure of this?" Cor pushes. "You know where this hiding place is located?"

"No," Shoe admits.

"Well then," Cor decides. "We will still try for East Oria."

Shoe nods. But the power of Story is bigger than any of them, and the Godmother serves its will with brutal resolve.

It doesn't really matter which way they go. It doesn't matter how hard they struggle. Their ending is coming, he is sure of it.

29

As long as we're on the river, we decide, we can stay ahead of the Godmother's footmen and trackers and Huntsmen. I sit at the tiller, keeping us in the fastest part of the river as best I can. Shoe takes a turn at the oars, rowing with the clean efficiency that I'm starting to expect in everything he does. While Shoe rows, Cor digs some blankets out of the supplies, makes a bed in the bow, and goes to sleep.

"My turn," I say, after Shoe has been rowing for what seems like a long time.

Panting, he rests, lifting the dripping oars from the water so the boat glides silently along. "All right," he says. He pulls the oars in and, crouching so as not to rock the boat, climbs over a pack to sit on the bench next to me. I take off my long hooded cloak and climb awkwardly to the next seat to take my place at the oars.

As I row, I have my back to the bow and am facing Shoe at the tiller in the stern of the boat. I watch him, and he finds ways to avoid meeting my eyes. Often he looks back along our wake to see if we're being pursued.

"Rowing is rather boring, isn't it?" I say, to distract him.

"I'm not bored at all," he says, and checks over his shoulder again. "And I've had enough excitement for a while, anyway."

I grin at him, and he blinks. "Tell me about the God-mother's fortress," I say, and take a stroke.

He frowns.

"Unless you don't want to think about it," I put in quickly.

"It's not a good memory," he says with half a shrug. "But it's yours, too. You need to know about it."

Shoe is a talker, it turns out, telling his story easily, with plenty of details so that I get a picture of what it was like in the Godmother's fortress. The bleak, gray monotony of the days, the hard work, the lentils and oats they ate, the guards and overseers. I get into a rhythm with the sound of his words and the stroke of the oars.

"None of it is familiar," I tell him. "It's all one big blank." My back aches as I continue to row. "How does she do it? Take away the memories?"

"With her thimble," Shoe answers. He touches a finger to his forehead. "Some kind of magic."

I wonder if my own thimble has that kind of magic in it.

I shake my head to clear the thought away. "The Pin you're telling me about—the seamstress. She seems like a completely different person from me."

His gaze is the green of the forest as he looks at me. "You're still yourself," he says quietly.

"I don't see how you can be so certain of that," I tell him.

"Well, I am," he says.

I remember a moment from when we first met, in my Stepmama's house. "Oh, that's right; I'd forgotten. You're stubborn, aren't you?"

He doesn't answer, just turns his head to look back at our wake. I study his profile, his fine features, the flush of red over his cheekbones as if he can feel me watching him. I hadn't realized it before, but Shoe is very handsome, in his own way. I'd been too distracted by Cor's more bold, flashing good looks. But Shoe . . . he draws my eyes. I wonder what it would be like if he ever smiled. Devastating, probably.

The boat rocks; I glance back to see Cor sitting up in the bow, awake from his nap. "Pen," he says, his voice rusty with sleep. "You shouldn't be doing that."

"It was my turn." I pause, the oar handles smooth under my hands.

"You're a lady," Cor protests. He gets to his feet, crouching in the bow as if he's going to make his way back to where I'm sitting. "It's not appropriate for you to row when Shoe and I can do it for you. And your hands will be blistered."

"I already have blisters on my hands," I tell him. Actually

I have calluses from working as a maid in my stepmother's house.

"Tell her, Shoe," Cor says.

"I don't see why she shouldn't," Shoe says. He is straightening the tiller to keep us in the middle of the current.

"Exactly," I say. "There's no reason I shouldn't take my turn." I smile at him. "But you're welcome to take yours now."

We rearrange ourselves so that it's me at the tiller, Cor at the oars, and Shoe asleep in the bow. All I can see of him is the top of his head and a hunched shoulder.

I watch the thickly forested banks slide past us under a lowering gray sky. I watch Cor, too. He has taken off his leather coat to row so I get to admire his broad shoulders as he reaches forward to take each stroke.

In turn, he studies me. I've pulled up the hood of my cape, so he must not be able to see much of my face, just shadows.

"You feel it too, don't you, Pen?" he asks. "That you and I are meant to be together?"

I look down at the smooth wood of the tiller. "I do feel a pull," I admit. "But I suspect that it's Story at work." I look up, and his blue eyes are so intense. "What do you think?"

"I know that we are far from the city now," he says, lifting the oars from the water and taking another stroke, "and I still feel drawn to you."

I feel it too. *Does* Story have power this far away from the

Godmother's city? Is what I feel for him real, true? Is it more than just simple attraction? "I want to . . . ," I begin, and then study my callused fingertips. "I want to . . . to"—to *love you*—"to care for you, Cor. But . . ."

This is not like me, to be so hesitant. I shake my head.

"Things are too uncertain," Cor says, his deep voice gentle.

"Yes," I say, relieved. "I need more time."

"We may not have much time," he says.

"I know." But I need to figure out who I am. I need to be certain before I can truly love someone else.

Another long silence, and the awkwardness grows.

"Shoe still calls you Pin, have you noticed?" Cor asks suddenly.

"Yes," I answer. I am not sure whether it bothers me or not.

"He is in love with Pin," Cor goes on.

My heart lurches. Shoe? In love with *me*? I can't help but think of our kiss in the hallway. I gather my wits. "No," I say, with much more certainty than I feel. "He's in love with the girl he told me about, the Pin who escaped with him from the Godmother's fortress, not with me. I am Pen now." And despite Shoe's stubbornness on this point, he does not know Pen very well at all.

Cor gives a satisfied nod, as if I have told him something he wanted to hear.

From the shadow of my hood, I study him. His mouth curves in a smile that looks almost smug. I don't like it. "Did Shoe tell you that he loves Pin?"

"Yes," Cor admits. He leans forward to take another stroke, the oars rattling in the oarlocks.

"Hmmm," I murmur.

Cor's shoulders stiffen. He pauses in his rowing and gives me a half bow—so princely polite. "You are right, of course, Pen. I should not have told you. Shoe told me in confidence, and I have betrayed that confidence. I will apologize to him at the first opportunity."

I find myself smiling. There's something endearing about his formality, his exquisite sense of honor. It's almost a shield for him, but I'm starting to get a good idea of the kind of man hiding behind it. A proud man who can admit when he's wrong. That makes him even more likeable to me.

Cor is about to say something else when I hold up my hand, silencing him. From ahead I can hear the faintest roaring sound. I cock my head, listening.

Cor hears it too. "What is that?"

In the bow, Shoe sits up, shedding the blankets, looking ahead. His sandy hair is tousled from sleep. "It's a waterfall," he says.

"We'll have to get off the river," Cor says, and starts rowing hard. Steering with the tiller, I take us out of the current and closer to the bank until we find a place to land. Shoe and Cor go first, and between them they pull the boat up; then I climb over the packed supplies and onto the rocky shore.

Hurrying, we unload the supplies and stuff them into the two knapsacks; Shoe rolls the blankets and straps them on, too. We don't talk, and our fingers fumble with haste. Once we're ready, Shoe shoves the lightened boat out into the river current again. "So it won't give away where we landed," he explains.

"Which way?" I ask. The riverbank is steep here, leading up like the side of a mountain, forested with pine trees spaced closely together, and choked below with brambles and ferns and other bushes. What looks like a path—it's a gap in the trees, anyway—leads straight up the hill, away from the river.

Cor is handing one of the packs to Shoe; then he slings the bigger pack over his shoulders. I have two water bottles to carry. "We'd better follow the river," Cor says, pointing. "The coast must be farther in that direction—as the river flows."

Shoe shrugs—I can see that he thinks it doesn't matter which way we go.

"Lead on, Cor," I say. We set off into the forest.

The farther we go, the denser the bushes become. There are brambles, too, and they tangle in my skirt and cloak, slowing me down. The pine trees crowd closer together; their thick branches cut off the light, so it is too dim to see the roots that reach up to grab my feet, tripping me. Cor is the biggest and strongest, so he goes first, breaking a path, Shoe trudging behind him with his head down. I rip the hem of my cloak out of yet another clump of brambles and wade through a waist-high stand of ferns.

I find myself watching Shoe. He is not so tall and broad as Cor, but he's slim and straight, and he stops sometimes to hold a branch out of my way, or checks over his shoulder to see that I'm keeping up, and I catch glimpses of his forest-green eyes. He is all grim purpose, no smiling, no flirtatious glances. Yet he loves me, Cor says. Or he loves Pin, I remind myself. The girl that I was. As I walk, I turn that idea over in my mind, and I'm not sure what to make of it.

After an afternoon of struggling, Cor pauses, and I catch up to him, panting. Shoe is looking back the way we came, then at the hill. I can see it too—the worst of the undergrowth has been ahead of us, so without quite realizing it we've been heading away from the river, uphill. We've been forced back around to the same path that led away from the river.

"The forest wants us to go that way," Shoe says, pointing.

"The forest?" Cor asks, his voice sharp with doubt. "It's some kind of magic?"

"I don't know," Shoe says. "Probably."

Cor's face creases with a frown. "The Godmother's magic," he pronounces.

"I don't think it is," Shoe contradicts.

"Nevertheless," Cor says, "we continue along the river."

And back we go down the hill, floundering through the grasping brambles, twisting our ankles on roots, squeezing through the narrow gaps between trees. We have the river in sight again—flowing gray and swift in gaps between the trees—when, just ahead of me, Shoe freezes.

"*Cor*," he whispers.

Cor turns.

"Get down." Pulling me with him, Shoe crouches among the ferns.

"What is it?" I whisper. Shoe shakes his head and reaches out to put his hand over my mouth. I can feel the calluses on his palm against my face.

Cor has hidden himself too.

Then I hear it and I freeze like a terrified rabbit. The knock and splash of oars and a harsh command. My eyes widen. I glance at Shoe and he nods, taking his hand away. Through the ferns and trees I see, on the river, a low boat crowded with men. Some of them wear the expected blue coats. Some are man-shaped, but I catch glimpses of furred naked backs and animal faces. They lean forward, eager, scanning the river banks. The Godmother's footmen. Another boat passes, and then another.

Then they are gone. Slowly we get to our feet.

"We follow the path," I say, knowing that Shoe is thinking the same thing.

Cor glances aside at Shoe. "We will do what the forest wants. Perhaps once we get away from the river we can turn toward East Oria again."

Now it is Shoe who leads the way up the steep hill, then along a ridge, and down the other side until we reach a valley. By this time twilight is coming on and the path is growing dim before our feet. Shoe leads us steadily on.

I am the only one of the three of us who didn't get to sleep in the boat and I am growing more and more tired, the straps from the heavy water bottles cutting into my shoulders, my stomach aching with emptiness.

Cor glances back at me, then stops; I stumble to a stop, too. "You're exhausted," he says, taking my hand.

Shoe goes on for a few steps, then pauses and looks back. "We have to go on," he says, his voice rough.

"We will rest here," Cor says. He slings the pack from his back. "It will soon grow too dark to see the path, anyway."

We settle in a circle and eat some of the food from the packs—cheese and bread and dried apple slices—and I pass around one of the water bottles. The night falls like a heavy curtain, completely dark, no moon and no stars. The air grows colder and damper and has a taste like metal.

"Pin," comes Shoe's voice out of the darkness.

"Her name is Pen," Cor corrects.

Shoe ignores him. I hear him shift and lean closer to me. "I've been thinking about your thimble."

I reach into my cloak pocket and pull it out. As always, it warms at my touch. When I confronted the Godmother it glowed with heat. Testing, I clench it in my fist and think *warmth* and *light.* I catch my breath as my hand begins to glow as if I'm holding a star. I cup it in my palms and look up to see Shoe's and Cor's faces, eyes wide in our bubble of warm, golden light.

"*Magic,*" Cor says, surprised.

Shoe nods. "The Godmother's thimble is ice, and yours is fire, Pin. Hers takes memories away. I'm wondering if yours could give them back."

"Oh," I breathe. "That's an excellent thought." I gaze down at the glowing thimble in my hands. Its warmth spreads through me. The night feels suddenly less damp and hopeless.

"You could try it and see if Cor's memories are real," Shoe goes on, "and then we'd know if East Oria is somewhere we can escape to." He shrugs. "If it's all right with you, Cor, that is."

"Yes, I'm willing, of course," Cor says. "How does it work?"

"The Godmother touches the thimble here," Shoe says, pointing to his own forehead. He shivers. "I don't know how she does it beyond that."

I give a decided nod. "We might as well try it." I slip the glowing thimble onto my finger and turn to Cor. He leans forward, then closer and touches his lips to mine. "For luck," he says softly, and pulls back again.

"Keep still," I order, but my lips tingle from his kiss. I raise my hand and gently brush aside a curl of his dark hair and place my thimble against his forehead. He closes his eyes.

Who are you, really, Cor? I find myself thinking. *Are you just a prince, or are you something more?*

As if in answer to my thought, the thimble blazes, a flash that scorches through me and into Cor. He flinches back and darkness falls again.

I blink the shadows out of my eyes and ask the thimble for light. As it begins to glow again, I see Cor rubbing his forehead and frowning.

"That was . . ." He pauses to clear his throat. "That was very odd."

"Did it work?" Shoe asks.

"I . . ." He blinks again. "Yes, I believe it did."

I hold my breath.

"My name is Cornelius," Cor says slowly, "and I am a prince of the realm, and my mother, the queen, lives in East Oria."

"You remembered that before," Shoe points out.

"Yes. But that is not all." Cor glances aside at Shoe, and I see that trace of haughtiness again. "I remember being taken from East Oria. I was on a hunt. The Godmother's footmen ambushed me and imprisoned me—and my dogs—in a carriage and brought me to her city. I remember the Godmother using her thimble—she must have ripped away my memory of being taken."

"She needed a prince for Story," Shoe says, "so she went and got a prince."

"Apparently," Cor says, still looking dazed. "Just as she found a shoemaker when she needed one, and the other servants who do her work for her."

The thimble's glow is fading. I want to think more about this, but I can't stay awake. I'm weary down to my bones. I slip the thimble into my pocket again and curl on my side on the pine-needly ground. As I drift into sleep, I catch bits and pieces of Cor and Shoe's conversation, something about the Godmother's half-animal, half-man footmen.

"It's a cruel thing to do to a dog," I hear Cor's deep voice say. "Dogs are perfectly content and complete in what they are. It's terrible to take that away from them."

"You know dogs very well," Shoe's lighter voice says.

"Better than people, I sometimes think." Cor's voice is rueful.

There is a long pause, and I drift closer to sleep.

Cor's deep voice drags me back to the surface again. "Shoe," he says formally. "I owe you an apology."

Shoe makes a sleepy, questioning noise.

"Yes. You told me that you were in love with Pen when she was Pin, and, well, I betrayed your trust."

There is a silence. When he speaks, Shoe's voice is muffled. "You told her?"

"Yes, I did. It was not . . . well, it was not noble of me. I've been taught better. Again, I am sorry."

A weary sigh from Shoe. "It's all right, Cor."

"Thank you," Cor says stiffly.

Then silence.

A HAND ON my shoulder wakes me. It is still dark, and I can tell from my gritty eyes that I haven't been asleep for very long. A blanket is over my shoulders and a coat is under my head, a pillow. The coat is leather—it must be Cor's.

"All right," Cor is saying from the darkness.

"I'm sorry, Pin," Shoe says softly. It is his hand that shook me awake. "The forest has given us a path again. We have to go on."

I sit up, rubbing my eyes. At first I can't see anything, but Shoe's hand bumps my face, and then he gently takes my chin and turns my head so I am looking in the right direction. Something on the ground—like a scattering of pearl buttons on black velvet—is glowing, leading into the darkness.

"Mushrooms," Shoe whispers. "They're marking the path."

I gather up my water bottles; I can hear Shoe and Cor packing up the supplies and Cor putting his coat on again. Shoe gets out a rope for us to hold in a line, first Cor, then Shoe, and then me. We are about to step onto the path again when, from far behind us, comes the faint echo of a howl.

"How far, do you think?" comes Shoe's voice out of the darkness.

"At the river," Cor answers. "They must have found the path."

My heart gives a stutter of fright, and then the rope jerks and we are off on the mushroom-marked trail.

We stumble along for the rest of the night. The air grows icy, and my hands are too numb with cold to grip the rope. After I've dropped it for the third time, Shoe takes my hand and pulls me behind him. In my other hand I hold the thimble, drawing strength from it. I consider using it to show our way, but its light could betray us to our pursuers, so I keep it clenched in my fist. On and on we go. I look back and see that the mushrooms marking our trail go dark after we have passed.

At last the sky grows pale with dawn. The forest takes shape around us—dark pine trees with moss clinging to every branch, more ferns and bushes. My legs feel heavy and sore as we crest a ridge. Cor keeps going, leading us. Shoe and I pause and, panting, we look back in the direction we've come. Behind us, dense white fog is flowing down the hill, slithering among the trees, gathering in the valley below.

Shoe's face is drawn and pale, his eyes smudged with weariness. I probably don't look any better. I dredge up a grin. "I suppose the fog will confound the trackers, don't you?"

"For a little while, maybe," he says.

As if in answer, a howl echoes from the valley. Another one answers, and then another. My stomach clenches. "That was closer than last night."

Shoe nods. He still has my hand in his. He steps closer. "Pin, if we don't—"

"But we will," I interrupt. He wants to say one last thing before we are captured, and I can't bear to hear it.

"No," he says, shaking his head. "You thought—when you were Pin, I mean—you thought there was something Before the Godmother's fortress, and you thought we could escape back to it. But I don't think we can. It's like . . ." He shakes his head. "Circles within circles. You climb over one wall, only to find yourself in a new prison."

"What?" I blink. "Are you saying this is all pointless? All this struggle, this pain?" Suddenly I am angry with him. "Are we just supposed to let go? To give up hope and let it take us?"

"I don't know," he answers. "We have to figure some way out that isn't escape."

"There is no other way," I insist. "We have to keep going. At least we know that East Oria is real—it's out there. And . . ." I don't know why my heart starts pounding. "And I want you to stop calling me Pin. I'm not that girl anymore. My name is Pen."

He gives me a searching look. "Yes, all right," he says quietly. "Pen."

I think he understands what I mean by this.

CHAPTER

30

ALL DAY, THE HOWLS OF THE TRACKERS GET CLOSER. COR pauses and pulls cheese and apples out of his pack, and they eat while walking. Shoe feels his shoulders hunching with every echoing howl, and he can't help but think about the ending that is waiting for him when they are caught—and if they keep trying to escape to East Oria they *will* be caught, he doesn't have any doubt about that. It will be the icy wind, the post, the pig-snouted guard taking practice swings with the whip. The Godmother waving a languid hand, her smile of triumph as they begin. And then trying to count how many lashes he's had so he'll know when it is over, and losing the number in a haze of blood and pain, realizing that this time they're not going to stop. Not until he is dead.

For Pin it will be just as bad. No, *Pen*. He shakes his

head and trudges on. The Godmother will take her memories again, he guesses, and Cor's, and she will become the blank-faced bride of an equally empty-headed prince. She'll be chewed up by the relentlessly turning gears of Story, and the shimmering, sharp flame of a girl that he knows will be no more.

Ahead of him Pen trips over a root, going to her knees. Two shuffling steps and he catches up in time to help her to her feet.

"Drat this dress," she says. Her face is stark white; her eyes are so shadowed they look bruised.

Ahead, Cor pauses and looks back. "Come on," he shouts. "They're coming."

"Yes, we noticed," Pen mutters, and this time she doesn't smile.

Without speaking Shoe takes her hand and they stumble on.

Cor's confession last night had shaken him—Pen knows that he loves her. But he can't bring himself to speak to her about it; it's like a loud, silent thing hanging between them, his keen awareness of her every breath, her every glance at him. With every step, he feels the urgency of their situation, and of needing to tell her. *Pen, you are Pin too, and I love you.*

But he can't. It wouldn't fair to burden her with it, not now. Pen thinks she doesn't know him; to her, he's practically a stranger, still. Doubtless she thinks much more about handsome Cor than about him.

So he'll have to love her—and stay silent until their ending catches up with them.

Overhead the sky is covered with dense gray clouds; the air gets colder until they are breathing out puffs of steam with every step. The clouds lower, hovering just above the tops of the pine trees, and it begins to snow, fat white flakes that fall so thickly that he can hardly see Cor's dark shape ahead of them. Within a few minutes the path is covered; a layer of white covers the trees. Blinking snowflakes from his lashes, Shoe checks the way they've come. Their footprints look black against the snow, a clear path for the trackers to follow.

Pen sees it too. "Oh, curse it," she says wearily. The shoulders and hood of her cloak are dusted with snow, and she is shivering.

"Maybe not," Shoe realizes. "The trackers won't smell as keenly in the snow. Can you use the thimble?"

She looks blankly at him; she's too tired to think.

"To erase the trail we're leaving," he explains.

She blinks. "I suppose I can try." She pulls the thimble from her pocket, puts it on her finger, and crouches. With a pale, shaking hand, she reaches out to touch one of her footprints. She closes her eyes. "It's as you said. It likes warmth better," she murmurs. "Cold is for the Godmother." She is silent for another long moment. Snow sifts down around them. "I think I can make it work," she says at last.

As he watches, a faint, warm wind swirls out from the tip of the thimble, brushing over the ground like an invisible broom. Where it touches, their footprints melt away. The wind sweeps back along their path, erasing their trail.

Pin plucks the thimble from her finger; Shoe bends and helps her stand. "That should help," she says, and casts him a brief smile. Seeing the grimness in his face she adds, "I know, you think we don't have a chance."

"We didn't last time," he says.

"I wasn't there last time," she reminds him.

Yes, Shoe decides. It's definitely better that he stays silent.

CHAPTER

31

COR COMES BACK TO URGE US ON. "PEN," HE PANTS. HIS black hair is dusted with snow. In the gray light, his eyes look pale, like ice.

"Yes, we're coming," I say. Scraping up the last of my strength, I straighten my spine.

"You need food," Cor says, and shares some dried apples. Without speaking we eat them and then drink ice-cold water from the bottles I've been carrying.

We turn to continue down the forest path when a creature, wraithlike and gray in the snow, appears on the path before us. It is man-shaped, with a dog's muzzle bent to the ground, sniffing; on its paw-like hands and feet it wears leather booties.

"Tracker," Cor says, drawing his knife. "Stay behind me."

Seeing us, the tracker freezes. Its muzzle sniffs the air. It is wearing a sort of rough woolen jacket buckled over its belly.

"Wait," Shoe says from beside me. "I think—"

A second tracker appears. It halts and cocks its head, alert.

Cor steps forward to meet them, his whole body tense, ready to fight; it is clear he's had training and knows what he's doing. His knife glints in the gray light.

"No," Shoe says more loudly. "Stop, Cor."

"What are you doing?" I ask, and try to grab Shoe's arm.

He twists out of my grasp and pushes past Cor. "Put the knife away," he says, and goes to the trackers, who pant up at him, their hot breath turning to smoke that wreathes their heads. "Jip, Jes," Shoe says. He peers down the path. "Where's your master?"

The trackers seem to grin up at Shoe; if they had tails, they'd be wagging them.

Shoe glances back at us. "They're friends," he says. He opens his mouth to say something else, when another dark shape looms out of the snow.

It is a huge man with a bristling mustache crusted with snow and ice, a knitted cap on his head, and an ax slung across his back. Without hesitation, he seizes Shoe's hand and shakes it, then claps his other hand on Shoe's shoulder. "I thought it must be you," he says in a deep, gravelly voice.

A friend?

Shoe turns back to me and Cor. "It's the Huntsman." He

sees my questioning look and explains. "The one I told you about, who has the hideout in the forest." He turns to the big man. "I didn't think we'd find you."

"Well, we've been keeping an eye out," he says. Both of the trackers are grinning up at him; he pats their heads. "This your girl? Pin?"

To my profound lack of surprise, Shoe flushes. "No," he says shortly. "Her name is Pen."

The Huntsman gives him a searching look, and then nods to me, then to Cor. "A prince, I'm thinking?"

Cor nods back and sheathes his knife. "You may call me Cor," he says.

"Right, well," the Huntsman says. "The forest isn't happy about them that are tracking you. We've got a clear line out if we go now, and they'll not be able to follow. Do you have another few hours in you?"

"Yes," I answer. I can find the strength somewhere if there's a promise of rest and rescue at the end of it.

"Yes, of course," Cor adds.

The Huntsman nods at Shoe. "He's not running into trees yet, is he?" he asks me.

"No," I answer, not sure what he's talking about.

"Not yet," Shoe answers.

"Stubborn, your lad Shoe," the Huntsman says to me.

"I've noticed," I say, and as Shoe turns an even more interesting shade of red, the Huntsman gives me a beaming smile.

Suddenly I like him enormously and give him a wicked grin in return. Because Shoe is wrong—there *is* escape, and we have found it.

"We'd best get on, then," he says, and takes the water bottles from me, and both Cor's and Shoe's packs, and slings them over his broad shoulders. "By night you'll have a hot fire and dinner in your bellies."

I WAKE UP in the morning and lie still, savoring the comfort of being warm and relatively safe, with the prospect of a good breakfast ahead of me. Far overhead is the rugged ceiling of a cave, the stone pale, like sand. Natural light is coming in from somewhere, and there are torches, too, the flickering flames making shadows dance against the cave's rough walls. I can hear the crackle of a fire and the murmur of voices. And I can smell sausages cooking.

I only remember snatches of the night before, trudging with my head down through the snow, the Huntsman and his trackers leading us on, Cor's strong arm around my shoulders toward the end, helping me along. Then a climb, my fingers numb against the rungs of a ladder, and the cave and a wooden bowl full of stew that I can't remember actually eating, and then nothing else. I must have fallen asleep.

"She's awake," says a harsh-sounding voice.

Stiff in every muscle, I sit up, pushing tangled hair out of my eyes.

Crouched next to my blankets is a young woman whose

face matches her voice. She is sturdy and short and has pock-marked brown skin and straight black hair pulled back into a braid; a jagged scar runs across her cheek almost to her ear; her dark eyes are narrowed, assessing me. She wears trousers, a close-fitting leather vest, and a shirt with the sleeves ripped off. Her bare arms ripple with muscle. "I'm Templeton," she says, and stands. She jerks a thumb over her shoulder. "That's Zel." The girl she is pointing to nods at me, and I blink. She's the most beautiful girl I've ever seen, blonde and blue-eyed, and taller than her friend, slim, and smoothly muscled. Her hair is shaved short, revealing the cool poise of her head and her long, slender neck.

"Breakfast?" Templeton asks.

"Yes indeed," I answer, and scramble out of bed. The floor of the cave is made of sand that feels soft under my bare feet.

Templeton looks me up and down. "Expect you'd like to clean up first." My dress is ragged around the hem and stiff with dirt and pine needles.

But *breakfast* . . . ! My stomach growls.

Templeton grins. "It'll still be there when you're done. Come on." She leads me into a corner of the sleeping area—which is curtained off from the rest of the cave with blankets pinned to a rope—where there's a wooden bucket full of water. Zel hands me a cloth and a cup full of slimy soap, and I strip down and wash, even sticking my head in to do my hair. "You're about Zel's size," Templeton says, coming up with a pile of folded clothes in her arms as I'm toweling myself dry. I put the clothes on—a shirt with cloth thin from washing, a leather vest like Templeton's that comes halfway down my thighs, and trousers, which I like, though I don't ever remember wearing them before, only dresses. I lace up my boots again, comb my fingers through my wet hair, and feel ready for anything.

They lead me into the rest of the cave. I can see now that the natural light is coming from a wide, flat opening high in one wall; a ladder leads down from it. In the middle of the cave is a bright fire with smoke drifting up to a natural chimney, a crack in the ceiling. People, all strangers except for Cor and the Huntsman, are sitting around the fire on sawed-off logs for chairs. The trackers are there too, curled together with another dog; all three look up alertly as I come in. Some of the people are drinking something hot from tin cups; others are eating sausages and thick slabs of toast with cheese. My stomach growls again.

"Good morning, Pen," Cor says, coming up to me, taking my hand. He looks hardly affected by our long flight; even his curly hair is neatly combed.

"Good morning," I say, looking past him. "Is there breakfast?"

The Huntsman gets up from his log chair. Now that he's not wearing his woolen cap, I can see that his head is completely bald—except for his eyebrows and his drooping mustache. "There is," he says in his deep voice, and hands me a plate of sausages and toast slathered with jam.

"Thank you," I say through a mouthful of toast. "How did you know I like jam?"

"Who doesn't like jam?" the Huntsman asks, and sits down again.

"I don't," Cor says. "I prefer butter."

While eating and listening to the Huntsman and Cor talk about toast, and about the dog and the trackers, I look around. The other people are watching me. None of them are Shoe. I open my mouth to ask where he is, but the Huntsman beats me to it.

"He's out with Tobias having a scout around," he says. "He'll be back soon."

"Come and sit down, Pen," Cor says, and guides me to a stool.

I sit and give my breakfast the attention it deserves. The sausages are delicious. The jam is raspberry. I eat every crumb, and the Huntsman hands me a cup of something hot that is not tea. I take a sip. Coffee. Mmm. I can't remember the last time I had coffee. I take another sip and finally pay attention to the others in the cave.

There is the Huntsman, talking quietly with Templeton and Zel by the fire. I see four redheaded girls who must be sisters—"there used to be twelve of us," one of them tells me—and a little hunchbacked old man with crooked fingers sits next to an old woman with a creased, smiling face. Another woman with a dress cut very low and tousled hair as if she's just gotten up from a long sleep bends over the fire, pouring herself a cup of coffee. Farther from the fire, two men are sitting shoulder to shoulder, their knees touching. One of them is ordinary-looking; the other has a wide, ugly mouth, a flat nose, a collection of warts on his chin, and a twinkling smile in his eyes. As I look at them, the ugly one gives a welcoming nod. There are a few others, too, and they all look . . . confident, somehow. Sure of who they are.

"He says they're people who have escaped from Story, or were hurt by it," Cor says to me in a low voice. "They are rebels, and the forest hides them from the Godmother."

"And now we're rebels too," I say, and drink more coffee.

"I am a prince," Cor corrects gently, "and I will make my way to East Oria."

"Story's not going to let you escape that easily, Cor."

"Nevertheless," he says. "I will go, and you should come with me. My mother, the queen, must know of these happenings."

I don't answer. At the mouth of the cave, two figures are climbing inside and down the ladder. They are both wrapped in warm coats with hats and scarves over their faces; I can tell which one is Shoe by the quick competence of his movements. He and the other young man come to the fire, pulling off their hats and unwrapping their scarves.

Shoe's face is bright with cold; seeing me with Cor, he nods. "Good morning, Pen. Did you sleep well?"

"I don't remember," I say, and smile at him. I am strangely glad to see him.

He blinks and swallows. "Um, this is—"

"I'm Tobias," says the boy who came in with him. He is taller than Shoe, and broad, with straw-colored hair and brown eyes. "Marya was my girl. A seamstress, like you."

I give my head a little shake.

"I told you, she doesn't remember," Shoe says to him. "Marya was another Seamstress in the Godmother's fortress," he explains. "Pin knew her." He glances aside at Tobias, who looks away.

Over by the fire, Templeton claps her hands loudly. The others around the fire stop talking; we all turn to face her. The Huntsman gets up from his seat and folds his arms.

"Well now," he says. "You've all seen our newcomers. Pen, there"—he points at me—"and you've met Shoe and Prince Cor." The others nod.

"The Godmother is tracking you," Templeton adds in her harsh voice. "Any sign of them?" she asks Shoe and Tobias.

"Nothing," Shoe answers. "It's cold out there, and quiet."

"Forest has taken care of 'em for now," Tobias adds.

"For now," Templeton repeats. Her eyes narrow and she studies me and Cor and Shoe. "She doesn't come after somebody that hard unless she's got a good reason. Actually, we've never seen her this keen on a hunt. Even when she was searching for past storybreakers."

"What do you mean—storybreakers?" Cor asks.

Templeton gives him a look of strong dislike. "Those who break the story they're in," she says disdainfully. I can almost hear the *you idiot* tacked on to the end of her sentence.

"The storybreaker must be me," I say. I pull the thimble out of my pocket and hold it up. It glimmers in the firelight. All of the others stare at it. "I can use it to do magic."

"Interesting," Templeton says. "But it's not you." She points at Shoe. "It's him."

Shoe, who has been studying the sandy floor under his feet, looks up, startled.

"There aren't many of us," Templeton goes on. "Not that survive it, anyway. We're the ones who mess things up, and the Godmother hates mess, doesn't she? We get into Story and jam up the wheels. When the wheels get caught, they grind. We usually have scars to show for it. Right?" she asks Shoe.

To my surprise, he nods.

"We do it for love, mostly," Templeton says. "But there are other reasons, too."

"I don't quite understand," Cor puts in. "Despite the amazing clarity of your explanation." His voice is sharp enough to cut glass. "Can you give us an example?"

"Well, like you," Templeton says. "The pattern was set. You and Pen were supposed to fall in love at first sight, right? Girl gets prince, turns into princess? Happily ever after? And Shoe here got in the way of it."

"It wasn't—" I start to interrupt.

"We are—" Cor says at the same time.

Shoe is looking intently at the floor again.

"Never mind," Templeton says, waving her hand. "I'll give you a better example." She nods at Zel, who, I realize, has not yet spoken a word. "Zel is gorgeous, as you can see. From birth, like an affliction. The Godmother took her away from her family, brought her here, did the thing with the thimble, you know what I mean?"

I nod, and so does Shoe.

"Takes her memories. Puts her in a little room in a tower like a pretty doll," Templeton goes on. She braces her hands on her hips and I notice again the strength of her arms. "So the Godmother's got a prince all picked out. He'll climb up the tower, rescue her, true love, the end. Doesn't matter what the prince really wants, or the pretty doll really wants. This is Story at work, you see?"

Cor and I nod. Shoe, I think, has already guessed how it comes out.

Templeton reaches out and takes Zel's hand; Zel's beauti ful mouth quirks into a smile. "But I got there first. I'd been visiting her every night. Zel grew her hair out long as a rope." She gives her arm muscles a proud flex. "We fell in love, and we wanted to be together, no matter Story's intentions. So I became a storybreaker. I climbed up, cut off her hair, and we used it to escape. Had a bit of a tussle with the prince first." She draws a finger along the scar that slashes across her cheek, and it makes me realize why she doesn't like Cor very much—all princes are the same, to her. "The forest led us here, and here we've been, ever since."

"Not exactly a happily-ever-after," I say.

"Oh, we're happy," Templeton says. "But it's not Story's ending, either."

Cor is shaking his head. "You call yourself a storybreaker. But Story is not actually broken, is it?"

"Zel's is," Templeton puts in. "But there are lots of stories within Story. It grinds on, even when one story falls out of the pattern."

"What about me?" I ask, and hold up the thimble, reminding her.

"You," Templeton says, nodding. "It's most likely that you are something else altogether. Where did you get that thimble?"

"It was my mother's," I tell her.

The Huntsman nods. "That's what we figured. Your mother worked inside Story. Trying to change it from within."

Shoe's head jerks up, and he stares at me as if something has clicked into place. He's smart, I realize. Always thinking one step ahead.

"That's right," Templeton says. "The Godmother works inside Story too, but her purpose is to make the right endings happen. Your mother opposed her."

"Pen's mother was the Witch?" Shoe interrupts.

Templeton cocks her head. "You've heard of her?"

Shoe nods. "From Natters and his Missus. They're friends of mine in the city. They told me how Story works and about the Godmother and the Witch."

My head whirls. "What does . . ." My voice shakes. "What does that mean, that she was a witch?"

"Not *a* witch," Templeton corrects. "*The* Witch. Your mother worked inside the stories, trying to prevent Story from gaining too much power. She did it by turning the Godmother's strengths against her. The Godmother likes thorny brambles—so your mother became the bad fairy, and used brambles to hide the sleeping girl in a tower, to protect her from any man passing by." Across the fire from me, the woman in the low-cut dress nods. So she was the sleeping girl? Templeton goes on. "The Godmother likes turning people into animals, so your mother used her thimble to turn a prince into a frog, to hide him from Story's intentions so that he could find out who truly loved him."

"And it wasn't a princess, either," puts in the man across the fire, the ordinary one who is sitting next to the man with the ugly, flat face. Had *he* been the frog?

"She was the Witch who gave the drugged apple to the girl in the glass coffin, in order to save her from the prince," the Huntsman adds. Then he adds in a low voice, "But that girl's storybreaker failed her, and she ended up with the prince, even though she was in love with someone else."

"She was brave, your mother," Templeton finishes.

"Did you know her?" I ask.

"Well, I did say that she worked *inside* Story," Templeton answers. "All of us here"—she waves her hand to include all the people gathered around the fire—"all of us managed to get ourselves *outside* of Story." She shrugs. "Some of us met her, when she was the witch in our stories, or the bad fairy or whatever, but she wasn't one of us."

But she'd had a daughter. She must have had some kind of life outside of Story. Where did we live? Did she spend much time with me, or was she always away, being the Witch, fighting against the Godmother?

Did she love me?

"Your mother fought inside Story for a long time," Templeton says, "though she usually lost. And in the end she lost her life, too."

"When?" I interrupt. "How long ago did it happen?"

"What do you think?" Templeton asks the Huntsman. "Last winter, maybe?"

"About that, I'd say," he answers.

My heart shivers with a sudden sense of loss. One year, that's all. One year ago I had a mother and a name and a place in the world, and now it's gone. The only memory I have of her is when she gave me the thimble. "The Godmother must have taken me then," I realize. "She worked her memory spell with the thimble and turned me into one of her seamstresses."

"That's likely what happened," Templeton says. "Since your mother was killed, the Godmother has prevailed. No one has escaped their story's ending and come here to hide. Many storybreakers have died. Story has grown stronger. There's none who can stop it now."

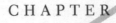

CHAPTER

32

Shoe stares down at the sandy floor of the cave listening to Templeton talking to Pen, his thoughts spinning, trying to parse the possibilities of what will happen next.

By the fire, the Huntsman clears his throat. "You are welcome to stay, Prince Cor, Shoe, and Pen. The forest used to be the Godmother's. Stories used to happen in the forest, but it grew too wild, too unmanageable, so she had to build her city."

"The forest is a rebel, too," Templeton puts in.

"That's right," the Huntsman goes on. "It hides us. The trackers will give up eventually, and you will be safe here."

Listening, Shoe gives a tiny shake of his head. As Templeton says, he is a storybreaker, and he knows how much the Godmother hates him and wants him crushed beneath the wheels of Story. And she wants Pen even more. This story—Pen's story—is crucial; Pen has a thimble and is the daughter of the Witch, so she is far more important to Story than she realizes. The Godmother is not going to give up her hunt this easily. If she has to, she will cover the entire forest with ice and snow until he and Pen and the rest of them are frozen and waiting for her footmen to find them.

"While I thank you for your offer," Cor says formally, "I must go to East Oria. And Pen, you should come with me."

"No," Shoe interrupts. "I don't think you should leave, either of you." This is not going to be good, but he has to say it. "Not yet, I mean," he adds.

"Explain, Shoe," Cor orders.

He nods, trying to think it through.

There's none who can stop Story now, Templeton had said. Circles within circles, he'd told Pen, and no escape except into another prison.

"Shoe?" the Huntsman prompts.

Shoe nods. What if there really is another way? He is a storybreaker. And Pen—with her thimble and the strength that is so much a part of her that she doesn't even realize it—she's even more powerful. "The Godmother's fortress," he says slowly. "It isn't far from here?"

"We're practically under her nose," Templeton says.

"Pen, I know you don't remember," Shoe says to her. "But the fortress is full of people like us. Like Marya." He nods at Tobias, who nods back. "The Godmother's thimble took away our memories, our pasts, and we were put to work." He gazes intently at Pen, willing her to understand. "You were a Seamstress. I was a Shoemaker." He remembers when he first met Pin in the fortress, when she'd whispered this in his ear, the soft caress of her cheek against his. "We didn't touch, or talk, or . . . or kiss, or fall in love. We were slaves to Story, that's all."

Pen is standing close beside Cor. She is staring at Shoe with her eyebrows raised; she doesn't remember any of this, of course.

She doesn't remember that moment during their escape when she'd promised aloud to go back to the fortress and rescue the Jacks who had helped them, and free the God-mother's other slaves, too. She doesn't remember the other Seamstress, Marya, who had died on the wall, impaled by thorns.

Marya, who had been loved by Tobias before she'd been turned into a Seamstress. Early that morning, Tobias had found Shoe in a corner of the cave where he'd been sleeping. "Come on," the other man had said, shaking him awake. "We'll go have a look around outside."

The snow had been blue with the shadows of the night as they climbed out of the cave and scouted for signs of the Godmother's trackers. The air had been bitterly cold; they'd tramped silently along, their breath puffing out as clouds of steam. The snow had turned pink as the sun rose, and then sparkling white, but the air didn't warm. They reached a high place and stopped to look out. The valley below them was absolutely still, the pines cloaked with snow.

Tobias pulled down the scarf covering his mouth. "You were there," he said, his broad farmer's face expressionless. "In the Godmother's fortress."

"Yes," Shoe said.

"I wandered into the forest from outside when I was searching for her. My girl, Marya. Was she there, in the fortress? The Godmother took her, for a seamstress most likely."

Shoe knew exactly who Tobias was talking about. He nodded.

Tobias looked steadily over the quiet valley. "She's still there?"

Shoe made the blow quick. "No. She's dead."

Tobias's face is grim. "Badly?"

"Yes," Shoe said. "I'm sorry."

There was a long silence. "Nothing you could have done about it, is there?" Tobias had said at last, not expecting an answer. "We'd best be getting back."

As they'd hiked back to the cave, Shoe had realized exactly what they needed to do to strike at the very heart of Story so that people like Marya and Tobias would never be hurt again.

Cor is staring at him impatiently. "Well, Shoe? We know already that you were a slave in the fortress."

Shoe nods. "Pin and I escaped from the Godmother's fortress, but we left people behind," he says. "We need to help her slaves escape, just like we did."

"Wait a moment," Templeton interrupts. "What are you talking about exactly here, Shoe?"

Shoe looks at her, then at the others gathered around the campfire. "I'm talking about invading the Godmother's fortress."

"*What?*" Templeton squawks. Beside her, Zel breaks into a silent laugh.

"For one thing," Shoe goes on stubbornly, "if we do it, we'll free her slaves. For another, it'll jam up the wheels of Story, taking away all the dresses and shoes and candles, and things—"

"And straw to be spun into gold," puts in the wizened little man across the fire unexpectedly.

"And dancing slippers," adds one of the four redheaded sisters; the other three nod.

"And glass coffins," finishes the Huntsman. "All of those things make Story turn."

"Right," Shoe goes on. Before anybody can object, he continues. "We should do it fast. We know the Godmother's in the city, not at the fortress. Her guards and footmen are all out searching. We've got Pen and her thimble. There are enough of us; together we might be able to invade the fortress, disarm the few guards and overseers left behind, and rescue her slaves."

The others are staring in disbelief.

Deciding to risk it all, he tells them the rest of the plan

he's been turning over in his head. "From there, we'd have enough people to go after the Godmother."

"You mean attack the city?" Cor asks, his voice strained.

Shoe nods. "Not just the city. Story itself."

They are all still staring as if he is crazy. Shoe feels a flush prickling his cheeks. He can see the shape of things now, and he knows the plan he's suggesting is the only way to truly escape the ending that is coming for all of them.

"You're not just *a* storybreaker," Templeton says at last. "You are *the* storybreaker."

"It would stir up a lot of trouble," says the Huntsman. His eyes are gleaming in the firelight.

"I think it's a terrible idea," Cor says, his voice deep and authoritative. "We should let my mother, the queen, deal with the Godmother, and with Story."

"No." Shoe shakes his head. "She never has before. People from East Oria must have been disappearing for years, but you didn't even know that Story existed, did you, hidden away in its city in the middle of the forest?"

"No," Cor admits.

"Then we can't wait any longer," Shoe says. "The time to do it is now."

There is a long silence. Shoe sneaks a glance at Pen, but she is staring down at her fingers, which are turning the thimble over and over.

"All right," Templeton says at last. She glances aside at Zel, who gives a decided nod. "We're in."

"As am I," the Huntsman says.

"I'm for it, too," Tobias says.

To Shoe's surprise, Pen looks up and gives a sudden laugh. "Oh, I think it's a wonderful idea," she says.

"Pen!" Cor protests.

"Cor, we'll never be free of Story unless we try to break it," she says. "I think it's brilliant. The Godmother will think we're running like scared rabbits. She'll never expect an attack. Well done, Shoe." She gives him a clean, clear smile, her gray eyes shining.

He finds himself smiling back at her.

Her eyes widen, and then she frowns. "I've never seen you do that before."

"Do what?" he asks, nervous. It's as if they're suddenly alone together, not in a cave crowded with other people.

"Smile, of course," she says.

"Oh." He thinks back. "I don't remember ever doing it before."

CHAPTER

33

Shoe tells us about the people in the city—*them that knows*, he calls them—who are willing to resist the Godmother. "They'll help us, I'm sure of it," he says. "If we could get them a message . . ."

"I'll take it," Tobias volunteers.

"Natters and his Missus," Shoe says. "Start with them. They're the leaders, and they'll know who else to contact."

"Good," I say. "If we manage to defeat the guards at the fortress, we'll move on the city. We'll need a signal." I glance at the group around the campfire to see if they have any suggestions.

"The fog," the Huntsman says. "The forest is on our side."

"All right," I say, with a decided nod. "When the fog rises, we will come."

We decide to give Tobias two days' head start before we invade the Godmother's fortress. That gives Cor and me and Shoe time to rest, and to make our plans.

After Tobias leaves, I corner Shoe and make him tell me everything he knows—or guesses—about Story. It gives me a lot to think about, but I'm still tired from the flight from the city, so I curl up in a corner to nap for a few hours. When I wake up, night has fallen outside the cave and I can hear the clash of metal on metal. I rub the sleep out of my eyes and get to my feet.

Out in the main part of the cave, by the light of lanterns set in a circle, Templeton and Zel are fighting each other with long, narrow swords that flash quick and silver in the dim light as they beat and parry. Their feet kick up little puffs of sand.

"Hah!" Templeton shouts, and lunges as keen as a thrown spear at Zel's heart.

Zel coolly parries Templeton's blade and, quicker than my eye can see, has her opponent on the floor with the sword blade at her throat.

Templeton smiles up at her. "Nicely done, love."

Smoothly Zel sheathes her blade, then bends and pulls Templeton to her feet.

They are good. Very, very good.

Templeton, dusting sand from her knees, catches sight of me. "What about you, Pen? Can you fight?"

"No," I admit. "But I want to learn."

"Ah, good," Templeton says, rubbing her hands together. "We love teaching people how to fight." Zel nods, grinning. "First we'll have to choose you a weapon."

Silently, Zel holds out her sword to me. The leather-wrapped hilt is warm from her hand; I grip it tightly. It feels awkward, and wrong somehow. "I don't know. . . ," I mutter.

"No, you're right," Templeton says. "Zel is all grace and quickness, but you need something more solid."

Zel raises her eyebrows and tilts her chin.

"No, not a knife," Templeton answers. "A pike, maybe?"

Zel gives her head a decided shake. No.

While talking, they've led me to the edge of the cave, to a pile of weapons, both edged and blunted for practice, a shield or two, spears, and a large wooden chest.

As if it knows something I don't, my hand reaches for a long staff that leans against the bumpy cave wall. It is made of smooth, darkened oak and is as thick as my wrist, with metal caps at each end. My hands close around it and my body moves to find its balance. I hold it easily, testing its weight.

"A staff. Right," Templeton says with a nod. "Let's see what you can do with it."

We go back to the sandy practice circle.

Around the fire, Shoe and Cor have their heads together with the Huntsman and a few of the others. As we step into the circle of lantern light, they look up.

I am so tired of being used by Story. For as long as I can remember—which isn't very long—I have been determined to fight the Godmother, to *do* something. Feeling the smooth wood of the staff under my fingers, I finally sense my chance for action gathering in my arms and legs, and in the strong center of my very self. I whirl the staff around my head and plant it in the sand, then take up a fighting stance.

Templeton grins and salutes me with the practice sword she selected from the pile of weapons. "Have at me, Pen!"

She doesn't wait for me, but launches herself into an attack, one as blunt and straightforward as I might expect from her. My body shifts; I raise the staff, blocking her blade, ducking her next blow. She lunges again, and I slide away, bring the staff around, and with a metal-capped end knock her on the elbow. With a yelp, she drops her sword onto the sand.

"Ooh," she says, shaking out her hand. Grinning, she picks up her sword again. "Zel, care to join us?"

Her eyes alight, Zel steps into the circle and raises her sword—an edged weapon, not just for practice. They circle me, testing for weakness, slow reactions, but my staff leaps out to meet every attack. I flow, block, thrust, always balanced, always ready. We spar until Templeton takes a blow to the shoulder, flings down her practice sword, ducks the staff, and barrels into me, bearing me to the sand. Zel stands over us, laughing silently.

"You are *good!*" Templeton says, pushing herself off of me. She leans down and pulls me to my feet.

Panting, I dust sand from my leather vest. She's right. I *am.*

Because I've done this before, of course. I had forgotten, but my body remembers. "My mother must have taught me," I realize.

"She knew what she was doing," Templeton says. Zel nods in agreement and raises her sword. "Again?" Templeton asks.

I find myself returning her grin. I love this feeling of strength and competence. "Again," I say with a nod.

We spar for another hour, working, too, on ways of fighting together against multiple opponents, until all three of us are exhausted. At last, sore and sweaty, I settle next to the Huntsman on the cool side of the training circle, away from the fire. Zel and Templeton have gone to inspect the weapons, to be sure all the edged ones are well sharpened.

In the circle, Cor shows Shoe how to hold a knife. "Think of it as an extension of your fist," Cor instructs, then demonstrates. "Don't think stab, think punch."

Watching intently, Shoe nods and then, perfectly balanced, he smoothly repeats the motion.

"Good," Cor approves.

I watch as Shoe follows Cor's instruction to keep the knife hidden as long as he can. In a knife fight, Cor explains to him, the one who strikes fast, without warning, is the one who wins.

The Huntsman hands me a tin cup of cooled tea. "So," he murmurs in his deep voice. "The plan?"

"We'll invade, free the slaves, and then use the fortress as a base from which to go after the Godmother," I say. "We'll strike fast and hard, assisted from within the city by the rebels that Tobias is contacting."

"Well enough," he says.

"I know it won't be straightforward or easy." I cast him a sidelong glance, seeing his concern. "But one of the advantages that we have over Story is that we don't have to do what's expected. Story has to follow a pattern. We don't. We'll be ready, whatever happens."

He looks a little more cheerful. "If you think so."

"I do." As I speak I realize that somehow I've become leader of this group. Me, who was so uncertain, so hesitant. I may not know who I am—*what* I am—but I am determined to win this fight. To take up where my mother left off. Maybe the others can sense that, and I hope they're not wrong.

Cor has finished teaching knifework to Shoe. They step out of the training circle and I go to meet them.

"You're surprisingly quick," Cor says to Shoe, with an approving nod. Shoe hands him the knife; Cor holds it up, inspecting its edge. "A bit more training, and you could be quite good."

With a ragged sleeve, Shoe wipes sweat from his forehead. "We don't have time for more training."

Cor shrugs. "At least you won't get killed in your first fight." He smiles at me. "You're very good too, Pen. And you will have me there to protect you."

"Apparently I'm capable of taking care of myself in a fight," I tell him, a little acerbically.

"Of course you are," Cor says, still smiling. He moves closer and puts a hand on my arm in an almost proprietary way. I give him a level look, and he takes his hand away. He knows I need more time.

Shoe picks up his sweater and pulls it on over his head. "Pen—" he begins, and then he folds his arms and frowns down at the cave floor.

His sandy hair hangs over his eyes; my fingers twitch, wanting to reach out and brush it aside so I can see him better. "Yes, Shoe?"

After a moment he gives a half shrug, as if deciding something, then looks up, meeting my eyes. "Your thimble. Would you use it to help me remember my Before?"

I take a quick breath. Then let it slowly out. "Yes, of course. I should have asked before this."

"You have been busy," Shoe says wryly.

Cor excuses himself, and as I lead Shoe over to the fire, my mind flounders. I used the thimble on Cor, but the Godmother hadn't taken much from him; he'd already known most of his Before. What if I use it on Shoe and it hurts him? What if he's lost too much? What if his life Before makes everything since then irrelevant? "Are you—" I stumble. "Are you certain? It might be best not to know."

"I need to know," Shoe says, sitting on one of the sawed-off logs the rebels use as chairs. "And it's not just for myself. If we know more about the Before, we could learn more about what we're dealing with."

I sit down facing him, our knees touching. Yes, of course Shoe needs to know. He's so clear-sighted. So . . . true. He's not going to stay blind to his Before just to—to what, protect himself? He needs to go into his future with his eyes wide open. "All right," I agree.

"Thank you," he says soberly. His face is very pale.

Now my fingers get what they want as I reach out and gently brush aside the hair that hangs over his green eyes. Those eyes fix warily on the thimble as I draw it out of my pocket. Then I pause. Moving closer, I bring my lips to his. "For luck," I whisper against his mouth. He leans in, and our kiss scorches through me. I jerk back. His gaze is so intense I can't bring myself to return it. Instead I look away, busying myself with polishing the thimble on my sleeve and putting it onto my finger. "Ready?" I ask, in a voice that isn't as steady as it should be.

"Yes," he says, his voice gruff.

I raise my hand and feel him control a flinch as I touch the thimble to his forehead. He closes his eyes.

I know you, Shoe, I think. *Remember.*

The thimble's dimpled silver warms and then glows dull orange, brightening to a red flame. I put my other hand on Shoe's shoulder, steadying him, or maybe myself. The thimble burns even brighter, then flashes with brilliantly white light, and goes dark.

Panting as if he's run a race, Shoe slumps until his head is resting against my shoulder.

I swallow down a strange, desperate feeling and ask, "Do you remember?"

He takes a ragged breath. "Yes," he whispers.

"Is he all right?" Cor's deep voice interrupts behind me.

"Yes, I think so," I answer. Shoe lifts his head from my shoulder.

"Let me guess," Cor says. "He remembers that he's a shoemaker."

I glance up at him; he's standing with his hands on his hips, frowning. It's not like him to be unkind. He's not jealous, is he? Pointing to another sawed-off log, I frown back at him. "Sit down, Cor, and stop looming over us."

Shoe has his elbows on his knees and the palms of his hands pressed over his eyes. "Yes, I was a shoemaker," he says, his voice muffled. Slowly he straightens and blinks dazedly. With a shaking hand, he rubs his forehead. The thimble's heat left no mark there at all. He glances over at Cor, then back at me.

"Well?" I prompt, growing impatient.

"Pen," he says, and something about the way he says my name assures me that knowing his Before has not changed the way he feels about me.

"Shoe," I say, smiling back at him.

He shakes his head. "No," he says wonderingly. "Not Shoe. My name is Owen. I'm from Westhaven." He glances at Cor. "Do you know it?"

"Yes," Cor answers. "It's a trading city about a day's sail down the coast from East Oria."

I nod and turn back to Shoe. To *Owen*. "Do you have family?" I ask.

He nods. "My dad is a blacksmith there, and my mum runs the shop." Then his eyes take on a faraway look; he's clearly remembering them. "I have four brothers and six sisters, all older." I find myself imagining a big, noisy family, sandy haired, green eyed, some of them strapping like their blacksmith father, or clever like their mother, with *Owen* as the youngest, maybe a bit quieter than the rest, but safe and well loved.

"How did the Godmother take you?" Cor asks.

The smile fades from Owen's eyes. "Oh," he says as he gets abruptly to his feet. "They must think I'm dead." He looks as if he's ready to run all the way to his true family in Westhaven. "It was, um . . . it was her footmen. I was running an errand for my master. I was apprenticed to a shoemaker," he adds. "They just took me off the street, stuffed me into a windowless carriage with five other people, and drove night and day until we arrived at the fortress." He frowns. "We didn't stop once. They must have killed the horses." He shivers. "They dragged us in to the Godmother. She . . ." He touches the center of his forehead, and his shiver turns to a shudder.

"She took your Before," I say.

He nods. "Pen, I was eleven years old. I was just a kid." He looks sick. "I was at the fortress for such a long time."

"Your family remembers you," I reassure him.

"I hope they do," he says. "I hope they're all right."

I am glad for him. Yet I feel just a little bereft. He has all that certainty. He knows he is loved; he knows he has a place in the world, if he can get to it. He knows who he is.

But me—I feel certain that I can't use the thimble on myself. I may never discover who I really am.

CHAPTER

34

THE GODMOTHER'S FORTRESS IS HALF A DAY AWAY, AND WE are ready. We set off at midday with packs of supplies on our backs, plenty of rope, and weapons. Templeton gives me a warm coat to wear, and a woolly scarf; I'm glad for the fur-lined boots that Shoe made for me. I carry my staff. The trackers go ahead and come back to show us the best paths to take to avoid any of the Godmother's men who are lurking about. We go single file, silently. Cor is ahead of me and Shoe a step behind, wearing an overlarge coat that the Huntsman lent him. I've never fought in a battle before—at least, not that I remember—and I feel a fizz of excitement mixed with nerves.

And I am confused about what is happening between me and Shoe. *Owen*, I remind myself. Like his smile, our kiss lasted for only a fleeting moment, but it hit me—like a knife, without warning. It made me feel off-balance. Pulled in two directions at once. It makes me acutely aware of him, as if there's a current running between us. It's different from the attraction I feel to Cor.

As we walk, Cor and Owen are arguing in low voices about the best way to get into the fortress. Owen thinks he should go over the wall first, alone, as a scout. "That way," he explains, "we can be sure most of the guards are away. I can get to her slaves, too, and tell them to be ready to fight for us when the time comes, and then I'll come back and report."

"I don't like this plan," Cor says firmly. He turns and stares past me, challenging Owen. "If you should be caught, we'll have to stage a rescue as well as everything else."

"I'll try not to get caught," Owen says, as if it's that simple.

"I'll go with you, Sh—Owen," I add.

Cor stops in his tracks. In the snowy late afternoon, his eyes look very blue. "Pen, no."

"It makes sense for me to go," I say. "I've got this." I heft my staff. "And I've got the thimble. It'll help us get in, and get away safely."

Owen steps up next to me. His face is grim again. "She's right, Cor," he says. "The last time we wouldn't have gotten out—Pin and I wouldn't, I mean—without the thimble."

We continue on, catching up to the rest of the rebels. I can see by the stiffness in Cor's back and in his meticulous politeness that he's not happy with me and my decision to go with Owen.

As twilight falls, staining the snow-covered forest with pink, and then gray, we reach the fortress walls. One moment we are among thick pine trees, the next we are facing a gray stone wall about the height of two men.

The Huntsman has been leading us; he's brought us to a place where a hook of some kind is stuck to the top of the wall; a lumpy rope hangs down from it.

Owen steps up beside me. "It's where Pin and I escaped before," he tells me.

I notice how careful he is to call me Pen. "You don't think it's a trap?"

He shakes his head. "I think it wouldn't occur to the Godmother or her guards that anyone would use it to get back into the fortress."

The Huntsman steps up to us. His brown skin is ruddy with cold. "We'll pull back into the trees to wait until night-fall," he says in a low voice. "All right?"

"All right," I say, and we tramp through the snow until we can't see the wall anymore. The others are brushing aside snow, making a clear place on the pine-needly ground to sit while waiting for Owen and me to return. They won't have a fire—it's too risky—but they pull cheese and bread from one of the packs and share it around. Templeton and Zel sharpen their blades and look competent; the rest seem ready and determined. Owen and I stand apart, eating our dinners and waiting for full night.

"I keep wanting to call you Shoe," I tell him, taking a

last bite of cheese sandwich.

"I keep thinking of you as Pin." He shakes his head. "But you're right to insist on Pen. Names matter."

I shove my bare hands into my coat pockets, gripping the thimble. I should have worn mittens. "I suppose they do."

He nods, and moves closer to me, as if for warmth. "A shoe is a thing, like a pin is a thing. It's a slave name." He looks in the direction of the fortress wall, though we can't see it through the fir trees and the gathering dusk. "I'm not a slave anymore."

"No," I say, leaning my shoulder companionably against his.

"But I can't pretend it never happened, either." He's quiet for a few moments, thinking. "I'll use both names. Owen Shoemaker."

"It's a good name," I tell him. I think, now, that it doesn't matter what name Owen uses for me, Pin or Pen. It's clear that he loves me either way. I wonder why he won't speak of it. I'm not sure if I want him to, or not.

Cor tramps through the snow to join us. When he speaks, a puff of steam comes out with his words; the air has gotten colder. "Are you absolutely determined to do this, Pen?"

Right, back to the job at hand. "Absolutely determined," I say, feeling almost cheerful.

"Then I will come too," he says. "Someone has to protect you both."

I glance aside at Owen; he gives me a little shrug. "I can protect myself," I tell Cor.

"You'll need me with you just in case you're discovered and attacked," Cor says, all honorable formality.

"If that happens," I argue, "having one more fighter with us is not going to make a difference."

Owen nods, agreeing.

"And," I add, bending to pick up my staff, which I'd set down at my feet, "I do have some training."

As I stand, Cor rests his hand on my arm. "Can I have a moment alone with you, Pen?" he asks.

"Of course," I say. "We'll be back soon," I say to Owen, handing him my staff, and Cor and I head farther into the forest. The branches hang down, heavy under their blankets of snow. The air is cold and crisp; a wind rushes in the tops of the pine trees, making a sound like ocean waves. It is a peaceful scene, but a bubble of excitement is trembling in my chest.

As we walk through the snow, Cor takes my hand, helping me over a fallen log. His hand is big and warm and it feels safe, somehow. When we're far enough away from the makeshift camp, he stops, still holding my hand. I gaze up into his eyes. "This is difficult for me," he says softly.

"What is difficult, exactly?" I ask.

He draws me closer to him. "Pen, during the past few days I've seen the best of you. You've been brave, and strong, and beautiful. And I have to admit that your legs in those trousers are any man's dream. I grow more and more certain that we are meant to be together. Am I wrong to hope that you have feelings for me too?"

I gaze up into his clear blue eyes. He doesn't bother with his practiced smile anymore. His truest self is shining through—his strength and his patience, and a code of honor that clearly makes things difficult for him sometimes.

"I've been thinking," he goes on, "about those broken stories in which the girls in the towers are saved from the princes. But Pen, I've been wondering. Doesn't the prince ever get to be loved?"

Oh, such a question. "Yes," I answer. I remember my stepsisters' keen interest in the prince, and the many people, mostly young women, who crowded around him at the ball. "Surely you've had lots of girls eager to fall in love with you."

He nods. "Yes. But none of them were like you. They were ladies."

I can't help but laugh. "And I'm not?"

A reluctant smile tugs at the corner of his mouth. "That's not what I meant. I could never be sure if they liked *me*, or the rest of it."

"The prince," I say. "But not the man."

"Yes." He brings my hand to his lips and kisses it, then holds it in both of his. "Could you love me, Pen?"

I *could* love a man like him. Except . . . "Cor," I start. "I—"

"Don't speak now," he interrupts. "It's not the right time. And—and I have seen the way you look at Shoe."

I blink. "How do I look at him?"

He glances aside and gives me only half an answer. "I

have not seen you look at me that way."

Unsure of what he means, I shake my head. "He's Owen now, remember? Not Shoe."

"Ah," Cor says. "Yes. Pen, when this ends, you will have to choose between us. All I want to say to you now is that I hope you will choose me."

"I don't *have* to choose anyone, Cor," I interrupt.

"Of course you don't," he says hurriedly. "Yet I still believe that we belong together." He puts his hands on my shoulders. "May I kiss you?" he asks.

He kissed me once before, on the terrace at the ball, but I hardly knew him then. I am curious to see if his kiss tastes different to me now, if it can measure up. "You may," I say, a little breathless.

He bends closer and places a kiss carefully at the corner of my mouth, then pulls me tightly to his chest and gives me as finely shaped and worthy and well considered a kiss as any girl could ever want.

AT NIGHTFALL IT is the Huntsman and Templeton who make Cor's decision for him. "It'd be stupid for three to go," Templeton says. Her dislike of Cor is palpable. "You'll just be clumping around in the dark getting the other two caught."

"At any rate," the Huntsman puts in, "we could better use your help here, readying the assault."

Cor capitulates, and that leaves me and Owen standing in

the darkness at the base of the wall around the Godmother's fortress. The sky is a deep blue-black, the night lit by a three-quarter moon that hangs low over the fortress. It gives plenty of light, reflecting off the snow.

It gives plenty of light for guards to spot us, too.

Owen has taken off his borrowed coat and wears just his dark clothes and sweater, which is starting to look a bit ragged. He has a long knife sheathed at his belt. Templeton has lent me a woolen sweater too, and I roll up the sleeves while contemplating our climb. The rope we'll use looks lumpy and black against the gray of the wall.

"Up we go," I whisper, gripping my staff. A puff of steam comes out with my words.

"If we wait a few minutes, the moon will set," Owen whispers back. In the moonlight his face is pale and crossed with shadows. "Pen, there are brambles on the other side of the wall. Be careful of them. They might try to stab you with thorns."

He told me this once before, at the castle ball as the clock struck midnight—that I got the scar on my wrist from climbing up this very wall. It feels strange to think that my body was in this place before, that it did this thing that I can't remember doing.

"All right," I whisper. "I'll be careful."

"It could be icy at the top, too." His voice is tense. His hands are in his pockets and his shoulders are hunched.

He is wound very tightly, I realize. Shivering, and not just with the cold. Going back over the wall and into the fortress where he was once a slave must be difficult for him. "Lots of bad memories in there?" I ask, with a nod toward the wall.

He jerks out a nod.

I try to make a joke. "I expect you wouldn't mind if the Godmother took them all away."

He looks up, suddenly intense. "Yes. I would mind very much."

Oh. "Because of Pin. You wouldn't want to forget her."

"No, I wouldn't."

"I know you loved her," I say.

"Yes," he says briefly, sadly.

"Did she . . ." I lean my staff against the wall and step closer to him. We are much of a height, and I can feel the warmth of his breath on my cold cheek. "Did she love you back?"

As if he can't help himself, he lifts his hand and with his fingers traces the line of my jaw. My skin tingles at his touch. "I don't know. I think so."

"She never said?"

"Pen, don't—" he starts.

But I am relentless. "Did you ever kiss her?"

His lips are on mine. "Yes," he breathes, and his arms come around me and the kiss we share is warm and deep and desperate. I know I shouldn't be doing this, but I can't help it. It is nothing at all like kissing Cor.

A shadow falls over us. We break the kiss. I can't tell if I am shaking or he is. The moon has gone down behind the fortress. The night is dark enough. I catch my breath. "Time to go," I whisper.

I can barely make out his face in the darkness, but I feel him nod back at me.

CHAPTER
35

THEY GET OVER THE WALL AND PAST THE BRAMBLES WITH-
out any trouble. The courtyard, covered with a pristine
blanket of snow, stretches before them, interrupted only by
the stark line of the post in the middle. Beyond it, the fortress
is a huge, dark, humped shape with lights burning in many
of its windows. The slaves to Story work day and night with
little rest. Owen can feel the weight of the place settle over
his shoulders.

But it's heavy in a way that is different from when he was
a slave. Then, he was ruled by his fear, and he had nothing to
fight for. Now he knows about his Before.

He thinks of his mother, tiny and brisk, wrapped in an
apron too large for her, always the center of their loud, ram-
bunctious family. He remembers that when he was eight

years old he'd been apprenticed to a shoemaker on the other side of Westhaven, and he'd crept away from the noise and bustle to worry about it. It was baking day, and the house was filled to bursting with the whole family, plus his third-oldest sister, Jenny, and her husband and new baby, and his oldest brother Charlie's two kids, but his mother had sought him out in a corner of the dark smithy. He remembers wrapping his arms around his knees and sniffing away tears. *What if I'm not any good at it, Mum? I don't want to go. What if I miss you too much?*

Ah now, his mum had said, settling beside him in the sooty corner and putting an arm around his narrow shoulders. *I know it's hard. But you're not going to hide here in the dark for the rest of your life, are you? Some things have to be faced up to. It will be all right. You'll see.*

She'd smelled of fresh bread and lavender soap, and she'd used a corner of her flour-dusted apron to dry his tears. Then she'd found the smithy cat for him to cuddle. *Come back into the house when you're ready, my dearest,* she'd said.

He'd loved her so much; he'd loved them all. He couldn't imagine a world without them in it. But he'd lived in that world for seven years.

What if his mother or his dad were taken by the God-mother? What about one of his brothers or sisters or one of their many children? All the blank-eyed people in the city, or the slaves in the fortress—they had all been somebody's son or daughter or mother or dearest love.

If he and Pen and the others fail, the Godmother will steal even more people away from their real lives. Story will turn again, and grow even stronger.

He can't hide away from that. He has to face up to it.

"I've got the thimble ready," Pen whispers.

Owen nods and they start across the courtyard. Anyone looking out the windows will see them, shadows against the snow. Their breaths huff in the icy air, and they hurry past the post to reach the fortress wall. There is no sound of alarm.

"Wait a moment," Pen pants. Handing him her wooden staff, she crouches in the snow. He sees the glint of her thimble as she touches it to their trail of footprints. The warm wind swirls out and brushes away their tracks, just as it did in the forest. She stands, swiping a lock of hair out of her eyes. "Onward," she says briskly, taking her staff back.

Her steady bravery makes him want to kiss her again, once more for luck, maybe, but there's no time for that. Now that they're over the wall, they have to move fast. They'll try first for the Jacks, the slaves whose dread of the post might make them most eager to escape. Skirting the fortress wall, Owen finds an open door—the same door he and Pin escaped through before. It is unguarded. He cracks the door open and peers inside.

Pen leans over his shoulder to see. "This is strange," she says, seeing the empty hallway that stretches before them, lit only by an oil lamp turned low.

Not if all the guards are out in the forest hunting for

them. "Maybe they're counting on the workers to guard themselves," he whispers. He knows what he'd been like as a slave. He'd sat hunched over his workbench working, working, working, terrified of drawing the Godmother's attention again. The possibility of escape would never have occurred to him without Pin.

"Owen, there must be guards in there somewhere," Pen whispers.

"You're probably right," he whispers back. But he's not afraid anymore. Just determined.

"Let's go," she says.

With a nod he pushes the door open and they pad down the hallway. Pen walks lightly, the staff held across her body, as if she's ready to fight. Owen listens for the sound of footsteps, an alert shout. But all is silent. They turn a corner, go down another hallway until they reach a series of closed doors. "This one," he remembers. "You can open it with the thimble."

Pen touches the door's knob with the thimble and he turns it and peers into the Jacks' workshop.

When he'd been here before with Pin, the air had been loud with bangs and clanks, and thick with sawdust, the Jacks hard at work. Now it is silent. He pushes the door open wider and steps inside.

The only light comes from a lantern set on a table; a pile of crumpled blue requisition slips is there too, overflowing onto the floor. The rest of the workshop is filled with shadows, the machines and workbenches and forge silent.

There is a rustling sound. Owen freezes.

"What . . ." Pen glances alertly around, raising her staff.

"Shh," he breathes, listening.

A scrabble, and a shadow twitches behind one of the workbenches.

They're in here. "Jacks," Owen says, and even though he keeps his voice low, it shatters the silence. The shadows quiver with held breaths. "I know you're in here," he says. "It's me, the Shoemaker."

Another scuffling sound, and one of the Jacks—the Jack who built them the grappling hook before—edges into the light. He holds himself stiffly; Owen knows that hunch-shouldered look. This Jack has been to the post. He's the one who will have to lead the other Jacks out.

"I remember you," the Jack says. "And her." He nods with his chin at Pen. "The Seamstress."

"You got into trouble because of us," Owen says.

Another glance over the shoulder. "Yes," the Jack answers.

"We're very sorry for that," Owen says, but goes on quickly. "We escaped, and we've come back for you now."

The Jack blinks.

"We haven't seen any guards or overseers," Owen adds. "And the outer door is open." He turns to Pen. "Tell him the signal?"

She nods and holds up the thimble. "A flash of flame."

"Wait by the outer door," Owen goes on, sounding more

confident than he actually feels. "When you see the flame you'll know it's time. We've brought people with us to help. We'll fight the rest of the guards and try to take over the fortress."

"Take over . . . ?" the Jack asks, his voice wavering.

"There are far more slaves here than guards," Owen says. "You have things here you can use as weapons, don't you?"

That decides it. The Jack gathers himself and says, "Yes," then glances to Pen and back to Owen. "You got away, you say?"

Owen can't take the time to explain that their escape wasn't really an escape at all. Instead he nods.

"Righty-o then," the Jack says, and he's standing straighter. "We're with you." Other Jacks creep from behind the workbenches, their eyes wide. "Wait for the signal, is that it?" he asks.

"Right," Owen answers. "The signal."

CHAPTER
36

FROM THERE WE MAKE THE ROUNDS, GOING FROM ONE workshop to the next, warning Lacemakers and Glovers and a surly old Shoemaker—a new man, a replacement for Owen— who tells us to go away and turns back to his work, and Bakers of gingerbread, and all the rest. Watch for the signal, we tell them. It's time to fight.

Nothing about the fortress is even remotely familiar to me. I thought I might remember the smell—musty—or the feel of the air—damp—yet it is as if I have never been here before.

Owen saves the Seamstresses for last. We are hurrying now, knowing that the Godmother's slaves are on the move, that we need to get to the wall and give the signal for the Huntsman and Templeton and Cor and the rest to come over.

"Here." Owen points to a door at the end of a hallway.

I open it. The room of the seamstresses is long and narrow with whitewashed walls and a low ceiling stained with candle smoke. At the table sit old women, hunched, squinting, their gnarled fingers gripping silver needles. There is no color in the room except for the brilliant cloth they are stitching into dresses—sapphire velvet, ruby silk, gold satin shot with silver threads.

As I step into the room, the old seamstresses peer up at me. I stare back at them.

I remember what Owen said to me out on the terrace, at the prince's ball. I was wearing the stunning flame dress that Lady Faye had given me. *Where did you get the dress?* he had asked. No, he'd demanded—and I hadn't understood; I hadn't seen why the dress mattered.

But now I know. These slaves of Story had made it. The Godmother had taken my measurements with her thimble, and these sad, bent women had measured the silk, cut it, and sewn it with stitches no bigger than a grain of sand. This is all they know. The endless labor, the pain of gnarled hands and hunched backs, and then . . . an ending.

Once I'd worked on dresses just like the one I'd worn to the prince's ball. I run my thumb over the calluses on my fingertips. For the first time Pin is physically real to me in a way she never was before. The memory of it takes shape, the ache in my hunched shoulders as I bent over my work, my eyes straining in the meager candlelight.

Then I feel Owen's steady strength at my side. "Tell them," he whispers.

My Pin-self fades away, and I straighten and feel my new calluses as I grip my staff. "Do you remember me?" I ask, even knowing how frightening any question about memory might be for them. "I was a Seamstress like you. I was a rebel, but I didn't end up stabbed by thorns on the wall. I got away. You can, too, if you come with us."

Even before I finish speaking, the old seamstresses are dropping their work, pushing themselves off their benches, hobbling toward us.

The oldest Seamstress pauses and squints up at me with watery blue eyes. "We remember," she says in a cracked voice. "We helped you find scraps of silk for the rope."

"The rope?" I glance questioningly at Owen.

"The one we used to scale the fortress wall," he tells me. "Pin made it. She persuaded the Jacks to make the grappling hook, too."

"Oh," I say, surprised. I'm starting to like Pin—her cleverness and resourcefulness.

"This way," Owen says, and we gently help the old Seamstresses out the door.

And then we hear it. A shout, and the sound of running footsteps. A scream echoes down a hallway.

"Hurry," Owen says, his voice tense, and the seamstresses shuffle faster. They go around a corner ahead of us, and Owen casts a look back the way we've come. He skids to a halt; I crash into his back and we both stumble.

Coming down the hallway behind us is a woman. I blink. The woman has lidless eyes with slits for pupils; her hands are covered with scales. As she sees us, her wide mouth opens and her forked tongue flickers in and out, tasting the air.

"The Seamstresses' Overseer," Owen whispers. "We have to hold her off so they can get away."

"Sahhh," the Overseer breathes. She glides closer on silent, scaly feet. "So, Seamstressss."

Owen and I back up a step.

Three pig-faced guards in blue uniforms lurch around a corner and run to join the Overseer.

Owen pulls the knife from the sheath at his back.

I dig into my trousers pocket for my thimble and slip it onto my finger. At the same moment, the three guards charge us. A tusked face pushes close to mine; strong hands seize me. I twist in their grip, and fire flashes from the thimble, and a pig-guard grunts and collapses. The two other guards duck past us, trying to attack from behind. I slip the thimble back into my pocket.

Gripping my staff, I take up a low guard stance, my back to Owen. He'll have to handle the Overseer while I deal with these two. The moves I've practiced come without thought. One guard lunges at me with a sword and it's as if the blade slows down. I see the glint of light on metal, the grimace on his pig-snouted face, and I am turning, blocking the blade and coming around to strike with the top of my staff, right in the middle of his chest. I feel the blow all the way up my arms, but I hold my ground. The guard falls to the floor, groaning. The other guard flails at me with his sword and I dispatch him, too, *block* and *thrust*.

Then I whirl, staff at the ready, and see the Overseer weaving closer. Her mouth gapes; her fangs drip with poison. Before I can move, Owen lunges at her with his knife. She writhes out of his way and strikes back. With a shout, I swing my staff around until it slams into the side of the Overseer's head; she crumples to the floor.

Owen and I stand next to each other, panting. "Did she get you?" I ask, checking his sweater for blood from the Overseer's bite.

"No." With steady hands, he resheathes the knife at his back. He's not afraid, I realize. Just determined to do whatever needs to be done.

A sudden silence falls. After a moment, I hear pounding feet in the distance, more guards shouting, then another scream.

"The outer door?" I ask. We must give the signal at once, or we risk losing before the battle's even begun.

Owen nods. "Come on." Taking the lead, he guides me through the fortress's winding passages. A guard looms up before us; I don't even hesitate. Using one strike I lunge past Owen and sweep the guard from our path.

"Well done," Owen says breathlessly, and leads us on.

When we reach the door, I expect to see the fortress slaves

waiting there for the signal, but apart from a tight knot of old seamstresses, only the Jacks have gathered. They are holding lengths of pipe, chunks of wood with nails hammered into them, and shards of glass, ready to fight. "Where are the rest?" I pant, pushing past them to the door.

"Too afraid," the lead Jack answers, and hefts an ax.

"This way," Owen says urgently, pointing at an outer door. "We have to give the signal!"

The Jacks and seamstresses and I stumble out of the fortress. With Owen at my side, I hold the thimble high, and a brilliant flash flares out, flooding the courtyard with light. "Come on!" I shout. In the light I can see that the wall around the fortress is crawling with brambles; the Huntsman and Cor and Templeton and the rest are fighting their way down it. I clench the thimble in my hand again and turn. Fortress guards are spilling into the courtyard, some with pig snouts, others with naked rat tails or furry ears, or paws bristling with claws.

I turn to Owen; his face is pale and determined. "Stay with the Seamstresses," I tell him. "Protect them." A swift nod, and he goes.

The guards, seeing how few we are, break out into howls of triumph.

The Jacks cringe; in a moment they will break, and flee.

"Come on, Jacks!" I shout, and step forward, swinging my staff. The lead Jack comes with me, and then the rest follow, and so do Owen with his knife and the seamstresses, armed only with needles. The fortress guards roar out a challenge and advance across the snow-covered ground to meet us.

I block and strike and try to keep the Jacks from losing their nerve. I catch a glimpse of Owen protecting the oldest Seamstress. A footman with hooves thrusts his jagged sword past him; the tip of the blade slashes across the Seamstress's arm. Drops of blood scatter, staining the snow; she collapses, and Owen stands over her, gripping his knife, outnumbered. The fight boils around us. I catch torchlit glimpses of horns, tails, claws, snarling mouths—we are surrounded.

Then, with a shout, the Huntsman pushes through the Jacks and bulls into the center of the fortress guards, swinging his ax. Behind him comes Templeton, screaming out a challenge, and Zel, whose blade flickers as she slices through the first line of guards.

There are still too many of them and not enough of us. We need more help; somebody has to rally the other slaves. The Jacks look to me for direction.

I fight my way over to Owen and pull the old Seamstress out of the worst of the fighting. As Owen gently eases her to the snowy ground, I catch sight of Cor's tall form. "Cor!" I shout over the crash and clash of weapons. He stabs a guard with his sword, follows up with a punch, and then glances my way. Owen stays with me like a shadow as I push past two Jacks until I reach his side. "Cor," I pant, my breath steaming in the cold air. "I have to go for help. Can you take the lead here?"

The Huntsman heaves up beside me; he bends to pick up a handful of snow and uses it to wipe off his bloody ax. "Where are the rest of the fortress slaves?" he rumbles.

"They're frightened," I snap back at him. "I'll go rally them in a moment. But first—"

"Pen!" Templeton shouts. "I need your thimble here."

"Coming," I answer over my shoulder, then I address Cor again. "Cor—"

"Yes, of course," he interrupts. "Go do what you have to do."

No protest that I need protecting; I feel a surge of appreciation for him. "We'll be back as quickly as we can."

Cor nods and, avoiding a cluster of snarling, goat-footed guards, grabs a few Jacks to ready an assault on the fortress door.

I TURN BACK to the fight. With Owen a steady presence at my side, I clear a way to where Templeton and Zel are fighting back to back against three guards and one snakelike overseer. "Pen!" Templeton shouts, catching sight of me. She ducks, and Zel reaches past her to block a guard's knife thrust. "We're being overrun. Go find more of the slaves to fight for us!"

"Right!" I shout back.

We manage to extricate ourselves from the fighting. A clot of guards is at the door that leads inside; we're blocked.

"There's another way in," Owen pants.

I follow him as he ducks into the shadows at the edge of the fortress wall; we make our way through the knee-deep snow to another door. Quietly Owen pushes it open and we step into a darkened hallway. The sound of the fight fades behind us. I pause for a moment to catch my breath and stamp snow from my boots.

"All right?" Owen asks, his voice rough.

"Yes." I'm so glad he's with me. Gripping my staff, I follow him at a jog down the long hallway to a door at the end; it opens onto another hallway, this one lit with torches and lined with open doors. From one door peers a ruddy-faced man built like a barrel; others crowd behind him, too afraid to step into the hallway.

"You!" I shout, and pick up my pace, passing Owen.

As I get to the door, it slams shut; from behind it comes a babble of voices.

"Who are you?" demands a loud voice from behind me. From one of the other doors comes a huge woman with red hair that hangs down her back in two long braids. In her burly arms she holds a three-legged spinning wheel. She scowls fiercely at us. "No, wait. I already know. You're the ones who escaped. Seamstress and Shoemaker? Caused a lot of trouble, didn't you?"

"And we've brought more trouble," I say. Beside me, Owen nods.

"Good!" she cheers. "This place needs trouble." Reaching

past me and Owen, she bangs on the door. "Hey, you in there. Open up! It's a Spinster here!" Then she glances at me. "Straw into gold is what we spin." She turns to the door again and pounds with a meaty fist.

The door cracks open. I see dozens of eyes peeking out.

"We need your help," I tell them. "I used to be a Seamstress, and Owen was the Shoemaker, and we're here with others who are freeing the slaves from the fortress. We need your help."

"No, no," one of the Candlemakers protests; behind him, others are shaking their heads. "It's too dangerous."

"If we light this wick, we're the ones who'll be burned," another puts in.

Owen turns his grim stare on the Candlemakers. "She has power, and strength, and she can lead us out of here." He nods at me. "Show them the thimble."

I draw it from my pocket and it flares with light. The Candlemakers understand light, I think, and flame; at first they flinch away, and then they stare, as if drawn toward my thimble. Urgency makes my voice shake. "We can be free," I tell them. "We just need you to help us."

Behind the door, the heads come together, and there's a babble of discussion.

Then, suddenly the Candlemakers' door opens wide, and the barrel-shaped man steps out. "Aye, we'll help." The other Candlemakers step into the hallway, carrying heavy iron pitchers, and a knife or two, and one edges past me with a pot that brims with hot, melted wax. As good a weapon as any, I suppose.

I turn to the Spinster. "And you'll come, too?"

She gives a fierce grin, and from the doorway behind her come five more Spinsters, all carrying spinning wheels or wickedly sharp spindles like weapons.

I feel a sudden flame of hope. This might be enough to push back the fortress guards. "To the fight!" I shout, and turn to show them the way.

Owen's hand comes down on my shoulder. "Wait," he says to me. "You go on," he tells the Spinster. "Go toward the noise of fighting. We'll catch up." Then he points with his chin farther down the hallway.

The Spinster nods, as if understanding, and hoists her spinning wheel. "Come on, you lot!" she shouts. "To trouble!"

With a clatter and a rush, the Candlemakers and Spinsters run to join the fight.

I pull myself out of Owen's grip. "We have to go with them," I protest.

"Not yet. There's one more, Pen." He hurries down the hallway.

"Fighters?" I ask, falling into step beside him.

He shakes his head. "I don't know. But you need to see them." He leads us to a door that opens onto a staircase that winds up into one of the fortress's blunt towers. Up we climb, round and round until I get dizzy, my breath tearing at my lungs. Can't stop to rest—have to rally these last slaves and get back to the battle.

At last we reach the top of the stairs. With his shoulder Owen shoves open the door, which opens onto a room that takes up the entire floor of the tower. The room is made all of stone and holds no furniture. It is crowded with people, maybe twenty-five in all.

They are naked. They stand with their arms hanging, not trying to cover themselves. Some are old, some are young. Their hair has been cut short, and they are very clean. All of them stare at us with blank, hopeless eyes.

I catch my breath. "Hello."

None of them reacts; it's as if they don't even hear me.

Oh. With a shiver, I realize what these are. They've been brought here recently. The Godmother has taken their Befores; she's storing these people here like . . . like cogs and gears and pistons, parts for a machine she has no use for yet, and she will soon return to assign the best craftsmen and women to their work in the fortress. If they don't have a special skill she can use here, they'll be sent to the city to serve Story's will.

I was once one of them. I stood in this very room, slack-mouthed and blank-eyed like a puppet with its strings cut. No. Not *me*, just my body. With no *me* in it at all? Just . . . Nothing?

Beside me, Owen takes my hand, offering his steady

strength. I turn to him and rest my head on his shoulder, hiding my eyes so I don't have to see. He was one of them too, once; it's just as hard for him. This is the dark truth of our Befores: we both come from this room, this beginning. And all that we have become denies this place. We truly are ourselves. Owen's arm comes around me, and I know that the Nothing has no power over either of us anymore.

"Can we—can we help them?" I ask, my voice muffled. I could give back their Befores. . . .

"No time," he says briefly.

And yes, he's right—I can feel the urgency of the battle calling to me. I'm needed there, even more than here. I take a deep breath and straighten, then hold up my thimble to get their attention. They cringe away.

"I'm not the Godmother," I reassure them. "My thimble won't hurt you. My friends and I are fighting for your freedom, and we need your help." I gaze around at them. Nothing. "All right," I finish, and back away. "We'll leave the door open. Come fight with us if you can."

With that, Owen and I turn and race down the stairs again.

THE BATTLE HAS moved from the courtyard into the fortress, to a huge, torchlit room that looks like some kind of dining hall. In its center, among a jumble of rough tables and benches, the fight surges. The rebels fight with swords and knives; I catch a glimpse of the Huntsman swinging his ax. More have joined us; I see slaves wielding cutting scissors and hammers and bags of flour; the burly Spinster sweeps her spinning wheel around herself, screaming wildly.

But it still isn't enough. Led by a tall, goat-horned brute, more guards—these without uniforms; just their fur, or scales, and carrying no weapons but their claws and fangs—pour into the room through another doorway. They shriek and howl, breaking through the line of storybreakers and slaves. A snarling mass of guards surges toward me.

There's no time to be frightened. I take up a fighting stance, spin my staff to clear a space around me, and let them come. A faltering moment, and then, I find the rhythm of block and thrust that my body knows so well; and then the Huntsman is beside me, swinging his ax, and Templeton, grinning and wild-eyed, and Zel with her flickering sword, and even the oldest Seamstress, with her own blood dripping down her arm, darting in to stab with her needle.

In the surge of the battle, Owen is separated from me. Missing his steadiness at my side, I glance wildly around the room, catching a glimpse of him and Cor near one of the doorways, fighting back to back against the goat-horned guard and six of the most savage of the other guards.

I start to fight my way toward him, when a guard with tusks and wildly rolling eyes springs at me, slashing with his clawed hands. I barely get my staff up to block him.

"Pen!" Templeton screams.

I whirl; two paces away, Templeton stands over Zel, who has blood spurting from a gash on her arm; she's dropped her sword and tries to cover the wound with her hand.

"Help me get her clear," Templeton pants, sheathing her sword and stooping to help Zel to her feet.

With my staff, I hold off the attacking guards. "There," I point, and we make our way to the wall, where a turned-over table makes a safe corner.

"Is it deep?" Templeton is asking, trying to push aside Zel's hand to see the wound.

Biting her lip, Zel nods. Then she looks desperately back at the fight.

"I know," Templeton says. "Just let me get this bandaged." With her teeth, she rips the bottom of Zel's shirt and tears off a strip of cloth, using it to bind up the gash. While they're doing this, I stand guard, my staff at the ready.

"All right?" Templeton asks, and I turn to see her brace Zel's shoulder, and then bring her forehead to Zel's, a snatched moment of intimacy. Zel nods. Templeton hands her the sword she'd dropped.

"Let's go," I say, suddenly worried about Owen, about being separated from him for too long.

"Wait," Templeton says, and grips my arm. Zel reaches out, and with bloody fingers, touches the tip of my finger, where it's gripping the staff.

"Yes," Templeton says, with a quick glance at the fight. "The thimble. It's our only hope."

Quickly I dig the thimble out of my pocket and put it on my finger. It burns fiercely.

The fortress guards are a wave that is about to crest and overwhelm us. Snarling clots of them surround our fighters. Owen and Cor are gone; their fight has spilled out of the room and into the hallway beyond; I hear shouts and the crash of weapons. I know Owen is quick with his knife, but I am desperate to get to him.

As one, Templeton, Zel, and I leap back into the fight.

This time, when I strike, a bolt of light and heat erupts from my staff and slams into my opponents; none of them get up after I have passed. Quickly I clear a space around me, and lead an advance. It is enough to turn the battle. Like a thunderstorm, I blow through the room, striking, rallying our fighters, driving the last of the guards to the walls. Some of them turn tail and flee; the ones too injured to run throw down their weapons and fall onto their knees. The rebels and slaves break into ragged cheers. As I stand among my friends, panting for breath, my hands trembling on the smooth wood of my staff, I cheer, too.

As if in answer, a deep boom echoes through the fortress, shaking the stones under our feet. It's followed by a rush of wind like air escaping from a bottle that's long been sealed. A thrill runs through me—I didn't *really* think we could do it. The fortress has fallen, I realize; the Godmother's circle of power is broken. From here, with the slaves helping us, we just might have a chance against the Godmother and her footmen in the city.

My eyes rove the room, looking for Owen. In the chaos of

injuries and fallen tables and benches, and the rebels collecting weapons from the surrendered guards, I don't see him. Or Cor. They must be out in the hallway, not far.

Templeton strides up to me, panic in her voice. "A big group of guards charged through a gap in the wall," she announces. "I think it opened when the spell on the fortress was broken. We need to go after them." Zel is at her shoulder; the makeshift bandage on her arm is stained with blood.

"No," I decide. The guards will run for the city, but we have enough to do here before we attack. We'll need supplies, plenty of food, and warm clothes. "Check all the guard rooms," I tell the burly Spinster, who is still carrying her spinning wheel over her shoulder. "Collect any weapons we can use when we go after the Godmother. We have to act quickly."

The Huntsman has some skill as a healer, and we brought medical supplies, so he is busy tending to the slaves and rebels who were injured in the fight. I comfort the three seamstresses who were wounded; they blink up at me from their blankets like owls with bloody feathers. I keep an eye out for Cor and Owen, but they don't come.

"I have to find Owen and Cor," I tell the Huntsman, feeling a sudden urgency. They should have reported in by now.

The Huntsman gives the Glover a reassuring pat and gets to his feet. "I'll come with you." He slings his bag of medicines over his shoulder.

I lead him out of the big room into the hallway, stepping

over a few wounded or dead guards, nodding to the rebels who are helping with the cleanup. He's not here.

"The courtyard, maybe?" the Huntsman suggests.

"He must be there," I mutter.

We go down the hallway and out into the courtyard. It is empty, the snow churned and spotted here and there with blood.

The thrill of winning the fight drains out of me. "He's not here."

"Pen," the Huntsman says from behind me.

When I turn, he holds up a sword. Cor's sword, I realize, its blade crusted with blood along one edge. "Templeton said a group of guards got out the break in the wall," he says, ashen.

A bolt of icy terror slams into me and I freeze. When I speak, my lips feel stiff. "They took him."

"Both of them," the Huntsman says grimly.

"Oh no. No." The Huntsman says something else, but I can't hear him through the fright that whirls through my head. The guards have him, and they'll take him straight to the city. To the Godmother. "She'll kill him," I whisper.

She will kill him.

CHAPTER
37

EVEN BEFORE HE COMES FULLY AWAKE, OWEN CAN FEEL the shooting pain from the wound in his shoulder. It aches in his bones, all the way down his arm and into his neck. The pain has a pattern, he realizes dimly. It's sharp, pulsing in time with the jolting bumps. No, not bumps, steps. He's being carried by somebody who is running; he is hanging head-down over a broad shoulder. He can't move his arms, and his mouth feels as if it's full of ashes. Carefully he cracks open his gritty eyes. It is daytime. That's not right—it was night when they attacked the fortress. Squinting, he focuses on the back of the man who is carrying him.

Light blue. A light-blue uniform. And it comes back to him. He and Cor, fighting in the crowded hallways, a knife held by a hairy fist punching into his shoulder, wrenching out again, the sick, dizzy realization that the guard had put poison on the blade . . . then darkness.

He feels the sinking weight of despair. Their invasion of the fortress must have failed. Pen was captured too, or—or—

Somebody shouts an unintelligible order and he's tipped off the guard's shoulder onto the ground.

It's enough to put him out again.

THE NEXT TIME he awakens, the pain from his wound has receded, but it's been replaced with other pain. It's dark again.

"Gerrup," snuffles a slurred voice.

A sharp pain—a kick in the ribs. Owen pries open his eyes. He's lying on his side on the snowy ground. His arms are bound behind him with chains that are bitterly cold.

"Gerrup," the voice repeats. "You 'wake, gerrup."

Gritting his teeth, Owen struggles to his knees in the snow. Furry paws jerk him to his feet; he stands, swaying. A guard with furred ears and a mouth too full of teeth grips his arm.

Blinking, Owen looks around, trying to see if Pen is here, hoping she is not. The light of a single torch shows him a mass of shadows and glaring eyes and panting mouths—the Godmother's guards in a tight circle around him. One of them shifts, and he sees Cor. The prince's hands are bound in front of him. He has a purple bruise across his temple, but he looks steady enough.

"Cor—" Owen starts. *Where is Pen*, he wants to ask.

The guard holding him jabs him in the shoulder, right where the poisoned knife struck him, and he goes down onto his knees, head whirling.

"Gerrup," the guard orders. When Owen moves too slowly, the guard snarls sharply, "Gerrup!" and pulls his arms until pain lances into his shoulders. There are barks and howls of harsh laughter as Owen struggles to his feet. One of the guards shoves him, and he staggers, but doesn't fall.

"Let him alone," Cor shouts.

A guard backhands Owen across the face and he goes down again.

A goat-horned guard stalks up to Cor. "You talk," he says, jabbing a finger into Cor's chest, "he gets it." He points at Owen.

Owen spits bloody snow out of his mouth. "It's all right, Cor," he pants.

It earns him another kick in the ribs. "*You* talk and you get it," the guard snarls, jerking Owen to his feet.

"You 'scaped," another guard taunts. The rest of the guards press closer, and Owen can smell their rank sweat, their rancid breath, and he can feel the heat of their bodies. "You 'scaped, Seamstress 'scaped," the guard growls. "You got 'way from fortress, *we* punished, now you caught, now *you* punished."

The horned guard shoves his face closer. "Godmother wants you." He opens his mouth, shows sharp, yellowed teeth. When he speaks, he enunciates the next word carefully.

"Sto-ry-break-er." He gives a harsh laugh. "Story break you, this time."

Owen nods, understanding. He is as good as dead. But they don't have Pen. Maybe the invasion hasn't failed after all, and that is enough.

The horned, goat-footed guard slurs out an order, and Owen is pushed into a shuffling run in the midst of the guards; Cor is somewhere ahead of him.

The rest of the night is a misery. When he falls, the guards kick him and drag him to his feet again, and they run on. As a gray dawn breaks, they stop to rest in a clearing surrounded by snow-covered pine trees. The guards slump on the ground, panting, and Cor is allowed to sit. He's given some dried meat and bread to eat, but they make Owen stand in the middle of the clearing. He closes his eyes, concentrating on staying on his feet, shaking with weariness and cold. Even his feet are numb inside the sturdy boots he made while a slave in the fortress.

If only he'd had time to send a message to his mum and dad, telling them he was still alive. It's too late for that now. And Pen. He'd been waiting, letting her find herself again.

I love you, Pen. He should have said it. Story pushes people together, but it is obedience and fear that oils its gears, not real, true love. If only he'd said it, and if Pen felt it too . . .

But it's too late.

The guards finish their break and drag him into a run again, and it should be more misery, but something has shifted. He feels distant from himself, as if he's stepped back and is watching this poor, stupid shoemaker caught up in something that is way, way too powerful for him to resist. It's always been too big for him; he was just too dumb to realize it. His ending is rushing toward him with massive inevitability. There's nothing he can do to change any of it, he can only go on for as long as he is able. And so he shuffles on, not hearing the taunts of the guards or feeling their blows. He doesn't even feel the cold anymore.

At last they come down a steep, forested hillside to the river. Some of the guards must be the footmen the Godmother sent after him and Pen and Cor from the city, because they know a boat is waiting on the bank. When they find it, they shove him into the bottom of the boat. The guards jump in, settle Cor with a blanket, then push off from the shore and start paddling upstream.

Slowly Owen comes back to himself, feels the icy bite of the cold again, the ache of his bound arms, the bruises from the guards' blows. Shivering, he lifts his face out of the freezing water that is pooled in the bottom of the boat and rests his aching head against the wooden side. He can hear the river rushing past, just under the keel. From where he's lying he can see two guards perched on a thwart, grunting as they dig their paddles into the water. Sitting against the other side of the boat, not an arm span away, is Cor.

The prince glances aside at the guards, then leans forward. "You all right?" he breathes.

Owen closes his eyes. "Well enough," he whispers. Things could be worse. He could be dead already.

"After we were captured, the guards took us and fled the fortress," Cor goes on. "They'd lost the battle; Pen and the others must have won."

Owen nods. Yes, he's figured that out.

Cor falls silent. Exhausted, Owen feels sleep creeping up on him.

"Listen," Cor whispers. "I think I can get us out of this."

Owen opens his eyes. "I doubt it."

"Why not let Story have its way?" Cor reasons. "It couldn't be worse than this. Once it has the ending it wants, and Pen and I are together, I can convince the Godmother to let you live, too. I am a prince, after all; my demands should mean something to her."

Owen gives his head a weary shake.

"Why not?" Cor persists. "Pen and I could be happy with each other. I know you don't want to lose her, but at least you'd be alive."

"No," Owen says. "Pen wouldn't want that." He casts a quick look to be sure the guards are still distracted. "She doesn't want that ending—she said so, back at her stepmother's house—you heard her. She doesn't believe that love is destined or meant to be, she wants to choose it for herself." He meets Cor's gaze, willing him to understand. "Cor, you *know* her."

Cor raises his bound hands to rub his forehead. "No," he says soberly, wincing. "I think *you* know her."

"She knows there's no happily-ever-after for any of us. Now that we've been taken, she'll know exactly what she has to do to break the story she's in." He knows what that means for him, too, but he still knows it's the right thing for her to do. "Story needs her to come to the city to play the role it assigned her. You'll see," he assures Cor. "Pen knows she has to stay away. She won't come after us."

CHAPTER

38

"WE HAVE TO GO AFTER THEM," I ANNOUNCE.

Templeton and Zel and the Huntsman are sitting around the hearth in a wide, high-ceilinged bedroom that must be the Godmother's, because it is decorated with swags of lace and blue silk that look incongruous against the stone walls. Somebody must have raided the Godmother's supplies; on a low table they've laid out wine and cheese and coffee, dried fruit and three kinds of nuts. The Huntsman's two trackers are stretched out before the fire sharing a bone.

They all stare at me where I'm standing in the doorway; I'm holding my staff and a knapsack that I've loaded with supplies.

Templeton swallows down a mouthful of cheese. She points with her chin at the window. "Pen, we're all worried about the boys, but it's the middle of the night."

"I know what time it is," I snap.

She raises her eyebrows and holds up her hands, as if in surrender.

"As long as you are away from the city, your story can't continue," the Huntsman points out.

"I know that! But she will kill him!" I take a shaky breath. "Sorry. I know—" I have to stop and clear my throat. "I know that the last thing I should do is go after them. I know that Story is weakened if my own story doesn't play out, and I know that I should stay here while you bring the battle to the city. Do you think I haven't thought that through?" I take a second deep breath to steady myself. "But I have to go after them."

"If you don't mind my asking," Templeton puts in, getting to her feet, "which *him* is it that you're so worried about?"

"What?!" I shake my head. "I'm worried about both of them, of course."

"Of course," Templeton repeats. She rubs the scar that slashes across her cheek; then she and Zel exchange a speaking look. "It's only that you said 'she will kill *him*,' and Story is pushing you and the prince together—we saw you going into the forest with him before we invaded the fortress."

I am not the blushing kind, I realize. I am the biting kind. "Yes, Templeton, I kissed the prince."

"So it's Cor you're worried about," Templeton pushes.

I shake my head in frustration. "What does it matter? We have to go after them. *Now.*"

"It matters a lot," Templeton says.

I am about to snap again, when the Huntsman interrupts. "Pen," he chides. "Tempy." Then he falls silent. "Let's just think about this."

"Yes, a little thinking would be good," Templeton says. "Before we all run off without a plan to rescue the boys, let's think. What does the Godmother want?"

"To serve Story, obviously," I say. I drop my knapsack on the floor and take three nervous paces into the room. "She'll use her thimble on me so I'll forget Owen and then she'll kill him and turn me into a happy-puppet who will marry the prince and live in the castle and smile for the rest of her life until she rips all of her hair out and dies."

"She just did it again, did you notice?" Templeton asks. Zel and the Huntsman nod.

"What did I do?" I ask, looking wildly around at them.

"Pen," Templeton asks with surprising gentleness, "are you aware that you are in love with Owen?"

"I'm not in love with Owen," I say. They all stare at me. Then I say it again slowly to convince them. "I am not. In love. With Owen." Zel cocks her head in a questioning way, so I add, "I just . . . I just can't stand the thought that the Godmother is going to kill him. She detests Owen, and she's not likely to kill Cor—he is a prince, after all. . . ."

"All right, if you insist," Templeton says. Zel rolls her eyes. "Here's what we know about the Godmother," Templeton goes on. "She is clever. She knows that this story—*your* story, Pen—is crucial. For years Story's power has been growing. You're the daughter of the Witch who opposed it for so long. If Story can force you into an ending, its power will never be broken. The Godmother must be under nearly unbearable pressure to complete your happily-ever-after. Soon she will know that she has lost this fortress and all the slaves she's got working for Story, and she will guess that we are coming to the city. She will want to have all the pieces in place for her ending. She needs you. And as long as she thinks she might find a use for Owen, she won't kill him. Or Cor, for that matter."

The Huntsman nods. "That's right. The Godmother will keep them on hand, just in case she needs them."

I take a moment to think about this. "All right," I say slowly. "This makes sense. But I'm coming. And we're leaving in the morning."

WE DON'T BOTHER with sleep. I spend hours with the blank-faced people in the tower, using the thimble to restore their Befores. Some of them are frozen with shock and fright, but some are able to come fully back to themselves. We find them clothes and invite them to fight Story with us. We are joined by the lead Jack, who won't put down his ax, and the slave with the spinning wheel, who wants to be called Spinner because she doesn't like the word *spinster*, and many of the other slaves. We make sure everybody has supplies to carry and some sort of weapon.

Nobody so much as looks at me cross-eyed, and as the

night sky lightens to gray we're ready to head out, climbing through the gap in the wall left by the broken spell. With the former slaves, including four of the spryer seamstresses, we have about seventy fighters. Not many, but if Tobias has gathered Natters and the Missus and they've rallied the people inside the city, it might be enough.

There shouldn't be any road through the forest—the Godmother has traveled here through magic—but as we step through the gap we find a wide path before us, unmarked by wagon wheels, smooth, dry, and edged with snow.

"The forest," the Huntsman says with a shrug. "It's no friend of the Godmother's, as you know."

I nod and set the pace, using my staff as a walking stick, the knapsack heavy on my shoulders; I'm wearing Owen's coat, the one he borrowed from the Huntsman, with the sleeves rolled up.

The Godmother is cruel, and her footmen are worse. Cor, I figure, is safe because he is a prince, and useful to her. Owen, though. I remember how the Godmother looked at him—with fury and venom and the promise of a *special ending*. I can't bear to think what might be happening to him at this moment. Instead I call up a better memory, a conversation we had in the rebels' cave.

We were sitting on the sandy floor with our backs against the cave wall; we had bread and a pot of raspberry jam, and we were sharing a tin cup of tea. Owen was still Shoe at that point; I hadn't given his Before back yet. He was having trouble keeping his eyes open because we'd arrived there late the previous night, and he'd been up at dawn to scout the forest with Tobias.

"Why does Story have so much power?" I wondered. I'd been thinking a lot about that, about where its power came from. If we could identify its source, we might be able to block it, somehow.

Shoe took a drink of tea, then passed me the cup. My fingers warmed where they touched his. "It's because people are afraid."

"Of what?" I asked.

He shrugged. "Because there's just one ending."

"Happily ever after," I said.

"No," he said. "Death. Death is the real ending."

I loaded another spoonful of jam on my bread and thought. Stories, I figured, offered people different endings— not death, but the possibility for happiness in the time that we have to live. *That* is why we like getting caught up in stories. They are bigger than we are. They help us understand the shape of our lives and the nature of our own endings.

"Story's not necessarily a bad thing," I said aloud. "Story doesn't want power. It's not evil, necessarily. Endings are just what Story *does*. That's its nature."

Shoe's head was tipped back against the wall and his eyes were closed. I nudged him. His eyes snapped open. "What?"

"We need stories, don't we?" I asked.

"Um. Yes," he said. "I think we do."

"Well, that's irony for you," I said.

For just an instant, Shoe looked stricken, but before I could ask him why he nodded and said, "Everything about this is ironic, Pen."

"It is!" I exclaimed. "We're fighting Story, Shoe, but its power comes from *us*. We've given it too much power, and we have to take some of it back. We have to make our own choices."

I know Owen. Bone-deep, I know him. I know that he's thought all along that Story's ending for him is not happiness, but death. He's struggled against Story and tried to break it, but it's too big for him. And no matter how desperately I want to help, I don't know if there's anything I can do about it.

THANKS TO THE forest's wide, smooth path, and our fear that Story is still turning, we make good time, hiking along the river, and then camping for the night.

"Stop pacing, Pen," Templeton says from where she's sitting on the ground by the campfire. Zel leans against her shoulder, eyes closed. The Huntsman crouches next to them, cooking our dinner in a pan. The trackers are curled together asleep, as close to the fire as they can get; other fires burn in the clearing.

I stand with hands fisted on my hips, staring out at the forest. It surrounds us, almost as if the trees are embracing us, keeping us safe. I wonder how far from the city we are. Surely we'll get there tomorrow. Where is he, right now? Is he still alive?

"Come now, Pen," the Huntsman adds.

I turn back to them. Seeking comfort, I take out my thimble, holding it in my hand.

Which reminds me of something I might not have another chance to do. "Do you want me to give back your Befores?" I ask them.

"No," Templeton says immediately, with a shrug that wakes Zel, who raises her head, blinking. "I love Zel," she goes on. "I don't want to know about anything that happened before her."

"Here," the Huntsman says, and holds out a tin plate of potatoes and bacon.

Taking it, and the fork he hands me, I sit across the fire from them. As I settle on the ground, I feel suddenly how weary I am. "How can you be so sure?" I ask.

Templeton rubs her blunt nose. "What, about loving her?" Zel smiles sleepily. "Love is pretty simple, Pen."

"No it isn't," I say. I take a bite of potatoes. They're peppery and hot. "I mean, if you don't know who you are, how can you love somebody else?"

Templeton starts to answer, but Zel reaches over and places a slim finger on her lips. Templeton falls silent. Turning to me, Zel puts one hand on her breast, over her heart; she puts the other hand over Templeton's heart. Bringing her hands together, she kisses them tenderly.

"See?" Templeton says. "Simple."

For them, maybe. Not for me.

"I don't want to know either," the Huntsman puts in. The firelight gleams on his bald head. He forks up a last bite of potatoes. "Figure I've got enough to think about right here, really."

Maybe they're right. There's my mother—the Witch—and my thimble, and I want to know what those things mean for me. But maybe all that doesn't matter, and who I was—Pin, or Pen, or someone with another Before—is less important than who I am *now*, what I choose to do *now*.

Maybe . . .

And maybe the person I am becoming can choose love.

THE NEXT DAY we continue through the forest until we hear a roaring in the distance. Coming around a bend, we see the waterfall slamming into the river with the city high on the cliff beyond. The sun is setting, and the waterfall looks like a veil of lace, and the white stone of the castle in the distance is tinged pink and gilded at its edges.

Then the sun drops out of the sky and the hollow boom of the castle clock rolls out—it is the sound of a gravedigger knocking on a tomb door.

CHAPTER

39

SNAKES OF FOG WRITHE AROUND OUR FEET AS IF THE FOR-est is impatient to begin. We will not wait until morning.

Surely the Godmother knows we are here, so we must be like a knife fight—strike first and fast, without warning. Quickly, in a dark clearing—we dare not show any lights—I give out orders. "When the fog rises," I tell the Jack and Spin-ner, "you'll lead an attack on the city gates closest to the lake." It's the main assault, I tell them, and it will prompt the rebels inside the city to start fighting too. That's the message Tobias took to the Missus and her people, and we've spoken to a mes-senger he sent to meet us. They are ready.

"Righty-o," says the Jack, hefting his ax, and he and Spin-ner lead the bulk of our force through the trees toward the city.

The Huntsman, Templeton, Zel, and I make our way along the pebbly bank of the lake. We are guided through the darkness by the sound of the waterfall and by the feel of spray on our faces. We find the steep stone stairway and start up it. The steps are slippery, and my fingers are numb with cold as I steady myself with my staff and continue climbing.

At the top, the stone steps turn into a narrow path, which then leads to an alley between what smells like a tannery and some kind of warehouse. The night is still and dark; the fog is thickening, and soon the attack outside the gates will begin. We have to get into place by then. At the edge of the alley, I stop with the others behind me and peer into the dark street, which is lined by shuttered shops.

"Tsssst," hisses a voice.

Templeton makes a quick move toward her sword, but I hold up a hand, stopping her. "Who's there?" I whisper.

From out of the shadows steps an old woman, nearly as wide as she is tall. She pauses and looks me up and down. "You're Shoe's Pen, are you?"

"I'm my own Pen, thank you," I answer.

Her eyes narrow. "So you are. I'm Natters's Missus, come to meet you." She glances behind me. "This the rest of your lot?"

"The ones that aren't at the gate, yes," I answer.

"Good." She gives a brisk nod and starts down the street, moving surprisingly fast for someone with such short legs. As we walk, she fills me in on what's been happening in the city. For the past few days, the Godmother's footmen have been extra vigilant. Houses have been raided, weapons confiscated; suspected rebels have gone to the post; one by one the prince's castle guards have been disappearing. The castle clock has struck the hour at shorter and shorter intervals. The city is wound up and terrified and waiting.

She glances again at the others. "I'm half surprised not to see Shoe with you."

The worry I've tried to set aside comes rushing back all at once. "He—" My voice trembles, and I fall silent. Owen must be in the Godmother's hands by now. I can't speak of it.

The Huntsman fills in my silence. "He was captured along with Prince Cornelius," he says.

The Missus stops suddenly, staring straight ahead. "The Godmother has him?" She closes her eyes, then lifts her fist and presses it into her forehead as if she can somehow push the thought of Owen's capture out of her mind. "I can't tell my Natters. We've lost two already; he can't bear to lose another."

She can't bear it either, I can see that clearly.

"We'd better get on," the Huntsman puts in gruffly. "It must be nearly time."

As he speaks, I look up to see a white wall rushing down the street toward us; a moment later, we are enveloped in a thick, damp fog that smells of the forest's snow and pine. In the distance is a sudden roar of sound. The battle has begun.

"Take hands," Missus Natters says, and I feel her

blunt-fingered hand seize mine; the Huntsman's big hand rests on my shoulder.

"Lead on," I say.

The Missus hurries us through the fog to a group of city rebels armed with staffs and swords and stout clubs. I catch a glimpse of the ratcatcher among them, the one who brought me the message from Owen; he winks and gives me a gap-toothed grin.

We attack the Godmother's footmen—the ones guarding the city gates—from behind so our rebels can bring the battle inside the city itself. We are quick and fast and our people flood in. I join in the battle, and it is a whirl of sound and strikes with my staff, and glimpses of snarling mouths with too many teeth in them. It seems like chaos at first, but just as it was in the fortress, I get a feel for the rhythm of the battle, its surges and sudden attacks. Every time I turn around the Huntsman is there, stalwart with his ax, protecting my back.

The Godmother has been busy, it is clear, because there are many, many footmen, most of them naked and half wild, and fanatically fierce. She must have found every dog and cat and rat in the city and used her thimble to bring them into her service. They emerge in snarling clots from the fog, striking us from the side, and we fight through them toward the castle. That's where we'll find the Godmother.

And, I hope, Cor and Owen.

I am in the midst of the fighting, striking with my staff, receiving reports from the Jacks and Spinner. We push on, and

I catch a glimpse of Anna and a footman from my stepmother's house fighting back to back against too many footmen; they are about to be overwhelmed. Then I hear a piercing shriek and my stepsister Dulcet is there, wildly swinging a staff; Precious, beside her, follows it with a precisely placed thrust. I step toward them to help, when suddenly there is a flurry of attacks and I find myself shoved aside and stumbling into an alley. From the other end of it comes a snarl; I whirl toward the sound.

"Come'n fight me, girlie," taunts a guttural voice.

I glance behind me, but the fighting is too close for me to plunge back into it. Gripping my staff, I pace toward the challenge. The fog swirls away from me and then closes in behind me again. I trail my hand against the brick wall to my left and peer ahead through the fog. There are lumps of trash on the ground, and here and there a doorway. The air smells of fires burning and of scorched metal; in the distance I hear the clash and crash of glass breaking, shouts, running footsteps. "Afraid, are you?" the voice taunts. I keep trying to catch it, but it recedes before me. Above the fog and the roofs of the city I can see the tower clock, its face shining luridly red, a kind of beacon, and a place of power. I head toward it.

At last I stumble out onto a wide street that leads directly toward the castle. As I orient myself, four naked footmen, half dog, half man, slink from the alley behind me. Fog smokes around them. They must have been following me, their paw-like feet silent on the cobblestoned street. I gulp and back away from them, holding my staff ready.

They lope toward me, their heads jutting forward, sniffing, ropes of drool trailing from their muzzle-like mouths. One of them lunges at me and I stumble back and swing with my staff, but he twists away, and then another nips at my side and I whirl and strike out and miss again. They growl and I back away again; with a glance over my shoulder, I see that I'm closer, now, to the castle, to a door at the base of the clock tower. The footmen dart in again, but they don't bite—they are herding me.

"Well, that's enough of that," I gasp. I give one last sweep with my staff and then turn and run straight for the tower door; snarling, they follow.

I am at the door, scrabbling for the latch, when the guards' strong, clawed hands grab my arms and shoulders.

A wave of cold air washes over me. I grope in my pocket for my thimble.

"Hello, my dear," the Godmother's voice says in my ear. "I have been waiting for you."

A touch of ice at my temple, and all goes dark.

I COME TO myself.

And I *am* myself. I am still Pen; she didn't take that away from me.

Something is wrapped tightly around my ribs, and I can barely catch my breath. I blink and a curved wall swims into focus. It is hung with paintings of blue flowers and girls in blue dresses. And there is—I blink my bleary eyes again—a mirror in a gilded frame.

I sit up straight, my head whirling. I am in the castle . . . in the clock tower. The chairs are covered with blue damask; candles gleam; a thick white carpet covers the floor. Shakily I get to my feet and catch a glimpse of myself in the mirror. I am wearing a dress of deep-blue velvet, cut low over my corseted breasts; the skirt is cut wide over layers of petticoats. My hair is held back from my face by two diamond-encrusted clasps. One of my feet is covered only by a pale-blue silk stocking; on my other foot is a thin slipper, replacing the sturdy boots that Owen made for me.

Owen.

He must be here, somewhere. I have to find him. Blinking black spots from my eyes, I see a door and stagger over to it, but the knob doesn't turn. Locked. Thimble. I need my thimble to open the door. I fumble at the stiff velvet of my skirt. "Bother this dress," I mutter. No pockets.

"It is not quite time yet," comes a voice from behind me.

I whirl. My head whirls too, and I lean against the door, dizzy.

Lady Faye—the Godmother—is standing behind a chair. She looks different. Story has taken its toll. Her white-blonde hair is now completely white, her mouth bracketed by wrinkles, her glittering eyes deep-set and shadowed. Her pursuit of us has not been easy on her. Yet she is impeccably dressed in ice-blue silk and her necklace of knucklebone diamonds.

"Where is he?" I gasp.

"I assume, of course, that you are speaking of the prince," she says. "Don't worry. You will see him very soon." She is trying to be smoothly controlled, but I can hear the edge of tension in her voice. "Won't you have some tea?"

"I don't mean—" I don't mean the prince. My head is so fuzzy, I'm not sure what is happening.

"I know exactly what you mean, my dear," the Godmother says, and goes to a tea table, where she pours out two cups of tea and sets one on a table beside the chair I was sitting in.

I try taking a deep breath to settle myself and feel the corset cutting into my ribs. I look around the room again. The walls, I realize, and the door against my back, are trembling with the faintest low thunder, just at the edge of hearing. There is a grinding edge to the noise, as of gears clashing.

"It won't be long now," the Godmother says, regarding me over the rim of her teacup.

I go to the table and pick up my cup with shaking fingers and take a long drink. I list my advantages. They are not many. I am still light-headed from the touch of the Godmother's thimble. I don't have my own thimble, or my staff. I am wearing this cumbersome dress and this cursed corset that is squeezing me into an uncomfortable shape. The door is locked and there is no other way to get out of this room. The Godmother is holding Owen prisoner somewhere and intends to kill him, and possibly Cor as well.

The advantages would seem to be all hers. There is no

hope of escape, and no one is going to rescue me.

My ears hear something faint, in the distance, but it sounds like shouting, the clash of swords. I hold my cup out for more, steadying my hand so that it does not shake. "It sounds as if the fighting is getting closer," I say, calm and even, trying to hide my hopeless desperation.

The Godmother pours more tea and hands the cup back to me, but I stay on my feet. The tea is clearing my head; I take another gulp.

She shrugs. "Everything will be settled soon." There is a low, heavy groan from the walls. "Ah." She sets down her teacup with an uncharacteristic clatter. "It is time. Come along, Penelope." She gets to her feet and shakes out her skirts. Moving stiffly—not her usual graceful self—she leads me to the door and opens it with her thimble. I am right on her heels as we come out into the hallway.

I can feel the floor trembling under my feet, especially the foot without a slipper. The low thunder has gotten louder. We go through another doorway and then up a narrow set of stairs that doubles back on itself, climbing higher and higher into the central tower of the castle.

By the time we reach the top I am panting for breath and cursing the corset and the petticoats that weigh heavily against my legs. We come out into a huge, high-ceilinged room that hums with power and seethes with shadows. One wall is taken up by an enormous clock face as luminous as the moon. Its hands are huge, taller than two men, and made of heavy iron. I can see that the hands have nearly met in the middle; it is a few minutes until midnight.

The *clock*, I realize. As its power has grown, Story has taken this huge, implacable shape, and with iron hands and grinding gears it has imposed its will on the city. It is as if we've stepped inside a giant machine, one with invisible wheels and pistons. The stone walls almost seem to breathe in and out with the rumblings of the gears of Story turning. I swallow and my ears pop from the pressure.

The next thing I see is Owen pinned against the stone wall just to the left of the clock face. Brambles grow from the stone and wrap around him so that he is bound to the wall and can't move. His head is lowered, but I can see that his face is ashen and bruised. Without the brambles holding him up, he would fall.

My heart twists in my chest. "*Owen*," I breathe.

He looks up, blinking. I see his cracked lips shape my name—*Pen*.

I take a quick step toward him, and the Godmother rests cold fingers against my shoulder. "Wait," she orders.

I shrug off her touch and start toward Owen again.

From one of the brambles gripping him a knifelike thorn erupts; he flinches as it slashes a deep cut along his ribs. Blood seeps out, staining his sweater.

"The next one may find his heart," says the Godmother from behind me.

I pause and feel as if I'm teetering on the edge of a cliff.

Under my feet, the floor shudders, and briars burst from the stone and wrap themselves around my legs under my skirt, holding me in place. My breath comes short. "No," I whisper.

"Ah," the Godmother says, as if confirming something. "I see."

I am about to speak when we are interrupted by the sound of footsteps on the stairs. Cor bursts into the room. He is breathing hard and holding a sword; he looks pale, and his eyes are deeply shadowed. "Pen!" he shouts.

"Good," the Godmother says. She raises her hands. "Hold there, prince," she orders.

Cor stops, panting. Beneath his feet, brambles twine from the stone and wrap around his ankles.

"He has come to complete your story, Penelope, do you see?" the Godmother says aside to me. "So brave, so noble." She raises her voice. "She is such a pretty girl, don't you think, Prince Cornelius?" She points at me, and I see now why she has dressed me so finely. We each have roles to play, the prince and I.

Cor finds his voice. "She is very much more than that," he says, regarding me steadily. "But pretty? No."

"Oh, well done," I say, releasing a breath of relief. Cor is himself, resisting the pull of Story toward an ending that I know he wants much more than I do.

The Godmother frowns. "We don't have time for this," she says impatiently. Moving with strange jerkiness, she crosses the room to where Cor stands. Brambles writhe up his legs, binding his sword arm to his side. Swiftly she raises her thimble. Cor struggles, but the vines grip him all the tighter. The Godmother holds her hand to his temple. Blue light flares and Cor goes still. "There," she says, satisfied. "Now let us try this again." She leans forward, slipping something— a shoe?—into Cor's coat pocket, then steps back. "She is a pretty girl, is she not, Prince Cornelius?" she prompts, pointing at me as she did before.

"She is," Cor says, staring blankly ahead. "You are so pretty, Pen."

"You know very well that I am not, Cor," I say desperately.

"You are pretty, Pen," he repeats woodenly, and I can see that he has no choice but to play his part.

We make a triangle—Cor near the door, Owen bound against the wall, and then me, all of us entangled with brambles. The walls are vibrating now; the huge clock face glows like a full moon. There is an immense grinding, groaning sound, and the clock's hands come together with a clang. From overhead the first strike of midnight rolls out with a thunderous *boom*.

When the Godmother speaks, her voice takes on the deep echoes of the clock's second strike. "It is time! We will take up your story again where we left off." She goes to stand at the center of the triangle; then she holds up her hand, the thimble on her finger glittering with an icy, blinding light.

The third strike roars out. *Boom.*

"Before the clock strikes twelve, you will go to your

prince!" she announces, taking a step toward me.

The briars holding Cor's arms loosen. His movements rough, he reaches into his coat pocket and pulls out the dainty dancing slipper that the Godmother had put there.

I finally understand. Owen interrupted this ending before; now I have to allow Cor to put the slipper on my foot and claim me as his own.

The clock strikes again and a swirl of a breeze tugs at the hem of my dress. "You will marry your prince." The Godmother points toward Cor, but takes another step toward me. Her words have power; they speak with the weight of a thousand happily-ever-afters. *Boom*, the fifth strike. The weight presses down on me; I can barely hold up my head beneath it.

"You will become his princess." The clock strikes again— *boom*—interrupting her. "Story will be satisfied!" As she speaks, she uses her thimble to trace a line in the air from me to Cor.

As the line connects us, I feel a powerful pull in his direction. "And if I don't?" I say through gritted teeth.

The seventh strike rolls out. *Boom*. Dust sifts down from the high ceiling. The Godmother steps closer and raises the thimble, and I feel an answering tingle of cold in my forehead. Then she turns the thimble on Owen with chilling precision. I gasp as another thorn rips into him, his arm this time. Blood drips. The eighth strike, and my ears are ringing so loudly that I almost can't hear the Godmother's answer. "If you refuse to play your part, the Shoemaker will die."

The Godmother's hair has come loose and writhes around her head; the thimble flashes with cold fire. The ninth strike booms and the walls tremble.

The tenth strike. *Doom.* The air around us cracks and shatters. I'm running out of time. The weight of Story is so heavy; I brace myself, trying to resist it. The brambles fall from my legs.

I so desperately want Owen to live, and in that wanting my body takes an involuntary step toward Cor. He opens his arms as if to welcome me, the slipper clenched in one hand, but the smile on his face is really a grimace of pain.

The eleventh strike rises from the stone floor, an all-encompassing sound that is like a blow against my ears. *Doom.* "Go to your prince!" the Godmother shrieks. "It is the only possible ending."

The silence before the last strike vibrates with anticipation. I take a deep breath. The *only* one? My arm weighs a hundred pounds, but I lift my hand to my face. I tap my chin with my finger. *"Do* I want that ending?" I tip my heavy head to the side, as if thinking. "I suppose I must choose."

"You do not choose," the Godmother says, and I see a flicker of unease cross her haggard face. "Story has chosen you. *Go to him!"*

Story grips me, huge, implacable. The air thickens; the weight of the last *boom* waiting to strike fills the room. I struggle to take a breath against it. "Oh my," I gasp. I give the Godmother my wickedest grin. I am my mother's daughter after all, the Witch, even without my thimble. A wind whips around me; dust whirls into my eyes. "But I hardly know what to say." I am stalling, not sure what to do, I only know that I can't cross the room. I cannot let Cor put the slipper on my foot. I glance at Owen, where he is bound against the wall.

You do the unexpected thing too, Pin, he said to me once. I can hear his voice as he says the words, feel the force of his steady gaze.

He knows me. And I know him. And oh, I am stupid, or slow, because Templeton was right. It is simple. Of *course* I love Owen. I love his steadiness and his stubbornness, the way his face shows his every thought, I love the way he thinks and the way he likes to talk, and the way he likes raspberry jam just as much as I do. I loved him when I was Pin, and I love him as Pen, and I love so much that he loves me, for who I am, because I am absolutely sure that he does.

As the joy of my realization washes through me, I turn back to the Godmother. "I can't go to the prince," I tell her, raising my leg and waggling my stockinged foot. "I rather like having just one shoe, you see." My eyes meet Owen's and I nod. *Yes,* it means. *You. I love you.* He's staring at me with grim intensity, but as he makes sense of my words, he blinks and—amazingly—a smile lightens his eyes. For a fleeting moment, we are the only two people in the entire world. Even across the room, I feel connected to him, as if we are one flame, burning.

"Stop looking at him!" the Godmother orders, and her voice has an edge of panic. The tension builds, and builds; the high-pitched whine of gears stressed beyond bearing fills the air, rising to a scream. She is close now, just an arm's length away. She raises the thimble and I could struggle, but I no longer fear her power to turn me into Nothing. I let her reach out and touch me, right in the center of my forehead.

A wave of sparkling cold flashes from the thimble, battering me with a blizzard's fury. It is icy, and dark, and empty, and it wants to drag me in and rip me away from myself and reshape me into a puppet that will allow herself to be pulled to the prince, allow herself to be fitted with the slipper. But I am Pin. I am Pen. And I am flame, and all the bitter cold of the thimble's nothingness cannot touch me. Story wants its ending? Let me give it a new ending, one shaped by my own choices. When I speak, my voice burns. "No," I shout, bracing myself. "I do not choose that ending."

The last *boom* of the castle clock strikes not with sound, but with silence, a muffling wave of noiseless thunder that fills the room until the walls shudder. The Godmother's mouth is stretched wide as if she is screaming, but no sound emerges. The waves of silence slam against me, but I stand firm, unwavering. Sparks and smoke seep from the floor, swirling around the room.

The two huge hands of the clock crack at their base and waver, and like two spears tip away and plunge toward the ground. Slowly, silently, the clock face rips itself from the wall. Trailing stones, it leans outward and goes suddenly dark, and there is one more long moment of ringing silence before all sound rushes back and I hear a resounding crash as it shatters on the ground far below.

CHAPTER

40

Freezing air rushes into the room through the gap left by the clock.

The brambles binding Owen to the wall turn to dust and he crumples to the floor.

"Pen," pants Cor, rushing to my side.

"See to Owen," I shout, without taking my eyes from the Godmother. This isn't over yet.

The Godmother stands in the middle of the floor. The icy wind swirls around her, ruffling her skirts and the ends of her snaky white hair. She stares back at me.

The thimble on her finger glows with a dull blue light.

"Story has its own shape, its own energy," the Godmother grinds out. "It will always return."

Maybe. I step closer to her. "Your story is over, at any rate," I say flatly.

She tips her head back as if trying to bring me into focus. She raises the hand holding the thimble, but she knows that its Nothing has no power over me anymore. Its light goes out. Her fingers look almost transparent, and they shake violently as if she is shivering with cold.

I reach out and take the thimble from her hand. Then, following a sense of heat and light, I dip my fingers into a pocket of her skirt and find the thimble that she had taken from me, my thimble. My hand closes over it, warming me, and I take it back.

She closes her eyes and releases a breath. Slowly she sinks to her knees before me. She looks old, faded, defeated. Broken.

I slip her thimble onto my own finger. It is sticky with cold; my finger feels frozen. Its glow intensifies again. I bend over the Godmother and brush a wisp of her dry white hair from her face.

"You can have it," the Godmother whispers, her voice thin. "The power is yours. Serve Story as I did."

"No," I tell her. "We have come to the end." Carefully I touch the thimble to the center of her forehead.

"Pen, don't do it." I glance over my shoulder. Owen has a bloodstained hand pressed to his side; only Cor's arm around his shoulders is keeping him on his feet.

I look away. "I have to."

"Pen, no," comes Owen's voice, cracked and weary.

I know why he's protesting. It's horrible to lose all your memories, all your past, your very self. She took all those things away from every slave in the fortress and in the city, and from Owen, and away from me.

"She deserves this ending," I say.

Calling up the power of the thimble, I press it to her forehead.

And I take it all away from her.

CHAPTER

41

PEN IS GONE, TAKING THE THIMBLES, TO SEE TO THE final defeat of the Godmother's footmen in the city.

Cor helps Owen from the clock tower with its gaping hole in the wall. He leads him to his own rooms, where the heavy wooden furniture is covered with dust shaken from the ceiling and the two dogs are cowering in a corner. He eases Owen onto the four-poster bed.

"There's a battle going on outside," Cor says. "There's got to be a healer around somewhere. Rest here. I'll be back."

Owen closes his eyes and floats. He remembers only snatches of the rest of the journey from the Godmother's fortress in the forest, and then blinking into consciousness in the clock room with the brambles wrapped around him. The moment where Pen broke Story. And then after.

The pain from his wounded shoulder and from the thorns that slashed his side and his arm ebbs. His throat is parched with thirst, but he can't summon the energy to get up and look for something to drink.

He fades out for a while, then comes back as someone lifts his head. "Drink this, lad," says a deep, rumbling voice. The Huntsman. He drinks, and feels liquid go down his throat and trickle down the side of his face and neck.

"Can you get his sweater off?" Cor's voice asks.

A jolt of pain, and he fades out again.

HE COMES BACK to himself. For the first time in a very long time, he is completely comfortable.

He remembers another time of perfect comfort, a moment that is lost to Pen forever. The two of them, him and Pin, fleeing from the Godmother's fortress, staggering with cold and hunger and fright, hiding in a hollow under the roots of a fallen tree. Then warmth and light and Pin across the fire from him. That moment, he realizes. As he watched her eat a bite of gingerbread. That was when he'd started falling in love with her. He knows that he will never stop falling in love with her, with Pin. With Pen.

And she loves him.

But it's all tangled up in the brambles of Story and the thimbles and what she'd done to the Godmother. It's not going to be that simple to figure each other out.

He opens his eyes.

The Huntsman is sitting on the bed, his back against one of the posts. His trackers sleep next to the fire with Cor's dogs.

Owen finds his voice. "Is Pen here?"

"She came to see you while you were out." The Huntsman gets off the bed and helps Owen sit up, stuffing another pillow behind his back. He turns away to pour something into a cup. "Can you manage this?" he asks.

"Yes," Owen answers, taking the cup. "Is she coming back?" He takes a drink. It's water with something in it. A healing herb, he guesses.

"Ah, well." The Huntsman settles on the bed again. He rubs a hand over his bald head. "She's gone with Prince Cor to East Oria to alert his mother, the queen, about what's been going on here. The prince was in a great hurry to be away."

"But she's coming back?" Owen asks.

"I don't know, lad," the Huntsman answers. "But she's given you something to see to while she's gone."

He nods. Anything.

THE NEXT DAY, when he can stay on his feet without falling over, the Huntsman fetches him from Cor's room. They walk slowly along a passageway, heading deeper into the castle.

"What will you do now?" Owen asks, as they stop to rest at the top of a stone staircase. He leans against the wall, feeling the pull of the bandages wrapping the cut on his ribs.

"Ah, well now." The Huntsman shrugs. "I was caught up in a story once, as you know."

Owen nods. "And it ended badly."

"For me it did," the Huntsman says. "And for the girl I loved. Bianca was her name. She ended up married to a prince she didn't love. I hear he died—took poison, they say—and she went to live in a cottage in the forest." He smiles beneath his bushy mustache. "Living there with a bunch of cats, I've heard. I've a mind to go and find her." He raises his eyebrows. "All right to go on?"

Owen nods, pushes himself from the wall he's been resting against, and they head down a set of narrow stone stairs, deep under the castle. The air is heavy and damp. A prison. The Huntsman nods to a guard, who opens a door and lets them pass. They go down another stairway and along a dark hallway lined with doors. In each door is a tiny window for looking at the prisoner inside.

The Huntsman stops them before one of the doors and opens the little window.

"You're to decide her punishment," the Huntsman says. "Her ending."

Owen peers into the cell, which is small, cold, and damp.

An old woman in the ragged remains of a blue silk dress sits on the floor, her back hunched against the stone wall. White hair hangs down around her face, which is pale and blank.

The Godmother.

Or what's left of her.

CHAPTER

42

I SPEND WEEKS WITH COR IN EAST ORIA, MEETING HIS
mother, the queen, and explaining to her during excruciatingly long and formal meetings what Story is and how
dangerous it can be. I show her my thimble and the Godmother's and tell her about their power. The queen doesn't
seem to realize how easily Story could rise again to threaten
the land, even though so many people from her own king-
dom disappeared, stolen out of their lives to serve in the city
or the fortress. "You might open your eyes," I tell her acerbically, "and look about your realm every now and then to see
what's been going on."

Obviously, we don't get along.

All the while I miss Owen. It's a constant, almost physical ache, this feeling, and I realize that when I first awoke in

the cinders in my stepmother's house it was Owen that I was grieving for. The loss of him, when we had only just discovered each other.

It is quite possible that I am going to lose him all over again.

Before leaving the Godmother's city, I went to Cor's room to tell Owen that I was going.

"He's still out," the Huntsman had said as he met me at the door. "He's a strong lad, but he was pushed too far this time."

Cor's room was full of dark wood, heavy tapestries, a wide fireplace. I only had eyes for Owen in the canopied bed. On quiet feet, I approached. He was so still, so pale. One of his hands was folded around a crumpled edge of the sheet, as if he'd fallen asleep while holding on to it. I could see bandages wrapped around his chest and his arm.

"Hello," I whispered. I sat on the bed and took his hand. Turning it over, I traced my fingers along the calluses that lined his palm. He was just a shoemaker, and he was so much more than that, too. He was everything. All I wanted to do was to crawl into the bed and wrap my arms around him; I wanted him to turn his face to me and open his eyes just for a moment.

But he slept on. With trembling fingers I reached out to brush aside the lock of sandy hair that had fallen over his closed eyes.

From the doorway I heard footsteps, and then the rustle

of movement as the Huntsmen got up to meet someone in the hall. A low murmur of voices. I was being summoned; it was time to go.

"Good-bye," I whispered, and I brought my face down and laid my cheek against his so that I could hear his quiet breaths in my ear. Then, softly, with a feather's touch, I kissed him. I got to my feet. And it felt as if I was tearing myself in half, but I did it; I went to the door, and I went out, and I left him.

NOW I AM so afraid that our time together has ended. Story treated Owen so cruelly; he might have already left the city to go back to his family in Westhaven. I wouldn't blame him if he did. And I did a terrible thing, taking the Godmother away from herself, even though he asked me not to. At the moment I did it, it seemed necessary. Now I'm not so certain. She had to be stopped, but maybe there was a better way.

Cor has made plans to come visit the city as soon as he can leave East Oria. He hopes to find homes for all the animals— especially the dogs—that the Godmother turned into footmen in her service, and who turned back when Story's power was broken. He's been helping the former slaves from the Godmother's fortress find new lives for themselves, too. Some of them returned to their Befores, but for others too much time had passed. They can only go on, not back.

AT LAST IT is time for me to return to the city. "We need to come up with a name for it," I tell Cor.

"Write to me when you get there," he suggests. His dog Bunny, who is expecting puppies, nudges his leg and he reaches down to stroke her long ears. "Tell me what the people are calling it."

He has given me a fine black mare to ride. Templeton and Zel are saddling their horses too, in the courtyard of the royal residence. They're to be my bodyguards on the ten-day trip.

Cor gives me a leg up into the saddle. Apparently I've ridden before, because my hands know just what to do with the reins, how to set my feet in the stirrups and balance my weight. I check my coat pocket for the thimbles. "Keep working on your mother," I tell him. "Try to convince her that she must remain vigilant."

"I will," he assures me. "I hope you and Owen will be very happy."

I nod, but I can't answer.

Because I know very well that making my own choices and living a real life is harder in some ways than living in Story. Owen can love me and I can love him, but we still might not be able to be together.

Templeton and Zel and I travel for four days through the queen's realm and then six more days through the forest. Every night when we stop, Templeton makes me practice my staff-work. "You never know when Story will rise again, Pen," she warns. "You'll have to be ready, just in case."

As we ride, I think about all the misery caused by Story

and the Godmother. The unhappiness of ordinary people, not just princes and princesses, but the ones trampled on or cast to the side or left behind. Marya and Tobias. Natters and his Missus and their apprentice who was like a son to them, who died in the Godmother's fortress. And all the other slaves kidnapped from their homes, their memories erased. The Huntsman and his lost Bianca. Lady Meister. Dulcet's beautiful voice silenced and Precious's talents, all set aside for the pursuit of an appropriate ending.

And Owen, with his scars, and his rare and fleeting smile.

I'M NOT QUITE sure what to expect when we arrive in the city. Before leaving with Cor, I'd spent two days using my thimble to give back the memories of everyone living there. They might have all gone back to their Befores; the city might be empty, abandoned.

We arrive on a bright afternoon on the edge of spring. To my surprise, the streets are bustling with people going about their business, looking perfectly content and normal. None of them are wearing blue. The streets of the upper city are not quite as terrifyingly clean as when I lived here before; the lower city seems not as dark and twisted. The air even smells different—dankly of the river, and of frying meat and baking bread, woodsmoke, and a faint whiff of drains. The castle has been repaired; new stone covers the huge hole in the tower where the clock face used to be.

While Templeton and Zel go to find us an inn and stable

9-15